DRAGON'S TEETH II.

In tragic times like these, an elderly
au thor has nothing to give but words.
This collection of words is dedicated
to the men and women in many parts
of the world who are giv ing their lives
in the cause of free dom and hu man decency.   - Upton Sinclair

Au tumn, 1941

World's End	1913 - 1919
Be tween Two Worlds	1919 - 1929
Drangon's Teeth	1929 - 1934
Wide is the Gate	1934 - 1937
Presidential Agent	1937 - 1938
Dragon Harvest	1938 - 1940
A World to Win	1940 - 1942
Presidential Mission	1942 - 1943
One Clear Call	1943 - 1944
O Shep herd, Speak!	1943 - 1946
The Return of Lanny Budd	1946 - 1949

Each vol ume is pub lished in two parts: I and II.

DRAGON'S TEETH II.

Upton Sinclair

Copy right © 1942 by Upton Sinclair

First pub lished in Jan u ary 1942

Re print 2001 by Si mon Pub li ca tions

LCCN: 67058718

ISBN: 1-931313-15-6

Dis tributed by Ingram Book Com pany

Printed by Light ning Source Inc., LaVergne, TN

Pub lished by Si mon Pub li ca tions, P.O. Box 321 Safety Har bor, FL

When I say "his to rian," I have a mean ing of my own. I por tray world events in story form, because that form is the one I have been trained in. I have sup ported my self by writ ing fic tion since the age of six teen, which means for forty-nine years.

... Now I re al ize that this one was the one job for which I had been born: to put the pe riod of world wars and rev o lu tions into a great long novel. ...

I can not say when it will end, be cause I don't know ex actly what the char - acters will do. They lead a semi-independent life, being more real to me than any of the people I know, with the single exception of my wife. ... Some of my char ac ters are peo ple who lived, and whom I had op por tu nity to know and watch. Oth ers are imag i nary—or rather, they are com plexes of many people whom I have known and watched. Lanny Budd and his mother and fa ther and their var i ous rel a tives and friends have come in the course of the past four years to be my daily and nightly com pan ions. I have come to know them so in ti mately that I need only to ask them what they would do in a given set of cir cum stances and they start to en act their roles. ... I chose what seems to me the most re veal ing of them and of their world.

How long will this go on? I can not tell. It de pends in great part upon two pub lic fig ures, Hit ler and Mus so lini. What are they go ing to do to man kind and what is man kind will do to them? It seems to me hardly likely that ei - ther will die a peace ful death. I am hop ing to out live them; and what ever happens Lanny Budd will be some where in the neigh bor hood, he will be "in at the death," ac cord ing to the fox-hunting phrase.

These two foxes are my quarry, and I hope to hang their brushes over my mantel.

In the course of this novel a num ber of well-known per sons make their ap -
pearance, some of them living, some dead; they appear under their own
names, and what is said about them is fac tu ally cor rect.

There are other char ac ters which are fic ti tious, and in these cases the au thor
has gone out of his way to avoid seem ing to point at real per sons. He has given
them un likely names, and hopes that no per son bear ing such names ex ist. But
it is im pos si ble to make sure; there fore the writer states that, if any such co in -
cidence occurs, it is accidental. This is not the customary "hedge clause"
which the author of a *ro man à clef* pub lishes for le gal pro tec tion; it means
what it says and it is in tended to be so taken.

Various European concerns engaged in the man u fac ture of mu ni tions have
been named in the story, and what has been said about them is also ac cord ing
to the re cords. There is one Amer i can firm, and that, with all its af fairs, is
imag i nary. The writer has done his best to avoid seem ing to in di cate any ac -
tual Amer i can firm or fam ily.

...Of course there will be slips, as I know from ex pe ri ence; but *World's End* is
meant to be a his tory as well as fic tion, and I am sure there are no mis takes of
im por tance. I have my own point of view, but I have tried to play fair in this
book. There is a var ied cast of char ac ters and they say as they think. ...

The Peace Con fer ence of Paris [*for example*], which is the scene of the last
third of *World's End*, is of course one of the greatest events of all time. A
friend on mine asked an au thor ity on mod ern fic tion a ques tion: "Has any -
body ever used the Peace Con fer ence in a novel?" And the re ply was: "Could
any body?" Well, I thought some body could, and now I think some body has.
The reader will ask, and I state ex plic itly that so far as con cerns his toric char -
ac ters and events my pic ture is cor rect in all de tails. This part of the manu -
script, 374 pages, was read and checked by eight or ten gen tle men who were
on the Amer i can staff at the Con fer ence. Sev eral of these hold im por tant po si -
tions in the world of troubled international affairs; others are college presi-
dents and professors, and I promised them all that their letters will be
con fi den tial. Suf fice it to say that the er rors they pointed out were cor rected,
and where they dis agreed, both sides have a word in the book.

Contents:

BOOK FOUR

As on a Darkling Plain

16

Root of All Evil

A WORLD conqueror had appeared in modern times. Alexander, Caesar, Attila, Genghis Khan, Napoleon—another such as these, appearing in the age of electricity, of rotary presses and radio, when nine men out of ten would have said it was impossible. A world conqueror has to be a man of few ideas, and those fixed; a peculiar combination of exactly the right qualities, both good and bad—iron determination, irresistible energy, and no scruples of any sort. He has to know what he wants, and permit no obstacle to stand in the way of his getting it. He has to understand the minds of other men, both foes and friends, and what greeds, fears, hates, jealousies will move them to action. He must understand the mass mind, the ideals or delusions which sway it; he must be enough of a fanatic to talk their language, though not enough to be controlled by it. He must believe in nothing but his own destiny, the glorified image of himself on the screen of history; whole races of mankind made over in his own image and according to his will. To accomplish that purpose he must be liar, thief, and murderer upon a world-wide scale; he must be ready without hesitation to commit every crime his own interest commands, whether upon individuals or nations. He must pave the highway for his legions with the bones of his enemies, he must float his battleships upon oceans of human blood, he must compose his songs of glory out of the groans and curses of mankind.

The singular advantage enjoyed by Adolf Hitler was that his own people believed what he said, while other peoples couldn't and wouldn't. The attitude of the outside world to him was that of the farmer who stared at a giraffe in the circus and exclaimed: "There ain't no sich animal!" The more Adolf told the world what he was and what he meant to do, the more the world smiled incredulously. There were men like that in every lunatic asylum; the type was so familiar that any psychiatrist could diagnose it from a single paragraph of a speech or a single page of a book. Sensible men said: "*Nut!*" and went on about their affairs, leaving Adolf to conquer the world. Here and there a man of social insight cried out warnings of what was going on; but these, too, were a well-known type and the psychiatrists had names for them.

Adolf Hitler got the mastery of the National Socialist Party because of his combination of qualities; because he was the most fanatical, the most determined, the most tireless, and at the same time the shrewdest, the most unscrupulous, the most deadly. From the beginning men had revolted against his authority, and while he was weak he had wheedled and cajoled them and when he became strong he had crushed them. There had been split after split in his movement, and he had gone after the leaders of the factions without ruth; even before he had got the authority of government in his hands, his fanatical Stormtroopers had been beating and sometimes murdering the opponents of this new dark religion of *Blut und Boden*, blood and soil. Work with Adolf Hitler and you would rise to power in the world; oppose him, and your brains would be spattered on the pavement, or you would be shot in the back and left unburied in a dark wood.

Hermann Göring, aviator and army officer, man of wealth, of luxurious tastes and insatiable vanities, hated and despised Joseph Goebbels, the blabbing journalist, the club-footed little dwarf with the venom-spitting tongue; and these sentiments were cordially reciprocated. Jupp would have thrown vitriol into Hermann's face, Hermann would have shot Jupp on sight—if either had dared. But the Führer needed Hermann as a master executive and Jupp as a master propagandist, and he put them into harness and drove them as a team. The same thing was true of hundreds of men in that party of madness and hate: World War victims, depression victims, psychopaths, drug addicts, perverts, criminals—they all needed Adolf a little more than Adolf needed them, and he welded them into something more powerful than themselves. Hardly one who wasn't sure that he was a greater man than Adolf, and better fitted to lead the party; in the old days many had patronized him, and in their hearts they still did so; but he had won out over them, because of the combination of qualities. He was the one who had persuaded the masses to trust him, and he was the one who could lead the N.S.D.A.P. and all its members and officials upon the road to conquest.

II

Adolf Hitler had watched Lenin, he now was watching Stalin and Mussolini, and had learned from them all. In June of the year 1924, when Lanny Budd had been in Rome, Benito Mussolini had been Premier of Italy for more than twenty months, but the Socialists were still publishing papers with several times as many readers as Mussolini's papers, and there was still freedom of speech in the Italian parliament and elsewhere; there was still an opposition party, there were labor unions and co-operatives and other means of resistance to the will of the Fascists. It had taken the murderer of Matteotti another year and more to accomplish his purpose of crushing opposition and making himself master of the Italian nation.

But Adolf's time-table was different from that. Adolf had a job to do in the outside world, and had no idea of dawdling for three years before beginning it. He knew how to wait, but would never wait an hour longer than necessary, and would be his own judge of the timing; he would startle the world, and even his own followers, by the suddenness and speed of his moves.

First, always first, the psychological preparation. Was he going to wipe out the rights of German labor, to destroy a movement which the workers had been patiently building for nearly a century? Obviously, then, the first step was to come to labor with outstretched hands, to enfold it in a brotherly clasp while it was stabbed in the back; to set it upon a throne where it could be safely and surely riddled with machine gun bullets.

Europe's labor day was the First of May, and everywhere over the continent the workers paraded, they held enormous meetings, picnics and sports, they sang songs and listened to speeches from their leaders, they heartened and inspired themselves for the three hundred and sixty-four hard days. So now, several weeks in advance, it was announced that the Hitler government was going to take over the First of May and make it the "Day of National Labor." This was a government of "true Socialism"; it was the friend of labor, it *was* labor, and no longer could there be a class struggle or any conflict of interest. The revolution having been accomplished, the workers would celebrate their conquest and the new and splendid future which lay before them. All these golden, glowing words —and all the power of press and radio to carry the message to every corner of the Fatherland. Also, of course, the power of the police and the private Nazi armies to terrify and crush anyone who might try to voice any other idea.

"Oh, Lanny, you should come to see it!" wrote Heinrich Jung, ecstatically. "It will be something the like of which has not been seen in the world before. All our youth forces will assemble in the Lustgarten in the morning and President Hindenburg himself will address us. In the afternoon there will be costume parades of every craft and trade, even every great factory in Germany. All will gather in the Tempelhof Airfield, and the decorations will exceed anything you could imagine. The rich are paying for them by buying tickets so as to sit near the Führer. Of course He will speak, and afterwards there will be fireworks like a battle—three hundred meters of silver rain! I beg you and your wife to come as my guests—you will always be glad that you witnessed these historic scenes. . . . P.S. I am sending you some literature about our wonderful new labor program. You cannot have any doubts after this."

Lanny wrote, acknowledging the letter and expressing his regrets. It cost nothing to keep in touch with this ardent young official, and the literature he sent might some day be useful to Rick. Lanny was quite sure that he wouldn't care to enter Germany so long as Adolf Hitler remained its Chancellor.

III

The celebration came off, with all the splendor which Heinrich had promised. Everything was the biggest and most elaborate ever known, and even the hardboiled foreign correspondents were awe-stricken; they sent out word that something new was being born into the world. On the enormous airfield three hundred thousand persons had assembled by noon, to sit on the ground and await ceremonies which did not begin until eight in the evening. By that time there were a million or a million and a half in the crowd, believed to be the greatest number ever gathered in one place. Hitler and Hindenburg drove side by side, the first time that had happened. They passed along Friedrichstrasse, packed to the curb with shouting masses, and hung with streamers reading: "For German Socialism," and "Honor the Worker." In front of the speaker's platform stood the new Chancellor, looking over a vast sea of faces. He stood under the spotlight, giving the Nazi salute over and over, and when at last he spoke, the amplifiers carried his voice to every part of the airfield, and wireless and cables carried it over the world.

The new Chancellor's message was that "the German people must learn to know one another again." The divisions within Germany had been invented "by human madness," and could be remedied "by human wisdom." Hitler ordained that from now on the First of May should be a day of universal giving of hands, and that its motto was to be: "Honor work and have respect for the worker." He told the Germans what they wanted most of all to hear: "You are not a second-rate nation, but are strong if you wish to be strong." He became devout, and prayed: "O Lord, help Thou our fight for liberty!"

Nothing could have been more eloquent, nothing nobler. Did Adi wink to his journalist and say: "Well, Juppchen, we got away with it," or some German equivalent for that slang? At any rate, on the following morning the labor unions of Germany, representing four million workers and having annual incomes of nearly two hundred million marks, were wiped out at one single stroke. The agents of the job were so-called "action committees" of the Shop-

Cell Organization, the Nazi group which had carried on their propaganda in the unions. Armed gangs appeared at the headquarters of all the unions, arrested officials and threw them into concentration camps. Their funds were confiscated, their newspapers suppressed, their editors jailed, their banks closed; and there was no resistance. The Socialists had insisted upon waiting until the Nazis did something "illegal"; and here it was.

"What can we do?" wrote Freddi to Lanny, in an unsigned letter written on a typewriter—for such a letter might well have cost him his life. "Our friends hold little meetings in their homes, but they have no arms, and the rank and file are demoralized by the cowardice of their leaders. The rumor is that the co-operatives are to be confiscated also. There is to be a new organization called the 'German Labor Front,' to be directed by Robert Ley, the drunken braggart who ordered these raids. I suppose the papers in Paris will have published his manifesto, in which he says: 'No, workers, your institutions are sacred and inviolable to us National Socialists.' Can anyone imagine such hypocrisy? Have words lost all meaning?

"Do not answer this letter and write us nothing but harmless things, for our mail is pretty certain to be watched. We have to ask our relatives abroad not to attend any political meetings for the present. The reason for this is clear."

An agonizing thing to Hansi and Bess, to have to sit with folded hands while this horror was going on. But the Nazis had made plain that they were going to revive the ancient barbarian custom of punishing innocent members of a family in order to intimidate the guilty ones. A man doesn't make quite such a good anti-Nazi fighter when he knows that he may be causing his wife and children, his parents, his brothers and sisters, to be thrown into concentration camps and tortured. Hansi had no choice but to cancel engagements he had made to play at concerts for the benefit of refugees.

"Wait at least until the family is out of Germany," pleaded Beauty; and the young Reds asked their consciences: "What then?" Did they have the right to go off on a pleasure yacht while friends and comrades were suffering agonies? On the other hand, what about Papa's need of rest? The sense of family solidarity is strong among the Jews. "Honor thy father and thy mother: that thy days may be long upon the land which the Lord thy God giveth thee." The Lord in His wisdom had seen fit to take away the land, but the commandment still stood, and Hansi thought of his father, who had given him the best of everything in the world, and now would surely get no rest if his oldest son should declare war upon the Nazis. Also, there was the mother, who had lived for her family and hardly had a thought of any other happiness. Was she to be kept in terror from this time on?

"What do you think, Lanny?" asked the son of ancient Judea who wanted to be artist and reformer at the same time. Lanny was moved to reveal to him the scheme which was cooking in his mind for the entrapment of Johannes and the harnessing of his money. Hansi was greatly pleased; this would put his conscience at rest and he could go on with his violin studies. But Bess, the tough-minded one, remarked: "It'll be just one more liberal magazine."

"You can have a Red section, and put in your comments," replied Lanny, with a grin.

"It would break up the family," declared the granddaughter of the Puritans.

IV

Johannes wrote that he had got passports for his party, and set the date for the yacht to arrive at Calais. Thence they would proceed to Ramsgate, run up to London for a few days, and perhaps visit the Pomeroy-Nielsons—for this was going to be a pleasure trip, with time to do anything that took anybody's fancy. "We have all earned a vacation," said the letter. Lanny reflected that this might apply to Johannes Robin—but did it apply to Mr. Irma Barnes?

He wrote in answer: "Emily Chattersworth has arrived at Les Forêts, and Hansi is to give her a concert with a very fine program. Why don't you and the family come at once and have a few days in Paris? We are extremely anxious to see you. The spring Salon is the most interesting I have seen in years. Zoltan is here and will sell you some fine pictures. Zaharoff is at Balincourt, and Madame is out there with him; I will take you and you can have a séance, and perhaps meet once more the spirits of your deceased uncles. There are other pleasures I might suggest, and other reasons I might give why we are so very impatient to see you."

Johannes replied, with a smile between the lines: "Your invitation is appreciated, but please explain to the spirits of my uncles that I still have important matters which must be cleared up. I am rendering services to some influential persons, and this will be to the advantage of all of us." Very cryptic, but Lanny could guess that Johannes was selling something, perhaps parting with control of a great enterprise, and couldn't let go of a few million marks. The spirits of his uncles would understand this.

"Do not believe everything that the foreign press is publishing about Germany," wrote the master of caution. "Important social changes are taking place here, and the spirit of the people, except for certain small groups, is remarkable." Studying that sentence you could see that its words had been carefully selected, and there were several interpretations to be put upon them. Lanny knew his old friend's mind, and not a few of his connections. The bankrupted landlords to whom he had loaned money, the grasping steel and coal lords with whom he had allied himself, were still carrying on their struggle for the mastery of Germany; they were working inside the Nazi party, and its factional strife was partly of their making. Lanny made note of the fact that the raids on the labor unions had been made by Robert Ley and his own gangs. Had the "drunken braggart" by any chance "jumped the gun" on his party comrades? If so, one might suspect that the steel hand of Thyssen had been at work behind the scenes. Who could figure how many billions of marks it would mean to the chairman of the Ruhr trust to be rid of the hated unions and safe against strikes from this day forth?

Robbie Budd wrote about this situation, important to him. He said: "There is a bitter fight going on for control of the industry in Germany. There are two groups, both powerful politically. It is Thyssen and Krupp vs. the Otto Wolff group. The latter is part Jewish, and the present set-up is not so good for them. Johannes believes he has friends in both camps, and I hope he is not fooling himself. He is sailing a small ship in a stormy sea."

Robbie also gave another item of news: "Father is failing and I fear you may not find him here when you arrive. It is no definite disease, just the slow breakdown of old age, very sad to witness. It means heavy responsibilities for me; a situation which I prefer not to write about, but will tell you when I see you. Write the old gentleman and assure him of your appreciation of his kindness to you; he tries to keep his hold on all the family as well as on the business. He forgets what I told him yesterday, but remembers clearly what happened long ago. That is hard on me, because I caused him a great deal of unhappiness in those days, whereas of late he had been learning to take me for what I am and make the best of it. I try not to grieve about him, because he has had more out of life than most men, and fate neither lets us live forever nor have our way entirely while we are here."

V

Adolf Hitler was the man who was having his own way, more than any who had lived in modern times. He was going ahead to get the mastery of everything in Germany, government, institutions, even cultural and social life. Every organization which stood in his way he proceeded to break, one after another, with such speed and ruthlessness that it left the opposition dizzy. The Nationalist party, which had fondly imagined it could control him, found itself helpless. Papen, Vice-Chancellor, was reduced to a figurehead; Göring took his place in control of the Prussian state. Hugenberg had several of his papers suppressed, and when he threatened to resign from the Cabinet, no one appeared to care. One by one the Nationalist members were forced out and Nazis replaced them. Subordinates were arrested, charged with defalcation or what not— the Minister of Information was in position to charge anybody with anything, and it was dangerous to answer.

On the tenth day of May there were ceremonies throughout Germany which riveted the attention of the civilized world. Quantities of books were collected from the great library of Berlin University, including most of the worthwhile books which had been written during the past hundred years: everything that touched even remotely upon political, social, or sexual problems. Some forty thousand volumes were heaped into a pile in the square between the University and the Opera House and drenched with gasoline. The students paraded, wearing their bright society caps and singing patriotic and Nazi songs. They solemnly lighted the pyre and a crowd stood in a drizzling rain to watch it burn. Thus modern thought was symbolically destroyed in the Fatherland, and a nation which had stood at the forefront of the intellectual life would learn to do its thinking with its "blood."

On that same tenth of May the schools of Germany were ordered to begin teaching the Nazi doctrines of "race." On that day the government confiscated all the funds belonging to the Socialist party and turned them over to the new Nazi-controlled unions. On that day Chancellor Hitler spoke to a Labor Congress, telling it that his own humble origin and upbringing fitted him to understand the needs of the workers and attend to them. On that day the correspondent of the *New York Times* was forbidden to cable news of the suicide of the daughter of Scheidemann, the Socialist leader, and of a woman tennis champion who had brought honor to Germany but who objected to the process of "co-ordinating" German sport with Nazi propaganda. Finally, on that day there was a parade of a hundred thousand persons down Broadway in New York, protesting against the treatment of German Jews.

VI

The members of the Budd family in Bienvenu and in Paris were packing and getting ready for a year's absence from home. What should they take and what leave behind? Everything that was going on board the yacht had to be marked for the cabins or the hold. What was to be sent from Paris to Bienvenu was left in charge of Jerry Pendleton, who would see to its packing and unpacking. The ex-tutor and ex-lieutenant had saved most of his year's salary, and would go back to the *pension* and wait for the tourists to return. Madame Zyszynski was to be loaned for a year to the munitions king—for the spirits of the Budds and Dingles appeared to have said their say, whereas the Duquesa Marqueni was still going strong. Bub Smith was to escort the priceless little Frances to the yacht and see her safely on board; then he would take a steamer and return to his job in Newcastle, until such time as the baby should arrive in the land of the gangsters and the home of the kidnapers.

The expedition from Bienvenu arrived in Paris by train: Hansi and Bess; Beauty and her husband; Marceline and her governess— the former nearly sixteen, an elegant young lady, but she would be made to study every day on the yacht, and if there was anything Miss Addington didn't know, she would look it up in the encyclopedia, or the all-knowing Lanny would tell it to her. Frances was now three years old, and her entourage was made up of Miss Severne, a nurse, and the ex-cowboy from Texas. These ten persons arrived in the morning, and there was fuss and clamor, because they all wanted this or that before they got onto a yacht, and it seemed that so many bags and boxes had never before been heaped up in the entrance hall of a palace.

In the evening the expedition entrained for Calais; four more of them now: Irma and her husband, her maid and her Feathers—who, as Irma said over and over, was a fool, but a good one, doing all the errands, the shopping, and telephoning; keeping the accounts and getting hopelessly mixed up in them; taking her scoldings with tears, and promising to reform and doing her best, poor soul, but not having it in her, since she had been brought up as a lady, and thought about her own ego more than she could ever think about her job.

There were now twice as many boxes and bags, and twice as much fuss, but carried on in low tones, because Irma was strict about having the dignity of the family preserved. It was a conspicuous family, and there were reporters at the station to see them off and to ask about their proposed trip. Millions of people would read about their doings and get vicarious thrills; millions would admire them and millions would envy them, but only a small handful would love them—such appeared to be the way of the world.

VII

Next morning the party emerged on the station platform of the ancient seaport and bathing resort. They waited while Lanny got busy on the telephone and ascertained that the yacht had not yet been reported. They were loaded into taxis and taken to the Hotel du Commerce et Excelsior, where the mountain of luggage was stacked in a room and Feathers set to watch over it. A glorious spring day, and the family set out to find a point of vantage from which they could watch the approach of the trim white *Bessie Budd*. Irma and Lanny had a memory of this spectacle, never to be forgotten: the day at Ramsgate when they had been trying to get married in a hurry, and the yacht and its gay-spirited owner had provided them with a way of escape from the dominion of the Archbishop of Canterbury.

Now the yacht was going to transport them to Utopia, or to some tropical isle with an ivory tower on it—any place·in the world where there were no Nazis yelling and parading and singing songs about Jewish blood spurting from the knife. Oil-burning vessels make no smudges of smoke on the horizon, so they must look for a dim speck that grew gradually larger. Many such appeared from the east, but when they got larger they were something else. So the party went to lunch, fourteen at one long table, and it was quite a job getting them settled and all their orders taken and correctly distributed. Belonging to the important classes as they did, neither they nor their servants must do anything to attract attention to themselves in public, and this was impressed on a member of the family even at the age of three. Hush, hush, Baby!

They sat on the esplanade and watched all afternoon. Some of them took a swim, some looked at the sights of the town—the four-hundred-year-old bastion, the citadel, the church of Notre Dame with a painting by Rubens. They bought postcards and mailed them to various friends. Every now and then they would inspect the harbor again, but still there was no trim white *Bessie Budd*. Again they had tables put together in the restaurant, and the fourteen had supper; they went out and watched till dark—but still no sign of the yacht.

They were beginning to be worried. Johannes had set a definite hour for leaving Bremerhaven, and he was a precise man who did everything on time and had his employees do the same. If anything unforeseen had turned up he would surely have telegraphed or telephoned. He had specified in his last letter what hotel they should go to, so that he would know where to look for them. They had sailed so often with him that they knew how many hours it would take to reach Calais, and it had been planned for the yacht to arrive simultaneously with the train from Paris. She was now twelve hours overdue.

Something must have happened, and they spent time discussing possibilities. Private yachts which are properly cared for do not have machinery trouble in calm weather, nor do they butt into the Frisian islands on the way from Germany to France. They travel as safely by night as by day; but of course some fisherman's boat or other obstruction might conceivably have got in the way. "Tire trouble!" said Lanny, the motorist.

VIII

When it was bedtime and still no word, he went to the telephone and put in a call for the yacht *Bessie Budd* at Bremerhaven—that being the quickest way to find out if she had taken her departure. Hansi and Bess sat with him, and after the usual delays he heard a guttural voice saying in German: "*Dieselmotorjacht Bessie Budd.*"

"*Wer spricht?*" inquired Lanny.

"*Pressmann.*"

"*Wer ist Pressmann?*"

"*Reichsbetriebszellenabteilung Gruppenführerstellvertreter.*" The Germans carry such titles proudly and say them rapidly.

"What are you doing on board the yacht?"

"*Auskunft untersagt*," replied the voice. Information forbidden!

"But the yacht was supposed to sail yesterday!"

"*Auskunft untersagt.*"

"*Aber, bitte——*"

"*Leider, nicht erlaubt*"—and that was all. "Sorry, not permitted!" The receiver clicked, and Lanny, aghast, listened on a dead wire.

"My God!" he exclaimed. "Can the Nazis have seized the *Bessie Budd?*" Hansi went white and Bess dug her nails into the palms of her hands. "Why would they do that!" she exclaimed.

"I don't know," answered Lanny, "unless one of them wanted a yacht."

"They have arrested Papa!" whispered Hansi. He looked as if he was about to keel over, and Bess caught him by the shoulders. "Oh, Hansi! Poor Hansi!" It was characteristic that she thought of him. He was the one who would suffer most!

It was as if a bolt of lightning had fallen from the sky and blasted their plans, turned their pleasures into a nightmare of suffering. Utter ruin, doom without escape—that was the way it appeared, and none could think of anything to say to comfort the others. More than thirty-six hours had passed since the scheduled sailing, and was it conceivable that Johannes would have delayed that length of time to get word to his friends? If any member of the family was at liberty, would that person have failed to communicate?

Just one other possibility: they might have been "tipped off" and have made their escape. They might be on their way out of Germany; or they might be hiding somewhere, not daring to wire. In the latter case they would use the method which they had already resorted to, of an unsigned letter. If such a letter was on the way it was to be expected in the morning.

"I'll try Berlin," said Lanny. Anything to break that dreadful spell of inaction! He put in a call for the Robin palace, and when he got the connection, an unfamiliar voice answered. Lanny asked if Johannes Robin was there, and the stranger tried to find out who was calling; when Lanny gave his name, the other started to put him through a questioning as to his reasons for calling. When Lanny insisted upon knowing to whom he was talking, the speaker abruptly hung up. And that again could mean only one thing: the Nazis had seized the palace!

"I must go and help Papa!" exclaimed Hansi, and started up as if to run to the station right away, or perhaps to the airplane field if there was one. Lanny and Bess caught him at the same moment. "Sit down," commanded the brother-in-law, "and be sensible. There's not a thing you can do in Germany but get yourself killed."

"I certainly must try, Lanny."

"You certainly must *not!* There's nobody they would better like to get hold of."

"I will go under another name."

"With false passports? You who have played on so many concert stages? Our enemies have brains, Hansi, and we have to show that we have some, too."

"He is right," put in Bess. "Whatever is to be done, I'm the one to do it."

Lanny turned upon her. "They know you almost as well as Hansi, and they will be looking for you."

"They won't dare do anything to an American."

"They've been doing it pretty freely. And besides, you're not an American, you're the wife of a German citizen, and that makes you one." All four of the Robins had made themselves citizens of the Weimar Republic, because they believed in it and planned to live their lives there. "So that's out," declared Lanny. "You both have to give me your word of honor not to enter Germany, and not to come anywhere near the border, where they might kidnap you. Then Irma and I will go in and see what we can find out."

"Oh, *will* you do it, Lanny?" Hansi looked at his brother-in-law with the grateful eyes of a dog.

"I promise for myself. I'm guessing that Irma will go along, but of course I'll have to ask her."

IX

Irma was in her room resting, and he went to her alone. He couldn't be sure how she would take this appalling news, and he wanted to give her a chance to make up her mind before it was revealed to anybody else. Irma was no reformer and no saint; she was a young woman who had always had her own way and had taken it for granted that the world existed to give it to her. Now fate was dealing her a nasty blow.

She sat staring at her husband in consternation; she really couldn't bring herself to realize that such a thing could happen in this comfortable civilized world, created for her and her kind. "Lanny, they *can't* do that!"

"They do what they see fit, dear."

"But it ruins our cruise! It leaves us stranded!"

"They probably have our friends in prison somewhere; and they may be beating and abusing them."

"Lanny, how perfectly unspeakable!"

"Yes, but that won't stop it. We have to figure out some way to save them."

"What can we do?"

"I don't know yet. I'll have to go to Berlin and see what has happened."

"Lanny, you *can't* go into that dreadful country!"

"I can't refuse, dear. Don't forget, we have been Johannes's guests; we were going to be his guests another whole year. How could we throw him down?"

She didn't know what to say; she could only sit staring at him. She had never thought that life could play such a trick upon her and her chosen playmate. It was outrageous, insane! Lanny saw her lips trembling; he had never seen her that way before, and perhaps she had never been that way before.

For that matter, he didn't like it any too well himself. But it was as if fate had got him by the collar, and he knew he couldn't pull loose. "Get yourself together, darling," he said. "Remember, Johannes is Hansi's father, and Hansi is my sister's husband. I can't let them see that I'm yellow."

"But Lanny, what on earth can you do? Those Nazis control everything in Germany."

"We know some influential people there, and I'll ask their advice.

The first thing, of course, is to find out what has happened, and why."

"Lanny, you'll be in frightful danger!"

"Not too great, I think. The high-ups don't want any scandals involving foreigners, I feel sure."

"What do you expect me to do? Go with you?"

"Well, it's not a holiday. You might prefer to go to Bienvenu with Baby. You could have your mother come; or you could take Baby and visit her."

"I wouldn't have a moment's peace, thinking you might be in trouble. I haven't the least idea what I could do, but I think I ought to be with you."

"I have no doubt there'll be ways to help. The fact that you have money impresses the Germans—and that includes the Nazis."

"Oh, Lanny, it's a horrid nuisance and a disappointment! I thought we were going to have such fun!"

"Yes, dear, but don't let Hansi or Bess hear you say that. Remember what it means to them."

"They should have thought of this long ago. But they wouldn't let anybody tell them. Now they see the results of their behavior—and we are expected to pay for it!"

"Dear, there's no reason to suppose that they have been the cause of the trouble."

"There must be some reason why Johannes is picked on, and not other rich Jews. The fact that one of his sons is a Communist and the other a Socialist certainly must have made him enemies."

Lanny couldn't deny that this was so; but he said: "Please don't mention it now, while Hansi and Bess are half beside themselves with grief. Let's go and get their family out, and then we'll be in position to talk to them straight."

"Yes, but you *won't!*" said Irma, grimly. She would go with him into the lion's den, but she wouldn't pretend that she liked it! And when it was over, she would do the talking herself.

X

The adult members of the family had no sleep that night. The six sat in conference, going over and over what meager data they had, trying to anticipate the future and to plan their moves. A distressing thing, to have their happiness for a year upset, and to be "stranded" here in Calais; but they were well-bred persons and concealed their annoyance. Beauty couldn't bear letting her darling go into danger, and for a while insisted that she must go along and put her social powers to work. But Lanny argued no—he wasn't in the least worried for himself, and in a few days the yacht might be freed and their plans resumed. Let the family stay here for a few days, and serve as a clearing house for communicating with their friends in the outside world. If the worst proved true, and a long siege was to be expected, Marceline and Frances could be taken back to Juan, and the Dingles and Hansi Robins could go to Paris—or perhaps Emily would shelter them at Sept Chênes.

Lanny got Jerry Pendleton on the phone in the middle of the night. Jerry was still in Paris, having bills to pay and other matters to settle. The plan had been for him to drive his car home, and the chauffeur to drive the Mercédès, the car of Irma and Lanny. But now Lanny ordered Jerry to remain in Paris, and the chauffeur to leave at once for Calais; with fast driving he could arrive before noon, and Lanny and Irma would take the car and set out for Berlin. They were going alone, since neither the chauffeur, Bub Smith, nor Feathers was any good for Germany, not knowing the language. "If you were worth your keep you would have learned it," said Irma to the secretary, taking out her irritation on this unfortunate soul.

Lanny sent cables to his father and to Rick, telling them what had happened. He guessed that in times such as these a foreign journalist might prove a powerful person, more so than an industrialist or an heiress. Lanny saw himself in a campaign to arouse the civilized world on behalf of a Jewish *Schieber* and his family. His head was boiling with letters and telegrams, manifestoes and appeals. Robbie would arouse the businessmen, Uncle Jesse the Communists, Longuet and Blum the Socialists, Hansi and Bess the musical world, Zoltan the art lovers, Parsifal the religious, Beauty and Emily and Sophie and Margy the fashionable, Rick the English press, Corsatti the American—what a clamor there would be when they all got going!

Taking a leaf from his father's notebook, Lanny arranged a code so that he could communicate with his mother confidentially. His letters and telegrams would be addressed to Mrs. Dingle, that being an inconspicuous name. Papa Robin would be "money" and Mama "corsets"—she wore them. Freddi would be "clarinet," and Rahel "mezzo." Lanny said it was to be assumed that all letters and telegrams addressed to him might be read by the Nazis, and all phone calls listened to; later he might arrange a secret way of communication, but nothing of the sort could come to the Hotel Adlon. If he had anything private to impart, he would type it on his little portable machine and mail it without signature in some out-of-the-way part of Berlin. Beauty would open all mail that came addressed to Lanny, and forward nothing that was compromising. All signed letters, both going and coming, would contain phrases expressing admiration for the achievements of National Socialism.

"Don't be surprised if you hear that they have converted me," said the playboy turned serious.

"Don't go too far," warned his mother. "You could never fool Kurt, and he's bound to hear about it."

"I can let him convert me, little by little."

Beauty shook her lovely blond head. She had done no little deceiving in her own time, and had no faith in Lanny's ability along that line. "Kurt will know exactly what you're there for," she declared. "Your best chance is to put it to him frankly. You saved his life in Paris, and you have a right to ask his help now."

"Kurt is a Nazi," said Lanny. "He will help no one but his party."

Irma listened to this conversation, and thought: "This can't be real; this is a melodrama!" She was frightened, but at the same time began to experience strange thrills. She wondered: "Could I pretend to be a Nazi? Could I fool them?" Her mind went on even bolder flights. "Could I be a vamp, like those I've seen on the screen? How would I set about it? And what would I find out?"

XI

They got the morning newspapers. Hard to imagine a millionaire's yacht and palace being seized, and no word of it getting to the outside world; but the rules were being changed in Naziland, and you didn't know what was possible until you saw it. They searched the French papers and found much news from Germany, having to do with the Conference on Arms Limitation at Geneva, and Germany's threats to withdraw from it. Hitler had unexpectedly summoned the Reichstag to meet, and the correspondents assumed that it was to give him a platform from which to address the world. All France was agog to know what he was going to say, and apparently that left the papers no space for the troubles of a Jewish *Schieber*.

The next chance was the mail. A letter mailed in Bremerhaven or Berlin on the day before yesterday might have arrived yesterday afternoon or it might not, but surely it would arrive this morning. Hansi was waiting downstairs at the hotel office; he couldn't think about anything else, not even Lanny's plans. He came rushing into the room, out of breath from running and from anxiety. "A letter in Mama's handwriting!" He handed it to Lanny, to whom it was addressed; his own sense of propriety had not permitted him to open it.

The letter had been scrawled in haste on a scrap of paper and mailed in a plain cheap envelope. Lanny tore it open, and his eyes took it in at a glance. He hated to read such words aloud, but there were five persons waiting in suspense. The letter was in German, and he translated it:

"Oh, Lanny, the Nazis have seized the boat. They have arrested Papa. They would not tell us a word what they will do. They will arrest us if we go near them, but they will not arrest you. We are going to Berlin. We will try to stay there and wait for you. Come to the Adlon, and put it in the papers, we will watch there. We are so frightened. Dear Lanny, do not fail poor Papa. What will they do to him? I am alone. I made the children go. They must not find us all together. God help us all. Mama."

So there it was! Those poor souls traveling separately, and doomed to spend their days and nights in terror for themselves and grief for what might be happening to the father of the family! Hansi broke down and cried like a child, and Beauty did the same. Bess sat twisting her hands together. The others found it difficult to speak.

Somebody had to take command of that situation, and Lanny thought it was up to him. "At least we know the worst," he said, "and we have something to act on. As soon as the car comes, Irma and I will drive to Berlin, not stopping for anything."

"Don't you think you ought to fly?" broke in Bess.

"It will make only a few hours' difference, and we shall need the car; it's the right sort, and will impress the Nazis. This job is not going to be one of a few hours, I'm afraid."

"But think what they may be doing to him, Lanny!"

"I've been thinking about it a lot, and I doubt if they'll do him serious harm. It must be money they're after, and the job will be one of bargaining."

"He's a Jew, Lanny."

"I know; but he has a great many friends at home and abroad, and the Nazis know it, and I don't believe they want any needless scandals. It's up to Irma and me to serve as mediators, as friends to both sides; to meet the right people and find out what it's going to cost."

"You'll be exhausted when you arrive," objected Beauty, struggling with tears. She wanted him to take the chauffeur.

"No," said Lanny. "We'll take turns sleeping on the back seat, and all we'll need when we get there is a bath, a shave for me and some make-up for Irma. If we drive ourselves we can talk freely, without fear of spies, and I wouldn't want to trust any servant, whether German or French. That goes for all the time we're in Naziland."

XII

There was a phone call for Lanny: Jerry Pendleton calling from Paris, to report that a letter from Germany had arrived. It bore no sender's name, but Jerry had guessed that it might have some bearing on the situation. Lanny told him to open and read it. It proved to be an unsigned letter from Freddi, who had reached Berlin. He wrote in English, telling the same news, but adding that he and his wife were in hiding; they were not free to give the address, and were not sure how long they could stay. If Lanny would come to the Adlon, they would hear of it and arrange to meet him.

To Jerry, Lanny said: "My family is coming to Paris at once. Do what you can to help them. I am telling them to trust you completely. You are to trust nobody but them."

"I get you."

"You are still *Contrôleur-Général*, and your salary goes on. Whatever expenses you incur will be refunded. Has the chauffeur left?"

"He left at four this morning. He thinks he can make it by ten."

"All right, thanks."

Lanny reported all this to the family, and his mother said: "You ought to get some sleep before you start driving."

"I have too many things on my mind," he replied. "You go and sleep, Irma, and you can do the first spell of driving."

Irma liked this new husband who seemed to know exactly what to do and spoke with so much decisiveness. She had once had a father like that. Incidentally, she was extremely tired, and glad to get away from demonstrative Jewish grief. Lanny said "Sleep," and she was a healthy young animal, to whom it came easily. She had been half-hypnotized watching Parsifal Dingle, who would sit for a long time in a chair with his eyes closed; if you didn't know him well you would think he was asleep, but he was meditating. Was he asking God to save Johannes Robin? Was he asking God to soften the hearts of the Nazis? God could do such things, no doubt; but it was hard to think out the problem, because, why had God made the Nazis in the beginning? If you said that the devil had made them, why had God made the devil?

There was no longer any reason for anyone's remaining in Calais, so Feathers went to buy tickets for Paris and arrange to have the mountain of luggage transported. Meanwhile Hansi and Bess and Lanny discussed the best way of getting Papa's misfortune made known to the outside world. That would be an important means of help—perhaps the most important of all. Lanny's first impulse was to call up the office of *Le Populaire;* but he checked himself, realizing that if he was going to turn into a Nazi sympathizer, he oughtn't to be furnishing explosive news items to a Socialist paper. Besides, this was not a Socialist or Communist story; it had to do with a leading financier and belonged in the bourgeois press; it ought to come from the victim's son, a distinguished person in his own right. Hansi and his wife should go to the Hotel Crillon, and there summon the newspaper men, both French and foreign, and tell them the news, and appeal for world sympathy. Lanny had met several of the American correspondents in Paris, and now he gave Hansi their names.

"The Nazis lie freely," said the budding intriguer, "and they compel you to do the same. Don't mention the rest of your family, and if the reporters ask, say that you have not heard from them and have no idea where they are. Say that you got your information by telephoning to the yacht and to the palace. Put the burden of responsibility off on *Reichsbetriebszellenabteilung Gruppenführerstellvertreter* Pressmann, and let his *Hauptgruppenführer* take him down into the cellar and shoot him for it. Don't ever drop a hint that you are getting information from your family, or from Irma or me. Make that clear to Jerry also. We must learn to watch our step from this moment on, because the Nazis want one thing and we want another, and if they win, we lose!"

17

Will You Walk into My Parlor?

MR. and Mrs. Lanning Prescott Budd of Juan-les-Pins, France, registered themselves at the Hotel Adlon, on Unter den Linden. That is where the rich Americans stop, and this richest of young couples were installed in a suite appropriate to their state. Every luxury was put at their command. Attendants took their car and serviced it promptly and faithfully; a maid and a valet came to unpack their things and to carry off their clothes and press them; a bellboy brought iced drinks and copies of various morning newspapers. Lanny sat down at once and made certain that these contained no mention of a confiscated palace and yacht. There might be ever so much clamor in the outside world, but the German people would know only what their new masters considered proper for them. It was the seventeenth of May, and the headlines were devoted to the speech which the Führer was to deliver to the Reichstag at three o'clock that afternoon, dealing with the Geneva Conference on Arms Limitation and the attitude of the German government to its proposals.

The telephone rang: a reporter requesting the honor of an interview with Mr. and Mrs. Budd. Lanny had wondered how it was going to be in this new world. Would money still make one a personage? Apparently it would. Tourist traffic, so vital to the German economy, had fallen off to a mere trickle as a result of the Jewbaiting, and the insulting of foreigners who had failed to give the Nazi salute on the proper occasions. The papers must make the most of what few visitors came to them.

Every large newspaper has a "morgue," in Germany called the

Archiv, from which one can ascertain without delay what has been published concerning any person. The reporter who receives an assignment of consequence consults this file before he sets out. So here was a smart young representative of the recently "co-ordinated" *Zeitung am Mittag,* fully informed as to the new arrivals, and asking the customary questions, beginning with: "What do you think of our country?"

Lanny said that they had motored to Berlin in twenty-four hours, so their impressions were fleeting. They had been struck by the order and neatness they had seen along the way. They were non-political persons, and had no opinions concerning National Socialism, but they were open-minded, and glad to be shown. Lanny winced as he spoke, thinking of his Socialist friends who would read this. When the reporter asked if the outside world believed the stories of atrocities and persecutions in Germany, Lanny said he supposed that some did and some did not, according to their predilections—*ihre Gesinnung,* he said. He and his wife had come to renew old friendships, and also to make purchases of old masters for American collectors.

All this would put him right with the Nazi world, and enable him to stay without exciting suspicion. Nothing was said about a Jewish brother-in-law or the brother-in-law's *Schieber* father, either by this reporter or by others who followed. They were made welcome and treated to cigars and drinks by two friendly and informal darlings of fortune. Delightful people, the Americans, and the Germans admired them greatly, went to see their movies, adopted their slang, their sports, their drinks, their gadgets and fashions.

II

It was Lanny's immediate duty to report himself to the Polizei-wache. He submitted the passports of himself and wife, and stated his business as art expert and his race as Aryan. Then he went back to the hotel, where he found a telegram from his mother in Paris: "Robbie reports grandfather died last night impossible Robbie

come now he is cabling embassy concerning you advises you report there immediately."

So the old Puritan armorer was gone! Lanny had thought of him
for so long as going that the news brought no shock. He had to
keep his mind on his Berlin job, and without delay he wrote notes
to Seine Hochgeboren the General Graf Stubendorf, to Oberst Emil
Meissner, and to Heinrich Jung. Irma, at his suggestion, wrote to
several of the ladies of prominence whom she had met. No Jews,
no *Schieberfrauen*, but the socially untainted!

By that time the afternoon papers were on the street, making
known Lanny's arrival, and he had reason to expect a telephone call.
It came, and he heard a voice saying: "I understand that you are
interested in the paintings of Alexander Jacovleff." Lanny replied
without hesitation that he was greatly interested, and the voice informed him: "There is some of his work at the Dubasset Galleries
which you should see."

"Very well," said Lanny. "Should I come at once?"

"If you please."

He had agreed with Irma that hotel rooms might have ears; so all
he said to her was: "Come." She looked at him, and he nodded.
Without another word she got up and slipped on a freshly pressed
spring costume. Lanny ordered his car, and in a short time they
were safe from prying ears. "Yes, it's Freddi," he said.

The art dealer's place was on Friedrichstrasse, only a short way
from the Adlon. Lanny drove slowly by, and there was a tall, dark
young Jew strolling. The Mercédès slowed up at the curb and he
stepped in; they went on down the street, and around several
corners, until they were certain that no car was following.

"Oh, I am so glad to see you!" Freddi's voice broke and he buried
his face in his hands and began to weep. "Oh, thank you, Lanny!
Thank you, Irma!" He knew he oughtn't to behave like that, but
evidently he had been under a heartbreaking strain.

"Forget it, kid," said the "Aryan." He had to drive, and keep
watch in the mirror of the car. "Tell us—have you heard from
Papa?"

"Not a word."

"Has anything been published?"

"Nothing."

"You have no idea where he's been taken?"

"No idea. We dare not go to the authorities, you know."

"Are Mama and Rahel and the baby all right?"

"They were when I left them."

"You're not staying together?"

"We're afraid of attracting attention. Mama is staying with one of our old servants. Rahel and the baby with her father's family."

"And you?"

"I slept in the Tiergarten last night."

"Oh, Freddi!" It was Irma's cry of dismay.

"It was all right—not cold."

"You don't know anyone who would shelter you?"

"Plenty of people—but I might get them into trouble as well as myself. The fact that a Jew appears in a new place may suggest that he's wanted—and you can't imagine the way it is, there are spies everywhere—servants, house-wardens, all sorts of people seeking to curry favor with the Nazis. I couldn't afford to let them catch me before I had a talk with you."

"Nor afterward," said Lanny. "We're going to get all of you out of the country. It might be wiser for you and the others to go at once—because it's plain that you can't do anything to help Papa."

"We couldn't go even if we were willing," replied the unhappy young man. "Papa had our exit permits, and now the Nazis have them."

He told briefly what had happened. The family with several servants had gone to Bremerhaven by the night train and to the yacht by taxis. Just as they reached the dock a group of Brown-shirts stopped them and told Papa that he was under arrest. Papa asked, very politely, if he might know why, and the leader of the troop spat directly in his face and called him a Jew-pig. They pushed him into a car and took him away, leaving the others standing aghast. They didn't dare go on board the yacht, but wandered along the docks, carrying their bags. They talked it over and decided that they could do no good to Papa by getting themselves arrested. Both Freddi and Rahel were liable to be sent to concentration camps on account of their Socialist activities; so they decided to travel separately to Berlin and stay in hiding until they could get word to their friends.

III

Freddi said: "I had only a little money when I was going on board the yacht, and I had to pay my fare back here."

Lanny took out his billfold and wanted to give him a large sum, but he said no, it might be stolen, or, if he was arrested, the Nazis would get it; better a little bit at a time. He started to say that Papa would make it all good, but Lanny told him not to be silly; whatever he needed was his.

"Where are you going to stay?" asked Irma, and he said he would join the crowd in *die Palme*, a refuge for the shelterless; it would be pretty bad, but it wouldn't hurt him, and no one would pay any attention to him there, no one would call him a Jew-pig. He hoped the wait wouldn't be too long.

Lanny had to tell him it might be quite a while. His activities would be in the higher circles, and things did not move rapidly there; you had to apply the social arts. Freddi said: "I hope poor Papa can stand it."

"He will be sure that we are doing our best," replied Lanny; "so at least he will have hope."

The American didn't go into detail concerning his plans, because he feared that Freddi might be tempted to impart some of it to his wife or his mother; then, too, there was the fearful possibility that the Nazis might drag something out of him by torture—and he surely wouldn't tell what he didn't know. Lanny said: "You can always write or call me at the hotel and make an appointment to show me some art."

They contrived a private code. Pictures by Bouguereau would mean that everything was all right, whereas Goya would mean danger. Lanny said: "Think of something to say about a painting that will convey whatever you have in mind." He didn't ask the addresses of the other members of the family, knowing that in case of need they, too, could write him or phone him about paintings. Freddi advised that they should meet as seldom as possible, because an expensive automobile driven by foreigners was a conspicuous object, and persons who got into it or out of it might be watched.

They stopped for a while on a quiet residence street and talked. Freddi's mind was absorbed by the subject of concentration camps; he had heard so many horrible stories, some of which he couldn't repeat in Irma's presence. He said: "Oh, suppose they are doing such things to Papa!" Later he said: "Have you thought what you would do if you had to stand such things?"

Lanny had to answer no, he hadn't thought much about it. "I suppose one stands what one has to."

Freddi persisted: "I can't help thinking about it all the time. No Jew can help it now. They mean it to break your spirit; to wreck you for the rest of your life. And you have to set your spirit against theirs. You have to refuse to be broken."

"It can be done," said Lanny, but rather weakly. He didn't want to think of it, at least not while Irma was there. Irma was afraid enough already. But the Jewish lad had two thousand years of it in his blood.

"Do you believe in the soul, Lanny? I mean, something in us that is greater than ourselves? I have had to think a lot about it. When they take you down into the cellar, all alone, with nobody to help you—you have no party, no comrades—it's just what you have in yourself. What I decided is, you have to learn to pray."

"That's what Parsifal has been trying to tell us."

"I know, and I think he is right. He's the one they couldn't conquer. I'm sorry I didn't talk more about it with him while I had the chance."

"You'll have more chances," said Lanny, with determination.

Parting is a serious matter when you have thoughts like that. Freddi said: "I oughtn't to keep you from whatever you're planning to do. Put me off near a subway entrance and I'll ride to *die Palme.*"

So they drove on. Lanny said: "Cheerio," English fashion, and the young Jew replied: "Thanks a million," which he knew was American. The car slowed up and he stepped out, and the great hole in the Berlin sidewalk swallowed him up. Irma had a mist in her eyes, but she winked it away and said: "I could do with some sleep." She too had learned to admire the English manner.

IV

The Reichstag met in the Kroll Opera House that afternoon and listened to Adolf Hitler's speech on foreign affairs. The speech took three-quarters of an hour and immediately afterward Göring moved approval, which was voted unanimously, and the Reichstag adjourned. Soon afterward the newsboys were crying the extra editions, and there was the full text, under banner headlines. Of course these *gleichgeschaltete* papers called it the most extraordinary piece of statesmanship.

Lanny glanced through it swiftly, and saw that it was a speech like none other in the Führer's career. It was the first time he had ever read a prepared address; as it happened, the Wilhelmstrasse, the German foreign office, had put pressure on him and persuaded him that there was real danger of overt action by France. The Fatherland had no means of resisting, and certainly it was the last thing the infant Nazi regime wanted.

So here was a new Hitler. Such a convenient thing to be able to be something new whenever you wished, unhampered by anything you had been hitherto! The Führer spoke more in sorrow than in anger of the wrongs his country had suffered, and he told the Reichstag that he was a man utterly devoted to peace and justice among the nations; all he asked of the rest of the world was that it should follow the example of Germany and disarm. There was to be no more "force" among the nations; he called this "the eruption of insanity without end," and said that it would result in "a Europe sinking into Communistic chaos."

France and Britain, which had been worried, breathed a sigh of relief. The Führer really wasn't as bad as he had been painted; his soup wasn't going to scald anybody's tongue. He would settle down and let others write his speeches for him and govern the country sanely. To the diplomats and statesmen of foreign lands it was obvious that a mere corporal and painter of picture-postcards couldn't manage a great modern state. That called for trained men, and Germany had plenty of them. In an emergency they would take control.

Lanny wasn't sure about it; but he saw that today's speech was the best possible of omens for the Robin family. Adi was singing low; he wouldn't want any family rows, any scandals going out to the world; he was in a position where he could be mildly and politely blackmailed, and Lanny had an idea how to set about it.

The telephone rang. His note to Heinrich Jung had been delivered promptly. Heinrich had attended the Reichstag meeting, and now he was taking the first opportunity to call his friend. "Oh, Lanny, the most marvelous affair! Have you read the speech?"

"Indeed I have, and I consider it a great piece of statesmanship."

"*Wundervoll!*" exclaimed Heinrich.

"*Kolossal!*" echoed Lanny. In German you sing it, with the accent on the last syllable, prolonging it like a tenor.

"*Ganz grosse Staatskunst!*"

"*Absolut!*" Another word which you accent on the last syllable; it sounds like a popgun.

"*Wirkliches Genie!*" declared the Nazi official.

So they chanted in *bel canto*, like a love duet in Italian opera. They sang the praises of Adolf, his speech, his party, his doctrine, his Fatherland. Heinrich, enraptured, exclaimed: "You really see it now!"

"I didn't think he could do it," admitted the genial visitor.

"But he *is* doing it! He will go on doing it!" Heinrich remained lyrical; he even tried to become American. "How is it that you say—*er geht damit hinweg?*"

"He is getting away with it," chuckled Lanny.

"When can I see you?" demanded the young official.

"Are you busy this evening?"

"Nothing that I can't break."

"Well, come on over. We were just about to order something to eat. We'll wait for you."

Lanny hung up, and Irma said: "Isn't that overdoing it just a little?"

Lanny put his finger to his lips. "Let's dress and dine downstairs," he said. "Your best clothes. The moral effect will be worth while."

V

There were three of them in the stately dining-room of the most fashionable hotel in Berlin; the American heiress in the showiest rig she had brought, Lanny in a "smoking," and Heinrich in the elegant dress uniform he had worn to the Kroll Opera House. *Die grosse Welt* stared at them, and the heart of Heinrich Jung, the forester's son, was bursting with pride—not for himself, of course, but for his Führer and the wonderful movement he had built. Respect for rank and station had been bred into the very bones of a lad on the estate of Stubendorf, and this was the highest he had ever climbed on the social pyramid. This smart American couple had been guests on two occasions at the Schloss; it might even happen that the General Graf would enter this room and be introduced to the son of his *Oberförster!* Lanny didn't fail to mention that he had written to Seine Hochgeboren at his Berlin palace.

The orchestra played softly, and the waiters bowed obsequiously. Lanny, most gracious of hosts, revealed his mastery of the gastronomic arts. Did Heinrich have any preference? No, Heinrich would leave it to his host, and the host said they should have something *echt berlinerisch*—how about some *Krebse*, billed as *écrevisses?* Heinrich said that these would please him greatly, and kept the dark secret that he had never before eaten them. They proved to be small crayfish served steaming hot on a large silver platter with a much embossed silver cover. The waiter exhibited the magnificence before he put some on separate plates. Heinrich had to be shown how to extract the hot pink body from the thin shell, and then dip it into a dish of hot butter. Yes, they were good!

And what would Heinrich like to drink? Heinrich left that, too, to his host, so he had Rheinwein, the color of a yellow diamond, and later he had sparkling champagne. Also he had wild strawberries with *Schlagsahne*, and tiny cakes with varicolored icing. "Shall we have the coffee in our suite?" said the heiress; they went upstairs, and on the way were observed by many, and Heinrich's uniform with its special insignia indicating party rank left no doubt that Mr. and Mrs. Irma Barnes were all right; the word would go through the hotel, and the reporters would hear of it, and the social doings of the young couple would be featured in the controlled press. The Nazis would not love them, of course; the Nazis were not sentimental. But they were ready to see people climbing onto their bandwagon, and would let them ride so far as suited the convenience of the bandwagon Führer.

VI

Up in the room they had coffee, also brandy in large but very thin goblets. Heinrich never felt better in his life, and he talked for a couple of hours about the N.S.D.A.P. and the wonders it had achieved and was going to achieve. Lanny listened intently, and explained his own position in a frank way. Twelve years ago, when the forester's son had first made known Adi Schicklgruber's movement, Lanny hadn't had the faintest idea that it could succeed, or even attain importance. But he had watched it growing, step by step, and of course couldn't help being impressed; now he had come to realize that it was what the German people wanted, and of course they had every right in the world to have it. Lanny couldn't say that he was a convert, but he was a student of the movement; he was eager to talk with the leaders and question them, so that he could take back to the outside world a true and honest account of the changes taking place in the Fatherland. "I know a great many journalists," he said, "and I may be able to exert a little influence."

"Indeed I am sure you can," responded Heinrich cordially.

Lanny took a deep breath and said a little prayer. "There's just one trouble, Heinrich. You know, of course, that my sister is married to a Jew."

"Yes. It's too bad!" responded the young official, gravely.

"It happens that he's a fine violinist; the best I know. Have you ever heard him?"

"Never."

"He played the Beethoven concerto in Paris a few weeks ago, and it was considered extraordinary."

"I don't think I'd care to hear a Jew play Beethoven," replied Heinrich. His enthusiasm had sustained a sudden chill.

"Here is my position," continued Lanny. "Hansi's father has been my father's business associate for a long time."

"They tell me he was a *Schieber*."

"Maybe so. There were plenty of good German *Schieber;* the biggest of all was Stinnes. There's an open market, and men buy and sell, and nobody knows whom he's buying from or selling to. The point is, I have ties with the Robin family, and it makes it awkward for me."

"They ought to get out of the country, Lanny. Let them go to America, if you like them and can get along with them."

"Exactly! That is what I've been urging them to do, and they wanted to do it. But unfortunately Johannes has disappeared."

"Disappeared? How do you mean?"

"He was about to go on board his yacht in Bremerhaven when some Brownshirts seized him and carried him off, and nobody has any idea where he is."

"But that's absurd, Lanny."

"I'm sure it doesn't seem absurd to my old friend."

"What has he been doing? He must have broken some law."

"I have no idea and I doubt very much if he has."

"How do you know about it, Lanny?"

"I telephoned to the yacht and a strange voice answered. The man said he was a *Reichsbetriebszellenabteilung Gruppenführerstellvertreter.*"

"That's a part of Dr. Ley's new Labor Front. What's he got to do with a Jewish *Schieber?*"

"You may do me a great favor if you'll find out for me, Heinrich."

"Well, you know what happens in revolutions. People take things into their own hands, and regrettable incidents occur. The Führer can't know everything that's going on."

"I'm quite sure of it," said Lanny. "The moment I heard about it, I said: 'I know exactly where to go. Heinrich Jung is the person who will understand and help me.' So here I am!"

VII

The young Nazi executive wasn't a fool, not even with the Rheinwein and the champagne and the brandy. He perceived at once why he had been receiving all this hospitality. But then, he had known Lanny Budd for some twelve years, and had had other meals at his expense and no favors asked. It is injurious to one's vanity to have to suspect old friends, and Heinrich had a naturally confiding disposition. So he asked: "What do you want me to do?"

"First, I want you to understand my position in this unhappy matter. I have many friends in Germany, and I don't want to hurt them; but at the same time I can't let a member of my family rot in a concentration camp without at least trying to find out what he's accused of. Can I, Heinrich?"

"No, I suppose not," the other admitted, reluctantly.

"So far, there hasn't been any publicity that I have seen. Of course something may break loose abroad; Johannes has friends and business associates there, and when they don't hear from him they, too, may get busy on the telephone. If that happens, it will make a scandal, and I think I'm doing a favor to you and to Kurt and to Seine Hochgeboren and even to the Führer, when I come and let you know the situation. The first person I meet in Berlin is likely to ask me: 'Where is Johannes?' And what am I to say? Since he is my sister's father-in-law and my father's associate, I'd be bound to call at his home, or at least telephone and let him know of my arrival."

"It's certainly awkward," conceded Heinrich.

"Another thing: when Seine Hochgeboren gets my letter in the morning he may call up. He's a friend of Johannes—in fact, it was at Johannes's palace that I first met him. Also, Irma expects to meet the Fürstin Bismarck tomorrow—perhaps you know her, a very charming Swedish lady. What is she going to say about the matter?"

Heinrich admitted that it was *verteufelt;* and Lanny went on: "If I tell these people what has happened, I am in the position of having come here to attack the *Regierung;* and that's the last thing I want to do. But the story can't be kept down indefinitely, and it's going to make a frightful stink. So I said to Irma: 'Let's get to Heinrich quickly, and have the thing stopped before it gets started.' Johannes is absolutely a non-political person, and he has no interest in spread-ing scandals. I'm sure he'll gladly agree to shut up and forget that it happened."

"But the man must have done something, Lanny! They don't just grab people in Germany and drag them to jail for nothing."

"Not even Jews, Heinrich?"

"Not even Jews. You saw how orderly the boycott was. Or did the foreign press lie to you about it?"

"I have heard terrible stories; but I have refused to believe them and I don't want to have to. I want to be able to go out and tell my friends that as soon as I reported this case to the Nazi authorities, the trouble was corrected. I offer you a chance to distinguish your-self, Heinrich, because your superiors will be grateful to you for helping to avoid a scandal in the outside world."

VIII

This conversation was being carried on in German, because Hein-rich's English was inadequate. Irma's German was even poorer, but she had the advantage of having been told Lanny's plan of campaign, and she could follow its progress on the young official's face. A well-chiseled Nordic face, with two sky-blue eyes looking earnestly out, and a crown of straw-colored hair shaved so that a *Pickelhaube* might fit over it—though Heinrich had never worn that decoration. The face had been pink with pleasure at the evening's start; it had become rosy with good food, wine, and friendship; now it appeared to be growing pale with anxiety and a crushing burden of thought.

"But what on earth could I do, Lanny?"

"It was my idea that you would help me to take the matter directly to the Führer."

"Oh, Lanny, I couldn't possibly do that!"

"You have access to him, don't you?"

"Not so much as I used to. Things have changed. In the old days he was just a party leader, but now he's the head of the government. You've no idea of the pressure upon him, and the swarms of people trying to get at him all the time."

"I can understand that. But here is an emergency, and surely he would thank you for coming to him."

"I simply wouldn't dare, Lanny. You must understand, I am nothing but an office-man. They give me a certain job, and I do it efficiently, and presently they give me more to do. But I have never had anything to do with politics."

"But is this politics, Heinrich?"

"You will soon find out that it is. If Dr. Ley has arrested a rich Jew, he has some reason; and he's a powerful politician, and has friends at court—I mean, near the Führer. If I go and butt in, it will be like walking into No Man's Land while the shooting is going on. What hold I have on the Führer is because I am an old admirer, who has never asked anything of him in all my life. Now, if I come to him, and he finds that I'm meddling in state affairs, he might be furious and say ''*Raus mit dir!*' and never see me again."

"On the other hand, Heinrich, if it should ever come to his ears that you had advance knowledge of this matter and failed to give him warning, he wouldn't think it was a high sort of friendship, would he?"

The young Nazi didn't answer, but the furrows on his brow made it plain that he was facing a moral crisis. "I really don't know what to say, Lanny. They tell me he's frightfully irritable just now, and it's very easy to make him angry."

"I should think he ought to feel happy after that wonderful speech, and the praise it is bound to get from the outside world. I should think he'd be more than anxious to avoid having anything spoil the effect of such a carefully planned move."

"*Du lieber Gott!*" exclaimed the other. "I ought to have the advice of somebody who knows the state of his mind."

Lanny thought: "The bureaucrat meets an emergency, and has no orders!" Aloud he said: "Be careful whom you trust."

"Of course. That's the worst of the difficulty. In political affairs you cannot trust anybody. I have heard the Führer say it himself." Heinrich wrinkled his brows some more, and finally remarked: "It seems to me it's a question of the effect on the outside world, so it might properly come before our Reichsminister of Public Enlightenment and Propaganda."

"Do you know him?"

"I know his wife very well. She used to work in Berlin party headquarters. Would you let me take you to her?"

"Certainly, if you are sure it's the wise step. As it is a matter of politics, you ought to consider the situation between Dr. Goebbels and Dr. Ley. If they are friends, Goebbels might try to hush it up, and perhaps keep us from seeing the Führer."

"*Gott im Himmel!*" exclaimed Heinrich. "Nobody in the world can keep track of all the quarrels and jealousies and intrigues. It is dreadful."

"I know," replied Lanny. "I used to hear you and Kurt talk about it in the old days."

"It is a thousand times worse now, because there are so many more jobs. I suppose it is the same everywhere in politics. That is why I have kept out of it so carefully."

"It has caught up with you now," said Lanny; but to himself. Aloud he remarked: "We have to start somewhere, so let us see what Frau Goebbels will advise."

IX

Heinrich Jung went to the telephone and called the home of Reichsminister Doktor Joseph Goebbels. When he got the Frau Reichsminister he called her "Magda," and asked if she had ever heard of Lanny Budd and Irma Barnes. Apparently she hadn't, for he proceeded to tell her the essential facts, which were how much money Irma had and how many guns Lanny's father had made; also that they had visited at Schloss Stubendorf and that Lanny had once had tea with the Führer. Now they had a matter of importance to the party about which they wished Magda's counsel. "We are at the Adlon," said Heinrich. "*Ja, so schnell wie möglich. Auf wiedersehen.*"

Lanny called for his car, and while he drove to the Reichstagplatz, Heinrich told them about the beauty, the charm, the warmth of heart of the lady they were soon to meet. One point which should be in their favor, she had been the adopted child of a Jewish family. She had been married to Herr Quandt, one of the richest men in Germany, much older than herself; she had divorced him and now had a comfortable alimony—while the man who paid it stayed in a concentration camp! She had become a convert to National Socialism and had gone to work for the party; a short time ago she had become the bride of Dr. Goebbels, with Hitler as best man, a great event in the Nazi world. Now she was "Frau Reichsminister," and ran a sort of salon—for it appeared that men cannot get along without feminine influence, even while they preach the doctrine of *Küche, Kinder, Kirche* to the masses.

"People accuse Magda of being ambitious," explained the young official. "But she has brains and ability, and naturally she likes to use them for the good of the cause."

"She will have a chance to do it tonight," replied Lanny.

They were escorted to the fashionable apartment where the lovely Frau Quandt had once lived with the elderly manufacturer. The "Frau Reichsminister" appeared in a cerise evening gown and a double string of pearls that matched Irma's; both strings were genuine, but each lady would have been interested to bite the other's to make sure. Magda had wavy fair hair, a sweet, almost childish face, and rather melancholy eyes with the beginning of dark rings about them. Lanny knew that she was married to one of the ugliest men in Germany; he could believe that she had needed the spur of ambition, and wondered if she was getting the satisfaction she craved.

It was growing late, and the visitors came to the point quickly. Knowing that the Minister of Popular Enlightenment and Propaganda was a bitter anti-Semite, Lanny said: "Whatever one's ideas may be, it is a fact that Hansi Robin is a musician of the first rank. The concert which he gave with the Paris Symphony this spring brought him a tremendous ovation. He has given similar concerts in London and in all the great cities of the United States, and that means that thousands of people will be ready to come to his defense. And the same thing is true about the business men who know his father. From the purely practical point of view, Frau Reichsminister, that is bad for your *Regierung*. I cannot see what you can possibly gain from the incarceration of Johannes Robin that can equal the loss of prestige you will suffer in foreign lands."

"I agree with you," said the woman, promptly. "It is one of those irrational things which happen. You must admit, Mr. Budd, that our revolution has been accomplished with less violence than any in previous history; but there have been cases of needless hardship which my husband has learned about, and he has used his influence to correct them. He is, of course, a very hard-pressed man just now, and it is my duty as a wife to shield him from cares rather than to press new ones upon him. But this is a special case, as you say, and I will bring it to his attention. What did you say was the name of the party organization which is responsible?"

"*Die Reichsbetriebszellenabteilung.*"

"I believe that has been taken into Dr. Ley's *Arbeitsfront*. Do you know Robert Ley?"

"I have not the honor."

"He is one of the men who came into our party from the air service. Many of our most capable leaders are former airmen: Gregor Strasser——"

"I have met him," said Lanny.

"Hermann Göring, Rudolph Hess—quite a long list. Airmen learn to act, and not to have feelings. Dr. Ley, like my husband, is a Rheinlander, and I don't know if you realize how it is in the steel country——"

"My father is a steel man, Frau Reichsminister."

"*Ach, so!* Then you can realize what labor is in the Ruhr. The Reds held it as their domain; it was no longer a part of Germany, but of Russia. Robert Ley got his training by raiding their meetings and throwing the speaker off the platform. Many a time he would have the shirt torn off his back, but he would make the speech. After ten years of that sort of fighting he is not always a polite person."

"I have heard stories about him."

"Now he is head of our *Arbeitsfront*, and has broken the Marxist unions and jailed the leaders who have been exploiting our German workers and tearing the Fatherland to pieces with class war. That is a great personal triumph for Dr. Ley, and perhaps he is a little too exultant over it—he has what you Americans call a 'swelled head.'" The Frau Reichsminister smiled, and Lanny smiled in return.

"I suppose he saw a rich Jew getting out of the country in a private yacht, obtained by methods which have made the Jews so hated in our country; and perhaps it occurred to him that he would like to have that yacht for the hospitalization of National Socialist party workers who have been beaten and shot by Communist gangsters."

"*Na also*, Frau Reichsminister!" said Lanny, laughing. "Heinrich assured me that if I came to you I would get the truth about the situation. Let the *Arbeitsfront* take the yacht and give me my brother-in-law's father, and we will call it a deal. *Wir werden es als ein gutes Geschäft betrachten.*"

X

There was the sound of a door closing, and Magda Goebbels said: "I think that is the Reichsminister now." She rose, and Heinrich rose, and Irma and Lanny followed suit; for when you are in Berlin you must do as Berliners do, especially when you are suing for favors from a Cabinet Minister who is more than royalty in these modern days.

"Juppchen" Goebbels appeared in the doorway of the drawing-room. He was small indeed, but not so small as he had seemed when Lanny had seen him standing on the platform at one of those colossal meetings. He had a clubfoot and walked with a limp which could not be concealed. He had a thin face built to a point in a sharp nose. He had a wide, tightly-drawn mouth which became like a Greek comic mask when he opened it for a speech. He had prominent eyes, black hair combed back from a receding forehead, and rather wide ears slightly hanging over at the top.

Also he had a brain and a tongue. The brain was superficial, but possessed of everything that was needed to delight a hundred thousand German *Kleinbürger* packed into a swastika-bedecked stadium. The tongue was as sharp as a snake's, and unlike a snake's it exuded venom. The Goebbels mind was packed with discreditable facts concerning every person and group and nation which offered opposition to National Socialism, and his eager imagination could make up as many new facts as any poet or novelist who had ever lived. The difference between fiction and fact no longer existed for Dr. Juppchen. Inside the German realm this grotesque little man had complete and unquestioned charge of newspapers, films, and radio, the stage, literature, and the arts, all exhibitions and celebrations, parades and meetings, lectures on whatever subject, school books, advertising, and cultural relations of whatever sort that went on between Germany and the outside world, including those organizations and publications which were carrying on Nazi propaganda in several score of nations. This ugly, dark, and pitiful deformity had a budget of a hundred million dollars a year to sing the praises of the beautiful, blond, and perfect Aryan.

In private life he was genial and witty, resourceful and quick in argument, and completely cynical about his job; you could chaff him about what he was doing, and he would even chaff himself. All the world's a stage and all the men and women on it merely players; how did you like my performance tonight? Like all truly great actors, Herr Reichsminister Doktor Goebbels worked terrifically hard, driven by an iron determination to get to the top of his profession and stay there in spite of all his rivals. At the beginning of his career he had been a violent opponent of the N.S.D.A.P., but the party had offered him a higher salary and he had at once become a convert. Now, besides being Minister of Popular Enlightenment and Propaganda, he was the party's *Gauleiter* of Berlin and director of *Der Angriff,* the powerful Nazi newspaper of the city.

He was pleased to find two rich and influential Americans in his home. One of his duties was to receive such persons and explain National Socialism to them. He was quick in reading their characters and in suiting what he told them to their positions and prejudices. For the third time that evening Lanny told his story, and the Reichsminister Doktor listened attentively. When he had heard to the end he turned to his wife. "*Na,* Magda, there you have it!" he said. "That pothouse brawler, that *Saalschlacht* hero, Ley! Such a *Grobian* to represent us to the outside world and involve us in his gangsterism!"

"*Vorsicht, Jockl!*" warned Magda.

But masterful Nazis are above heeding the warnings of their wives. Goebbels persisted: "A drunken rowdy, who wishes to control all German labor but cannot control himself! Have you seen that great organizer of ours, Mr. Budd?"

"Not that I know of, Herr Reichsminister."

"A pot-bellied, roaring braggart who cannot live without his flagon at his side. He likes to tell jokes, and he explodes with laughter and a fine spray flies over the surrounding company. You know that he is building the new Labor Front, and it must be done with melodrama—he personally must raid the union headquarters here in Berlin. Revolvers and hand grenades are not enough, he has to have machine guns mounted in front of the doors—for the arresting of cowardly fat labor parasites who find it difficult to rise out of their swivel-chairs without assistance! That is the way it goes in our land of *Zucht und Ordnung*—we are going to turn Berlin into another Chicago, and have bandits and kidnapers operating freely in our streets! I hope I do not offend you by the comparison, Mr. Budd."

"Not at all," laughed Lanny. "The home of my forefathers is a thousand miles from Chicago—and we, too, have sometimes observed the imperfections of human nature manifesting themselves in our perfect political system."

"*Na!*" said the Reichsminister Doktor. Then, becoming serious: "I leave the administration of justice to the proper authorities; but where the matter concerns a person with international reputation, I surely have a right to be consulted. I promise you that I will look into the matter the first thing in the morning and will report to you what I find."

"Thank you very much," said Lanny. "That is all I could ask."

The little great man appeared to notice the look of worry on his wife's gentle features; he added: "You understand, I do not know what crime your Jewish friend may be accused of, nor do I know that the overzealous Dr. Ley really has anything to do with it. Let us hold our minds open until we know exactly what has happened."

"What you have said will go no further, I assure you," declared Lanny, promptly. "I am not here to make gossip but to stop it."

XI

The Reichsminister of Popular Enlightenment and Propaganda relaxed in his chair and sipped the wine which his wife poured out for him and for the guests. "*Na!*" he exclaimed. "Tell me what you think of our Führer's speech."

Lanny started to repeat what he had said to the forester's son, and the *bel canto* duet was sung over again. Juppchen proved an even more romantic tenor than Heinrich; there was no language too ardent for him to employ in praise of Hitler. Lanny realized the situation; a deputy was free to criticize his fellow deputies, the Leys and the Strassers, the Hesses and the Röhms, but the Great One was perfection, and on him the butter of flattery was laid thickly. Heinrich had informed Lanny that the Goebbels home had become Adi's favorite haunt when he was in Berlin; here Magda caused to be prepared for him the vegetable plates which he enjoyed, and afterward he relaxed, listened to music, and played with her two children. Lanny didn't have to be told that the wily intriguer would use the occasion to fill his Chief's mind with his own views of the various personalities with whom their lives were involved. So it is that sovereigns are guided and the destinies of states controlled.

The Reichsminister of Popular Enlightenment and Propaganda enjoyed every aspect of his job and worked at it day and night.

Here he had two rich and well-dressed Americans, and at least one of them appeared to be intelligent. He thought just what Heinrich had been thinking for the past twelve years—to send Lanny Budd out as a missionary to spread the faith in the lands where he was at home. Said Goebbels: "All that we National Socialists want is to be left alone, so that we can reorganize our country's industry, solve the problem of unemployment by public works, and show the world what a model state can be. We have absolutely nothing to gain by forcing our ideas upon other peoples."

Said Lanny: "Ten years ago Mussolini told me that *Fascismo* was not for export. But since then I have seen him export it to Germany."

The Reichsminister Doktor perceived that this was indeed an intelligent young man, in spite of his well-tailored clothes and rich wife. "We have learned where we could," he admitted.

"Even from Lenin," smiled the other.

"If I answered that, Mr. Budd, it would have to be, as you Americans say, off the record."

"Naturally, Herr Reichsminister. I ought to explain to you that I had the good fortune to be secretary and translator to one of the experts on the American staff at the Peace Conference. I learned there how international business is carried on, and to keep my own counsel."

"Are you older than your years, Mr. Budd—or is it that you are older than your looks?"

"I was only nineteen at the time, but I had lived all over Europe, and knew the languages better than a geographer from what we call a 'fresh-water college' in the Middle West."

"*Eine frisch-Wasser-Universität?*" translated the Minister of Enlightenment, puzzled; and when Lanny explained, "*Süsswasser*," he said: "One thing that I envy you Americans is your amusing forms of speech."

"Other people laugh at us," responded Lanny; "they fail to realize that we are laughing at ourselves."

"I perceive that you are a philosopher, Mr. Budd. I, too, had aspirations in that direction, but the world of affairs has claimed me.

Tell me honestly, without any evasion, what will Europe and America make of the Führer's speech?"

"They will be pleased, of course, but surprised by its tone of politeness. The skeptical ones will say that he wishes to have no trouble until Germany has had time to rearm."

"Let them learn one of his sentences: 'that Germany wishes nothing but to preserve her independence and guard her borders.'"

"Yes, Herr Reichsminister; but there are sometimes uncertainties as to where borders are or should be."

The other could not fail to smile. But he insisted: "You will see that all our arming is defensive. We are completely absorbed in the problems of our own economy. We mean to make good the Socialism in our name, and show the outside world as well as our own people that the problems of unemployment can be solved. In five years—no, I dare say in three—there will not be a single man desiring work in Germany and not finding it."

"That indeed will be something to watch, Herr Reichsminister."

The great man started to explain how it could be done; and from that abnormally wide mouth there poured a torrent of words. Lanny had observed the same thing with Hitler and Mussolini and many lesser propagandists—they forgot the difference beween an audience of four and an audience of four million, and were willing to expend as much energy on the former as on the latter. Crooked Juppchen went on and on, and perhaps would have talked all night; but his tactful wife chose an opportunity when he was taking in breath, and said: "The Herr Reichsminister Doktor has a hard day's work behind him and has another before him. He ought to have some sleep."

The others started to their feet at once; and so they missed hearing about the *Autobahnen* which the new government was going to build all over Germany. They thanked both host and hostess, and took their departure quickly. After they had delivered Heinrich to his home and were safely alone in their car, Irma said: "Well, do you think you got away with it?"

"We can't tell a thing, in this world of intrigue. Goebbels will think the matter over and decide where his interests lie."

Irma had understood a little of the conversation here and there. She remarked: "At least you got the dirt on Dr. Ley!"

"Yes," replied her husband; "and if we have the fortune to meet Dr. Ley, we'll get the dirt on Dr. Goebbels!"

18

I Am a Jew

I

LANNY wasn't taking his father's suggestion of reporting to the American Embassy. The attaché who was Robbie's old friend was no longer there. The Ambassador was a Hoover appointee, a former Republican senator from Kentucky and Robbie Budd's type of man; but he was ill, and had gone to Vichy, France, from which place he had given an interview defending the Nazi regime. As for Lanny himself, he didn't expect any serious trouble, but if it came, he would put it up to the Embassy to get him out. He had agreed with Irma that when he went out alone he would set a time for his return; if anything delayed him he would telephone, and if he failed to do this, she would report him as missing.

In the morning they took things easy; had breakfast in bed and read the papers, including interviews with themselves, also full accounts of the Reichstag session and other Nazi doings. Their comments were guarded, for they had to expect some form of spying. Except when they were alone in their car, everything in Germany was to be wonderful, and only code names were to be used. Heinrich was "Aryan," Goebbels was "Mr. Mouth," and the Frau Minister "Mrs. Mouth." Disrespectful, but they were young and their manners were "smart."

There came a telephone call from Freddi; he gave no name, but Lanny, knowing his voice, said promptly: "We saw some fine Bouguereau paintings last night, and are waiting for a call telling us the price. Call later." Then he settled down and wrote a note to Mrs. Dingle, in Paris, enclosing various newspaper clippings, and saying: "The picture market appears promising and we hope to make purchases soon. The clarinet and other instruments are in good condition."

While he was writing, one of Irma's friends, the Fürstin Donnerstein, called up to invite the young couple to lunch. Lanny told Irma to accept for herself. It was a waste of time for her to sit through long interviews with officials in the German language; let her go out and spread the news about Johannes, and find out the reaction of "society" to the disappearance of a Jewish financier. Lanny himself would wait in their suite for messages.

They were dressing, when the telephone rang. The "personal secretary" to Herr Reichsminister Doktor Goebbels announced: "The Herr Reichsminister wishes you to know that he has taken entire charge of the matter which you brought to his attention, and he will report to you as soon as he has completed investigations."

Lanny returned his thanks, and remarked to his wife: "We are getting somewhere!"

Irma replied: "He was really a quite agreeable person, Lanny." He looked at her, expecting a small fraction of a wink; but apparently she meant it. He would have liked to say: "Too bad his public speeches aren't as pleasant as his private conversation." But that could be said only in the car.

He added a postscript to the note to his mother: "I have just been given reason to hope that our deal may go through quickly." He was about to offer to accompany Irma to the luncheon, when there came a tap upon the door, and a bellboy presented a card, reading: "*Herr Guenther Ludwig Furtwaengler. Amtsleiter Vierte Kammer: Untersuchungs- und Schlichtungsausschuss N.S.D.A.P.*" Lanny didn't stop to puzzle out this jet of letters, but said: "Bring the Herr up." Studying the card, he could tell something about the visitor, for the

Germans do not customarily put the title "Herr" on their cards, and this was a crudity.

The officer entered the reception room, clicked his heels, bowed from the waist, and remarked: "*Heil Hitler. Guten Morgen, Herr Budd.*" He was a clean-cut youngish man in the black and silver uniform of the S.S. with the white skull and crossbones. He said: "Herr Budd, I have the honor to inform you that I was yesterday appointed to the personal staff of the Reichsminister and Minister-Präsident of Prussia, Hauptmann Göring. I have the rank of Ober-leutnant, but have not had time to have new cards engraved. Seine Exzellenz wishes to invite you and Frau Budd to his inauguration ceremonies, which take place the day after tomorrow."

"We are greatly honored, Herr Oberleutnant," said Lanny, concealing his surprise.

"I present you with this card of admission. You understand it will be necessary to have it with you."

"Assuredly," said Lanny, and put the treasure safely into the inside breast pocket of his coat.

The other went on: "Seine Exzellenz the Minister-Präsident wishes you to know that he is giving immediate personal attention to the matter of Johannes Robin."

"Well, thank you, Herr Oberleutnant," said the American. This time his surprise couldn't be concealed. He explained: "Only a few minutes ago I had a call from the office of another Reichsminister, and was told that *he* had the matter in charge."

Said the officer: "I am instructed to inform you that if you will accompany me to the residence of Seine Exzellenz the Minister-Präsident, he personally will give you information about the matter."

"I am honored," replied Lanny, "and of course pleased to come. Excuse me while I inform my wife."

Irma paled when told this news, for she had heard about Göring, who had so far no rival for the title of the most brutal man in the Nazi government. "Can this be an arrest, Lanny?"

"It would be extremely bad form to suggest such an idea," he smiled. "I will phone you without fail at the Fürstin Donnerstein's by two o'clock. Wait there for me. If I do not call, it will be serious. But meantime, don't spoil your lunch by worrying." He gave her a quick kiss and went down to the big official car—a Mercédès, as big as a tank, having six wheels. It had a chauffeur and guard, both in Nazi uniforms. Lanny thought: "By heck! Johannes must be richer than I realized!"

II

A short drive up Unter den Linden and through the Brandenburger Tor to the Minister-Präsident's official residence, just across the way from the Reichstag building with its burned-out dome. Lanny had heard no end of discussion of the three-hundred-foot tunnel which ran under the street, through which the S.A. men were said to have come on the night when they filled the building with incendiary materials and touched them off with torches. All the non-Nazi world believed that Hermann Wilhelm Göring had ordered and directed that job. Certainly no one could question that it was he who had ordered and directed the hunting down and killing, the jailing and torturing, of tens of thousands of Communists and Socialists, democrats and pacifists, during the past three and a half months. In his capacity of Minister without Portfolio of the German Reich he had issued an official decree instructing the police to co-operate with the Nazi forces, and in a speech at Dortmund he had defended his decree:

"In future there will be only one man who will wield power and bear responsibility in Prussia—that is myself. A bullet fired from the barrel of a police pistol is my bullet. If you say that is murder, then I am a murderer. I know only two sorts of law because I know only two sorts of men: those who are with us and those who are against us."

With such a host anything was possible, and it was futile for Lanny to try to guess what was coming. How much would the Commandant of the Prussian Police and founder of the "Gestapo," the Secret State Police, have been able to find out about a Franco-American Pink in the course of a few hours? Lanny had been so indiscreet as to mention to Goebbels that he had met Mussolini.

Would they have phoned to Rome and learned how the son of Budd's had been expelled from that city for trying to spread news of the killing of Giacomo Matteotti? Would they have phoned to Cannes and found out about the labor school? To Paris and learned about the Red uncle, and the campaign contributions of Irma Barnes which had made him a Deputy of France? Lanny could pose as a Nazi sympathizer before Heinrich Jung—but hardly before the Führer's head triggerman!

It was all mystifying in the extreme. Lanny thought: "Has Goebbels turned the matter over to Göring, or has Göring grabbed it away from Goebbels?" Everybody knew that the pair were the bitterest of rivals; but since they had become Cabinet Ministers their two offices must be compelled to collaborate on all sorts of matters. Did they have jurisdictional disputes? Would they come to a fight over the possession of a wealthy Jew and the ransom which might be extorted from him? Göring gave orders to the Berlin police, while Goebbels, as *Gauleiter* of Berlin, commanded the party machinery, and presumably the Brownshirts. Would the cowering Johannes Robin become a cause of civil war?

And then, still more curious speculations: How had Göring managed to get wind of the Johannes Robin affair? Did he have a spy in the Goebbels household? Or in the Goebbels office? Or had Goebbels made the mistake of calling upon one of Göring's many departments for information? Lanny imagined a spiderweb of intrigue being spun about the Robin case. It doesn't take long, when the spinning is done with telephone wires.

III

Flunkies bowed the pair in, and a secretary led Lanny up a wide staircase and into a sumptuous room with a high ceiling. There was the great man, lolling in an overstuffed armchair, with a pile of papers on a small table beside him, and another table with drinks on the other side. Lanny had seen so many pictures of him that he knew what to expect: a mountain of a man, having a broad sullen face with heavy jowls, pinched-in lips, and bags of fat under the eyes. He was just forty, but had acquired a great expanse of chest and belly, now covered by a resplendent blue uniform with white lapels. Suspended around his neck with two white ribbons was a golden star having four double points.

The ex-aviator's love of power was such that he was assuming offices one after another: Minister without Portfolio of the Reich, Minister-Präsident of Prussia, Air Minister, Commander-in-Chief of the German Air Force, Chief Forester of the Reich, Reich Commissioner. For each he would have a new uniform, sky blue, cream, rose-pink. It wouldn't be long before some Berlin wit would invent the tale of Hitler attending a performance of *Lohengrin*, and falling asleep; between the acts comes the tenor in his gorgeous swanboat costume, wishing to pay his respects to•the Führer; Hitler, awakened from his nap, rubs his eyes and exclaims: *"Ach, nein, Hermann! That is too much!"*

Next to his chief, Göring was the least unpopular of the Nazis. He had been an ace aviator, with a record of devil-may-care courage. He had the peculiar German ability to combine ferocity with *Gemütlichkeit*. To his cronies he was genial, full of jokes, a roaring tankardman, able to hold unlimited quantities of beer. In short, he was one of the old-time heroes of Teutonic legend, those warriors who could slaughter their foes all day and at night drink wassail with their unwashed bloody hands; if they were slain, the Valkyries would come on their galloping steeds and carry them off to Valhalla to drink wassail forever after.

IV

Lanny's first thought: "The most repulsive of men!" His second thought, close on its heels: "I admire all Nazis!" He bowed correctly and said: *"Guten Morgen, Exzellenz."*

"Guten Morgen, Mr. Budd," said the Hauptmann, in a rumbling bull voice. *"Setzen Sie sich."*

He indicated a chair at his side and Lanny obeyed. Having met many of the great ones of the earth in his thirty-three years, Lanny had learned to treat them respectfully, but without obsequiousness.

It was the American manner, and so far had been acceptable. He knew that it was up to the host to state why he had summoned him, and meantime he submitted to an inspection in silence.

"Mr. Budd," said the great man, at last, "have you seen this morning's Paris and London newspapers?"

"I do not have the advantage of possessing an air fleet, Exzellenz." Lanny had heard that Göring possessed a sense of humor.

"Sometimes I learn about them by telephone the night before," explained the other, with a smile. "They carry a story to the effect that the Jewish moneylender, Johannes Robin, has disappeared in Germany. We do not care to have the outside world get the impression that we are adopting American customs, so I had the matter investigated at once, and have just informed the press that this *Schieber* has been legally arrested for attempting to carry a large sum of money out of the country on board his yacht. This, as you may know, is forbidden by our law."

"I am sorry to hear that news, Exzellenz."

"The prisoner is liable to a penalty of ten years at hard labor—and it will be very hard indeed, I can assure you."

"Naturally, Exzellenz, I cannot say anything about the matter until I have heard Johannes's side of the story. He has always been a law-abiding citizen, and I am sure that if he broke the law it was by oversight. He was setting out on a yachting cruise, and one cannot sail to strange lands without having cash on board to purchase food and fuel."

"It is absolutely requisite to have a permit from the Exchange Control Authority, and our records show that no such document had been issued. The law has been on the books for more than a year, and has been well advertised. We cannot afford to have our country drained of wealth, nor our currency depreciated on the world markets. At the present time, owing to the scoundrelism of the Marxist-Jews who have ruled Germany, our gold reserve is down to eight and one-half per cent, and the very life of our state is imperiled by the activities of these *Schieberschweine*. I would consider myself justified in proceeding against Johannes Robin for high treason, and may decide to do so."

"Naturally, Exzellenz, I am distressed to hear all this. Is it your intention to grant me the privilege of an interview with the prisoner?"

"There is something even more important than the protection of the Reich's currency and that is the protection of its good name. We are indignant concerning the slanders which have been broadcast by the enemies of our *Regierung,* and we intend to take all possible steps against these devils."

"So far as Johannes is concerned, Exzellenz, I can assure you positively that he has no such motives. He is an entirely non-political person, and has gone to extremes to keep friendly. He has always supposed that he had friends inside the N.S.D.A.P."

"I am taking steps to find out who they are," replied the head of the Prussian state. "When I do, I shall shoot them."

It was, in a way, as if he had shot Lanny. From behind those rolls of fat the American saw cold blue eyes staring at him, and he realized that this war-eagle was a deadly bird of prey.

"Let us get down to business, Mr. Budd. I am willing to negotiate with you, but I require your word of honor as a gentleman that whatever information I impart and whatever proposals I make will be strictly between us, now and for the future. That means exactly what it says, and the reason I am seeing you is that I have been told that you are a man who will keep his bargain."

"I do not know who has spoken that good word for me, Exzellenz, but I assure you that I have no desire in this matter except to help an old friend and connection by marriage out of the trouble into which he has stumbled. If you will enable me to do this, you may be sure that neither Johannes nor I will have any interest in making publicity out of the unfortunate affair."

"It happens that this matter was started by other persons, but now I have taken charge of it. Whatever you have heard to the contrary you are to disregard. Johannes Robin is my prisoner, and I am willing to turn him loose on certain terms. They are Nazi terms, and you won't like them, and certainly he won't. You may take them to him, and advise him to accept them or not. I put no pressure upon you, and make only the condition I have specified: the matter will be under the seal of confidence. You will agree never to reveal the facts to anyone, and Johannes will make the same agreement."

"Suppose that Johannes does not wish to accept your terms, Exzellenz?"

"You will be bound by your pledge whether he accepts or rejects. He will be bound if he accepts. If he rejects, it won't matter, because he will never speak to anyone again."

"That is clear enough, so far as regards him. But I don't understand why you have brought me in."

"You are in Berlin, and you know about the case. I am offering you an opportunity to save your friend from the worst fate which you or he can imagine. A part of the price is your silence as well as his. If you reject the offer, you will be free to go out to the world and say what you please, but you will be condemning your Jew to a death which I will make as painful as possible."

"That is clear enough, Exzellenz. It is obvious that you have me as well as Johannes. I can do nothing but accept your proposition."

V

Lanny knew that this man of *Blut und Eisen* was engaged in turning the government of Germany upside down. He was kicking out officials of all sorts, police chiefs, mayors, even professors and teachers, and replacing them with fanatical Nazis. This very day, the papers reported, the lower legislative chamber of the Prussian state was scheduled to meet and tender its collective resignation, so that Göring might replace them with his party followers. But with all this on his hands he had time to explain to a young American visitor that he, the head of the Prussian state, was not to be numbered among the anti-Jewish fanatics; his quarrel with them was the purely practical one, that they had swarmed upon the helpless body of postwar Germany to drain her white. They had been speculators in marks who had profited by the most dreadful national calamity of modern times. "You can look at our school children, Mr. Budd and have no difficulty in picking out those who were born in the years from 1919 to 1923, because of their stunted size."

Lanny would have liked to say that he knew many Germans who had sold marks; but it would have been the worst of blunders to get into an argument. He listened politely while the head of the Prussian government employed barrack-room phrases, some of which an American esthete had never heard before.

Suddenly the heavy fat fist of the thunder-god Thor came down with a bang on the table. "*Jawohl!* To business! The Jew who has fattened himself upon our blood is going to disgorge. His yacht shall serve as a means of recreation for deserving party members. His palace shall become a public museum. I understand that it contains a well-chosen collection of old masters."

"I appreciate the compliment, Exzellenz. Or do you know that I had the pleasure of selecting them?"

"*Ach, so!* Shall I call it the Lanning Budd Museum?" The hard blue eyes twinkled between the heavy layers of fat.

"The museum should be named for the one who institutes it, Exzellenz. Johannes has often told me that he planned to leave it to the public. But now you are doing it."

"I intend to go about these matters with all proper formality," said Göring, still with the twinkle. "Our Führer is a stickler for legality. The papers will be prepared by our Staatsanwalt, and the *Schieber* will sign them before a notary. For the sum of one mark his yacht, for another his palace, and for yet other marks his shares in our leading industrial enterprises and banks. In payment for my services in the above matters, he will give me checks for the amount of his bank deposits—and be sure that I shall cash them before he gets away."

"You intend to leave him nothing, Exzellenz?"

"Each business transaction shall be for the sum of one mark, and those marks will be his inalienable personal property. For the rest—naked came he into Germany, and naked will he go out."

"Pardon me if I correct you, sir. I happen to know that Johannes was a rich man when he came into Germany. He and my father had been business associates for several years, so I know pretty well what he had."

"He made his money trading with the German government, I am informed."

"In part, yes. He sold things which the government was glad to have in wartime; magnetos which you doubtless used in the planes in which you performed such astounding feats of gallantry."

"You are a shrewd young man, Mr. Budd, and after this deal is over, you and I may be good friends and perhaps do a profitable business. But for the moment you are the devil's advocate, predestined to lose your case. I could never understand why our magnetos so often failed at the critical moment, but now I know that they were sold to us by filthy Jewish swine who probably sabotaged them so that we would have to buy more." The great man said this with a broad grin; he was a large and powerful cat playing with a lively but entirely helpless mouse. On the rug in front of his chair lay a half-grown lion-cub, which yawned and then licked his chops as he watched his master preparing for a kill. Lanny thought: "I am back among the Assyrians!"

VI

The visitor had the feeling that he ought to put up some sort of fight for his friend's fortune, but he couldn't figure out how to set about it. He had never met a man like this in all his life, and he was completely intimidated—not for himself, but for Johannes. Your money or your life!

"Exzellenz," he ventured, "aren't you being a trifle harsh on one unfortunate individual? There are many non-Jewish *Schieber;* and there are rich Jews in Germany who have so far managed to escape your displeasure."

"The *Schweine* have been careful not to break our laws. But this one has broken the eleventh commandment—he has been caught. *Man muss sich nicht kriegen lassen!* And moreover, we have use for his money."

Lanny was thinking: "It isn't as bad as it might be, because so much of Johannes's money is abroad." He decided not to risk a fight, but said: "I will transmit your message."

The head of the Prussian government continued: "I observe that you avoid mentioning the money which this *Schieber* has already shipped out and hidden in other countries. If you know the history of Europe you know that every now and then some monarch in need of funds would send one of the richest of his Hebrews to a dungeon and have him tortured until he revealed the hiding-places of his gold and jewels."

"I have read history, Exzellenz."

"Fortunately nothing of the sort will be needed here. We have all this scoundrel's bank statements, deposit slips, and what not. We have photostat copies of documents he thought were safe from all eyes. We will present checks for him to sign, so that those funds may be turned over to me; when my agents have collected the last dollar and pound and franc, then your Jew relative will have become to me a piece of rotten pork of which I dislike the smell. I will be glad to have you cart him away."

"And his family, Exzellenz?"

"They, too, will stink in our nostrils. We will take them to the border and give each of them a kick in the tail, to make certain they get across with no delay."

Lanny wanted to say: "That will be agreeable to them"; but he was afraid it might sound like irony, so he just kept smiling. The great man did the same, for he enjoyed the exercise of power; he had been fighting all his life to get it, and had succeeded beyond anything he could have dared expect. His lion-cub yawned and stretched his legs. It was time to go hunting.

"Finally," said Göring, "let me make plain what will happen to this *Dreck-Jude* if he ventures to defy my will. You know that German science has won high rank in the world. We have experts in every department of knowledge, and for years we have had them at work devising means of breaking the will of those who stand in our path. We know all about the human body, the human mind, and what you are pleased to call the human soul; we know

how to handle each. We will put this pig-carcass in a specially constructed cell, of such size and shape that it will be impossible for
him to stand or sit or lie without acute discomfort. A bright light
will glare into his eyes day and night, and a guard will watch him
and prod him if he falls asleep. The temperature of the cell will be
at exactly the right degree of coldness, so that he will not die, but
will become mentally a lump of putty in our hands. He will not
be permitted to commit suicide. If he does not break quickly enough
we will put camphor in his *Harnröhre*—you understand our medical
terms?"

"I can guess, Exzellenz."

"He will writhe and scream in pain all day and night. He will
wish a million times to die, but he will not even have a mark on
him. There are many other methods which I will not reveal to you,
because they are our secrets, gained during the past thirteen years
while we were supposed to be lying helpless, having the blood
drained out of our veins by filthy, stinking Jewish-Bolshevik vam-
pires. The German people are going to get free, Mr. Budd, and the
money of these parasites will help us. Are there any other questions
you wish to ask me?"

"I just want to be sure that I understand you correctly. If
Johannes accepts your terms and signs the papers which you put
before him, you will permit me to take him and his family out of
Germany without further delay?"

"That is the bargain. You, for your part agree that neither you
nor the Jew nor any member of his family will say anything to anybody about this interview, or about the terms of his leaving."

"I understand, Exzellenz. I shall advise Johannes that in my opinion he has no alternative but to comply with your demands."

"Tell him this, as my last word: if you, or he, or any member
of his family breaks the agreement, I shall compile a list of a hundred of his Jewish relatives and friends, seize them all and make
them pay the price for him. Is that clear?"

"Quite so."

"My enemies in Germany are making the discovery that I am the
master, and I break those who get in my way. When this affair

has been settled and I have a little more leisure, come and see me again, and I will show you how you can make your fortune and have an amusing life."

"Thank you, sir. As it happens, what I like to do is to play the works of Beethoven on the piano."

"Come and play them for the Führer," said the second in command, with a loud laugh which somewhat startled his visitor. Lanny wondered: Did the eagle-man take a patronizing attitude toward his Führer's fondness for music? Was he perchance watching for the time when he could take control of affairs out of the hands of a sentimentalist and *Schwärmer*, an orator with a gift for rabble-rousing but no capacity to govern? Had the Minister-Präsident's Gestapo reported to him that Lanny had once had tea with the Führer? Or that he had spent part of the previous evening in the Führer's favorite haunt?

When Lanny rose to leave, the lion-cub stretched himself and growled. The great man remarked: "He is getting too big, and everybody but me is afraid of him."

VII

Four days and nights had passed since Johannes Robin had been taken captive; and Lanny wondered how he was standing it. Had they been giving him a taste of those scientific tortures which they had evolved? Or had they left him to the crude barbarities of the S.A. and S.S. such as Lanny had read about in the Manchester *Guardian* and the Pink weeklies? He hadn't thought it wise to ask the General, and he didn't ask the young Schutzstaffel Oberleutnant who sat by his side on their way to visit the prisoner.

Furtwaengler talked about the wonderful scenes on the National Socialist First of May. His memories had not dimmed in eighteen days, nor would they in as many years, he said. He spoke with the same naïve enthusiasm as Heinrich Jung, and Lanny perceived that this was no accident of temperament, but another achievement of science. This young man was a product of the Nazi educational technique applied over a period of ten years. Lanny questioned him and

learned that his father was a workingman, killed in the last fighting
on the Somme—perhaps by a bullet from the rifle of Marcel Detaze.
The orphan boy had been taken into a Hitler youth group at the
age of fifteen, and had had military training in their camps and war
experience in the street fighting of Moabit, Neuköln, Schöneberg,
and other proletarian districts of Berlin. He was on his toes with
eagerness to become a real officer, like those of the Reichswehr;
the S.S. aspired to replace that army, considering such transfer of
power as part of the proletarian revolution. Oberleutnant Furtwaengler wanted to click his heels more sharply and salute more
snappily than any regular army man; but at the same time he couldn't
help being a naïve workingclass youth, wondering whether he was
making the right impression upon a foreigner who was obviously
elegant, and must be a person of importance, or why should the
Minister-Präsident of Prussia have spent half an hour with him on
such a busy morning?

They were now being driven in an ordinary Hispano-Suiza, not
a six-wheeled near-tank; but again they had a chauffeur in uniform
and a guard. There were hundreds of such cars, of all makes, including Packards and Lincolns, parked in front of the Minister-
Präsident's official residence and other public buildings near by. Such
were the perquisites of office; the reasons for seizing power and the
means of keeping it. Leutnant Furtwaengler was going to have a
new uniform, as well as new visiting cards; it was a great day in
the morning for him, and his heart was high; he needed only a
little encouragement to pour out his pride to an American who must
be a party sympathizer—how could anyone fail to be? Lanny did
his best to be agreeable, because he wanted friends at court.

Johannes had been taken out of the Nazi barracks, the so-called
Friesen Kaserne, to the main police headquarters, the Polizeipräsidium; but he was still in charge of a special group of the S.S.
It was like the Swiss Guard of the French kings, or the Janissaries
of the Turkish sultans—strangers to the place, having a special duty
and a special trust. Johannes represented a treasure of several tens
of millions of marks—Lanny didn't know how many, exactly. If he
should take a notion to commit suicide, Minister-Präsident Göring

would lose all chance of getting that portion of the treasure which had been stored abroad, nor could he get the part stored in Germany without violating his Führer's "legality complex."

VIII

The car stopped before a great red brick building in the Alexanderplatz, and Lanny was escorted inside. Steel doors clanged behind him—a sound which he had heard in the building of the Sûreté Générale in Paris and found intensely disagreeable. He was escorted down a bare stone-paved corridor, with more doors opening and clanging, until he found himself in a small room with one steel-barred window, a table, and three chairs. *"Bitte, setzen Sie sich,"* said the Oberleutnant. The chair which Lanny took faced the door, and he sat, wondering: "Will they have shaved his head and put him in stripes? Will he have any marks on him?"

He had none; that is, unless you counted spiritual marks. He was wearing the brown business suit in which he had set out for his yacht; but he needed a bath and a shave, and came into the room as if he might be on the way to a firing-squad. When he saw his daughter-in-law's half-brother sitting quietly in a chair, he started visibly, and then pulled himself together, pressing his lips tightly, as if he didn't want Lanny to see them trembling. In short, he was a thoroughly cowed Jew; his manner resembled that of an animal which had been mistreated—not a fighting animal, but a tame domestic one.

"Setzen Sie sich, Herr Robin," ordered the Oberleutnant. On Lanny's account he would be polite, even to a *Missgeburt.* Johannes took the third chair. *"Bitte, sprechen Sie Deutsch,"* added the officer, to Lanny.

Two S.S. men had followed the prisoner into the room; they closed the door behind them and took post in front of it. As Lanny was placed he couldn't help seeing them, even while absorbed in conversation. Those two lads in shining black boots and black and silver uniforms with skull and crossbones insignia stood like two monuments of Prussian militarism; their forms rigid, their chests thrust out, their guts sucked in—Lanny had learned the phrase from his ex-sergeant friend Jerry Pendleton. Their hands did not hang by their sides, but were pressed with palms open and fingers close together, tightly against their thighs and held there as if glued. Not the faintest trace of expression on the faces, not the slightest motion of the eyes; apparently each man picked out a spot on the wall and stared at it continuously for a quarter of an hour. Did they do this because they were in the presence of an officer, or in order to impress a foreigner—or just because they had been trained to do it and not think about it?

"Johannes," said Lanny, speaking German, as requested, "Irma and I came as soon as we heard about your trouble. All the members of your family are safe and well."

"*Gott sei Dank!*" murmured the prisoner. He was holding onto the chair in which he had seated himself, and when he had spoken he pressed his lips together again. For the first time in his life Johannes Robin seemed an old man; he was sixty, but had never shown even that much.

"The situation is a serious one, Johannes, but it can be settled for money, and you and your family are to be allowed to go to France with us."

"I don't mind about the money," said the Jew, quickly. He had fixed his eyes on Lanny's face and never took them away. He seemed to be asking: "Am I to believe what you tell me?" Lanny kept nodding, as if to say: "Yes, this is real, this is not a dream."

"The charge against you is that you tried to carry money out of the country on your yacht."

"*Aber*, Lanny!" exclaimed the prisoner, starting forward in his chair. "I had a permit for every mark that I took!"

"Where did you put the permit?"

"It was in my pocket when I was arrested."

"Are you sure of that?"

"Absolutely. I would have been mad to try to carry money out of Germany without it."

Lanny was not too much surprised by this. "We have to assume that some malicious person destroyed the paper, Johannes."

"Yes, but there will be a record of it in the office of the Exchange Control Authority."

"I have been told on the best possible authority that no such record exists. I am afraid we shall have to assume that some mistake has been made, and that you had no valid permit."

Johannes's eyes darted for the fraction of a second toward the S.S. officer. Then he said, as humbly as any moneylender in a medieval dungeon: "Yes, Lanny, of course. It must be so."

"That makes a very serious offense, and the punishment, I fear, would be more than your health could stand. The only alternative is for you to part with your money. All of it."

Lanny was prepared for some anguish, some kind of Shylock scene. "Justice! the law! my ducats, and my daughter!" But Johannes sank back in his chair and resumed his dull tone. "I have been expecting that, Lanny. It is all right."

The man's aspect and manner revealed even more than his words. Lanny knew how he loved his money; how hard he had worked for it, how many plans he had for the use of it. But here he was kissing it good-by, as casually as if he had been a darling of fortune whose interest was dancing, playing the piano, and listening to parlor Pinks discussing the expropriation of the expropriators!

What had happened to him to produce such a change? Had he been worked over with rubber hose, which leaves few marks? Had he seen his fellow Jews being compelled to lash one another's faces with whips? Had he lain awake all night listening to the screams of men with camphor injected in their urinary ducts? Something of the sort must have happened.

IX

The visitor had to leave no uncertainty in his friend's mind. He had to be as implacable as Minister-Präsident Göring himself. He said: "It means everything you have, Johannes—both here and abroad."

"I understand."

"They have had a man in your office and have all the records."

"I had become aware of that."

"I have gone into the situation carefully, and I'm afraid you will have to give up."

"If they will really let me go, and my family, they may have everything."

"I have the word of Minister-Präsident Göring, and I believe that he means what he says. He has explained in the clearest language that he has no interest in you or yours, and will be glad to be rid of you."

"I am sure that Minister-Präsident Göring is a man of honor, and I accept his promise."

"He wants your money to use for the upbuilding of National Socialism. From his point of view that is, of course, a worthy purpose."

"The money would be of no use to me in this place."

"Exactly, Johannes. We can go abroad and you and Robbie can start business again. Irma will back you."

"Thank you, Lanny. I'll get along, I am sure."

"I have had to agree, and you have to agree, not to say a word about the case to anybody. We'll just get out and forget it."

"God knows I don't want to talk about it, Lanny. What good would that do me?"

"All right, then. Papers will be brought for you to sign."

"I will sign them."

"Some papers must go to New York, you know. It should take a week or two. Irma and I will wait here, and take you and the others out with us."

"I will never be able to express my gratitude, Lanny."

"Don't waste any energy on that. All we want is to have the family with us on the Riviera. We can have a good time without so much money. Are you being treated reasonably well?"

"I have no complaint."

"Is there anything I could send you—assuming I can get permission?"

"I have everything I need—everything unless perhaps some red ink."

Johannes said this without the flicker of an eyelash; and Lanny answered, without change of tone or expression: "I will see if it is possible to get some."

Rote Tinte! "Oh, the clever rascal!" Lanny thought. "His mind works like greased lightning." Johannes could sit there in the presence of a Schutzstaffel officer and two privates, and with all this pressure of terror and grief upon him—in the midst of having to make the most fateful decision of his life—he could think up a way to tell Lanny what he wished him to know, and without the slightest chance of his enemies' guessing what he had said!

For fifteen years Lanny and his old friend had been watching the experiment in the Soviet Union and arguing about it. Johannes, taking the negative, had delighted himself by collecting ironical stories, to be repeated to the credulous Lanny, and over Lanny's shoulder to Johannes's two misguided sons. One such story had to do with two German business men, one of whom was going to make a trip into the proletarian paradise, and promised his friend to write a full account of what he found there. "But," objected the friend, "you won't dare to write the truth if it's unfavorable." The other replied: "We'll fix it this way. I'll write you everything is fine, and if I write it in black ink it's true, and if in red ink the opposite is true." So he went, and in due course his friend received a letter in black ink, detailing the wonders of the proletarian paradise. "Everybody is happy, everybody is free, the markets are full of food, the shops well stocked with goods—in fact there is only one thing I cannot find, and that is red ink."

While Lanny and the Oberleutnant were driving to the hotel, the latter inquired: "What does he want red ink for?"

Lanny, who wasn't slow-minded himself, explained: "He keeps a diary, and writes it in red ink to keep it separate from his other papers."

The officer replied: "One cannot keep a diary in prison. They will surely take it away from him."

X

It was the Oberleutnant's duty to report to his superior, and mean while Lanny had to wait. He was deposited at his hotel a few minutes before two o'clock, and called his wife and told her: "I have seen our friend and he is all right. I think matters can be arranged. Take your time." To his mother, his father, and Rick he sent telegrams. "Have seen our friend. Believe matters arranged." He decided against using code names; if the Gestapo was interested, let them know what he was saying, and to whom. He called Heinrich and reported: "I think that matters are being arranged, and I am grateful for the help of yourself and your friends. I have been asked to keep the matter confidential, so I cannot say any more." That was satisfactory to a perfect young bureaucrat.

The afternoon papers contained the story of the arrest of Johannes Robin, made public by the Prussian government. Eighty million Germans, minus the infants and a few malcontents, would learn that a Jewish *Schieber* had been caught trying to smuggle money out of the country on his yacht. Eighty million Germans, minus the infants and malcontents, would continue every day to believe statements issued on official authority, which statements would be carefully contrived fiction. It was a new kind of world to be living in, and for the present Lanny had but one desire, to get out of it.

Irma came home in the middle of the afternoon and he took her for a drive. He didn't feel in any way bound by promises made to a bandit, so he told her the story, adding: "If you drop a hint of it to anybody here it may cost Johannes and his family their lives." Irma listened in wide-eyed horror. It was like the things you read about the Borgias. He answered that there was nothing in history to compare it to, because never before had barbarians commanded the resources of modern science.

"Do you suppose Göring is taking that money for himself?" she asked.

"It's all the same thing," he told her. "Göring is Germany, and Germany will be Göring, whether it wishes to or not. The Nazis will spend everything the Germans have."

"But the money abroad! What will he do about that?"

"They have a network of agents in other countries, and doubtless they will have more. Also, if things should go wrong, and Göring has to take a plane some day, it will be nice to have a nest-egg, and be able to spend a comfortable old age in Paris or Buenos Aires."

"What perfect agony it must be to Johannes to turn all that money loose! My father would have died first!"

"Your father wouldn't have got into this position. Johannes was too trusting. He thought he could handle matters by diplomacy; but these fellows have knocked over the conference table. They have the advantage that nobody can realize how bad they are. If you and I were to go to Paris or London tomorrow and tell this story, the Nazis would call us liars and nine people out of ten would believe them."

XI

They went back to the hotel, expecting Freddi to call. But he didn't, and in the evening Colonel Emil Meissner came to dinner. He had read about the Robin case, and it did not occur to him to doubt his government's word. He said there had been a great deal of graft and favoritism under the Republic, but now, apparently, the laws were going to be enforced against rich as well as poor. This tall, severe-looking Prussian officer expressed polite regret that such misfortune should have fallen upon a relative of Lanny's. The host contented himself with replying that he had reason to hope matters would soon be straightened out, and that he had been asked to consider it confidential. Emil accepted this just as Heinrich had; all good Germans would accept it.

Emil talked freely about the new *Regierung*. He had despised the Republic, but had obeyed its orders because that was the duty of an army officer. Now Adolf Hitler had become his Commander-in-chief, and it was necessary to obey him, however one might privately dislike his manners. But Emil was sure that the stories of abuse of power had been greatly exaggerated, and for malicious purposes. There were bound to be excesses in any governmental overturn; the essential thing was that Germany had been saved from the clutches of the Reds, and every civilized person owed the new Chancellor a debt of gratitude for that. Lanny indulged in no Pink arguments, but said that he and his wife had been greatly impressed by what they had found in the country.

They waited late for a call from Freddi, but none came, and they went to bed speculating about it. Doubtless he was avoiding risks, and perhaps also afraid of bothering them; but it was too bad they couldn't give him the news which would so greatly relieve his mind. Lanny was prepared to state that he had come upon a wonderful Bouguereau!

Morning came, and the papers had editorials about the case of the Jewish *Schieber;* in Hitlerland all news stories were editorials, and were full of rancid hatred and venomous threats. At last the sneaking traitors were feeling the stern hand of the law; at last the vile Semitic parasites were being shaken from the fair body of Germania! *Der Angriff* was especially exultant. Here was proof to all the world that National Socialism meant what it said, that the stealthy influence of the Jewish plutocracy was no longer to rule the Fatherland! Lanny translated the words, which really seemed insane in their virulence. "Mr. Mouth doesn't sound so pleasant in print," he remarked.

Breakfast, and still no call from Freddi. They didn't like to go out until they had heard from him. Irma had her hair dressed and got a manicure; Lanny read a little, wrote a few notes, roamed about, and worried. They had a luncheon engagement at the Berlin home of General Graf Stubendorf, and they had to go. Irma said: "Clarinet can call again; or he can drop us a note."

Driving to the palace, they were free to discuss the various possibilities. Göring might have had Freddi arrested; or the Brownshirts might have picked him up, without Göring's knowing anything about it. Freddi was a Jew and a Socialist, and either was enough. Irma suggested: "Mightn't it be that Göring wants to keep the whole family in his hands until he's ready to put them out?"

"Anything is possible," said Lanny; "except that I can't imagine Freddi delaying this long to call us if he is free."

It rather spoiled their lunch. To tell the truth it wasn't an especially good lunch, or very good company—unless it was enough for you to know that you were the guest of a high-up Junker. The General Graf's attitude was the same as Emil's; he was a cog in the Reichswehr machine, and he obeyed orders. His special concern was get-

ting his home district out of the clutches of the Poles; he knew that
Lanny sympathized with this aim, but even so, he could talk about
it only guardedly, for the Chancellor had given the cue by a pacific
speech, so it was the duty of good Germans to let the subject of
boundary lines rest and to concentrate on the right of the Fatherland to equality of armaments. Having expressed regret over the
plight of Lanny's Jewish relative, the General Graf Stubendorf
talked about other friends, and about the condition of his crops and
the market for them, and what did Lanny's father think about the
prospects for world recovery?

Lanny answered with one part of his mind, while the other part
was thinking: "I wonder if Freddi is calling now!"

But Freddi wasn't calling.

19

No Peace in Zion

I

WHEN Mr. and Mrs. Irma Barnes had visited Berlin a year previously, they had been the darlings of the smart set, and all the important people had been glad to entertain them. But now the social
weather had changed; a thunderstorm was raging, and nobody could
be sure where the lightning might strike. The story of Johannes
Robin was known to the whole town; and who could guess what
confessions he might have made, or what might have been found in
his papers? Many persons have dealings with moneylenders which
they don't care to have become known. Many have affairs of various
sorts which they prefer not to have looked into by the Secret State

Police, and they carefully avoid anyone who might be under sur-
veillance by that dreaded body.

Moreover, Irma and Lanny were worried, and when you are worried you are not very good company. Another day passed, and another, and they became certain that something terrible must have
happened to Freddi. Of course he might have been knocked down
by a truck, or slugged and robbed by one of the inmates of an
Asyl für Obdachlose who suspected that he had money. But far
more likely was the chance that a Jew and Socialist had fallen into
the clutches of the Brown Terror. Their problem was, did Göring
know about it, and if so was it a breach of faith, or merely a precaution against a breach of faith on their part? Would Göring be
content to keep his hostage until the bargain was completed? Or
was Freddi to remain in durance for a long time?

The more Lanny thought about it, the more complications he
discovered. Could it be that there was a war going on between the
two powerful Nazi chiefs? Had Goebbels becomes furious because
Göring had taken the prisoner? Had he grabbed Freddi in order to
thwart Göring and keep him from carrying out his bargain? If
so, what was Lanny supposed to do? What part could a mere man
play in a battle of giants—except to get his head cracked by a flying
rock or uprooted tree? Lanny couldn't go to Goebbels and ask,
because that would be breaking his pledge to Göring.

No, if he went to anybody it must be to Göring. But was he
privileged to do this? Had it been a part of the bargain that the
Minister-Präsident of Prussia and holder of six or eight other important posts was to lay aside his multifarious duties and keep track
of the misfortunes of a family of Jewish *Schieber?* All Göring was
obligated to do was to let them alone; and how easy for him to say:
"Mr. Budd, I know nothing about the matter and have no desire to."
Was Lanny to reply: "I do not believe you, Exzellenz!"?

It seemed clear that all Lanny could accomplish was to center the
attention of the Gestapo upon the Robin family. If they set out to
look for Freddi they would have to inquire among his friends. They
might ask Lanny for a list of these friends; and what could Lanny
say? "I do not trust you, *meine Herren von der Geheimen Staats-*

Polizei"? On the other hand, to give the names might condemn all these friends to concentration camps. The wife of Johannes was hiding with one of her former servants. The Gestapo would get a list of these and hunt them out—Jews, most of them, and doubtless possessing secrets of Johannes and his associates. Who could guess what they might reveal, or what anybody might invent under the new scientific forms of torture?

II

Lanny and his wife attended the very grand inauguration ceremonies of the Minister-Präsident of Prussia. They were met by Oberleutnant Furtwaengler and introduced to Ministerialdirektor Doktor X and General Ritter von Y. They were surrounded by Nazis in magnificent uniforms covered with medals and orders, behaving themselves with dignity and even with charm. Very difficult indeed to believe that they were the most dangerous miscreants in the world! Irma in her heart couldn't believe it, and when she and Lanny were driving afterward they had a bit of an argument, as married couples have been known to do.

Irma was a daughter of civilization. When she suspected a crime she went to the police. But now, it appeared, the police were the criminals! Irma had listened to Lanny's Red and Pink friends denouncing the police of all lands, and it had annoyed her more than she had cared to say; there were still traces of that annoyance in her soul, and Lanny had to exclaim: "My God, didn't Göring tell me with his own lips that he would find a hundred of Johannes's relatives and friends and torture them?"

"Yes, darling," replied the wife, with that bland manner which could be so exasperating. "But couldn't it have been that he was trying to frighten you?"

"Jesus!" he exploded. "For years I've been trying to tell the world what the Nazis are, and now it appears that I haven't convinced even my own wife!" He saw that he had offended her, and right away was sorry.

He had been through all this with his mother, starting a full decade ago. Beauty had never been able to believe that Mussolini was as bad as her son had portrayed him; she had never been able to think of an Italian refugee as other than some sort of misdoer. Beauty's own friends had come out of Italy, reporting everything improved, the streets clean, the trains running on time. Finally, she had gone and seen for herself; had she seen anybody beaten, or any signs of terror? Of course not!

And now, here was the same thing in Germany. Wherever you drove you saw perfect order. The people were clean and appeared well fed; they were polite and friendly—in short, it was a charming country, a pleasure to visit, and how was anybody to credit these horror tales? Irma was in a continual struggle between what she wanted to believe and what was being forced upon her reluctant mind. Casting about for something to do for poor Freddi, she had a bright idea. "Mightn't it be possible for me to go and talk to Göring?"

"To appeal to his better nature, you mean?"

"Well, I thought I might be able to tell him things about the Robins."

"If you went to Göring, he would want just one thing from you, and it wouldn't be stories about any Jews."

What could Irma say to that? She knew that if she refused to believe it, she would annoy her husband. But she persisted: "Would it do any harm to try?"

"It might do great harm," replied the anti-Nazi. "If you refused him, he would be enraged, and avenge the affront by punishing the Robins."

"Do you really know that he's that kind of man, Lanny?"

"I'm tired of telling you about these people," he answered. "Get *rhe Fürstin Donnerstein off in a corner and ask her to give you the dirt!"

III

Any pleasure they might have got out of a visit to Berlin was ruined. They sat in their rooms expecting a telephone call; they waited for every mail. They could think of nothing to do that might not make matters worse; yet to do nothing seemed abominable. They thought: "Even if he's in a concentration camp, he'll find some way to smuggle out a message! Surely all the guards can't be loyal, surely some one can be bribed!"

Lanny bothered himself with the question: was he committing an act of bad faith with Johannes in not informing him of this new situation? He had assured Johannes that the family was all well. Was it now his duty to see the prisoner again and say: "Freddi has disappeared"? To do so would be equivalent to telling the Gestapo—and so there was the same round of problems to be gone over again. Even if he told Johannes, what could Johannes do? Was he going to say: "No, Exzellenz, I will not sign the papers until I know where my younger son is. Go ahead and torture me if you please." Suppose Göring should answer: "I have no idea where your son is. I have tried to find him and failed. Sign—or be tortured!"

The agonizing thing was that anywhere Lanny tried asking a question, he might be involving somebody else in the troubles of the Robin family. Friends or relatives, they would all be on the Gestapo list—or he might get them on! Was he being followed? So far he had seen no signs of it, but that didn't prove it mightn't be happening, or mightn't begin with his next step outdoors. The people he went to see, whoever they were, would know about the danger, and their first thought would be: "*Um Gottes Willen*, go somewhere else."

Rahel's parents, for example; he knew their names, and they were in the telephone book. But Freddi had said: "Don't ever call them. It would endanger them." The family were not Socialists; the father was a small lawyer, and along with all the other Jewish lawyers, had been forbidden to practice his profession, and thus was deprived of his livelihood. What would happen if a phone call were overheard and reported? Or if a rich American were to visit a third-class apartment house, where Jews were despised and spied upon, where the Nazis boasted that they had one of their followers in every building, keeping track of the tenants and reporting everything suspicious or even unusual? The Brown Terror!

Was Lanny at liberty to ignore Freddi's request, even in an effort

to save Freddi's life? Would Freddi want his life saved at the risk
of involving his wife and child? Would he even want his wife to
know about his disappearance? What could she do if she knew it,
except to fret herself ill, and perhaps refuse to let Lanny and Irma
take her out of the country? No, Freddi would surely want her to
go, and he wouldn't thank Lanny for thwarting his wishes. Possibly
he hadn't told Rahel where Lanny and Irma were staying, but she
must have learned it from the newspapers or from her parents; and
surely, if she knew where Freddi was, and if he needed help, she
would risk everything to get word to Lanny. Was she, too, in an
agony of dread, hesitating to communicate with Lanny, because
Freddi had forbidden her to do so?

IV

Lanny bethought himself of the Schultzes, the young artist couple.
Having got some of Trudi's work published in Paris, he had a legitimate reason for calling upon her. They lived in one of the industrial districts, desiring to be in touch with the workers; and this
of course made them conspicuous. He hesitated for some time, but
finally drove to the place, a vast area of six-story tenements, neater
than such buildings would have been in any other land. Almost without exception there were flower-boxes in the windows; the German
people didn't take readily to the confinements of city life, and each
wanted a bit of country.

A few months ago there had been civil war in these streets; the
Brownshirts had marched and the workers had hurled bottles and
bricks from the rooftops; meetings had been raided and party workers dragged away and slugged. But now all that was over; the promise of the *Horst Wessel Lied* had been kept and the streets were free
to the brown battalions. The whole appearance of the neighborhood
had changed; the people no longer lived on the streets, even in this
brightest spring weather; the children stayed in their rooms, and
the women with their market-baskets traveled no farther than they
had to, and watched with furtive glances as they went.

Lanny parked his car around the corner and walked to the house.

He looked for the name Schultz and did not find it, so he began knocking on doors and inquiring. He couldn't find a single person who would admit having heard of Ludi and Trudi Schultz. He was quite sure from their manner that this wasn't so; but they were afraid of him. Whether he was a Socialist or a spy, he was dangerous, and "*Weiss nichts*" was all he could get. Doubtless there were "comrades" in the building, but they had "gone underground," and you had to know where to dig in order to find them. It was no job for "parlor Pinks," and nobody wanted one to meddle with it.

V

Lanny went back to the hotel and continued his vigil. Sooner or later a note or a telephone message was bound to come, and this painful business of guessing and imagining would end. He went downstairs for a haircut, and when he came back he found his wife in a state of excitement. "Mama called!" she whispered. "She has to buy some gloves at Wertheim's, and I'm to meet her there in half an hour."

Irma had already ordered the car, so they went down, and while they were driving they planned their tactics. Irma would go in alone, because the meeting of two women would be less conspicuous. "Better not speak to her," suggested Lanny. "Let her see you and follow you out. I'll drive round the block and pick you up."

The wife of Johannes Robin didn't need any warning as to danger; she was back in old Russia, where fear had been bred into her bones. When Irma strolled down the aisle of the great department store, Mama was asking prices, a natural occupation for an elderly Jewish lady. She followed at a distance, and when Irma went out onto the street and Lanny came along they both stepped into the car. "Where is Freddi?" she whispered with her first breath.

"We have not heard from him," said Lanny, and she cried: "*Ach, Gott der Gerechte!*" and hid her face in her hands and began to sob.

Lanny hastened to say: "We have got things fixed up about Papa. He's all right, and is to be allowed to leave Germany, with you and the others." That comforted her, but only for a minute. She was like the man who has an hundred sheep, and one of them has gone astray, and he leaves the ninety and nine and goeth into the mountains, and seeketh that which is gone astray. "Oh, my poor lamb, what have they done to him?"

The mother hadn't heard a word from her son since he had called Lanny, and then written her a comforting note. She had been doing just what Lanny had been doing, waiting, numb with fear, imagining calamities. Freddi had forbidden her to call the Budds or to go near them, and she had obeyed for as long as she could stand it. "Oh, my poor darling, my poor baby!"

It was a painful hour they spent. The good soul, usually so sensible, so well adjusted to her routine of caring for those she loved, was now in a state of near distraction; her mind was as if in a nightmare, obsessed by all the horror stories which were being whispered among the Jews in the holes where they were hiding, apart from the rest of Germany. Stories of bodies found every day in the woods or dragged out of the lakes and canals of Berlin; suicides or murdered people whose fates would never be known, whose names were not mentioned in the press. Stories of the abandoned factory in the Friedrichstrasse which the Nazis had taken over, and where they now brought their victims to beat and torture them. The walls inside that building were soaked with human blood; you could walk by it and hear the screams—but you had best walk quickly! Stories of the concentration camps, where Jews, Communists, and Socialists were being made to dig their own graves in preparation for pretended executions; where they underwent every form of degradation which brutes and degenerates were able to devise—forced to roll about in the mud, to stick their faces into their own excrement, to lash and beat one another insensible, thus saving labor for the guards. "*Oi, oi!*" wailed the poor mother, and begged the *Herrgott* to let her son be dead.

Only one thing restrained her, and that was consideration for her kind friends. "I have no right to behave like this!" she would say. "It is so good of you to come and try to help us poor wretches. And of course Freddi would want us to go away, and to live the best we can without him. Do you really believe the Nazis will turn Papa loose?"

Lanny didn't tell her the story; he just said: "It will cost a lot of money"—he guessed that would help to make it real to her mind. She couldn't expect any kindness of these persecutors, but she would understand that they wanted money.

"Oh, Lanny, it was a mistake that we ever had so much! I never thought it could last. Let it all go—if only we can get out of this terrible country."

"I want to get you out, Mama, and then I'll see what can be done about Freddi. I haven't dared to try meantime, because it may make more trouble for Papa. If I can get four of you out safely, I know that is what Freddi would want."

"Of course he would," said Mama. "He thought about everybody in the world but himself. *Oi*, my darling, my little one, my *Schatz!* You know, Lanny, I would give my life in a minute if I could save him. Oh, we must save him!"

"I know, Mama; but you have to think about the others. Papa is going to have to start life over, and will need your counsel as he did in the old days. Also, don't forget that you have Freddi's son."

"I cannot believe any good thing, ever again! I cannot believe that any of us will ever get out of Germany alive. I cannot believe that God is still alive."

V I

Oberleutnant Furtwaengler telephoned, reporting that the prisoner had signed the necessary documents and that the arrangements were in process of completion. He asked what Lanny intended to do with him, and Lanny replied that he would take the family to Belgium as soon as he was at liberty to do so. The businesslike young officer jotted down the names of the persons and said he would have the exit permits and visas ready on time.

It would have been natural for Lanny to say: "Freddi Robin is missing. Please find him and put me in touch with him." But after thinking and talking it over for days and nights, he had decided that if Freddi was still alive, he could probably survive for another week or two, until the rest of his family had been got out of the country.

Lanny had no way to hold Göring to his bargain if he didn't choose to keep it, and as half a loaf is better than no bread, so four-fifths of a Jewish family would be better than none of them—unless you took the Nazi view of Jewish families!

However, it might be the part of wisdom to prepare for the future, so Lanny invited the Oberleutnant to lunch; the officer was pleased to come, and to bring his wife, a tall sturdy girl from the country, obviously very much flustered at being the guest of a fashionable pair who talked freely about Paris and London and New York, and knew all the important people. The Nazis might be ever so nationalistic, but the great world capitals still commanded prestige. Seeking to cover up his evil past, Lanny referred to his former Pinkness, and said that one outgrew such things as one grew older; what really concerned him was to find out how the problem of unemployment could be solved and the products of modern machinery distributed; he intended to come back to Germany and see if the Führer was able to carry out his promises.

A young devotee could ask no more, and the Oberleutnant warmed to his host and hostess. Afterward Irma said: "They really do believe in their doctrine with all their hearts!" Lanny saw that she found it much easier to credit the good things about the Hitler system than the evil. She accepted at face value the idea current among her leisure-class friends, that Mussolini had saved Italy from Bolshevism and that Hitler was now doing the same for Germany. "What good would it do to upset everything," she wished to know, "and get in a set of men who are just as bad as the Nazis or worse?"

One little hint Lanny had dropped to the officer: "I'm keeping away from the Robin family and all their friends, because I don't want to involve myself in any way in political affairs. I am hoping that nothing of an unhappy nature will happen to the Robins while we are waiting. If anything of the sort should come up I will count upon Seine Exzellenz to have it corrected."

"*Ja, gewiss!*" replied the officer. "Seine Exzellenz would not permit harm to come to them—in fact, I assure you that no harm is coming to any Jewish persons, unless they themselves are making some sort of trouble."

The latter half of this statement rather tended to cancel the former half; it was a part of the Nazi propaganda. That was what made it so difficult to deal with them; you had to pick every sentence apart and figure out which portions they might mean and which were bait for suckers. The Oberleutnant was cordial, and seemed to admire Lanny and his wife greatly; but would this keep him from lying blandly, if, for example, his chief was holding Freddi Robin as a hostage and wished to conceal the fact? Would it keep him from committing any other act of treachery which might appear necessary to the cause of National Socialism? Lanny had to keep reminding himself that these young men had been reared on *Mein Kampf;* he had to keep reminding his wife, who had never read that book, but instead had heard Lord Wickthorpe cite passages from Lenin, proclaiming doctrines of political cynicism which sounded embarrassingly like Hitler's.

VII

Heinrich Jung also had earned a right to hospitality, so he and his devoted little blue-eyed *Hausfrau* were invited to a dinner which was an outstanding event in her life. She had presented the Fatherland with three little Aryans, so she didn't get out very often, she confessed. She exclaimed with naïve delight over the wonders of the Hotel Adlon, and had to have Irma assure her that her home-made dress was adequate for such a grand occasion. Heinrich talked N.S.D.A.P. politics, and incidentally fished around to find out what had happened in the case of Johannes Robin, about which there was no end of curiosity in party circles, he reported. Lanny could only say that he had orders not to talk. A little later he asked: "Have you seen Frau Reichsminister Goebbels since our meeting?"

Yes, Heinrich had been invited to tea at her home; so Lanny didn't have to ask who had manifested the curiosity in party circles. Presently Heinrich said that Magda had wished to know whether Mr. and Mrs. Budd would care to be invited to one of her receptions. Irma hastened to say that she would be pleased, and Heinrich undertook to communicate this attitude. So it is that one advances in *die grosse Welt;* if one has money, plus the right clothes and manners, one can go from drawing-room to drawing-room, filling one's stomach with choice food and drink and one's ears with choice gossip.

Hugo Behr, the *Gausportführer*, had expressed his desire to meet Lanny again. Heinrich, reporting this, said: "I think I ought to warn you, Lanny. Hugo and I are still friends, but there are differences of opinion developing between us." Lanny asked questions and learned that some among the Nazis were impatient because the Führer was not carrying out the radical economic planks upon which he had founded the party. He seemed to be growing conservative, allying himself with Göring's friends, the great industrialists, and forgetting the promises he had made to the common man. Heinrich said it was easy to find fault, but it was the duty of good party members to realize what heavy burdens had been heaped upon the Führer's shoulders, and to trust him and give him time. He had to reorganize the government, and the new men he put in power had to learn their jobs before they could start on any fundamental changes. However, there were people who were naturally impatient, and perhaps jealous, unwilling to give the Führer the trust he deserved; if they could have their way, the party would be destroyed by factional strife before it got fairly started.

Heinrich talked at length, and with great seriousness, as always, and his devoted little wife listened as if it were the Führer himself speaking. From the discourse Lanny gathered that the dissension was really serious; the right wing had won all along the line, and the left was in confusion. Gregor Strasser, who had taken such a dressing down from Hitler in Lanny's presence, had resigned his high party posts and retired to the country in disgust. Ernst Röhm, Chief of Staff of the S.A. and one of Hitler's oldest friends, was active in protest and reported to be in touch with Schleicher, the "labor general," whom Hitler had ousted from the chancellorship. A most dangerous situation, and Hugo was making a tragic mistake in letting himself be drawn into it.

"But you know how it is," Heinrich explained. "Hugo was a Social-Democrat, and when the Marxist poison has once got into your veins it's hard to get it out."

Lanny said yes, he could understand; he had been in that camp a while himself; but there was no use expecting everything to be changed in a few months. "You have two elements in your party, Nationalism and Socialism, and I suppose it isn't always easy to preserve the balance between them."

"It will be easy if only they trust the Führer. He knows that our Socialism must be German and fitted to the understanding of the German people. He will give it to them as rapidly as they can adjust themselves to it."

After their guests had left, Lanny said to his wife: "If we want to collect the dirt, Hugo's the boy to give it to us."

VIII

Mama had agreed with Lanny and Irma that there was nothing to be gained by telling the family in Paris about Freddi's disappearance. They could hardly fail to talk about it, and so imperil the fate of Johannes. It might even be that Hansi or Bess would insist on .coming into Germany—and the least hint of that threw poor Mama into another panic. So Lanny wrote vague letters to his mother: "Everything is being arranged. The less publicity the better. Tell our friends to go to Juan and rest; living is cheap there, and I feel sure that times are going to be hard financially." Little hints like that!

Beauty herself didn't go to Juan. Her next letter was written on stationery of the Château de Balincourt. "Do you remember Lady Caillard? She is the widow of Sir Vincent Caillard, who was one of Sir Basil's closest associates in Vickers. She is an ardent spiritualist, and has published a pamphlet of messages received from her husband in the spirit world. She is immensely impressed by Madame, and wants to borrow her for as long as Sir Basil will spare her. He invited me out here, and we have had several séances. One thing that came up worries me. Tecumseh said: 'There is a man who speaks German. Does anyone know German?' Sir Basil said: 'I know a little,' and the control said: '*Clarinet ist verstimmt.*' That was all. Madame began to moan, and when she came out of the trance she was greatly depressed and could do no more that day. I didn't get the idea for a while. Now I wonder, can there be anything the matter with *your* Clarinet? I shall say nothing to anybody else until I hear from you."

So there it was again; one of those mysterious hints out of the subconscious world. The word *verstimmt* can mean either "out of tune" or "out of humor." Beauty had known that "Clarinet" meant Freddi, and it was easy to imagine Tecumseh getting that out of her subconscious mind; but Beauty had no reason to imagine that Freddi was in trouble. Was it to be supposed that when Beauty sat in a "circle," her subconscious mind became merged with her son's, and his worries passed over into hers? Or was it easier to believe that some Socialist had been kicked or beaten or shot into the spirit world by the Nazis and was now trying to bring help to his comrade?

Lanny sent a telegram to his mother: "Clarinet music interesting send more if possible." He decided that here was a way he could pass some time while waiting upon the convenience of Minister-Präsident Göring. Like Paris and London, Berlin was full of mediums and fortune tellers of all varieties; it was reported that the Führer himself consulted an astrologer—oddly enough, a Jew. Here was Lanny, obliged to sit around indefinitely, and with no heart for social life, for music or books. Why not take a chance, and see if he could get any further hints from that underworld which had surprised him so many times?

Irma was interested, and they agreed to go separately to different mediums, thus doubling their chances. Maybe not all the spirits had been Nazified, and the young couple could get ahead of Göring in that shadowy realm!

IX

So there was Lanny being ushered into the fashionable apartment of one of the most famous of Berlin's clairvoyants, Madame Diseuse. (If she had been practicing in Paris she would have been Frau Wahrsagerin.) You had to be introduced by a friend, and sittings were by appointment, well in advance; but this was an emergency call, arranged by Frau Ritter von Fiebewitz, and was to cost a hundred marks. No Arabian costumes, or zodiacal charts, or other hocus-pocus, but a reception-room with the latest furniture of tubular light metal, and an elegant French lady with white hair and a St. Germain accent. She sometimes produced physical phenomena, and spoke with various voices in languages of which she claimed not to know a word. The séance was held in a tiny interior room which became utterly dark when a soft fluorescent light was turned off.

There Lanny sat in silence for perhaps twenty minutes, and had about concluded that his hundred marks had been wasted, when he heard a sort of cooing voice, like a child's, saying in English: "What is it that you want, sir?" He replied: "I want news about a young friend who may or may not be in the spirit world." After another wait the voice said: "An old gentleman comes. He says you do not want him."

Lanny had learned that you must always be polite to any spirit. He said: "I am always glad to meet an old friend. Who is he?"

So came an experience which a young philosopher would retain as a subject of speculation for the rest of his life. A deep masculine voice seemed to burst the tiny room, declaring: "Men have forgotten the Word of God." Lanny didn't have to ask: "Who are you?" for it was just as if he were sitting in the study of a rather dreary New England mansion with hundred-year-old furniture, listening to his Grandfather Samuel expounding Holy Writ. Not the feeble old man with the quavering voice who had said that he would not be there when Lanny came again, but the grim gunmaker of the World War days who had talked about sin, knowing that Lanny was a child of sin—but all of us were that in the sight of the Lord God of Sabaoth.

"All the troubles in the world are caused by men ceasing to hear the Word of God," announced this surprising voice in the darkness. "They will continue to suffer until they hear and obey. So is it, world without end, amen."

"Yes, Grandfather," said Lanny, just as he had said many times in the ancestral study. Wishing to be especially polite, he asked: "Is this really you, Grandfather?"

"All flesh is grass, and my voice is vain, except that I speak the words which God has given to men. I have been young, and now am old; yet have I not seen the righteous forsaken, nor his seed begging bread."

Either that was the late president of Budd Gunmakers, or else a highly skilled actor! Lanny waited a respectful time, and then inquired: "What is it you wish of me, Grandfather?"

"You have not heeded the Word!" exploded the voice.

Lanny could think of many Words to which this statement might apply; so he waited, and after another pause the voice went on: "Swear now therefore unto me by the Lord, that thou wilt not cut off my seed after me."

Lanny knew only too well what that meant. The old man had objected strenuously to the practice known as birth control. He had wanted grandchildren, plenty of them, because that was the Lord's command. Be fruitful and multiply and replenish the earth. It had been one of Samuel Budd's obsessions, and the first time Irma had been taken to see him he had quoted the words of old King Saul to David. But Irma had disregarded the injunction; she didn't want a lot of babies, she wanted to have a good time while she was young. The price which nature exacts for babies is far too high for fashionable ladies to pay. So now the old man had come back from the grave!

Or was it just Lanny's subconscious mind? His guilty conscience —plus that of Irma's, since she was defying not merely Lanny's grandfather in the spirit world, but her own mother in this world! A strange enough phenomenon in either case.

"I will bear your words in mind, Grandfather," said Lanny, with the tactfulness which had become his very soul. "How am I to know that this really is you?"

"I have already taken steps to make sure that you know," replied the voice. "But do not try to put me off with polite phrases."

That was convincing, and Lanny was really quite awestricken. But still, he wasn't going to forget about Freddi. "Grandfather, do you remember Bess's husband, and his young brother? Can you find out anything about him?"

But Grandfather could be just as stubborn as Grandson. "Remember the Word of the Lord," the voice commanded; and then no more. Lanny spoke two or three times, but got no answer. At last he heard a sigh in the darkness, and the soft fluorescent light was switched on, and there sat Madame Diseuse, asking in a dull, tired voice: "Did you get what you wanted?"

X

Lanny arrived at the hotel just a few minutes before Irma, who had consulted two other mediums, chosen from advertisements in the newspapers because they had English names. "Well, did you get anything?" she asked, and Lanny said: "Nothing about Clarinet. Did you?"

"I didn't get anything at all. It was pure waste of time. One of the mediums was supposed to be a Hindu woman, and she said I would get a letter from a handsome dark lover. The other was a greasy old creature with false teeth that didn't fit, and all she said was that an old man was trying to talk to me. She wouldn't tell me his name, and all he wanted was for me to learn some words."

"Did you learn them?"

"I couldn't help it; he made me repeat them three times, and he kept saying: 'You will know what they mean.' They sounded like they came from the Bible."

"Say them!" exclaimed Lanny.

"And that thou wilt not destroy my name out of my father's house."

"Oh, my God, Irma! It's a cross-correspondence!"

"What is that?"

"Don't you remember the first time you met Grandfather, he quoted a verse from the Bible, telling you to have babies, and not to interfere with the Lord's will?"

"Yes, but I don't remember the words."

"That is a part of what he said. He came to me just now and gave me the beginning of it. 'Swear now therefore unto me by the

Lord, that thou wilt not cut off my seed after me, and that thou wilt not destroy my name out of my father's house.' "

"Lanny, how perfectly amazing!" exclaimed the young wife.

"He said he had already taken steps to convince me that it was really he. He had probably already talked to you."

Irma had been living with the spirits now for nearly four years, and had got more or less used to them; but this was the first time she had come upon such an incident. Lanny explained that the literature of psychical research was full of "cross-correspondences." Sometimes one part of a sentence would be given in England and another in Australia. Sometimes there would be references by page and line to a book, and through another medium references to some other book, and when the words were put together they made sense. It seemed to prove that whatever intelligence was at work was bound by none of the limitations of time and space. The main trouble was, it was all so hard to believe—people just couldn't and wouldn't face it.

"Well," said Lanny, "do you want to have another baby?"

"What do you suppose Grandfather will do if we don't?"

"You go and ask him," chuckled Lanny.

Irma didn't. But a day or two later came a letter from Robbie, telling what the old gentleman would do if they obeyed him. He had established in his will a trust fund for Frances Barnes Budd to the amount of fifty thousand dollars, and had provided the same amount for any other child or children Irma Barnes Budd might bear within two years after his death. The old realist had taken no chances, but added: "Lanny Budd being the father."

XI

The golden-haired and blue-eyed young sports director, Hugo Behr, came to see his American friend, and was taken for a drive. Hugo didn't need any urging to induce him to "spill the dirt" about the present tendencies of his National Socialist Party; he said he had joined because he had believed it was a Socialist party and there were millions who felt as he did—they wanted it to remain Socialist.

and they had a right to try to keep it so, and have it carry out at least part of the program upon which it had won the faith of the German masses. Breaking up the great landed estates, socializing basic industries and department stores, abolishing interest slavery—these were the pledges which had been made, millions of times over. But now the party was hand in glove with the Ruhr magnates, and the old program was forgotten; the Führer had come under the spell of men who cared only about power, and if they could have their way, all the energies of the country would go into military preparation and none into social welfare.

"Yes," said Hugo, "many of the leaders feel as I do, and some of them are Hitler's oldest party comrades. It is no threat to his leadership, but a loyal effort to make him realize the danger and return to the true path." The young official offered to introduce Lanny to some of the men who were active in this movement; but the visitor explained the peculiar position he was in, with a Jewish relative in the toils of the law and the need of being discreet on his account.

That led to the subject of the Jews, and the apple-cheeked young Aryan proved that he was loyal to his creed by denouncing this evil people and the part they had played in corrupting German culture. But he added he did not approve the persecution of individual Jews who had broken no law, and he thought the recent one-day boycott had been silly. It represented an effort on the part of reactionary elements in the party to keep the people from remembering the radical promises which had been made to them. "It's a lot cheaper and easier to beat up a few poor Jews than to oust some of the great Junker landlords."

Lanny found this conversation promising, and ventured tactfully to give his young friend some idea of the plight in which he found himself. His brother-in-law's brother had been missing for more than a week, but he was afraid to initiate any inquiry for fear of arousing those elements about which Hugo had spoken, the fanatics who were eager to find some excuse for persecuting harmless, idealistic Jews. Lanny drew a picture of a shepherd boy out of ancient Judea, watching his flocks, playing his pipe, and dreaming of the

Lord and His angels. Freddi Robin was a Socialist in the high sense
of the word; desiring justice and kindness among men, and willing
to set an example by living a selfless life here and now. He was a
fine musician, a devoted husband and father, and his wife and
mother were in an agony of dread about him.

"*Ach, leider!*" exclaimed the sports director, and added the formula which Lanny already knew by heart, that unfortunate incidents
were bound to happen in the course of any great social overturn.

"For that reason," said Lanny, "each of us has to do what he can
in the cases which come to his knowledge. What I need now is
some person in the party whom I can trust, and who will do me the
service to try to locate Freddi and tell me what he is accused of."

"That might not be easy," replied the other. "Such information
isn't given out freely—I mean, assuming that he's in the hands of
the authorities."

"I thought that you, having so many contacts among the better
elements of the party, might be able to make inquiries without attracting too much attention. If you would do me this favor, I would
be most happy to pay you for your time——"

"Oh, I wouldn't want any pay, Herr Budd!"

"You would certainly have to have it. The work may call for a
lot of time, and there is no other way I can make it up to you.
My wife is here, and neither of us can enjoy anything, because
of worrying about this poor fellow. I assure you, she would consider a thousand marks a small price to pay for the mental peace she
would get from even knowing that Freddi is still alive. If only I can
find out where he is and what he's accused of, I may be able to go
to the proper authority and have the matter settled without any
disagreeable scandal."

"If I could be sure that my name wouldn't be brought into the
matter—" began the young official, hesitatingly.

"On that I will give you my word of honor," said Lanny.
"Nothing will induce either my wife or myself to speak your name.
You don't even have to give it when you call me on the phone;
just tell me that you have, say, an Arnold Boecklin painting to show
me, and tell me some place to meet you, and I'll come. Be so good

as to accept two hundred marks for a start—on the chance that you may have to pay out sums here and there."

XII

Minister-Präsident Hermann Wilhelm Göring flew to Rome unexpectedly. He had been there once before and hadn't got along very well with his mentor, the Blessed Little Pouter Pigeon; they were quarreling bitterly over the question of which was to control Austria. But they patched it up somehow, and the newspapers of the world blazed forth a momentous event: the four great European nations had signed a peace pact, agreeing that for a period of ten years they would refrain from aggressive action against one another and would settle all problems by negotiation. Mussolini signed for Italy, Göring for Germany, and the British and French ambassadors to Vienna signed for their governments. Such a relief to the war-weary peoples of the Continent! Göring came home in triumph; and Irma said: "You see, things aren't nearly as bad as you've been thinking."

The couple went to a reception at the home of the Frau Reichsminister Goebbels, where they met many of the Nazi great ones. Lanny, who had read history, remembered the Visigoths, who had conquered ancient Rome with astonishing ease, and wandered about the splendid city, dazed by the discovery of what they had at their disposal; he remembered Clive, who had been similarly stunned by the treasures of Bengal, and had said afterward that when he considered what his opportunities had been, he was astonished at his own moderation.

So it was now with the members of the N.S.D.A.P.; not the moderation, but the opportunities. Men who a few years ago had been without the price of a meal or a place to lay their heads had suddenly come into possession of all Germany. They wore the finest uniforms that Berlin's tailors could design, and their women displayed their charms in the latest Paris models. Orders and medals, orchids and sparkling jewels—did they get all that out of party salaries, or the stipends of office in the Deutsches Reich or Preussischer Staat? Or had each one got busy on his own? They wouldn't have to rob, or even to threaten; they would only have to keep their hands out and the possessors of wealth and privilege would come running to fill them.

Here were the friends and camp followers of Juppchen Goebbels, frustrated journalist from the Rheinland, now master of his country's intellectual life. His word could make or break anyone in any profession; an invitation to his home was at once a command and the highest of opportunities. Men bowed and fawned, women smiled and flattered—and at the same time they watched warily, for it was a perilous world, in which your place was held only by sleepless vigilance. Jungle cats, all in one cage, circling one another warily, keeping a careful distance; the leopard and the jaguar would have tangled, had not both been afraid of the tiger.

But they were civilized cats, which had learned manners, and applied psychology, pretending to be gentle and harmless, even amiable. The deadliest killers wore the most cordial smiles; the most cunning were the most dignified, the most exalted. They had a great cause, an historic destiny, a patriotic duty, an inspired leader. They said: "We are building a new Germany," and at the same time they thought: "How can I cut out this fellow's guts?" They said: "Good evening, *Parteigenosse*," and thought: "*Schwarzer Lump*, I know what lies you have been whispering!" They said: "*Guten Abend, Herr Budd*," and thought: "Who is this *Emporkömmling*, and what is he doing here?" One would whisper: "The Chief thinks he can make use of him," and the other would be thinking: "The Chief must be plucking him good and plenty!"

XIII

"*Seien Sie willkommen, Herr Budd*," said the hostess, with the loveliest of her smiles. "You have been moving up in the world since we last met."

"Don't say that, Frau Reichsminister!" pleaded Lanny. "I beg you to believe that what happened was totally unforeseen by me, and unsought." Would she believe it? Of course she wouldn't— unless she happened to have inside information.

"Aren't you going to tell me about it?" A mischievous request, and therefore the way to disguise it was with the most mischievous of smiles. On the same principle that you spoke the truth only when you didn't wish to be believed.

Lanny, who had learned about intrigue when he was a tiny boy hearing his mother and father discussing the landing of a munitions contract—Lanny Budd, grandson of Budd Gunmakers, knew nothing better to do in a crisis than to be honest. "*Liebe Frau Reichsminister*," he said, "I beg you to be kind to a stranger in a strange land. I am in a painful position. I receive orders from those in authority, and I dare do nothing but obey."

"If I give you orders, will you obey, Herr Budd?" The wife of a Cabinet Minister apparently knew other ways to deal with one in a painful position. "What you call authority has a way of shifting suddenly in times like these. You had better give me an opportunity to advise you."

"Indeed, Frau Reichsminister, I will avail myself of your kindness." He had meant to say: "As soon as I am free to do so," but he decided to leave himself free to think it over.

Irma was being entertained by "Putzi" Hanfstaengl, wealthy art-publisher's son who played clown to Hitler and staff; half American and a Harvard graduate, he was tall and big and waved his arms like a windmill; for a while he was solemn, and then suddenly he danced, capered, made jokes, and laughed at them so loudly that everybody else laughed at him. The younger men were curious about the famous heiress, and she enjoyed herself as she generally did in company. Elegant, uniformed men bowed attendance and flattered her, bringing food and over-strong drink—many of them had too much of it, but that was nothing new in smart society, and Irma knew how to deal with such men.

Driving home in the small hours of the morning she was a bit fuddled and sleepy. Next morning, or rather much later that same morning, they sat in bed sipping their coffee, and Irma said what she thought of the affair. She had met agreeable people and couldn't believe they were as bad as they were painted. Lanny had to wait until they were in the car before getting in his side, which was: "I felt as if I were in a rendezvous of pirates."

Said Irma: "Listen, darling; did you ever meet a company of politicians in the United States?"

He had to admit that he lacked any basis of comparison, and his wife went on:

"They used to come to Father's house quite often, and he used to talk about them. He said they were natural-born hijackers. He said that no one of them had ever produced anything—all they did was to take it away from business men. He said they wouldn't stop till they got everything in their clutches."

"The prophecy has come true in Germany!" said Lanny.

20

Sufferance Is the Badge

I

A LONG letter from Robbie Budd, telling of the situation resulting from his father's death. The old gentleman had held on to his power up to the last moment, but had failed to decide the question of who was to be his successor. Long ago he had tried to settle the quarrel between his oldest and his youngest sons; then he had given up, and left them to fight it out—and they were doing so. Each wanted to become head of Budd's, and each was sure that the other was unfitted for the task. "I suppose," said Robbie, bitterly, "Father didn't consider either of us fitted."

Anyhow, the question was going to be settled by the stockholders. It so happened that an election of directors was due, and for the next sixty days Robbie and Lawford would be lobbying, pulling wires, trying to corral votes. They had been doing this in underground ways for years, and now the fight was in the open. Meanwhile the first vice-president was in charge—"holding the sponge," as Robbie phrased it. He was Esther Budd's brother, son of the president of the First National Bank of Newcastle. "The thing the old gentleman always dreaded," wrote Robbie; "the banks are taking us over!" Lanny knew this was said playfully, for Robbie and "Chassie" Remsen got along reasonably well, and the two couples played bridge one evening every week.

What really worried Robbie was the possibility of some Wall Street outfit "barging in." Budd's had been forced to borrow from one of the big insurance companies; it was either that or the Reconstruction Finance Corporation, which meant putting yourself at the mercy of the politicians. Robbie was in a dither over what the new administration was doing; Roosevelt had had three months in which to show his hand, and apparently the only thing he knew was to borrow money and scatter it like a drunken sailor. Of course that was just putting off the trouble, throwing the country into debt which the future would have to pay; incidentally it meant teaching everybody to come to Washington—"like hogs to the trough," said the munitions salesman, who chose the most undignified metaphors whenever he referred to his country's governmental affairs. Everything which gave power to the politicians meant debts, taxes, and troubles.

But Robbie didn't go into that subject now; he had his own immediate problems. "If only I could raise the cash to buy some Budd stock that I know of, I could settle the matter of control. Tell our friend that I want to hear from him the moment he has time to spare. I can make him a proposition which he will find advantageous." This had been written before the receipt of an unsigned note in which Lanny conveyed the news that "our friend" was being separated from every dollar he owned in the world. Poor Johannes—and poor Robbie!

The ever-discreet father didn't need any warning to be careful what he wrote about matters in Germany. His letter was a model of vagueness. He said: "There is a great deal of new business being done in Europe this year, and I ought to be there getting contracts. Once our problems at home are settled, I'll get busy." Lanny knew what this meant—the rearmament of Germany was beginning, and what the Nazis couldn't yet manufacture for themselves they would buy through intermediaries in Holland, Switzerland, Sweden. The factory chimneys of Newcastle would begin to smoke again—and it wouldn't mean a thing to Robbie Budd that he was putting power into the hands of Hitler, Göring, and Goebbels. It was the salesman's first axiom that all European nations were equally bad, and that whether the jaguar, the leopard, or the tiger came out on top was of no concern to anybody outside the jungle.

Lanny read this letter to his wife, who said: "Don't you think it might be a good idea for me to help your father?"

"You know, dear," he answered, "I have never been willing to exploit my marriage."

"Yes, but be sensible. I own a lot of stocks and bonds, and why shouldn't I exchange some of them for Budd's?"

"Your father chose those investments very shrewdly, Irma. Some of them are still paying large dividends, and Budd's isn't paying any."

"Yes, but the prices seem to find their level, according to the earnings." Irma had been putting her mind on her financial affairs ever since she had got that terrific jolt in the panic. "If we could get Budd stock at its present price, wouldn't it be safe to hold?"

"It wouldn't worry you to be financing munitions?"

"Why should it? Somebody's going to do it."

So there it was: everybody was "sensible" but Lanny. If the Nazis wanted automatics and machine guns, there were many makes on the market, and why shouldn't Budd's get the business as well as Vickers or Bofors or Skoda or Schneider-Creusot? Irma settled the matter. "When we get this business out of the way, we'll run over to New York and get Robbie and Uncle Joseph together and see what can be worked out."

Lanny said: "It's very kind of you." He knew it would have been unkind of him to say anything else.

II

A letter from Kurt, begging them to drive to Stubendorf in this very lovely season of the year. Kurt had no car, and couldn't afford the luxury of hopping about; but Seine Hochgeboren had told him that any time Irma and Lanny would come, the Schloss was at their disposal. Lanny hadn't told Kurt about Freddi. Now he was discussing whether to do it, and what to say, when the telephone rang, and he heard the voice of Oberleutnant Furtwaengler: "Herr Budd, I am happy to inform you that the government is prepared to release Johannes Robin."

Lanny's heart gave a thump. "That is certainly good news to me, Herr Oberleutnant."

"It is still your plan to drive him and his family to Belgium?"

"Whenever I am free to do so."

"You have the other members of the family with you?"

"I know where they are—at least, all but one of them. I am sorry to report that I have not heard from the son, Freddi, for a long time."

"You have no idea where he has gone?"

"Not the slightest."

"Why didn't you let me know this?"

"I have been thinking that I would surely hear from him, and I didn't want to bother you or the Minister-Präsident. I was sure that if he was a prisoner of the government, he would be released along with his father."

"I cannot say anything about it, because I do not know the circumstances. An investigation will have to be made. What do you wish to do about the others in the meantime?"

"I wish to take them out as soon as I am permitted to do so. I can come back for Freddi if you find him."

"There would be no need for you to come unless you wished. We will surely send him out if we find him."

"Very well. Shall I call at the Polizeipräsidium for Johannes?"

"That will be satisfactory."

"You understand that we wish very much to avoid newspaper

reporters, especially the foreign correspondents. For that reason it would be wise to leave as quickly as possible."

"We shall be pleased to co-operate with you to that end. We have the passports and exit permits ready."

"Does that include the visas for Belgium?"

"Everything has been foreseen. We do things that way in Germany."

"I know," said Lanny. "It is one of your great virtues."

"I bid you farewell, Herr Budd, and hope to have the pleasure of seeing you when you again visit Berlin."

"The same to you, Herr Oberleutnant. I am grateful for your many courtesies through this somewhat trying affair."

"Not at all, Herr Budd. Allow me to say that your handling of the matter has been most exemplary, and Seine Exzellenz wishes me to assure you of his sincere appreciation."

So they buttered each other, and clicked heels and bowed and scraped over the telephone; when Lanny hung up, he turned to his wife and said: "Chuck your things into the bags and we'll get going!"

He hastened to call the home of Rahel's parents, and she herself answered. "Good news," he said. "Papa is to be released at once and I am going to get him at the prison. Is Mama far from you?"

"A ten-minute drive."

"Call a taxi, take the baby and your bags, pick up Mama, and come to the Hotel Adlon as quickly as you can. Irma will be waiting for you. We are leaving at once. Is that all clear?"

"Yes; but what—" He hung up quickly, for he knew she was going to ask about Freddi, and he didn't care to impart this news. Let Mama have the painful duty!

III

Lanny drove to the great red brick building on the Alexanderplatz. Many who entered there had not come out as quickly as they had hoped; but he with his magical American passport would take a chance. He discovered that the well-known German *Ordnung* was in operation; the officer at the desk had received full instructions. *"Einen Moment, Herr Budd,"* he said, politely. *"Bitte, setzen Sie sich."*

He gave an order, and in a few minutes Johannes was brought in. Apparently he had been told what was going to happen; he had got a shave, and appeared interested in life again. The odds and ends of property which he had had upon his person were restored to him; he signed a receipt, bade a courteous *Lebewohl* to his jailers, and walked briskly out to the car.

Lanny had the painful duty of knocking this newborn happiness flat. "Painful news, my friend. Freddi has been missing for two weeks, and we have no idea what has become of him." The poor father sat in the car with tears streaming down his cheeks while Lanny told about the last meeting with Freddi, the arrangements which had been made, and the dead silence which had fallen. Lanny couldn't bear to look at him—and had a good excuse, having to drive through busy traffic.

He explained his decisions, and the heartbroken father replied: "You did what was best. I shall never be able to tell you how grateful I am."

"I'm only guessing," Lanny continued; "but I think the chances are that Göring has Freddi and intends to keep him until the scandal will no longer be news. Our only chance is to comply strictly with the terms of the understanding. It seems to me the part of wisdom for us to tell no more than we have to, even to the family. The less they know, the less trouble they will have in keeping secrets."

"You are right," agreed the other.

"I think we should say we feel certain that Freddi is a hostage, and that, since he is some day to be released, he is not apt to be mistreated. That will make it easier for them all to get over the shock."

"I will tell them that I have had an intimation to that effect," said Johannes. "Anything to get Rahel quieted down. Otherwise she might insist upon staying. We must take her at all hazards, for she can do nothing here."

When they got to the hotel they found that Mama had already

imparted the news, Irma had confirmed it, and the young wife had had her first spell of weeping. It wasn't so bad, for she had made up her mind for some days that the worst must have happened. Her father-in-law's kind "intimation" helped a little; also Lanny's promise to keep up the search. The determination of the others to get her and her child out of Naziland was not to be resisted.

It wasn't exactly a fashionable autoload which departed from under the marquee of the Adlon Hotel. The magnificent uniformed personage who opened the car doors was used to seeing independent young Americans driving themselves, but rarely had he seen three dark-eyed Jews and a child crowded into the back seat of a Mer- cédès limousine about to depart for foreign lands. Both Lanny and Irma were determined to finish this job, and not let their periled friends out of sight until they were safe. In the breast pocket of Lanny's tan linen suit were stowed not merely the passports of himself and wife, but a packet of documents which had been deliv- ered by messenger from the headquarters of Minister-Präsident Göring, including four passports and four exit permits, each with a photograph of the person concerned. Lanny realized that the gov- ernment had had possession of all the papers in the Robin yacht and palace. He remembered Göring's promise of a "kick in the tail," but hoped it was just the barrack-room exuberance of a *Hauptmann* of the German Air Force.

The family were not too badly crowded in that rear seat. The three adults had each lost weight during the past weeks; and as for luggage, they had the suitcases they had carried away after Johannes's arrest; that was all they owned in the world. As for Little Johannes, it was no trouble taking turns holding him in their laps; each would have been glad to hold him the entire time, until they had got him to some place where the cry of *Juda verrecke* was unknown.

IV

Irma and Lanny meant to go as they had come, straight through. Lanny would buy food ready prepared and they would eat it in the car while driving; they would take no chance of entering a restaurant, and having some Brownshirt peddling Nazi literature stop in front of them and exhibit a copy of *Der Stürmer* with an obscene cartoon showing a Jew as a hog with a bulbous nose; if they declined to purchase it, likely as not the ruffian would spit into their food and walk away jeering. Such things had happened in Berlin, and much worse; for until a few days ago these peddlers of literature had gone armed with the regulation automatic revolver and hard rubber club, and in one café where Jewish merchants had been accustomed to eat, a crowd of the S.A. men had fallen upon them and forced them to run the gantlet, kicking and clubbing them insensible.

Drive carefully, but fast, and stop only when necessary! The roads were good and the route familiar, and meantime, safe from prying ears, they had much to talk about. The Robins were informed that they owned some money which the Nazis had not been able to keep track of—those sums which Johannes had spent in entertaining Irma Barnes. They would be repaid in installments, as the family needed it, and the money was not to be considered a loan or a gift, but board and passenger fares long overdue. Irma said this with the decisiveness which she was acquiring; she had learned that her money gave her power to settle the destinies of other people, and she found it pleasant exercising this power—always for their own good, of course.

There was the estate of Bienvenu with nobody in it but Hansi and Bess and Baby Frances with her attendants. Mama and Rahel and her little one were to settle down in the Lodge and learn to count their blessings. Johannes would probably wish to go to New York with Irma and Lanny, for they had some business to transact with Robbie, and Johannes might be of help. Lanny gave him Robbie's letter to read, and the spirits of this born trader began to show faint signs of life. Yes, he might have ideas about the selling of Budd products; if Robbie should get charge of the company, Johannes would offer to take his job as European representative. Or, if Robbie preferred, he would see what he could do with the

South American trade—he had sold all sorts of goods there, including military, and had much information about revolutions, past, present, and to come.

"Sufferance is the badge of all our tribe." So Shylock had spoken, and now these three wearers of the badge confronted their future, for the most part in silence. Their long siege of fear had exhausted them, and they still found it hard to believe that they were free, that the papers which Lanny was carrying would actually have power to get them over the border. They thought about the dear one they were leaving in the Hitler hell, and the tears would steal down their cheeks; they wiped them away furtively, having no right to add to the unhappiness of friends who had done so much for them. They ate the food and drank the bottled drinks which Lanny put into their hands; a lovely dark-eyed little boy with curly black hair lay still in his mother's or his grandmother's arms and never gave a whimper of complaint. He was only three years and as many months old, but already he had learned that he was in a world full of mysterious awful powers, which for some reason beyond his comprehension meant to harm him. Sufferance was his badge.

V

They were traveling by way of Hanover and Cologne. The roads were perfect, and three or four hundred miles was nothing to Lanny; they reached Aachen before nightfall, and then came the border, and the critical moment—which proved to be anticlimactic. The examination of baggage and persons for concealed money was usually made as disagreeable as possible for Jews; but perhaps there was some special mark on their exit permits, or perhaps it was because they were traveling in an expensive car and under the chaperonage of expensive-looking Americans—anyhow the questioning was not too severe, and much sooner than anyone had expected the anxious refugees were signaled to proceed across the line. The inspection of their passports on the Belgian side was a matter that took only a minute or two; and when the last formality was completed and the car rolled on through a peaceful countryside that wasn't Nazi, Mama broke down and wept in the arms of her spouse. She just hadn't been able to believe that it would happen.

They spent the night in the city of Liége, where Lanny's first duty was to send telegrams to his mother and father, to Hansi, to Zoltan and Emily and Rick. In the morning they drove on to Paris; and from there he telephoned to his friend Oberleutnant Furtwaengler in Berlin. What news was there about Freddi Robin? The officer reported that the young man was nowhere in the hands of the German authorities; unless by chance he had given a false name when arrested, something which was often attempted but rarely successful. Lanny said he was quite certain that Freddi would have no motive for doing this. The Oberleutnant promised to continue the search, and if anything came of it he would send a telegram to Lanny at his permanent address, Juan-les-Pins, Cap d'Antibes, Frankreich.

Lanny hung up and reported what he had heard. It meant little, of course. Long ago Lanny had learned that diplomats lie when it suits their country's purposes, and police and other officials do the same; among the Nazis, lying in the interest of party and *Regierung* was an heroic action. The statement of Göring's aide meant simply that if Göring had Freddi he meant to keep him. If and when he released him, he would doubtless say that an unfortunate mistake had been made.

Beauty had gone to London with her husband, as guests of Lady Caillard. She now wired Lanny to come and see if he could get any hints through Madame. Since it was as easy to go to New York from England as from France, they decided upon this plan. But first they must run down to Juan, because Irma couldn't cross the ocean without having at least a glimpse of her little daughter. Also it would be "nice" for Johannes to see Hansi and Bess. In general it was "nice" for people to dart here and there like humming-birds, sipping the honey of delight from whatever flower caught the eye. So next morning the four Robins were again loaded into the back seat, and in the evening they rolled through the gates of Bienvenu amid a chorus of delighted cries in English, German, and Yiddish; cries mostly in the treble clef, but with an undertone in the bass, because of the one sheep which had strayed and might already have been devoured by the wolves.

VI

Once again the young couple had a debauch of parental emotions; Irma hugged little Frances against all rules, talked baby-talk which interfered with the maturing of her speech, gave her foods which were unwholesome, let her stay up too late—in short disarranged all schedules and spread demoralization. She even talked about taking the whole entourage to Long Island—it would give such pleasure to the grandmother. Lanny argued against it—the child had everything that a three-year-old could really appreciate, and now was enjoying the companionship of a young Robin. Lanny and Irma were planning only a short stay, and why incur all the added expense, at a time when everything was so uncertain? Lanny was always trying to economize with the Barnes fortune—overlooking the fact that the only fun in having a fortune is if you don't economize. Just now he had the idea that they might have to buy Freddi out of Germany; and who could guess the price?

All right, Irma would stay another day, and then tear herself loose. She would lay many injunctions upon Bub Smith, the dependable bodyguard, and extract promises from Miss Severne to cable her at the smallest symptom of malaise. "Do you realize how many millions this tiny being represents?" Irma didn't say those crude words, but it was the clear implication of every command, and of the circumstances surrounding Frances Barnes Budd. "The twenty-three-million-dollar baby" was her newspaper name. The twenty-three-million-dollar baby had set out on a yachting cruise, and the twenty-three-million-dollar baby had unexpectedly returned to Bienvenu. All the expenses of maintaining the twenty-three-million-dollar baby might have been collected in admission fees from tourists who would have flocked to see her if arrangements had been made.

The men of the family had a conference in Lanny's studio.

Johannes hadn't been willing to tell the ladies what had happened to him in Germany, but he told Hansi and Lanny how he had been taken to the S.A. barracks in Bremerhaven and there subjected to a long series of indignities, obviously intended to break his spirit. They had given him strong purgatives, and amused themselves by forcing him to paddle other prisoners in the same plight, and to be paddled by them in turn, until all of them were a mess of one another's filth. While they did this they had to shout: *"Heil lieber Reichskanzler!"* As a climax they had been forced to dig a long trench, and were lined up to be shot and dumped into it—so they were told. It was only a mock execution, but they had died psychologically, and Johannes had by then become so sick with horror and pain that he had welcomed the end. He said now that he would never be the same man again; he would go on living because of his family and friends, but the game of making money would never hold the same zest. He said that, but then, being a clear-sighted man, he added: "It's a habit, and I suppose I'll go on reacting in the old way; but I can't imagine I'll ever be happy."

They talked about the problem of the missing one, and what was to be done. Lanny had promised not to name Hugo Behr, and he didn't, but said that he had a confidential agent at work, and had given him the Juan address. Hansi was to open all mail that might come from Germany, and if it contained anything significant, he was to cable it. Johannes said that Hansi and Bess would have to give up the pleasure of playing music at Red meetings, or doing anything to advertise their anti-Nazi views. They were still Göring's prisoners; and that was, no doubt, the way Göring intended it to be.

Hansi was "broke" because he and Bess had been spending all their money on refugees. That, too, would have to stop. Since it would do no good to sit around and mourn, Hansi decided to cable his New York agent to arrange a concert tour of the United States in the fall. Meantime, Irma would open an account for him at her bank in Cannes. "But remember," she said, "no more Reds and no Red talk!" Irma laying down the law!

All problems thus settled, one bright morning Irma and Lanny, with Papa in the back seat, set out amid more cries in English, German, and Yiddish—this time not so happy. They arrived in Paris and had dinner with Zoltan Kertezsi, and in the morning drove to Les Forêts, and told Emily Chattersworth as much of their story as was permitted. In the afternoon they set out for Calais, place of bitter memories forevermore. They took the night ferry, drove through England in the loveliest of all months, and arrived at the Dorchester Hotel amid the gayest of all seasons.

VII

Sir Vincent Caillard, pronounced French-fashion, Ky-yahr, had been one of Zaharoff's associates from the early days when they had bought Vickers; in the course of the years he had become one of the richest men in England. Also, strangely enough, he had been a poet, and had set Blake's *Songs of Innocence* to music; he had bequeathed these interests to his wife, along with a huge block of Vickers shares. So it had come about that an elderly, gray-haired lady, rather small, pale, and insignificant-looking, wielded power in London, and concentrated upon herself the attention of a swarm of eccentric persons, some of them genuine idealists, more of them genuine crooks.

She had purchased a large stone church in West Halkin Street and made it over into one of the strangest homes ever conceived by woman. The gallery of the church had been continued all around it and divided into bedrooms and bathrooms. The organ had been retained, and when it was played all the partitions of the rooms seemed to throb. On the ground floor was a grand reception room with art treasures fit for a museum; among them was a splendid collection of clocks; a large one struck the quarter-hours, and the front of the clock opened and a gold and ivory bird came out and sang lustily. Lady Caillard also collected scissors. Whoever came to that home was at once presented with a copy of the late husband's poems, also a copy of her ladyship's pamphlet entitled: *Sir Vincent Caillard Speaks from the Spirit World.* If you could devise a new kind of praise for either of these volumes it would be equivalent to a meal-ticket for the rest of your life—or, at any rate, of Lady Caillard's life.

Mr. and Mrs. Dingle and Madame Zyszynski were comfortably ensconced in this former house of God, and Beauty had had time to collect all the delicious gossip concerning its affairs. Pausing only for a tribute of grief to Freddi, she opened up to her son a truly thrilling line of conversation. Lady Caillard had become a convert to spiritualism, and now lived as completely surrounded by angels and ministers of grace as William Blake in his most mystical hours. She maintained a troop of mediums, and one of the spirits had directed the invention of a machine called the "Communigraph," whereby Sir Vincent, called "Vinny," could send messages to his wife, called "Birdie." The machine had been set up in "The Belfry," as this home was called, and had been blessed by Archdeacon Wilberforce in a regular service; thereafter the séance room, known as the "Upper Room," was kept sacred to this one purpose, and at a regular hour every Wednesday evening Sir Vincent gave his wife a communication which he signed V.B.X., meaning "Vinnie, Birdie, and a Kiss." These messages were now being compiled into a book entitled *A New Conception of Love.*

But, alas, love did not rule unchallenged in these twice-consecrated premises. There was a new favorite among the mediums, a woman whom the others all hated. Beauty's voice fell to a whisper as she revealed what huge sums of money this woman had been getting, and how she had persuaded her ladyship to bequeath her vast fortune to the cause of spiritualism, with the spirits to control it. Lady Caillard's two children, lacking faith in the other world, wanted their father's money for themselves, and had quarreled with their mother and been ousted from her home; they had got lawyers, and had even called in Scotland Yard, which couldn't help. There was the most awful pother going on!

Into this seething caldron of jealousies and hatreds had come Mabel Blackless, alias Beauty Budd, alias Madame Detaze, alias Mrs. Dingle, herself an object of many kinds of suspicion; also her husband, teaching and practicing love for all mankind, including both adventuresses and defrauded children; also a Polish woman medium with an unspellable name. Beauty, of course, was looked upon as an interloper and intriguer, Parsifal Dingle's love was hypocrisy, and Madame's mediumship was an effort to supplant the other possessors of this mysterious gift. Beauty was as much pleased over all this as a child at a movie melodrama. Her tongue tripped over itself as she poured out the exciting details. "Really, my dears, I wouldn't be surprised if somebody tried to poison us!" Her manner gave the impression that she would find that a delightful adventure.

One of the guests in this strange ex-church was the Grand Officer of the Légion d'Honneur and Knight Commander of the Bath. He appeared to be failing; his skin had become yellowish brown, with the texture of parchment; his hands trembled so that he kept them against some part of his body, and would not attempt to write in the presence of anyone. He had grown much thinner, which accentuated the prominence of his eagle's beak. As usual, Zaharoff kept himself out of all sorts of trouble, and took no sides in this family row; his interest was in getting messages from the duquesa, and he would sit tirelessly as long as any medium would stand it. But he still hadn't made up his mind entirely; he revealed that to Lanny, not by a direct statement, but by the trend of the questions he kept putting to the younger man.

It was permissible for Lanny to mention that a young friend of his had not been heard from in Germany; whereupon this hiveful of mediums set to work secreting wax and honey for him. Most of it appeared to be synthetic; Lanny became sure that some clever trickster had guessed that the missing person was a relative of Johannes Robin, himself recently named in the newspapers as missing, and now suddenly arriving with the Budds. Since Hansi had been interviewed in Paris on the subject, it couldn't be he who was lost. Since Freddi had been in London and was known to all friends of the Budds, it really wasn't much of a detective job to get his name. Every issue of the *Manchester Guardian* was full of stories about concentration camps and the mistreatment of the Jews; so the spirits began pouring out details—the only trouble being that no two of them agreed on anything of importance.

There was only one medium whom Lanny knew and trusted,

and that was Madame; but her control, Tecumseh, was still cross
with Lanny and wouldn't take any trouble for him. In New York
the control had been willing to repeat French sentences, syllable by
syllable, but now he refused to do the same for German. He said
it was too ugly a language, with sounds that no civilized tongue
could get round—this from a chieftain of the Iroquois Indians!
Tecumseh said that Freddi was not in the spirit world, and that
the spirits who tried to talk about Freddi didn't seem to know anything definite. Tecumseh got so that he would say to a sitter: "Are
you going to ask me about that Jewish fellow?" It threatened to
ruin Madame's mediumship and her career.

VIII

Marceline had been invited to spend the summer with the
Pomeroy-Nielsons, as a means of making up for the yacht cruise
which had been rudely snatched away. Marceline and Alfy, having
the same sixteen years, were shooting up tall and what the English
call "leggy." It is the age of self-consciousness and restlessness; many
things were changing suddenly and confusing their young minds.
With other friends of the same age they played with delicate inti-
mations of love; they felt attraction, then shied away, took offense
and made up, talked a great deal about themselves and one another,
and in various ways prepared for the serious business of matrimony.
Marceline exercised her impulse to tease Alfy by being interested
in other boys. She had a right to, hadn't she? Did she have to fall
in love the way her family expected? What sort of old-fashioned
idea was that? The future baronet was proud, offended, angry, then
exalted. *Himmelhoch jauchzend, zum Tode betrübt!*

Irma and Lanny motored up for a week end, to see how things
were going. A lovely old place by the Thames, so restful after the
storms and strains of the great world; especially after Berlin, with
its enormous and for the most part tasteless public buildings, its
statues, crude and cruel, celebrating military glory. Here at The
Reaches everything was peaceful; the little old river seemed tame
and friendly, safe to go punting on, just right for lovers and poets.

It had been here a long time and would stay while generation after generation of baronets appeared, grew up and studied at the proper schools, wore the proper comfortable clothes, established "little theaters," and wrote articles for newspapers and weeklies proving that the country was going to pot.

Here was Sir Alfred, tall, somewhat eccentric, but genial and full of humor; his hair had turned gray while his mustache remained black. Excessive taxes had completely ruined him, he declared, but he was absorbed in collecting records of twentieth-century British drama for a museum which some rich friend was financing. Here was his kind and gentle wife, the most attentive of hostesses. Here was Nina, helping to run this rambling old brick house, built onto indefinitely by one generation after another and having so many fireplaces and chimneys that in wintertime it would take one maid most of her time carrying coal-scuttles. Here were three very lovely children, eager and happy, but taught to be quieter than any you would find in America.

Finally here was the lame ex-aviator whom Lanny considered the wisest man he knew, the only one with whom he could exchange ideas with complete understanding. Rick was one who had a right to know everything about Lanny's German adventure, and they went off on the river where nobody could hear them if they talked in low tones, and Lanny told the story from beginning to end. It would be better that not even Nina should hear it, because there is a strong temptation for one woman to talk to the next, and so things get passed on and presently come to the ears of some journalist. After all, Johannes was a pretty important man, and his plundering would make a rare tale if properly dressed up.

Rick was quite shocked when he learned how Lanny had permitted the Berlin newspapers to publish that he was a sympathetic inquirer into National Socialism. He said that a thing like that would spread and might blacken Lanny forever; there would be no way to live it down, or to get himself trusted again. Lanny said he didn't mind, if he could save Freddi; but Rick insisted that a man had no right to make such a sacrifice. It wasn't just a question of saving one individual, but of a cause which was entitled to defense. Socialism had to be fought for against the monstrosity which had stolen its name and was trying to usurp its place in history. Lanny had thought of that, but not enough, apparently; he felt rather bad about it.

"Listen, Rick," he said; "there have to be spies in every war, don't there?"

"I suppose so."

"What if I were to go into Germany and become a friend of those higher-ups, and get all the dope and send it out to you?"

"They would soon get onto it, Lanny."

"Mightn't it be possible to be as clever as they?"

"A darned disagreeable job, I should think."

"I know; but Kurt did it in Paris, and got away with it."

"You're a very different man from Kurt. For one thing, you'd have to fool him; and do you think you could?"

"Beauty insists that I couldn't; but I believe that if I took enough time, and put my mind to it, I could at least keep him uncertain. I'd have to let him argue with me and convince me. You know I have a rare good excuse for going; I'm an art expert, and Germany has a lot to sell. That makes it easy for me to meet all sorts of people. I could collect evidence as to Nazi outrages, and you could make it into a book."

"That's already been done, you'll be glad to hear." Rick revealed that a group of liberal Englishmen had been busy assembling the data, and a work called *The Brown Book of the Hitler Terror* was now in press and shortly to be published. It gave the details of two or three hundred murders of prominent intellectuals and political opponents of the Nazi *Regierung*.

Lanny said: "There'll be other things worth reporting. If I go back to Germany on account of Freddi, I'll get what facts I can and it'll be up to you to figure out what use to make of them."

IX

Lanny didn't mention the name of his German agent, Hugo Behr, but he was free to tell about the left-wing movement developing inside the Nazi party. He thought it was of great importance. It was the class struggle in a new and strange form; the war between the haves and the have-nots, which apparently couldn't be kept out of any part of modern society. A leader might sell out a popular movement, but could he carry his followers along? Many people in Germany thought that Hitler could take his party wherever he chose, but Lanny saw it differently—he said that Hitler was extraordinarily sensitive to the pressure of his followers, and agile in keeping the lead wherever they were determined to go. "He got money from the biggest industrialists, and Johannes insists that he's their man; but I believe he may fool them and jump some way they have no idea of."

"Isn't there a third power," ventured Rick—"the army? Can anybody in Germany do anything without the consent of the Reichswehr?"

Lanny told of his talk with Emil and with Stubendorf, both of whom had agreed that they would obey the government loyally. Rick said: "Emil, yes; he's a subordinate. But would Stubendorf tell you his real thoughts? My guess is that he and his Junker crowd will serve Hitler so long as Hitler serves them; that is, to bring about rearmament, and get the Corridor and the lost provinces back into the Fatherland."

"Naturally," admitted Lanny, "Stubendorf thinks first about his own property. What he'd do after that I don't know."

"All Germans put their army first," insisted Rick. "The Social-Democrats brought about the revolution with the help of the common soldiers, but right away they became prisoners of the officer caste and never made any real change in the army's control. The Finance Minister of the Republic always had to be a man satisfactory to the Reichswehr, and no matter how much the politicians talked about social reforms they never made any cuts in the military budget."

Rick listened to all that his friend had to tell, and asked many questions, but refused to believe that Hitler could be pushed or dragged to the left. "No revolutionist who has become conservative ever goes back," he said, and added with a wry smile: "He learns to know the left too well, and has made too many enemies among them."

Lanny asked: "Won't he go if he sees another wave of revolt on the way?"

"He won't see it, because it won't be coming. One wave is enough for one generation. Strasser and Röhm and your friend Hugo may shout their heads off, but when Adolf tells them to shut up they will shut. And it's my belief that whatever 'socializing' Adolf does in Germany will be to make the Nazi party stronger, and enable him to smash Versailles more quickly and more surely."

X

The Conference on Limitation of Armaments was practically dead, after more than a year of futile efforts. But the nations couldn't give up trying to stop the general breakdown, and now sixty-six of them were assembled in a World Economic Conference. It was meeting in South Kensington with the usual fanfare about solving all problems. Rick, ever suspicious of what he called capitalist statesmanship, said that it was an effort of the Bank of England to get back on the gold standard, with the support of the United States, and of France, Switzerland, Holland, and the few nations still ruled by their creditor classes. While Lanny was watching this show and renewing old acquaintances among the journalists, President Roosevelt issued a manifesto refusing to be tied to this gold program. His action was called "torpedoing" the Conference, which at once proceeded to follow all the others into the graveyard of history.

Lord Wickthorpe was back at home, and desirous of repaying the hospitality which he had enjoyed in Paris; the more so when he learned that his American friends had just returned from Germany and had been meeting some of the Nazi head men. The young couple were invited to spend several days at Wickthorpe Castle, one of the landmarks of England. It was of brown sandstone, and the central structure with two great crenelated towers dated from Tudor days; two wings and a rear extension had been added in the time of Queen Anne, but the unity of style had been preserved. The ancient oaks were monuments of English permanence and solidity; the lawns were kept green by rains and fogs from several seas, and kept smooth by flocks of rolypoly sheep. Irma was fascinated by the place, and pleased her host by the naïveté of her commendations. When she heard that the estate had had to be broken up and tracts sold off to pay taxes, she counted it among the major calamities of the late war.

The Dowager Lady Wickthorpe kept house for her bachelor son. There was a younger brother whom Lanny had met at Rick's, and he had married an American girl whom Irma had known in café society; so it was like a family party, easy and informal, yet dignified and impressive. It was much easier to run an estate and a household in England, where everything was like a grandfather's clock which you wound up and it ran, not for eight days but for eight years or eight decades. There was no such thing as a servant problem, for your attendants were born, not made; the oldest son of your shepherd learned to tend your sheep and the oldest son of your butler learned to buttle. All masters were kind and all servants devoted and respectful; at least, that was how it was supposed to be, and if anything was short of perfection it was carefully hidden. Irma thought it was marvelous—until she discovered that she was expected to bathe her priceless self in a painted tin tub which was brought in by one maid, followed by two others bearing large pitchers of hot and cold water.

After the completion of this ceremony, she inquired: "Lanny, what do you suppose it would cost to put modern plumbing into a place like this?"

He answered with a grin: "In the style of Shore Acres?"—referring to his own bathroom with solid silver fixtures, and to Irma's of solid gold.

"I mean just ordinary Park Avenue."

"Are you thinking of buying this castle?"

Irma countered with another question. "Do you suppose you would be happy in England?"

"I'm afraid you couldn't get it, darling," he evaded in turn. "It's

bound to be entailed." He assured her with a grave face that everything had to be handed down intact—not merely towers and oaks
and lawns, but servants and sheep and bathing facilities.

XI

Neighbors dropped in from time to time, and Lanny listened to
upper-class Englishmen discussing the problems of their world and
his. They were not to be persuaded to take Adolf Hitler and his
party too seriously; in spite of his triumph he was still the clown,
the pasty-faced, hysterical tub-thumper, such as you could hear in
Hyde Park any Sunday afternoon; "a jumped-up house-painter,"
one of the country squires called him. They were not sorry to
have some effective opposition to France on the continent, for it
irked them greatly to see that rather shoddy republic of politicians riding on the gold standard while Britain had been ignomini-
ously thrown off. They were interested in Lanny's account of
Adolf, but even more interested in Göring, who was a kind of man
they could understand. In his capacity as Reichsminister, he had
come to Geneva and laid down the law as to Germany's claim to
arms equality. Wickthorpe had been impressed by his forceful personality, and now was amused to hear about the lion cub from
the Berlin zoo and the new gold velvet curtains in the reception
room of the Minister-Präsident's official residence.

Lanny said: "The important thing for you gentlemen to remember is that Göring is an air commander, and that rearmament for
him is going to mean fleets of planes. They will all be new and of
perfected models."

Eric Vivian Pomeroy-Nielson, ex-aviator, had laid great stress
upon this, but Lanny found it impossible to interest a representative of the British Foreign Office. To him airplanes were like Adolf
Hitler; that is to say, something "jumped-up," something cheap,
presumptuous, and altogether bad form. Britannia ruled the waves,
and did it with dignified and solid "ships of the line," weighing
thirty-five thousand tons each and costing ten or twenty million
pounds. An American admiral had written about the influence of

sea power upon history, and the British Admiralty had read it, one of the few compliments they had ever paid to their jumped-up cousins across the seas. Now their world strategy was based upon it, and when anyone tried to argue with them it was as if they all burst into song: "Britannia needs no bulwarks, no towers along the steep!"

Irma listened to the discussions, and afterward, as they drove back to London, they talked about it, and Lanny discovered that she agreed with her host rather than with her husband. She was irresistibly impressed by the dignity, stability, and self-confidence of this island nation; also by Lord Wickthorpe as the perfect type of English gentleman and statesman. Lanny didn't mind, for he was used to having people disagree with him, especially his own family. But when he happened to mention the matter to his mother, she minded it gravely, and said: "Doesn't it ever occur to you that you're taking an awful lot for granted?"

"How do you mean, old darling?"

"Take my advice and think seriously about Irma. You're making her a lot unhappier than you've any idea."

"You mean, by the company I keep?"

"By that, and by the ideas you express to your company, and to your wife's."

"Well, dear, she surely can't expect me to give up my political convictions as the price of her happiness."

"I don't know why she shouldn't—considering how we're all more or less dependent upon her bounty."

"Bless your heart!" said Lanny. "I can always go back to selling pictures again."

"Oh, Lanny, you say horrid things!"

He thought that she had started the horridness, but it would do no good to say so. "Cheer up, old dear—I'm taking my wife off to New York right away."

"Don't count on that too much. Don't ever forget that you've got a treasure, and it calls for a lot of attention and some guarding."

BOOK FIVE

This Is the Way the World Ends

21

In Friendship's Name

I

IRMA and Lanny guessed that the feelings of Fanny Barnes were going to be hurt because they weren't bringing her namesake to see her; to make up for it they had cabled that they would come first to Shore Acres. The Queen Mother was at the steamer to meet them with a big car. She wanted the news about her darling grandchild, and then, what on earth had they been doing all that time in Germany? Everybody was full of questions about Hitlerland, they discovered; at a distance of three thousand miles it sounded like Hollywood, and few could bring themselves to believe that it was real. The newspapers were determined to find out what had happened to a leading German-Jewish financier. They met him at the pier, and when he wouldn't talk they tried everyone who knew him; but in vain.

At Shore Acres, things were going along much as usual. The employees of the estate were doing the same work for no wages; but with seventeen million unemployed in the country, they were thankful to be kept alive. As for Irma's friends, they were planning the customary round of visits to seashore and mountains; those who still had dividends would play host to those who hadn't, and everybody would get along. There was general agreement that business was picking up at last, and credit for the boom was given to Roosevelt. Only a few diehards like Robbie Budd talked about the debts being incurred, and when and how were they going to be paid. Most people didn't want to pay any debts; they said that was what had got the country into trouble. The way to get out was to borrow and spend as fast as possible; and one of the things to

441

spend for was beer. Roosevelt was letting the people buy it instead of having to make it in their bathtubs.

Robbie came into the city by appointment, and in the office of the Barnes estate, he and Irma and Lanny sat down to a conference with Uncle Joseph Barnes and the other two trustees. Robbie had a briefcase full of figures setting forth the condition of Budd Gunmakers, a list of directors pledged to him, the voting shares which he controlled, and those which he could purchase, with their prices. The trustees presented a list of their poorest-paying shares, and weighed them in the balance. Under the will the trustees had the right to say no; but they realized that this was a family matter, and that it would be a distinguished thing to have Irma's father-in-law become president of a great manufacturing concern. Also, Irma had developed into a young lady who knew what she wanted, and said it in the style of the days before parliamentary control of the purse had been established.

"There's no use going into it unless you go heavily enough to win," cautioned Uncle Joseph.

"Of course not," said Irma, promptly. "We have no idea of not winning." *L'état, c'est moi!*

"If you pay more than the market for Budd stocks, it will mean that you are reducing the principal of your estate; for we shall have to list them at market value."

"List them any way you please," said Irma. "I want Robbie to be elected."

"Of course," said Mr. Barnes, timidly, "you might make up the principal by reducing your expenditures for a while."

"All right," assented Her Majesty—"but it will be time enough to do that when you get me a bit more income."

II

Johannes went to Newcastle to visit the Robbie Budds. The firm of R and R had many problems to talk out, and when Irma and Lanny arrived the pair were deeply buried in business. Robbie considered Johannes the best salesman he had ever known, bar none, and was determined to make a place for him with Budd's. If Robbie won out, Johannes would become European representative; if Robbie lost, Johannes would become Robbie's assistant on some sort of share basis. Robbie had a contract with the company which still had nearly three years to run and entitled him to commissions on all sales made in his territory. These matters Robbie put before his friend without reserve; he did it for medico-psychological reasons as well as financial—he wanted to get Johannes out of his depression, and the way to do it was to put him to work.

Robbie added: "Of course, provided there's anything left of business." America was in the throes of an extraordinary convulsion known as "the New Deal," which Robbie described as "government by college professors and their graduate students." They were turning the country upside down under a scheme called "N.R.A." You had to put a "blue eagle" up in your window and operate under a "code," bossed by an army general who swore like a trooper and drank like the trooper's horse. New markets for goods were being provided by the simple process of borrowing money from those who had it and giving it to those who hadn't. One lot of the unemployed were put to work draining swamps to plant crops, while another lot were making new swamps for wild ducks. And so on, for as long as Robbie Budd could find anybody to listen to him.

Everybody in Newcastle was glad to see the young couple again; excepting possibly Uncle Lawford, who wasn't going to see them. The only place they had met was in church, and Irma and Lanny were going to play golf or tennis on Sunday mornings—Grandfather being out of the way. Or was he really out of the way? Apparently he could only get at them if they went to a medium! Lanny remarked: "I'd like to try the experiment of sleeping in his bed one night and see if I hear any raps." Irma said: "Oh, what a horrid thought!" She had come to believe in the spirits about half way. Subtleties about the subconscious mind didn't impress her very much, because she wasn't sure if she had one.

The usual round of pleasure trips began. They motored to Maine, and then to the Adirondacks. So many people wanted to see them; Irma's gay and bright young old friends. They had got used to her husband's eccentricities, and if he wanted to pound the piano while they played bridge, all right, they would shut the doors between. He didn't talk so "Pink" as he had, so they decided that he was getting sensible. They played games, they motored and sailed and swam, they flirted a bit, and some couples quarreled, some traded partners as in one of the old-fashioned square dances. But they all agreed in letting the older people do the worrying and the carrying of burdens. "I should worry," —meaning that I won't— and "Let George do it," —so ran the formulas. To have plenty of money was the indispensable virtue, and to have to go to work the one unthinkable calamity. "Oh, Lanny," said Irma, after a visit where an ultra-smart playwright had entertained them with brilliant conversation—"Oh, Lanny, don't you think you could get along over here at least part of the time?"

She wanted to add: "Now that you're being more sensible." She didn't really think he had changed his political convictions, but she found it so much pleasanter when he withheld them, and if he would go on doing this long enough it might become a habit. When they passed through New York he didn't visit the Rand School of Social Science, or any of those summer camps where noisy and mostly Jewish working people swarmed as thick as bees in a hive. He was afraid these "comrades" might have learned what had been published about him in the Nazi papers; also that Nazi agents in New York might report him to Göring. He stayed with his wife, and she did her best to make herself everything that a woman could be to a man.

It worked for nearly a month; until one morning in Shore Acres, just as they were getting ready for a motor-trip to a "camp" in the Thousand Islands, Lanny was called to the telephone to receive a cablegram from Cannes, signed Hansi, and reading: "Unsigned unidentifiable letter postmarked Berlin text Freddi ist in Dachau."

III

Their things were packed and stowed in the car, and the car was waiting in front of the mansion. Irma was putting the last dab of powder on her nose, and Lanny stood in front of her with a frown of thought upon his face: "Darling, I don't see how I can possibly take this drive."

She knew him well, after four years of wifehood, and tried not to show her disappointment. "Just what do you want to do?"

"I want to think about how to help Freddi."

"Do you suppose that letter is from Hugo?"

"I had a clear understanding with him that he was to sign the name Boecklin. I think the letter must be from one of Freddi's comrades, some one who has learned that we helped Johannes. Or perhaps some one who has got out of Dachau."

"You don't think it might be a hoax?"

"Who would waste a stamp to play such a trick upon us?"

She couldn't think of any answer. "You're still convinced that Freddi is Göring's prisoner?"

"Certainly, if he's in the concentration camp, Göring knows he's there, and he knew it when he had Furtwaengler tell me that he couldn't find him. He had him sent a long way from Berlin, so as to make it harder for us to find out."

"Do you think you can get him away from Göring if Göring doesn't want to let him go?"

"What I think is, there may be a thousand things to think of before we can be sure of the best course of action."

"It's an awfully nasty job to take on, Lanny."

"I know, darling—but what else can we do? We can't go and enjoy ourselves, play around, and refuse to think about our friend. Dachau is a place of horror—I doubt if there's any so dreadful in the world today, unless it's some other of the Nazi camps. It's an old dilapidated barracks, utterly unfit for habitation, and they've got two or three thousand men jammed in there. They're not just holding them prisoners—they're doing what Göring told me with his own mouth, applying modern science to destroying them, body, mind, and soul. They're the best brains and the finest spirits in Germany, and they're going to be so broken that they can never do anything against the Nazi regime."

"You really believe that, Lanny?"

"I am as certain of it as I am of anything in human affairs. I've been studying Hitler and his movement for twelve years, and I really do know something about it."

"There's such an awful lot of lying, Lanny. People go into politics, and they hate their enemies, and exaggerate and invent things."

"I didn't invent *Mein Kampf*, nor the Brownshirts, nor the murders they are committing night after night. They break into people's homes and stab them or shoot them in their beds, before the eyes of their wives and children; or they drag them off to their barracks and beat them insensible."

"I've heard those stories until I've been made sick. But there are just as many violent men of the other side, and there have been provocations over the years. The Reds did the same thing in Russia, and they tried to do it in Germany——"

"It's not only the Communists who are being tortured, darling; it's pacifists and liberals, even church people; it's gentle idealists, like Freddi—and surely you know that Freddi wouldn't have harmed any living creature."

IV

Irma had to put down her powder-puff, but was still sitting on the stool in front of her dressing-table. She had many things that she had put off saying for a long time; and now, apparently, was the time to get them off her mind. She began: "You might as well take the time to understand me, Lanny. If you intend to plunge into a thing like this, you ought to know how your wife feels about it."

"Of course, dear," he answered, gently. He could pretty well guess what was coming.

"Sit down." And when he obeyed she turned to face him. "Freddi's an idealist, and you're an idealist. It's a word you're fond

of, a very nice word, and you're both lovely fellows, and you
wouldn't hurt anybody or anything on earth. You believe what
you want to believe about the world—which is that other people
are like you, good and kind and unselfish—idealists, in short. But
they're not that; they're full of jealousy and hatred and greed and
longing for revenge. They want to overthrow the people who
own property, and punish them for the crime of having had life
too easy. That's what's in their hearts, and they're looking for
chances to carry out their schemes, and when they come on you
idealists, they say: 'Here's my meat!' They get round you and
play you for suckers, they take your money to build what they
call their 'movement.' You serve them by helping to undermine
and destroy what you call capitalism. They call you comrades for
as long as they can use you, but the first day you dared to stand
in their way or interfere with their plans, they'd turn on you like
wolves. Don't you know that's true, Lanny?"

"It's true of many, I've no doubt."

"It would be true of every last one, when it came to a show-
down. You're their 'front,' their stalking horse. You tell me what
you heard from Göring's mouth—and I tell you what I've heard
from Uncle Jesse's mouth. Not once but a hundred times! He
says it jokingly, but he means it—it's his program. The Socialists
will make their peaceable revolution, and then the Communists will
rise up and take it away from them. It'll be easy because the Socialists are so gentle and so kind—they're idealists! You saw it happen in Russia, and then in Hungary—didn't I hear Károlyi tell you
about it?"

"Yes, dear——"

"With his own mouth he told you! But it didn't mean much to
you, because it isn't what you want to believe. Károlyi is a gentleman, a noble soul—I'm not mocking—I had a long talk with him,
and I'm sure he's one of the most high-minded men who ever
lived. He was a nobleman and he had estates, and when he saw the
ruin and misery after the war he gave them to the government. No
man could do more. He became the Socialist Premier of Hungary,
and tried to bring a peaceful change, and the Communists rose up

against his government—and what did he do? He said to me in these very words: 'I couldn't shoot the workers.' So he let the Communist-led mob seize the government, and there was the dreadful bloody regime of that Jew—what was his name?"

"Béla Kun. Too bad he had to be a Jew!"

"Yes, I admit it's too bad. You just told me that you didn't invent *Mein Kampf* and you didn't invent the Brownshirts. Well, I didn't invent Béla Kun and I didn't invent Liebknecht and that Red Rosa Jewess who tried to do the same thing in Germany, nor Eisner who did it in Bavaria, nor Trotsky who helped to do it in Russia. I suppose the Jews have an extra hard time and that makes them revolutionary; they haven't any country and that keeps them from being patriotic. I'm not blaming them, I'm just facing the facts, as you're all the time urging me to do."

"I've long ago faced the fact that you dislike the Jews, Irma."

"I dislike some of them intensely, and I dislike some things about them all. But I love Freddi, and I'm fond of all the Robins, even though I am repelled by Hansi's ideas. I've met other Jews that I like——"

"In short," put in Lanny, "you have accepted what Hitler calls 'honorary Aryans.'" He was surprised by his own bitterness.

"That's a mean crack, Lanny, and I think we ought to talk kindly about this problem. It isn't a simple one."

"I want very much to," he replied. "But one of the facts we have to face is that the things you have been saying to me are all in *Mein Kampf,* and the arguments you have been using are the foundation stones upon which the Nazi movement is built. Hitler also likes some Jews, but he dislikes most of them because he says they are revolutionary and not patriotic. Hitler also is forced to put down the idealists and the liberals because they serve as a 'front' for the Reds. But you see, darling, the capitalist system is breaking down, it is no longer able to produce goods or to feed the people, and some other way must be found to get the job done. We want to do it peaceably if possible; but surely the way to do it cannot be for all the men who want it done peaceably to agree to shut up and say nothing, for fear of giving some benefit to the men of violence!"

V

They argued for a while, but it didn't do any good; they had said it before, many times, and neither had changed much. In the course of four years Irma had listened attentively while her husband debated with many sorts of persons, and unless they were Communists she had nearly always found herself in agreement with the other persons. It was as if the ghost of J. Paramount Barnes were standing by her side telling her what to think. Saying: "I labored hard, and it was not for nothing. I gave you a pleasant position, and surely you don't wish to throw it away!" The ghost never said, in so many words: "What would you be without your money?" It said: "Things aren't so bad as the calamity-howlers say; and anyhow, there are better remedies." When Lanny, vastly irritated, would ask: "What are the remedies?" the ghost of the utilities king would fall silent, and Irma would become vague, and talk about such things as time, education, and spiritual enlightenment.

"It's no good going on with this, dear," said the husband. "The question is, what are we going to do about Freddi?"

"If you would only tell me any definite thing that we can do!"

"But that isn't possible, dear. I have to go there and try this and that, look for new facts and draw new conclusions. The one thing I can't do, it seems to me, is to leave Freddi to his fate. It's not merely that he's a friend; he's a pupil, in a way. I helped to teach him what he believes; I sent him literature, I showed him what to do, and he did it. So I have a double obligation."

"You have an obligation to your wife and daughter, also."

"Of course, and if they were in trouble, they would come first. But my daughter is getting along all right, and as for my wife, I'm hoping she will see it as I do."

"Do you want me to come with you again?"

"Of course I want you; but I'm trying to be fair, and not put pressure upon you. I want you to do what seems right to you."

Irma was fond enough of having her own way, but wasn't entirely reconciled to Lanny's willingness to give it to her. Somehow it bore too close a resemblance to indifference. "A woman wants to be wanted," she would say.

"Don't be silly, darling," he pleaded. "Of course I want your help. I might need you badly some time. But ought I drag you there against your will, and feeling that you're being imposed on?"

"It's a horrid bore for me to be in a country where I don't understand the language."

"Well, why not learn it? If you and I would agree not to speak anything but German to each other, you'd be chattering away in a week or two."

"Is that what I do in English, Lanny?" He hastened to embrace her, and smooth her ruffled feelings. That was the way they settled their arguments; they were still very much in love, and when he couldn't bring himself to think as she did, the least he could do was to cover her with kisses and tell her that she was the dearest woman in the world.

The upshot of the discussion was that she would go with him again, but she had a right to know what he was going to do before he started doing it. "Of course, darling," he replied. "How else could I have your help?"

"I mean, if it's something I don't approve of, I have a right to say so, and to refuse to go through with it."

He said again: "Haven't you always had that right in our marriage?"

VI

Johannes had established himself in New York, where he was running errands for Robbie, and incidentally trying to "pick up a little business," something he would never fail to do while he lived. Lanny phoned to his father, who motored in, and the four had a long conference in Johannes's hotel room. They threshed out every aspect of the problem and agreed upon a code for communicating with one another. They agreed with Lanny that if Freddi was a prisoner of the government, the Minister-Präsident of Prussia knew it, and there could be no gain in approaching him, unless it was to be another money hold-up. Said Johannes: "He is doubtless informed as to how much money Irma has."

Perhaps it was up to Irma to say: "I would gladly pay it all." But she didn't.

Instead, Robbie remarked to his son: "If you let anybody connected with the government know that you are there on account of Freddi, they will almost certainly have you watched, and be prepared to block you, and make trouble for anyone who helps you."

"I have a business," replied Lanny. "My idea is to work at it seriously and use it as a cover. I'll cable Zoltan and find out if he'd be interested to give a Detaze show in Berlin this autumn. That would make a lot of publicity, and enable me to meet people; also it would tip off Freddi's friends as to where and how to get in touch with me. All this will take time, but it's the only way I can think of to work in Hitler Germany."

This was a promising idea, and it pleased Irma, because it was respectable. She had had a very good time at the London showing of Marcel's paintings. It was associated in her mind with romantic events; getting married in a hurry and keeping the secret from her friends—she had felt quite delightfully wicked, because nobody could be sure whether they were really married or not. Also the New York show had been fun—even though the Wall Street panic had punctured it like a balloon.

Lanny said that before sailing they should take some time and drum up business; if he had American dollars to pay out for German art treasures, the most fanatical Nazi could find no fault with him. Irma had so far looked upon the picture business as if it were the vending of peanuts from a pushcart; but now it became part of a melodrama—as if she were dressing up as the peanut vender's wife! But without really sacrificing her social prestige; for the richest and most fastidious persons wouldn't suspect that the daughter of J. Paramount Barnes was peddling pictures for the money. It would be for love of *les beaux arts*, a fine and dignified thing.

When Lanny telegraphed some client that he and his wife were about to leave for Germany and would like to motor out and discuss the client's tastes and wishes, the least the person could do was to invite them to tea, and often it would be to spend the night in some showplace at Bar Harbor or Newport, in the Berkshires or up the Hudson.

So, when the young couple boarded a steamer for Southampton, they really had an excellent pretext for a sojourn in Naziland. They sailed on a German liner, because Irma had set out to learn the language and wanted opportunities to "chatter." They landed in England because their car had been stored there, and because Lanny wanted a conference with Rick before taking the final plunge. Zoltan was in London, and had answered Lanny's cable with an enthusiastic assent. He was a shrewd fellow, and knowing about Freddi Robin, had no trouble in guessing what was in their heads; but he was discreet, and said not a word.

Beauty had gone back to Juan, and of course the young couple wanted to see little Frances, and also to talk things over with the Robins and make them acquainted with the code. On the way they stopped to see Emily and get her wise advice. One bright moonlit night they arrived at Bienvenu, amid the powerful scent of orange and lemon blossoms. *Kennst du das Land, wo die Zitronen blühn?* It seemed to Irma that she wanted nothing ever again but to stay in that heaven-made garden.

For three days she was in ecstasies over their darling little girl, calling Lanny's attention to every new word she had learned. Lanny, duly responsive, wondered what the little one made of these two mysterious, godlike beings called mother and father, who swooped down into her life at long intervals and then vanished in a roar of motors and clouds of dust. He observed that the child was far more interested in the new playmate whom fate permitted her to have without interruption. Baby Freddi was blooming like a dark velvet rose in the hot sunshine of the Midi, for which he had been destined many centuries ago; fear was being forgotten, along with his father. Irma withheld her thought: "I must get those two apart before they come to the falling-in-love age!"

VII

All preparations having been made as for a military campaign, at the beginning of September the young couple set out for Berlin by way of Milan and Vienna. Lanny knew of paintings in the latter city, and the art business could be made more convincing if he stopped there. He had written letters to several of his friends in Germany, telling of his intention to spend the autumn in their country; they would approve his business purpose, for he would be contributing foreign exchange to the Fatherland, and with foreign exchange the Germans got coffee and chocolate and oranges, to say nothing of Hollywood movies and Budd machine guns. To Frau Reichsminister Goebbels he wrote reminding her of her kind offer to advise him; he told of the proposed Detaze exhibit and enclosed some photographs and clippings, in case the work of this painter wasn't already known to her. Carefully wrapped and stowed in the back of the car were several of Marcel's most famous works—not the *Poilu*, not those sketches satirizing German militarism, but *Pain*, and *Sister of Mercy*, so gentle, yet moving, adapted to a nation which had just signed a pact renouncing war; also samples of the land- and sea-scapes of that romantic Riviera coast which so many Germans had visited and come to love. *Kennst du das Land!*

On the drive through Italy, safe from possible eavesdropping, they discussed the various possibilities of this campaign. Should they try to appeal to what sense of honor the Commander of the German Air Force might have? Should they try to make friends with him, and to extract a favor from him, sometime when they had him well loaded up with good liquor? Should they make him a straight-out cash proposition? Or should they try to get next to the Führer, and persuade him that they were the victims of a breach of faith? Should they play the Goebbels faction, or find somebody in power who needed cash and could pull hidden wires? Should they try for a secret contact with some of the young Socialists, and perhaps plan a jailbreak? These and many more schemes they threshed out, and would keep them in mind as they groped their way into the Nazi jungle. One thing alone was certain; whatever plan they decided upon they could carry out more safely if they were established in Berlin as socially prominent and artistically distinguished, the heirs and interpreters of a great French painter, the patrons and friends of a German Komponist, and so on through various kinds of glamour they might manage to wrap about themselves.

In Vienna it wasn't at all difficult for Lanny to resume the role of art expert. In one of those half-dead palaces on the Ringstrasse he came upon a man's head by Hobbema which filled him with enthusiasm; he cabled to a collector in Tuxedo Park, the sale was completed in two days, and thus he had earned the cost of a long stay in Berlin before he got there. Irma was impressed, and said: "Perhaps Göring might let you sell for him those paintings in the Robin palace. Johannes would be getting his son in exchange for his art works!"

VIII

A detour in order to spend a couple of days at Stubendorf; for Kurt Meissner was like a fortress which had to be reduced before an army could march beyond it. No doubt Heinrich had already written something about Lanny's becoming sympathetic to National Socialism, and it wouldn't do to have Kurt writing back: "Watch out for him, he doesn't really mean it." If Lanny was to succeed as a spy, here was where he had to begin, and the first step would be the hardest.

A strange thing to be renewing old friendships and at the same time turning them into something else! To be listening to Kurt's new piano concerto with one half your mind, and with the other half thinking: "What shall I say that will be just right, and how shall I lead up to what I want to tell him about the Robins?"

Was it because of this that Kurt's music seemed to have lost its vitality? In the old days Lanny's enthusiasm had been unrestrained; all his being had flowed along with those sweeping melodies, his feet had marched with those thundering chords, he had been absolutely certain that this was the finest music of the present day. But now he thought: "Kurt has committed himself to these political fanatics, and all his thinking is adjusted to their formulas. He is trying to pump himself up and sound impressive, but really it's old stuff. He has got to the stage where he is repeating himself."

But Lanny mustn't give the least hint of that. He was an intriguer, a double-dealer, using art and art criticism as camouflage for *his* kind of ideology, *his* set of formulas. He had to say: "Kurt, that's extraordinary; that *finale* represents the highest point you have ever attained; the *adagio* weeps with all the woe of the world." How silly these phrases of musical rapture sounded; saying them made a mockery of friendship, took all the charm out of hospitality, even spoiled the taste of the food which the *gute verständige Mutter*, Frau Meissner, prepared for her guests.

But it worked. Kurt's heart was warmed to his old friend, and he decided that political differences must not be allowed to blind one to what was fine in an opponent. Later on, Lanny went for a walk in the forest, leaving Irma to have a heart-to-heart talk with Kurt, and tackle a job which would have been difficult for Lanny. For, strangely enough, Irma was play-acting only in part. She said things to this German musician which she hadn't said to anybody else, and hadn't thought she would ever say; so she assured him, and of course it touched him. She explained that Lanny was honest, and had dealt with her fairly, telling her his political convictions before he had let her become interested in him. But she had been ignorant of the world, and hadn't realized what it would mean to be a Socialist, or one sympathetic to their ideas. It meant meeting the most dreadful people, and having them interfere in your affairs, and your being drawn into theirs. Not merely the sincere ones, but the tricksters and adventurers who had learned to parrot the phrases! Lanny could never tell the difference—indeed, how could anybody tell? It was like going out into the world with your skin off, and any insect that came along could take a bite out of you.

"And not only Socialists," said the young wife, "but Communists, all sorts of trouble-makers. You know Uncle Jesse, how bitter he is, and what terrible speeches he makes."

"We had millions like him in Germany," replied Kurt. "Thank God that danger is no more."

"I've been pleading and arguing with Lanny for more than four years. At one time I was ready to give up in despair; but now I really begin to believe I am making some headway. You know how Lanny is, he believes what people tell him; but of late he seems to be realizing the true nature of some of the people he's been helping. That's why I wanted to ask you to talk to him. He has such a deep affection for you, and you may be able to explain what is going on in Germany, and help him to see things in their true light."

"I've tried many times," said Kurt; "but I never seemed to get anywhere."

"Try once more. Lanny is impressionable, and seeing your movement going to work has given a jolt to his ideas. What he wants more than anything is to see the problem of unemployment solved. Do you think the Führer will really be able to do it?"

"I have talked with him, and I know that he has practical plans and is actually getting them under way."

"Explain that to Lanny, so that while he's here with Marcel's pictures he'll watch and understand. It may seem strange to you that I'm letting him sell pictures when I have so much money of my own; but I've made up my mind that he ought to have something to do, and not have the humiliation of living on his wife's money."

"You're absolutely right," declared the musician, much impressed by the sound judgment of this young woman, whom he had imagined to be a social butterfly. "Lanny is lucky to have a wife who understands his weaknesses so well. Make him stick at some one thing, Irma, and keep him from chasing every will-o'-the-wisp that crosses his path."

IX

So these two boyhood friends got together and renewed their confidences. Life had played strange tricks upon them, beyond any foreseeing. Back in the peaceful Saxon village of Hellerau where they had met just twenty years ago, dancing Gluck's *Orpheus*, suppose that somebody had told them about the World War, less than a year off, and five years later Kurt in Paris as a German secret agent, passing ten thousand francs at a time to Uncle Jesse to be used in stirring up revolt among the French workers! Or suppose they had been told about a pitiful artist *manqué*, earning his bread and sausage by painting picture postcards, sleeping at night among the bums and derelicts of Vienna— and destined twenty years later to become the master of all Germany! What would they have said to that?

But here was Adolf Hitler, the one and only Führer of the Fatherland, sole possessor of a solution to the social problem and at the same time of the power to put it into effect. Kurt explained what Adi was doing and intended to do, and Lanny listened with deep attention. "It sounds too good to be true," was the younger man's comment.

The Komponist replied: "You will see it, and then you will believe." To himself he said: "Poor Lanny! He's good, but he's a weakling. Like all the rest of the world, he's impressed by success." Having been Beauty's lover for eight years, Kurt knew the American language, and thought: "He is getting ready to climb onto the bandwagon."

So, when the young couple drove away to Berlin, they left everything at Stubendorf the way they wanted it. Kurt was again their friend, and ready to accept whatever good news might come concerning them. They could ask him for advice, and for introductions, if needed; they could invite him to Berlin to see the Detaze show, and exploit his musical reputation for their own purposes. Lanny didn't let this trouble his conscience; it was for Freddi Robin, not for himself. Freddi, too, was a musician, a child of Bach and Beethoven and Brahms just as much as Kurt. Many compositions those two Germans had played together, and the clarinetist had given the Komponist many practical hints about writing for that instrument.

When Lanny had mentioned to Kurt that Freddi had been missing since the month of May, Kurt had said: "Oh, poor fellow!"

—but that was all. He hadn't said: "We must look into it, Lanny, because mistakes are often made, and a harmless, gentle idealist must not be made to pay the penalties for other people's offenses." Yes, Kurt should have said that, but he wouldn't, because he had become a full-fledged Nazi, despising both Marxists and Jews, and unwilling to move a finger to help even the best of them. But Lanny was going to help Freddi—and take the liberty of making Kurt take part in the enterprise.

X

On the day that Irma and Lanny arrived at the Hotel Adlon, another guest, an elderly American, was severely beaten by a group of Brownshirts because he failed to notice that a parade was passing and to give the Nazi salute. When he went to the Polizeiwache to complain about it, the police offered to show him how to give the Nazi salute. Episodes such as this, frequently repeated, had had the effect of causing the trickle of tourists to stop; and this was fortunate for an art expert and his wife, because it made them important, and caused space to be given to Detaze and his work. Everybody desired to make it clear that the great art-loving public of Berlin was not provincial in its tastes, but open to all the winds that blew across the world.

Lanny talked about his former stepfather who had had his face burned off in the war and had done his greatest painting in a white silk mask. His work was in the Luxembourg, in the National Gallery of London, and the Metropolitan Museum of New York; now Lanny was contemplating a one-man show in Berlin, and had invited the famous authority Zoltan Kertezsi to take charge of it. Before giving out photographs or further publicity concerning the matter, he wished to consult Reichsminister Doktor Joseph Goebbels, and be sure that his plans were agreeable to the government. That was the proper way to handle matters with a controlled press; the visitor's tact was appreciated, and the interviews received more space than would have been given if he had appeared anxious to obtain it.

Lanny had already sent a telegram to Magda Goebbels, and her secretary had telephoned an appointment for the next day. While Irma stayed in her rooms and practiced her German on maids and manicurists and hair-dressers, Lanny drove to the apartment in the Reichstagplatz, and bowed and kissed the hand of the first lady of the Fatherland—such was, presumably, her position, Hitler being a bachelor and Göring a widower. Lanny had brought along two footmen from the hotel, bearing paintings, just as had been done in the days of Marie Antoinette, and those of her mother, the Empress Maria Theresa of Austria. The *Sister of Mercy* was set up in a proper light and duly admired; when the Frau Reichsminister asked who it was, Lanny did not conceal the fact that it was his mother, or that she was well known in Berlin society.

He explained his own position. He had enjoyed the advantage of having these great works explained to him by his stepfather, and so had been a lover of art since his boyhood. He had helped to select several great collections in the United States, which would some day become public property. It was pleasant to earn money, but it was even more so to be able to gratify one's taste for beautiful things; Lanny was sure the Frau Reichsminister would understand this, and she said that she did. He added that while a few of the Detazes would be sold, that was not the purpose of the exhibition, and he would not ask to take money out of the country, for he had commissions to purchase German art works for Americans, in amounts greatly exceeding what he was willing to sell. He told how he had just purchased a Hobbema in Vienna; contrary to his usual custom he named both parties to the transaction, and it was impressive.

The upshot was that Magda Goebbels declared the proposed show a worthy cultural enterprise. She said that the Führer had very decided tastes in art, he despised the eccentric modern stuff which was a symptom of pluto-democratic Jewish decadence. Lanny said he had understood that this was the case and it was one of his reasons for coming to Berlin. The work of Detaze was simple, like most great art; it was clean and noble in spirit. He would be happy to take specimens of it to show to the Führer in advance, and the Frau Reichsminister said that possibly this might be arranged. He offered to leave the paintings and photographs for the Herr Reichsminister to inspect, and the offer was accepted. He took his departure feeling hopeful that Marcel Detaze might become a popular painter among the Germans. He wondered, had Marcel heard about the Nazis in the spirit land, and what would he make of them? Lanny would have liked to go at once to consult Madame Diseuse—but who could guess what his irreverent ex-stepfather might blurt out in the séance room!

XI

Lanny's second duty was to get in touch with Oberleutnant Furtwaengler and invite him and his wife to dinner. He explained that it was his wish to show the paintings to Seine Exzellenz, the Herr Minister-Präsident General Göring. Such was now the title—for the newspapers had just made known that the Reichspräsident Feldmarschall von Hindenburg had been pleased to make the Minister-Präsident into a General of the Reichswehr. The Oberleutnant confirmed the news and showed pride in the vicarious honor; it had been somewhat awkward having his chief a mere Hauptmann while in command of several generals of the Prussian Polizei.

Lanny said he was sure that Seine Exzellenz must be a lover of art; he assumed that the new furnishings in the official residence—that great black table and the gold velvet curtains—must represent Seine Exzellenz's taste. The staff officer admitted that this was so, and promised to mention Detaze to the great man. Lanny said that during the past three months he had been in London, Paris, New York, Cannes, and Vienna; the young Nazi, who had never been outside of Germany, was impressed in spite of himself, and wanted to know what the outside world was saying about the Führer and his achievements. Lanny said he was afraid they were not getting a very fair picture; apparently the National Socialist representatives abroad were not serving their cause too efficiently. He told of things he had heard, from various persons having important titles and positions; also of efforts he had made to explain and justify—

the latter being in reality things that he had heard Lord Wick-thorpe say. Lanny added that he had some suggestions which he would be glad to make to Seine Exzellenz if this busy man could spare the time to hear them. The young staff officer replied that he was sure this would be the case.

Not once did Lanny mention the name of Robin. He wanted to see if the Oberleutnant would bring it up; for that would give him an idea whether Göring had taken the staff officer into his confidence. Near the end of the evening, while Irma was off practicing her German on the tall and rather gawky country lady who was the Frau Oberleutnant, the officer said: "By the way, Herr Budd, did you ever hear any more from your young Jewish friend?"

"Not a word, Herr Oberleutnant."

"That is certainly a strange thing."

"I had been hoping for some results from the inquiries which you were kind enough to say you would carry on."

"I have done all that I could think of, Herr Budd, but with no results."

"It was my idea that in the confusion of last spring, various groups had been acting more or less independently, and the records might be imperfect."

"I assure you we don't do things that way in Germany, Herr Budd. In the office of the Geheime Staats-Polizei is a complete card-file covering every case of any person who is under arrest for any offense or under any charge of even the remotest political nature. I don't suppose that your friend could have been arrested, say for drunk driving."

"He does not drink and he does not drive, Herr Oberleutnant. He plays delicately and graciously upon the clarinet, and is a devoted student of your classics. If you should give him the beginning of any quotation from Goethe he would complete it and tell you in what work it was to be found."

"It is really too bad, Herr Budd. If there is anything you can suggest to me——"

"It has occurred to me that the young man might be in some place of confinement outside of Prussia, and so might not appear in your police card-file. Suppose, for example, that he was in Dachau?"

Lanny was watching his dinner companion closely; but if the officer smelled the rat, he was a skillful actor. "Your friend could not be in Dachau," he declared, "unless he were a Bavarian. Being a Berliner, he would be in Oranienburg or some other place near by. However, if you wish, I will cause an inquiry to be made through the *Reichsregierung,* and see if anything can be turned up."

"That is most kind of you," declared Lanny. "It is more than I should have ventured to ask in a time when you and your associates have your hands so full. Permit me to mention that while the young man's name is actually Freddi, some official may have assumed it to be Friedrich, or they might have listed him as Fritz. Also it is conceivable that some one may have set him down as Rabinowitz, the name which his father bore in the city of Lodz."

The staff officer took out his notebook and duly set down these items. "I will promise to do my best, Herr Budd," he declared.

"Perhaps it will be better if you do not trouble Seine Exzellenz with this matter," added the visitor. "I know that he must be the busiest man in the world, and I do not want him to think that I have come to Berlin to annoy him with my personal problems."

Said the staff officer: "He is one of those great men who know how to delegate authority and not let himself be burdened with details. He has time for social life, and I am sure he will be interested to hear what you have to report from the outside world."

Said the undercover diplomat: "I got some reactions of the British Foreign Office to Seine Exzellenz's speech in Geneva. Lord Wickthorpe was really quite stunned by it. You know how it is, the British have been used to having their own way of late years—perhaps much too easily, Herr Leutnant. I doubt if it is going to be so easy for them in future!"

22

Still Get Money, Boy!

I

I T WAS Lanny's hope that as soon as his arrival was announced in the papers he would receive some sort of communication from whoever had taken the trouble to write that Freddi was in Dachau. He was careful in his newspaper interviews to declare himself a non-political person, hoping that some of his former acquaintances among the Social-Democrats would take the hint. But the days passed, and no letter or telephone call was received. Lanny had got from Rahel a list of Freddi's former comrades; most of them would probably be under arrest, or in hiding, "sleeping out," as it was called, never two nights in the same place. Before trying to meet any of them, it seemed wiser for Lanny to try out his Nazi contacts. It would be difficult to combine the two sorts of connections.

He went to call on Heinrich Jung, who burst into his customary excited account of his activities. He had recently come back from the *Parteitag* in Nürnberg; the most marvelous of all *Parteitage*—it had been five days instead of one, and every one of the hundred and twenty hours had been a new climax, a fresh revelation of *das Wunder, die Schönheit, der Sieg* hidden in the soul of National Socialism. "Honestly, Lanny, the most cynical persons were moved to tears by what they saw there!" Lanny couldn't summon any tears, but he was able to bring smiles to his lips and perhaps a glow to his cheeks.

"Do you know Nürnberg?" asked Heinrich. Lanny had visited that old city, with a moat around it and houses having innumerable sharp gables, crowded into narrow streets which seldom ran straight for two successive blocks. An unpromising place for the convention of a great political party, but the Nazis had chosen it because of its historic associations, the memories of the old Germany they meant to bring back to life. Practical difficulties were merely a challenge to their powers of organization; they would show the world how to take care of a million visitors to a city whose population was less than half that. Suburbs of tents had been erected on the outskirts, and the Stormtroopers and Hitler Youth had slept on straw, six hundred to each great tent, two blankets to each person. There had been rows of field kitchens with aluminum spouts from which had poured endless streams of goulash or coffee. Heinrich declared that sixty thousand Hitler Youth had been fed in half an hour—three half-hours per day for five days!

These were specially selected youth, who had labored diligently all year to earn this reward. They had been brought by special trains and by trucks, and had marched in with their bands, shaking the air with songs and the great Zeppelin Meadow with the tramp of boots. For five days and most of five nights they had shouted and sung themselves hoarse, making up in their fervor for all the other forty-four political parties which they had wiped out of existence in Germany. Only one party now, one law, one faith, one baptism! A temporary hall had been built, accommodating a small part of the hundred and sixty thousand official delegates; the others listened to loud-speakers all over the fields, and that served just as well, because there didn't have to be any voting. Everything was settled by the Führer, and the million others had only to hear the speeches and shout their approval.

Heinrich, now a high official in the Hitler Youth, had been among those admitted to the opening ceremonies. He lacked language to describe the wonders, he had to wave his arms and raise his voice. The frenzied acclaim when the Führer marched in to the strains of the *Badenweiler Marsch*—did Lanny know it? Yes, Lanny did, but Heinrich hummed a few bars even so. After Hitler had reached the platform the standards were borne in, the flags consecrated by being touched with the Blood Flag, which had been borne in the Munich civil struggle. Heinrich, telling about it, was like a good Catholic witnessing the sacred mystery of the Host. He told how Ernst Röhm had called the roll of those eighteen martyrs, and of all the two or three hundred others who had died during the party's long struggle for power. Muffled drums beat softly, and at the end the S.A. Chief of Staff declared: "*Sie marschieren mit uns im Geist, in unseren Reihen.*"

Five days of speechmaking and cheering, marching and singing by a million of the most active and capable men in Germany, nearly all of them young. Heinrich said: "If you had seen it, Lanny, you would know that our movement has won, and that the Fatherland is going to be what we make it."

"I had a long talk with Kurt," said Lanny. "He convinced me that you and he have been right." The young official was so delighted that he clasped his friend's hand and wrung it. Another Hitler victory. *Sieg Heil!*

II

Most of Irma's fashionable acquaintances had not yet returned to the city, so she employed her spare time accustoming her ears to the German language. She struck up an acquaintance with the hotel's manicurist, a natural blonde improved by art, sophisticated as her profession required, but underneath it naïve, as all Germans seemed to Irma. An heiress's idea of how to acquire knowledge was to hire somebody to put it painlessly into her mind; and who could be a more agreeable injector than a young woman who had held the hands of assorted millionaires and celebrities from all parts of the world, chattering to them and encouraging them to chatter back? Fräulein Elsa Borg was delighted to sell her spare hours to Frau Budd, *geborene* Barnes, and to teach her the most gossipy and idiomatic Berlinese. Irma practiced laboriously those coughing and sneezing sounds which Tecumseh had found too barbarous. To her husband she said: "Really the craziest way to put words together! I will the blue bag with the white trimmings to the hotel room immediately bring let. I will the eggs without the shells to be broken have. It makes me feel all the time as if children were making it up."

But no one could question the right of Germans by the children their sentences to be shaped let, and Irma was determined to speak properly if at all; never would she consent to sound to anybody the way Mama Robin sounded to her. So she and the manicurist talked for hours about the events of the day, and when Irma mentioned the *Parteitag*, Elsa said yes, her beloved *Schatz* had been there. This "treasure" was the block leader for his neighborhood and an ardent party worker, so he had received a badge and transportation and a permit to leave his work, also his straw and two blankets and goulash and coffee—all free. Irma put many questions, and ascertained what the duties of a block leader were, and how he had a subordinate in every apartment building, and received immediate reports of any new person who appeared in it, and of any whose actions were suspicious, or who failed to contribute to the various party funds, the *Büchsen*, and so on..All this would be of interest to Lanny, who might use a block leader, perhaps to give him information so that he could outwit some other block leader in an emergency.

Elsa's "treasure" afforded an opportunity to check on the claims of Heinrich and to test the efficiency of the Nazi machine. One of a hundred clerks in a great insurance office, Elsa's Karl worked for wretched wages, and if it had not been for his "little treasure" would have had to live in a lodging-house room. Yet he was marching on air because of his pride in the party and its achievements. He worked nights and Sundays at a variety of voluntary tasks, and had never received a penny of compensation—unless you counted the various party festivals, and the fact that the party had power to force his employers to grant him a week's holiday to attend the *Parteitag*. Both he and Elsa swelled with pride over this power, and a word of approval from his party superior would keep Karl happy for months. He thought of the Führer as close to God, and was proud of having been within a few feet of him, even though he had not seen him. The "treasure" had been one of many thousands of Brownshirts who had been lined up on the street in Nürnberg through which the Führer made his triumphal entrance. It had been Karl's duty to hold the crowds back, and he had faced the crowds, keeping watch lest some fanatic should attempt to harm the holy one.

Elsa told how Karl had seen the Minister-Präsident General Göring riding in an open car with a magnificent green sash across his brown party uniform. He had heard the solemn words of Rudolf Hess, Deputy of the Führer: "I open the Congress of Victory!" He had heard Hitler's own proud announcement: "We shall meet here a year from now, we shall meet here ten years from now, and a hundred, and even a thousand!" And Reichsminister Goebbels's excoriation of the foreign Jews, the busy vilifiers of the Fatherland. "Not one hair of any Jewish head was disturbed without reason," Frau Magda's husband had declared. When Irma told Lanny about this, he thought of poor Freddi's hairs and hoped it might be true. He wondered if this orgy of party fervor had been paid for out of the funds which Johannes Robin had furnished. Doubtless that had been "reason" enough for disturbing the hairs of Johannes's head!

III

Lanny took Hugo Behr for a drive, that being the only way they could talk freely. Lanny didn't say: "Did you write me that letter?" No, he was learning the spy business, and letting the other fellow do the talking.

Right away the sports director opened up. "I'm terribly embarrassed not to have been of any use to you, Lanny."

"You haven't been able to learn anything?"

"I would have written if I had. I paid out more than half the money to persons who agreed to make inquiries in the prisons in Berlin, and also in Oranienburg and Sonnenburg and Spandau. They all reported there was no such prisoner. I can't be sure if they did what they promised, but I believe they did. I want to return the rest of the money."

"Nonsense," replied the other. "You gave your time and thought and that is all I asked. Do you suppose there is any chance that Freddi might be in some camp outside of Prussia?"

"There would have to be some special reason for it."

"Well, somebody might have expected me to be making this inquiry. Suppose they had removed him to Dachau, would you have any way of finding out?"

"I have friends in Munich, but I would have to go there and talk to them. I couldn't write."

"Of course not. Do you suppose you could get leave to go?"

"I might be able to think up some party matter."

"I would be very glad to pay your expenses, and another thousand marks for your trouble. Everything that I told you about the case applies even more now. The longer Freddi is missing, the more unhappy the father grows, and the more pressure on me to do something. If the Detaze show should prove a success in Berlin, I may take it to Munich; meantime, if you could get the information, I could be making plans."

"Have you any reason to think about Dachau, especially?"

"I'll tell you frankly. It may sound foolish, but during the World War I had an English friend who was a flyer in France, and I was at my father's home in Connecticut, and just at dawn I was awakened by a strange feeling and saw my friend standing at the foot of the bed, a shadowy figure with a gash across his forehead. It turned out that this was just after the man had crashed and was lying wounded in a field."

"One hears such stories," commented the other, "but one never knows whether to believe them."

"Naturally, I believed this. I've never had another such experience until the other night. I was awakened, I don't know how, and lying in the dark I distinctly heard a voice saying: 'Freddi is in Dachau.' I waited a long time, thinking he might appear, or that I might hear more, but nothing happened. I had no reason to think of Dachau— it seems a very unlikely place—so naturally I am interested to follow it up and see if I am what they call 'psychic.' "

Hugo agreed that he, too, would be interested; his interest increased when Lanny slipped several hundred-mark notes into his pocket, saying, with a laugh: "My mother and stepfather have paid much more than this to spiritualist mediums to see if they could get any news of our friend."

IV

Hugo also had been to the *Parteitag*. To him it was not merely a marvelous demonstration of loyalty, but a call to every *Parteigenosse* to see that the loyalty was not wasted. Those million devoted workers gave their services without pay, because they had been promised a great collective reward, the betterment of the lot of the common man in Germany. But so far they had got nothing; not one of the promised economic reforms had been carried out, and indeed many of the measures which had been taken were reactionary, making the reforms more remote and difficult. The big employers had got a commanding voice in the control of the new shop councils—which meant simply that wages would be frozen where they were, and the workers deprived of all means of influencing them. The same was true of the peasants, because prices were being fixed. "If this continues," said Hugo, "it will mean a slave system, just that and nothing else."

To Lanny it appeared that the young sports director talked exactly like a Social-Democrat; he had changed nothing but his label. He insisted that the rank and file were of his way of thinking, and that what he called the "Second Revolution" could not be more than a few weeks off. He pinned his hopes upon Ernst Röhm, Chief of Staff and highest commander of the S.A., who had been one of the ten men tried for treason and imprisoned after the Beerhall Putsch; a soldier and fighter all his life, he had become the hero of those who wanted the N.S.D.A.P. to remain what it had been and to do what it had promised to do. The Führer must be persuaded, if necessary he must be pushed; that was the way it was in politics—it was no drawing-room affair, but a war of words and ideas, and if need be of street demonstrations, marching, threats. None knew this better than Hitler himself.

Lanny thought: "Hugo is fooling himself with the Chief of Staff, as earlier he fooled himself with the Führer." Ernst Röhm was a homosexual who had publicly admitted his habits; an ignorant rough fellow who rarely even pretended to social idealism. When he denounced the reactionaries who were still in the Cabinet, it was because he wanted more power for his Brownshirts and their commander. But it wasn't Lanny's business to hint at this; he must find out who the malcontents were—and especially whether any of them were in power at Dachau. Such men want money for their pleasures, and if they are carrying on a struggle for power they want money for that. There might be a good chance of finding one who could be paid to let a prisoner slip through the bars.

Their conference was a long one, and their drive took them into the country; beautiful level country, every square foot of it tended like somebody's parlor. No room for a weed in the whole of the Fatherland, and the forests planted in rows like orchards and tended the same way. It happened to be Saturday afternoon, and the innumerable lakes around Berlin were gay with tiny sailboats, the shores lined with cottages and bathhouses. The tree-lined paths by the roads were full of *Wandervögel,* young people hiking—but it was all military now, they wore S.A. uniforms and their songs were of defiance. Drill-grounds everywhere, and the air full of sharp cries of command and dust of tramping feet. Germany was getting ready for something. If you asked what, they would say "defense," but they were never clear as to who wished to attack them—right after signing a solemn pact against the use of force in Europe.

Another way in which Hugo resembled the Social-Democrats rather than the Nazis—he hated militarism. He said: "There are two ways the Führer can solve the problem of unemployment; one is to put the idle to work and make plenty for all, including themselves; the other is to turn them over to the army, to be drilled and sent out to take the land and resources of other peoples. That is the question which is being decided in the inner circles right now."

"Too bad you can't be there!" remarked Lanny; and his young friend revealed what was in the depths of his mind. "Maybe I will be some day."

V

Seine Exzellenz, Minister-Präsident General Göring, was pleased to invite Mr. and Mrs. Lanny Budd to lunch at his official residence. He didn't ask them to bring their paintings, and Lanny wasn't sorry about it, for somehow he couldn't see the *Sister of Mercy* in company with a lion cub. He doubted very much if Seine Exzellenz was being deceived as to the real reason for Lanny's coming to Berlin; and anyhow, the Commander of the German Air Force was having his own art made to his own order—a nude statue of his deceased wife, made from photographs and cast in solid gold!

At least that was what the Fürstin Donnerstein had told Irma. There was no stopping the tongues of these fashionable ladies; the Fürstin had poured out the "dirt," and Irma had collected it and brought it home. The good-looking blond aviator named Göring, after being wounded in the Beerhall Putsch, had fled abroad and married a Swedish baroness; the lady was an epileptic and her spouse a morphia addict. There could be no doubt about either of these facts, for they had been proved in court when the baroness was refused custody of her son by a former marriage. Later on, the lady had died of tuberculosis, and Göring, returning to Germany, had chosen Thyssen and the former Crown Prince for his cronies, and the steel king's sister for his "secretary"; the quotation marks were indicated by the Fürstin's tone as she said the last word. It had been assumed that he would marry this Anita Thyssen, but it hadn't come off; perhaps he had become too great—or too fat! At the moment Anita was "out," and the "in" was Emmy Sonnemann, a blond Nordic Valkyrie who acted at the State Theater and could have any role she chose. "But that doesn't exclude other *Damen*," added the serpent's tongue of Fürstin Donnerstein. "*Vorsicht, Frau Budd!*"

So Irma learned a new German word.

VI

The utility king's daughter had lived most of her life in marble halls, and wasn't going to be awed by the livery of Göring's lackeys or the uniforms of his staff and self. The lion cub was not for ladies, it appeared—and she didn't miss him. The great ebony table with gold curtains behind it was really quite stunning; they made Irma think of Dick Oxnard's panels, and she couldn't see why Lanny had made fun of them. Pink jackets and white silk pumps and stock-ings for footmen—yes, but hardly in the daytime; and the General's medals seemed more suited to a state dinner than a private luncheon.

However, the ex-aviator was very good company; he spoke English well, and perhaps wanted to prove it. He did most of the talking, and laughed gaily at his own jokes. There was nobody else present but Furtwaengler and another staff officer, and needless to say they laughed at the jokes and didn't tell any of their own. Apparently it was a purely social affair; not a word about ransoms or hostages, Jews or concentration camps. No need for Lanny to say: "I hope you have noticed, Exzellenz, that I have kept my agreement." The fact that he was here, being served cold-storage plovers' eggs and a fat squab was proof enough that he had kept it and that his host had made note of the fact.

The assumption was that the holder of eight or ten of the most responsible positions in the "Third Reich" enjoyed nothing so much as sipping brandy and chatting with two idle rich Americans; it was up to Lanny to play his role, and let it come up quite by accident that he and his wife had visited Lausanne in the early days of the Conference on Arms Limitation, and could tell inside stories about the prominent personalities there, including the German. This led to the mention that Lanny had been on the American staff at Paris, and had met many of the men, and had helped a German agent to escape to Spain. He knew leading members of several of the French parties, including Daladier, the Premier, and he had visited in the homes of some of the British Foreign Office set—yes, there could be no doubt that he was a young man of exceptional opportunities, and could be very useful to a Reichsminister without Portfolio if he happened to be well disposed! Not a word was spoken, but always there was floating in the air the thought: "Why not take a chance, Exzellenz, and turn loose my Jewish *Schiebersohn?*"

VII

Herr Reichsminister Joseph Goebbels was so gracious as to indicate his opinion that the work of Marcel Detaze was suitable for showing in Germany; quite harmless, although not especially distinguished. Lanny understood that he could expect no more for a painter from a nation which the Führer had described as "Negroid." It was enough, and he wired Zoltan to come to Berlin.

What did one do to obtain publicity with a *gleichgeschaltete Presse?* Lanny found out, even before his friend arrived. A young-ish, very businesslike gentleman called; one of those Berliners who wear a derby hat, and on a hot day a vest-clip on which they may hang the hat, thus preserving comfort and respectability at the same time. His card made him known as Herr Privatdozent Doktor der Philosophie Aloysius Winckler zu Sturmschatten. In a polite philo-sophical voice he informed Lanny that he was in position to pro-mote the reputation of Detaze—or otherwise. The Privatdozent spoke as one having both authority and determination; he didn't evade or drop his eyes, but said: *"Sie sind ein Weltmann, Herr Budd.* You know that a great deal of money can be made from the sale of these paintings if properly presented; and it happens that I am a *Parteigenosse* from the early days, the intimate friend of persons of great influence. In past times I have rendered them serv-ices and they have done the same for me. You understand how such things go."

Lanny said that he understood; but that this was not entirely a commercial undertaking, he was interested in making known the work of a man whom he had loved in life and admired still.

"Yes, yes, of course," said the stranger, his voice as smooth and purring as that of a high-priced motor-car. "I understand what you want, and I am in position to give it to you. For the sum of twenty thousand marks I can make Marcel Detaze a celebrated painter, and for the sum of fifty thousand marks I can make him the initiator of a new era in representational art."

"Well, that would be fine," said Lanny. "But how can I know that you are able to do these things?"

"For the sum of two thousand marks I will cause the publication of an excellent critical account of Detaze, with reproductions of a couple of his works, in any daily newspaper of Berlin which you may select. This, you understand, will be a test, and you do not have to pay until the article appears. But it must be part of the understanding that if I produce such an article, you agree to go ahead on one of the larger projects I have suggested. I am not a cheap person, and am not interested in what you Americans call *kleine Kartoffeln*. You may write the article yourself, but it would be wiser for you to provide me with the material and let me prepare it, for, knowing the Berlin public, I can produce something which will serve your purposes more surely."

So it came about that the morning on which Zoltan Kertezsi arrived at the hotel, Lanny put into his hands a fresh newspaper containing an account of Detaze at once critically competent and journalistically lively. Zoltan ran his eyes over it and exclaimed: "How on earth did you do that?"

"Oh, I found a competent press agent," said the other. He knew that Zoltan had scruples, whereas Zoltan's partner had left his in the Austrian town whence he had crossed into Naziland.

Later that morning the Herr Privatdozent called and took Lanny for a drive. The stepson of Detaze said that he wanted his stepfather to become the initiator of a new era in representational painting, and offered to pay the sum of ten thousand marks per week for one week preceding the show and two weeks during it, conditioned upon the producing of publicity in abundant quantities and of a standard up to that of the sample. The Herr Privatdozent accepted, and they came back to the hotel, where Zoltan, possibly not so innocent as he appeared, sat down with them to map out a plan of campaign.

VIII

Suitable showrooms were engaged, and the ever dependable Jerry Pendleton saw to the packing of the pictures at Bienvenu. He hired a *camion*, and took turns with the driver, sleeping inside and coming straight through with that precious cargo. Beauty and her husband came by train—there could have been no keeping her away, and anyhow, she was worth the expenses of the journey as an auxiliary show. She was in her middle fifties, and with Lanny at her side couldn't deny it, but she was still a blooming rose, and if you questioned what she had once been, there were two most beautiful paintings to prove it. Nothing intrigued the crowd more than to have her standing near so that they could make comparisons. The widow of this initiator of a new era, and her son—but not the painter's son —no, these Negroid races run to promiscuity, and as for the Americans, their divorces are a joke, they have a special town in the wild and woolly West where the broken-hearted ladies of fashion stay for a few weeks in order to get them, and meantime are consoled by cowboys and Indians.

For the "professional beauty" it was a sort of public reception, afternoons and evenings for two weeks, and she did not miss a minute of it. A delightfully distinguished thing to be able to invite your friends to an exhibition of which you were so unique a part: hostess, biographer, and historian, counselor and guide—and in case of need assistant saleslady! Always she was genial and gracious, an intimate of the great, yet not spurning one lowly lover of *die schönen Künste*. Zoltan paid her a memorable compliment, saying: "My dear Beauty Budd, I should have asked you to marry me and travel about the world promoting pictures." Beauty, with her best dimpled smile, replied: "Why didn't you?" (Mr. Dingle was off visiting one of his mediums, trying to get something about Freddi, but instead getting long messages from his father, who was so happy in the spirit world, and morally much improved over what he had been—so he assured his son.)

There were still rich men in Germany. The steelmasters of the Ruhr, the makers of electrical power, the owners of plants which could turn out the means of defense—all these were sitting on the top of the Fatherland. Having wiped out the labor unions, they could pay low wages without fear of strikes, and thus count upon profits in ever-increasing floods. They looked about them for sound investments, and had learned ten years ago that one inflation-proof material was diamonds and another was old masters. As a rule the moneylords didn't possess much culture, but they knew how to read, and when they saw in one newspaper after another that a new school of representational art had come to the front, they decided that they ought to have at least one sample of this style in their collections. If they were elderly and retired they came to the show;

if they were middle-aged and busy they sent their wives or daughters. Twenty or thirty thousand marks for a landscape did not shock them, on the contrary it made a Detaze something to brag about.

So it was that the profits of Lanny, his mother, and his half-sister —less the ten per cent commission of Zoltan—covered twenty times over what they had paid to the efficient Herr Privatdozent, and Zoltan suggested that they should pay this able promoter and continue the splurge of glory for another week. Even Irma was impressed, and began to look at the familiar paintings with a new eye. She wondered if it mightn't be better to save them all for the palace with modern plumbing which she meant some day to have in England or France. To her husband she remarked: "You see how much better everything goes when you settle down and stop talking like a Red!"

IX

The Detaze show coincided in time with one of the strangest public spectacles ever staged in history. The Nazis had laid the attempt to burn the Reichstag upon the Communists, while the enemies of Nazism were charging that the fire had been a plot of the Hitlerites to enable them to seize power. The controversy was brought to a head by the publication in London of the *Brown Book of the Hitler Terror*, which charged that the Nazi Chief of Police of Breslau, one of the worst of their terrorists, had led a group of S.A. men through the tunnel from Göring's residence into the Reichstag building; they had scattered loads of incendiary materials all over the place, while another group had brought a half-witted Dutch tramp into the building by a window and put him to work starting fires with a domestic gas-lighter. This was what the whole world was coming to believe, and the Nazis couldn't very well dodge the issue. For six or seven months they had been preparing evidence, and in September they began a great public trial. They charged the Dutchman with the crime, and three Bulgarian Communists and a German with being his accessories. The issue thus became a three-months' propaganda battle, not merely in Germany but wherever news was read and public questions discussed. Ten thousand pages of testimony were taken, and seven thousand electrical transcriptions made of portions of the testimony for broadcasting.

The trial body was the Fourth Criminal Senate of the German Supreme Court in Leipzig; oddly enough, the same tribunal before which, three years previously, Adolf Hitler had proclaimed that "heads will roll in the sand." Now he was going to make good his threat. Unfortunately he had neglected to "co-ordinate" all five of the court judges; perhaps he didn't dare, because of world opinion. There was some conformity to established legal procedure, and the result was such a fiasco that the Nazis learned a lesson, and never again would political suspects have a chance to appear in public and cross-question their accusers.

In October and November the court came to Berlin, and it was a free show for persons who had leisure; particularly for those who in their secret hearts were pleased to see the Nazis humiliated. The five defendants had been kept in chains for seven months and wore chains in the courtroom during the entire trial. The tragedy of the show was provided by the Dutchman, van der Lubbe, half-blind as well as half-witted; mucus drooled from his mouth and nose, he giggled and grinned, made vague answers, sat in a stupor when let alone. The melodrama was supplied by the Bulgarian Dimitroff, who "stole the show"; a scholar as well as a man of the world, witty, alert, and with the courage of a lion, he turned the trial into anti-Nazi propaganda; defying his persecutors, mocking them, driving them into frenzies of rage. Three times they put him out of the room, but they had to bring him back, and again there was sarcasm, defiance, and exposition of revolutionary aims.

It soon became clear that neither Dimitroff nor the other defendants had ever known van der Lubbe or had anything to do with the Reichstag fire. The mistake had arisen because there was a parliamentary archivist in the Reichstag building who happened to resemble the half-witted Dutchman, and it was with him that the Communist Torgler had been seen in conversation. The proceedings gradually turned into a trial of the *Brown Book*, with the unseen British committee as prosecutors and the Nazis as defendants.

Goebbels appeared and denounced the volume, and Dimitroff mocked him and made him into a spectacle. Then came the corpulent head of the Prussian state; it was a serious matter for him, because the incendiaries had operated from his residence and it was difficult indeed to imagine that he hadn't known what was going on. Under the Bulgarian's stinging accusations Göring lost his temper completely and had to be saved by the presiding judge, who ordered Dimitroff dragged out, while Göring screamed after him: "I am not afraid of you, you scoundrel. I am not here to be questioned by you . . . You crook, you belong to the gallows! You'll be sorry yet, if I catch you when you come out of prison!" Not very dignified conduct for a Minister-Präsident of Prussia and Reichsminister of all Germany!

X

During these entertaining events two communications came to Lanny Budd at his hotel. The first was painful indeed; a cablegram from his father, saying that the newly elected directors of Budd Gunmakers had met, and that both Robbie and his brother had been cheated of their hopes. Seeing the younger on the verge of victory, Lawford had gone over to a Wall Street group which had unexpectedly appeared on the scene, backed by the insurance company which held the Budd bonds. The thing which Grandfather Samuel had dreaded and warned against all his life—Budd's had been taken out of the hands of the family!

"Oh, Lanny, how terrible!" exclaimed Irma. "We should have been there to attend to it."

"I doubt if we could have done anything," he replied. "If Robbie had thought so, he would surely have cabled us."

"What Uncle Lawford did was an act of treason to the family!"

"He is that kind of man; one of those dark souls who commit crimes. I have often had the thought that he might shoot Robbie rather than let him get the prize which both have been craving all their lives."

"What does he get out of the present arrangement?"

"The satisfaction of keeping Robbie out; and, of course, the Wall Street crowd may have paid him. Anyhow, Robbie has his contract, so they can't fire him."

"I bought all that stock for nothing!" exclaimed the young wife.

"Not for nothing, but for a high price, I fear. You had best cable Uncle Joseph to look into the matter thoroughly and advise you whether to sell it or hold on. Robbie, no doubt, will be writing us the details."

The other communication was very different; a letter addressed to Lanny in his own handwriting, and his heart gave a thump when he saw it, for he had given that envelope to Hugo Behr. It was postmarked Munich and Lanny tore it open quickly, and saw that Hugo had cut six letters out of a newspaper and pasted them onto a sheet of paper—a method of avoiding identification well known to kidnapers and other conspirators. "*Jawohl*" can be one word or two. With space after the first two letters, as Hugo had pasted them, it told Lanny that Freddi Robin was in Dachau and that he was well.

So the American playboy forgot about his father's lost hopes and his own lost heritage. A heavy load was lifted from his mind, and he sent two cablegrams, one to Mrs. Dingle in Juan—the arrangement being that the Robins were to open such messages—and the other to Robbie in Newcastle: "Clarinet music excellent," that being the code. To the latter message the dutiful son added: "Sincere sympathy don't take it too hard we still love you." Robbie would take this with a grin.

Irma and Lanny tore Hugo's message into small pieces and sent it on its way to the capacious sewers of Berlin. They still had hope of some favor to be gained from the head of the Prussian government. At any moment Leutnant Furtwaengler might show up and announce: "We have found your Yiddisher friend." Until then, Lanny could only wait; for when you are cultivating acquaintances in *die grosse Welt*, you don't say to these persons: "I have made certain that you are lying to me, and propose that we now proceed to negotiate upon that basis." No, Lanny couldn't even say: "I have doubts." For right away the Oberleutnant would look sur-

prised and ask: "What is the basis of them?" Lanny couldn't even
say: "I urge you to try harder"; for important persons must be
assumed to have their hands full.

XI

The sum of more than four hundred thousand marks which had
been paid for Detaze pictures had been deposited in Berlin banks.
It would be up to Lanny and Zoltan to use those marks in purchasing art works for their American clients, who would make their
payments in New York; thus the pair would have to ask no favors
of the Nazis. Lanny had obtained information from a list of clients
in America, and Zoltan had a list which he had been accumulating
over a period of many years; so there would be no difficulty in
doing a sufficient amount of business. They had agreed to go fifty-
fifty on all transactions.

Lanny had suggested taking the show to Munich for a week, and
his friend had approved. Here was a great art-loving public, and
sales were certain; moreover, Beauty got fun out of it, and Lanny
knew of pictures which might be bought there. Jerry Pendleton,
who had been waiting in Berlin to take the unsold Detazes back to
France, would see to packing and transporting them to Munich.
The Herr Privatdozent assured them that he enjoyed even more
influence in the Bavarian city, the cradle of National Socialism. He
would be paid another fifteen thousand marks for his services, plus
his expenses for two weeks. He was planning to live high.

Hugo Behr returned to Berlin, reporting that he had made contact with an old party acquaintance who was now one of the S.A.
guards in the camp of Dachau. To this man Hugo had explained
that he had a friend who was owed money by a young Jew, and
wondered if the debtor was still alive and if there was any prospect
of his coming out. The report had been that Freddi Robin had been
in the camp for four or five months; had been pretty roughly
treated before he came there, and now was kept by himself, for
what reason the S.A. man didn't know. What he had meant by
reporting Freddi as "well" was that he was alive and not being

abused, so far as the informant had heard. Nobody was happy in Dachau, and least of all any Jew.

Hugo added: "We might be able to trust that fellow, because I had a long talk with him and he feels about events pretty much as I do. He's sick of his job, which isn't at all what he bargained for. He says there are plenty of others who feel the same, though they don't always talk. You know, Lanny, the Germans aren't naturally a cruel people, and they don't like having the most brutal and rowdyish fellows among them picked out and put in charge."

"Did he say that?" inquired Lanny.

"He said even more. He said he'd like to see every Jew put out of Germany, but he didn't see any sense in locking them up and kicking them around, just for being what they were born. I told him my idea that the party is being led astray and that it's up to the rank and file to set it straight. He was interested, and maybe we'll have an organized group in Dachau."

"That's fine," commented the American; "and I'm ever so much obliged to you. I'm going to Munich pretty soon and perhaps you can come again, and I'll have some other message for your friend." At the same time he took a little roll of hundred-mark notes out of his pocket and slipped them into his friend's—a matter of only a few inches as they sat side by side in the car.

XII

To his wife Lanny said: "There might be a possibility of getting Freddi out without waiting forever on the fat General."

"Oh, do be careful!" exclaimed Irma. "That would be a fearful risk to take!"

"Only as a last resort. But I really think Göring has had time enough to peer into all the concentration camps in the Reich."

He made up his mind to call up Oberleutnant Furtwaengler and inquire concerning the promised investigation. But he put it off till the next morning, and before he got round to it the young staff officer was announced and ushered up to the suite. "Herr Budd," he said, "are you free for the next two or three days?"

"I could get free."

"Seine Exzellenz has earned a holiday after the strain of his court appearances." The serious young officer said this without the least trace of a smile, and Lanny assented with the gravest of nods. "Seine Exzellenz is taking a shooting trip to the estate of Prinz von Schwarzerober in the Schorfheide, and would be pleased if you would accompany him."

"That is very kind indeed," replied the American, with a carefully measured amount of cordiality. "I appreciate the honor and will enjoy the opportunity to know the General better."

"Unfortunately," added the other, "this is what you Americans, I believe, call a 'stag' affair."

"A stag affair in two senses of the word," smiled Lanny, who knew about shooting in the German forests. "My wife won't object to staying here, for she has friends who keep her entertained."

"Very well, then," replied the Oberleutnant. "The car will call for you at fifteen o'clock tomorrow."

Later, the young couple went driving and talked over the situation. "He wants something," declared the husband. "I suppose I'm going to find out about it now."

"Let him do the talking," cautioned Irma. "You saw that he expects it." She was nine years younger than her husband, and had met the General only once, but she knew all about his *Prunksucht*, his delight in self-display, both physical and mental. "He has to prove that he's the greatest man in the company, the greatest in the government, perhaps the greatest in the world. He will do anything for you if you convince him you believe that."

Lanny's mother had been supplying him with that sort of instruction all through his life. He wondered: had Irma got it from Beauty —or from the Great Mother of them all?

23

All the Kingdoms of the World

I

LANNY in his boyhood had observed the feudal system operating in Stubendorf, and had found it paternal and pleasant; so he could understand how the Nazis had made the same discovery. The party was bound for the hunting preserve of one of those great landlords who had been the friends of Hauptmann Göring in the days when he was an ace aviator, successor to von Richthofen in command of that famous squadron. These wealthy Junkers had allied themselves with the Hitler party upon Göring's assurance that they would be properly cared for, and Göring now was seeing that the pledge was kept. There wasn't going to be any "Second Revolution" in Prussia if the head of the government could prevent it, and he thought that he could.

The party traveled in that six-wheeled Mercédès which Lanny had come to call "the tank." The chauffeur and the guard who rode beside him were black-uniformed Schutzstaffel men, both well armed. The very large General lolled in the back seat, with Lanny in the place of honor beside him. In two retractable seats rode Oberst Siemans, a Reichswehr officer who was a World War buddy of the General's, and Hauptmann Einstoss, an S.A. man who had accompanied Göring in his flight to Switzerland after the Beerhall Putsch. A second car followed with Furtwaengler and another staff officer, a secretary, a telephone operator, and a valet.

The party in the "tank" talked about the trial. Lanny wished he might hear what they would have said if he hadn't been along, but there was no way to arrange that. They talked on the assumption that the five prisoners were the spawn of Satan, and that the

General had completely annihilated Dimitroff. When they asked Lanny what would be the opinion of the outside world, he replied that all people were inclined to believe what it was in their interest to believe, and the outside world was afraid of the Nazis because it suspected that they meant to rearm Germany. Thus, if one was cautious, it was possible to avoid lying and at the same time avoid giving offense.

They drove at high speed, with a powerful horn giving notice to all the world to clear the way. Toward dusk they left the highway and entered a heavy forest; they drove many miles on a private road before coming to a hunting lodge, well lighted for their reception. A spacious hall, with bearskins on the floor and trophies on the walls; a glass-cased rack of guns at one end, a banquet-table at the other, and a great stone fireplace with logs blazing. There was no host—the place had been turned over to the General. Servants in green foresters' uniforms brought drinks, and when Seine Exzellenz called for supper there came a procession of men, each bearing a silver platter: the first containing a huge roasted boar's head, steaming hot, the second a haunch of venison, the third several capercailzie, a kind of grouse bigger than any chicken, and the fourth some fricasseed hares. Lanny, dining under the feudal system, could only laugh and beg for mercy. His host, proud of his prowess as a trencherman, was not displeased to have others take an attitude of inferiority.

It was the same with the drinking. Hot punch and cold Moselle, burning brandy sauces, cocktails, beer—there was apparently no ordained sequence; the valiant air commander took everything that he saw and called for more. The way Lanny saved himself was by music; when they started singing he took his glass of punch to the piano and played and sang: "Show me the way to go home, boys," and other "college songs" which he had learned as a boy from his father. The General was amused, and Lanny kept him entertained with various kinds of American humor: "Yankee Doodle" and "Down Went McGinty" and "There'll be a Hot Time in the Old Town Tonight." Whether they all knew the language didn't matter, for pretty soon they didn't know what they knew. He played "My

Old Kentucky Home" and they wept; he played "The Arkansas Traveler" and "Turkey in the Straw" and they tried to dance. Lanny cut his capers on the keyboard, and the head of the Prussian state approved of him so ardently that he wouldn't let his own valet help him upstairs, but insisted upon having the young American on one side and a blue-eyed Wendish damsel on the other.

This was another aspect of the feudal system about which Lanny had heard talk and which he now saw in action. The men servants who had brought in the heavy dishes had disappeared, and desserts and coffee and various drinks were served by young women in peasant costumes with flaxen hair in heavy braids down their backs. They were not prostitutes, but daughters of the servants and retainers; they curtsied to these high-born great gentlemen in uniforms, danced with them when invited, and were prepared to be honored by their further attentions. Not much flirtation or cajoling was called for; they obeyed commands. Fortunately for Lanny there were not enough to go around, and his renunciation was appreciated.

The party arose late next day. There was no hurry, for this kind of shooting proceeds according to the convenience of the shooters and not of the game. After a "fork breakfast" they set out to stands in the forests, and beaters drove stags and buffalo and boar out of the thickets into the open ranges. Lanny had the honor of being posted with the General, and he waited respectfully while the great man shot, and when he was told that it was his turn he upheld the reputation of Budd Gunmakers. It was worth while for him to do so, for he guessed it wouldn't be long before Robbie would be making use of these valuable connections.

II

. Having obtained recreation and exercise by pulling the trigger of a rifle, Seine Exzellenz returned to the hunting lodge and took up the reins of government. Apparently he had had a private wire run into the estate, and for a couple of hours he listened to reports and gave orders. He sounded angry most of the time—or was that just his way of governing? It was almost as if he were trying to communicate with Berlin by the medium of the air instead of by a copper wire. His bellowing echoed through the house, and Lanny, anxious not to overhear, went into the billiard room and watched the two junior officers winning small sums from each other. Now and then, when the tones rose especially loud, they would grin at Lanny and he would grin back—this being a privilege of subordinates.　　　　　　　　　.

The guest would have liked to walk in that lovely deep forest, but had the idea that he should hold himself at the disposal of his host; and sure enough, after the State of Prussia had received its marching orders for the morrow, Lanny was summoned to the Presence, and found out why he had been taken on a shooting trip. Reclining at ease in a sky-blue silk dressing gown with ermine trimmings, the portly Kommandant of the German Air Force led the conversation into international channels, and began explaining the difficulties of getting real information as to the attitude of ruling circles in other European capitals. He had agents aplenty, paid them generous salaries, and allowed them to pad their expense accounts; but those who were the most loyal had the fewest connections, while those who really had the connections were just as apt to be working for the other side.

"Understand me, Budd"—he had got to that stage of intimacy— "I am not so foolish as to imagine that I could employ you. I know you have a well-paying profession, not to mention a rich wife. I also had one, and discovered that such a spouse expects attentions and does not leave one altogether free. But it happens that you go about and gather facts; and no doubt you realize when they are important."

"I suppose that has happened now and then," said Lanny, showing a coming-on disposition, but not too much.

"What I should like to have is, not an agent, but a friend; a gentleman, whose sense of honor I could trust, and who would not be indifferent to the importance of our task in putting down the Red menace in Germany, and perhaps later wiping out the nest where those vipers are being incubated. Surely one does not have to be a German in order to approve such an aim."

"I agree with you, Exzellenz."

"Call me Göring," commanded the great one. "Perhaps you can understand how tired one gets of dealing with lackeys and flatterers. You are a man who says what he thinks, and when I box with you I get some competition."

"Thank you, Ex–Göring."

"I am sure you understand that we Nazis are playing for no small stakes. You are one of the few who possess imagination enough to know that if you become my friend you will be able to have anything you care to ask for. I am going to become one of the richest men in the world—not because I am greedy for money, but because I have a job to do, and that is one of the tools. We are going to build a colossal industry, which will become the heritage of the future, and most certainly we are not going to leave it in the hands of Jews or other Bolshevist agencies. Sooner or later we shall take over the industry of Russia and bring it into line with modern practices. For all that we need brains and ability. I personally need men who see eye to eye with me, and I am prepared to pay on a royal scale. There is no limit to what I would do for a man who would be a real associate and partner."

"I appreciate the compliment, my dear Göring, but I doubt my own qualifications for any such role. Surely you must have among your own Germans men with special training——"

"No German can do what I am suggesting to you—an American, who is assumed to be above the battle. You can go into France or England and meet anybody you wish, and execute commissions of the most delicate sort without waste of time or sacrifice of your own or your wife's enjoyment. Be assured that I would never ask you to do anything dishonorable, or to betray any trust. If, for example, you were to meet certain persons in those countries and talk politics with them, and report on their true attitudes, so that I could know which of them really want to have the Reds put down and which would rather see those devils entrench themselves than to see Germany get upon her feet—that would be information almost priceless to me, and believe me, you would have to do no more than hint your desires. If you would come now and then on an art-buying expedition to Berlin and visit me in some quiet retreat like this, the information would be used without any label upon it, and I would pledge you my word never to name you to anyone."

III

Lanny perceived that he was receiving a really distinguished offer, and for a moment he was sorry that he didn't like the Nazis. He had a feeling that Irma would be willing for him to say yes, and would enjoy helping on such international errands. Doubtless the General had invited her to lunch in order that he might size her up from that point of view.

"My dear Göring," said Irma's husband, "you are paying me a compliment, and I wish I could believe that I deserve it. To be sure, I sometimes meet important persons and hear their talk when they are off their guard; I suppose I could have more such opportunities if I sought them. Also I find Berlin an agreeable city to visit, and if I should run over now and then to watch your interesting work, it would be natural for you to ask me questions and for me to tell you what I had heard. But when you offer to pay me, that is another matter. Then I should feel that I was under obligations; and I have always been a *Taugenichts*—even before I happened to acquire a rich wife I liked to flit from one place to another, look at pictures, listen to good music or play it not so well, chat with my friends, and amuse myself watching the human spectacle. It happens that I have made some money, but I have never felt that I was earning it, and I would hate to feel that I had to."

It was the sort of answer a man would make if he wished to raise his price; and how was a would-be employer to know? "My dear Budd," said the General, in the same cautious style, "the last thing in the world I desired was to put you under any sense of obligation, or to interfere with your enjoyments. It is just because of that way of life that you could be of help to me."

"It would be pleasant indeed, Exzellenz, to discover that my weaknesses have become my virtues."

The great man smiled, but went on trying to get what he wanted.

"Suppose you were to render me such services as happened to amuse you, and which required no greater sacrifice on your part than to motor to Berlin two or three times a year; and suppose that some day, purely out of friendship, I should be moved to present you with a shooting preserve such as this, a matter of one or two hundred square kilometers—surely that wouldn't have to be taken as a humiliation or indignity."

"*Gott behüte!*" exclaimed the playboy. "If I owned such a property, I would have to pay taxes and upkeep, and right away I should be under moral pressure to get some use out of it."

"Can you think of nothing I might do for you?"

Lanny perceived that he was being handled with masterly diplomacy. The General wasn't saying: "You know I have a hold on you, and this is the way you might induce me to release it!" He wasn't compelling Lanny to say: "You know that you are holding out on me and not keeping your promise!" He was making things easy for both of them; and Lanny was surely not going to miss his chance! "Yes, Göring," he said, quickly, "there is one thing—to have your wonderful governmental machine make some special effort and find that young son of Johannes Robin."

"You are still worried about that Yiddisher?"

"How can I help it? He is a sort of relative—my half-sister is married to his brother, and naturally the family is distressed. When I started out for Berlin to show my Detaze paintings, I had to promise to do everything in my power to find him. I have hesitated to trouble you again, knowing the enormous responsibilities you are carrying——"

"But I have already told you, my dear Budd, that I have tried to find the man without success."

"Yes, but I know how great the confusion of the past few months has been; I know of cases where individuals and groups have assumed authority which they did not legally possess. If you want to do me a favor I shall never forget, have one of your staff make a thorough investigation, not merely in Berlin but throughout the Reich, and enable me to get this utterly harmless young fellow off my conscience."

"All right," said the Minister-Präsident; "if that is your heart's desire, I will try to grant it. But remember, it may be beyond my power. I cannot bring back the dead."

IV

Back in Berlin, Lanny and his wife went for a drive and talked out this new development. "Either he doesn't trust me," said Lanny, "or else I ought to hear from him very soon."

"He must pretend to make an investigation," put in Irma.

"It needn't take long to discover a blunder. He can say: 'I am embarrassed to discover that my supposed-to-be-efficient organization has slipped up. Your friend was in Dachau all along and I have ordered him brought to Berlin.' If he doesn't do that, it's because he's not satisfied with my promises."

"Maybe he knows too much about you, Lanny."

"That is possible; but he hasn't given any hint of it."

"Would he, unless it suited his convenience? Freddi is his only hold on you, and he knows that. Probably he thinks you'd go straight out of Germany and spill the story of Johannes."

"That story is pretty old stuff by now. Johannes is a poor down-and-out, and I doubt if anybody could be got to take much interest in him. The *Brown Book* is published and he isn't in it."

"Listen," said the wife; "this is a question which has been troubling my mind. Can it be that Freddi has been doing something serious, and that Göring knows it, and assumes that you know it?"

"That depends on what you mean by serious. Freddi helped to finance and run a Socialist school; he tried to teach the workers a set of theories which are democratic and liberal. That's a crime to this *Regierung*, and people who are guilty of it are luckier if they are dead."

"I don't mean that, Lanny. I mean some sort of plot or conspiracy, an attempt to overthrow the government."

"You know that Freddi didn't believe in anything of the sort. I've heard him say a thousand times that he believed in government by popular consent, such as we have in America, and such as the Weimar Republic tried to be—or anyhow, was supposed to be."

"But isn't it conceivable that Freddi might have changed after the Reichstag fire, and after seeing what was done to his comrades? It wouldn't have been the Weimar Republic he was trying to overthrow, but Hitler. Isn't it likely that he and many of his friends changed their minds?"

"Many did, no doubt; but hardly Freddi. What good would he have been? He shuts his eyes when he aims a gun!"

"There are plenty of others who would do the shooting. What Freddi had was money—scads of it that he could have got from his father. There were the months of March and April—and how do you know what he was doing, or what his comrades were planning and drawing him into?"

"I think he would have told us about it, Irma. He would have felt in honor bound."

"He might have been in honor bound the other way; he couldn't talk about those comrades. It might even be that he didn't know what was going on, but that others were using him. Some of those fellows I met at the school—they were men who would have fought back, I know. Ludi Schultz, for example—do you imagine he'd lie down and let the Nazi machine roll over him? Wouldn't he have tried to arouse the workers to what they call 'mass action'? And wouldn't his wife have helped him? Then again, suppose there was some Nazi agent among them, trying to lure them into a trap, to catch them in some act of violence so that they could be arrested?"

"The Nazis don't have to have any excuses, Irma; they arrest people wholesale."

"I'm talking about the possibility that there might be some real guilt, or at any rate a charge against Freddi. Some reason why Göring would consider him dangerous and hold onto him."

"The people who are in the concentration camps aren't those against whom they have criminal charges. The latter are in the prisons, and the Nazis torture them to make them betray their associates; then they shoot them in the back of the neck and cremate them. The men who are in Dachau are Socialist politicians and editors and labor leaders—intellectuals of all the groups that stand for freedom and justice and peace."

"You mean they're there without any charge against them?"

"Exactly that. They've had no trial, and they don't know what they're there for or how long they're going to stay. Two or three thousand of the finest persons in Bavaria—and my guess is that Freddi has done no more than any of the others."

Irma didn't say any more, and her husband knew the reason—she couldn't believe what he said. It was too terrible to be true. All over the world people were saying that, and would go on saying it, to Lanny's great exasperation.

V

The days passed, and it was time for the Munich opening, and still nobody had called to admit a blunder on the part of an infallible governmental machine. Lanny brooded over the problem continually. Did the fat General expect him to go ahead delivering the goods on credit, and without ever presenting any bill? Lanny thought: "He can go to hell! And let it be soon!"

In his annoyance, the Socialist in disguise began thinking about those comrades whom he had met at the school receptions. Rahel had given him addresses, and in his spare hours he had dropped in at place after place, always taking the precaution to park his car some distance away and to make sure that he was not followed. In no single case had he been able to find the persons, or to find anyone who would admit knowing their whereabouts. In most cases people wouldn't even admit having heard of them. They had vanished off the face of the Fatherland. Was he to assume that they were all in prisons or concentration camps? Or had some of them "gone underground"? Once more he debated how he might find his way to that nether region—always being able to get back to the Hotel Adlon in time to receive a message from the second in command of the Nazi government!

Irma went to a *thé dansant* at the American Embassy, and Lanny went to look at some paintings in a near-by palace. But he didn't find anything he cared to recommend to his clients, and the prices seemed high; he didn't feel like dancing, and could be sure that his wife had other partners. His thoughts turned to a serious-minded young "commercial artist" who wore large horn-rimmed spectacles and hated his work—the making of drawings of abnormally slender Aryan ladies wearing lingerie, hosiery, and eccentric millinery. Also Lanny thought about the young man's wife, a consecrated soul, and an art student with a genuine talent. Ludwig and Gertrude Schultz —there was nothing striking about these names, but Ludi and Trudi sounded like a vaudeville team or a comic strip.

Lanny had phoned to the advertising concern and been informed that the young man was no longer employed there. He had called the art school and learned that the former student was no longer studying. In neither place did he hear any tone of cordiality or have any information volunteered. He guessed that if the young people had fled abroad they would surely have sent a message to Bienvenu. If they were "sleeping out" in Germany, what would they be doing? Would they go about only at night, or would they be wearing some sort of disguise? He could be fairly sure they would be living among the workers; for they had never had much money, and without jobs would probably be dependent upon worker comrades.

VI

How to get underground! Lanny could park his car, but he couldn't park his accent and manners and fashionable little brown mustache. And above all, his clothes! He had no old ones; and if he bought some in a secondhand place, how would he look going into a de luxe hotel? For him to become a slum-dweller would be almost as hard as for a slum-dweller to become a millionaire playboy.

He drove past the building where the workers' school had been. There was now a big swastika banner hanging from a pole over the door; the Nazis had taken it for a district headquarters. No information to be got there! So Lanny drove on to the neighborhood where the Schultzes had lived. Six-story tenements, the least "slummy" workingclass quarter he had seen in Europe. The people still stayed indoors as much as they could. Frost had come, and the window-boxes with the flowers had been taken inside.

He drove past the house in which he had visited the Schultzes. Nothing to distinguish it from any other house, except the number. He drove round the block and came again, and on a sudden impulse stopped his car and got out and rang the *Pförtner's* bell. He had already made one attempt to get something here, but perhaps he hadn't tried hard enough.

This time he begged permission to come in and talk to the janitor's wife, and it was grudgingly granted. Seated on a wooden stool in a kitchen very clean, but with a strong smell of pork and cabbage, he laid himself out to make friends with a suspicious woman of the people. He explained that he was an American art dealer who had met an artist of talent and had taken some of her work and sold it, and now he owed her money and was troubled because he was unable to find her. He knew that Trudi Schultz had been an active Socialist, and perhaps for that reason did not wish to be known; but he was an entirely non-political person, and neither Trudi nor her friends had anything to fear from him. He applied what psychology he possessed in an effort to win the woman's confidence, but it was in vain. She didn't know where the Schultzes had gone; she didn't know anybody who might know. The apartment was now occupied by a laborer with a family of several children. "*Nein,*" and then again "*Nein, mein Herr.*"

Lanny gave up, and heard the door of the *Pförtnerin* close behind him. Then he saw coming down the stairway of the tenement a girl of eight or ten, in a much patched dress and a black woolen shawl about her head and shoulders. On an impulse he said, quickly: "*Bitte, wo wohnt Frau Trudi Schultz?*"

The child halted and stared. She had large dark eyes and a pale undernourished face; he thought she was Jewish, and perhaps that accounted for her startled look. Or perhaps it was because she had never seen his kind of person in or near her home. "I am an old friend of Frau Schultz," he continued, following up his attack.

"I don't know where she lives," murmured the child.

"Can you think of anybody who would know? I owe her some money and she would be glad to have it." He added, on an inspiration: "I am a comrade."

"I know where she goes," replied the little one. "It is the tailorshop of Aronson, down that way, in the next block."

"*Danke schön*," said Lanny, and put a small coin into the frail hand of the hungry-looking little one.

He left his car where it stood and found the tailorshop, which had a sign in Yiddish as well as German. He walked by on the other side of the street, and again regretted his clothes, so conspicuous in this neighborhood. "Aronson" would probably be a Socialist; but maybe he wasn't, and for Lanny to stroll in and ask for Trudi might set going some train of events which he could not imagine. On the other hand, he couldn't walk up and down in front of the place without being noticed—and those inside the shop no doubt had reasons for keeping watch.

What he did was to walk down to the corner and buy a *Bonbon-Tüte* and come back and sit on a step across the street from the shop but farther on so that he was partly hidden by a railing. Sitting down made him less tall, and holding a bag of candy and nibbling it certainly made him less fashionable. Also it made him interesting to three children of the tenement; when he shared his treasure, which they called *Bom-bom*, they were glad to have him there, and when he asked their names, where they went to school, what games they played, they made shy answers. Meanwhile he kept his eyes on the door of Aronson's tailorshop.

Presently he ventured to ask his three proletarian friends if they knew Trudi Schultz. They had never heard of her, and he wondered if he was on a wild-goose chase. Perhaps it would be more sensible to go away and write a note; not giving his name, just a hint: "The friend who sold your drawings in Paris." He would add: "Take a walk in front of the enormous white marble Karl der Dicke (the Stout), in the Siegesallée at twenty-two o'clock Sunday." With one-third of his mind he debated this program, with another he distributed *Leckereien* to a growing throng, and with the remaining third he watched the door of "*Aronson: Schneiderei, Reparatur.*"

VII

The door opened suddenly, and there stepped forth a young woman carrying a large paper bundle. Lanny's heart gave a jump, and he handed the almost empty *Tüte* to one of his little friends, and started in the same direction as the woman. She was slender, not so tall as Lanny, and dressed in a poor-looking, badly-faded brown coat, with a shawl over her head and shoulders. He couldn't see her hair, and being somewhat behind her he couldn't see her face, but he thought he knew her walk. He followed for a block or so, then crossed over and came up behind her and to her side. Her face was paler and thinner than when he had last seen her; she appeared an older woman; but there was no mistaking the finely chiseled, sensitive features, which had so impressed him as revealing intelligence and character. "*Wie geht's, Trudi?*" he said.

She started violently, then glanced at him; one glance, and she turned her face to the front and walked steadily on. "I am sorry, *mein Herr*. You are making a mistake."

"But Trudi!" he exclaimed. "I am Lanny Budd."

"My name is not Trudi and I do not know you, sir."

If Lanny had had any doubt as to her face, he would have been sure of her voice. It had rather deep tones, and gave an impression of intense feelings which the calm features seemed trying to repress. Of course it was Trudi Schultz. But she didn't want to know him, or be known.

It was the first time Lanny had met a Socialist since he set out to save the Robin family. He had kept away from them on purpose; Rick had warned him what he might be doing to his own reputation, and now here he saw it! He walked by this devoted comrade's side, and spoke quickly—for she might come to her destination and slam a door in his face, or turn away and forbid him to follow her. "Trudi, please hear what I have to say. I came to Germany to try to save the Robins. First I got Johannes out of jail, and I took him and his wife with Rahel and the baby, out to France. Now I have come back to try to find Freddi and get him free."

"You are mistaken, sir," repeated the young woman. "I am not the person you think."

"You must understand that I have had to deal with people in authority here, and I couldn't do it unless I took an attitude acceptable to them. I have no right to speak of that, but I know I can trust you, and you ought to trust me, because I may need your help—I am a long way from succeeding with poor Freddi. I have tried my best to find some of his old friends, but I can't get a contact anywhere. Surely you must realize that I wouldn't be dropping my own affairs and coming here unless I was loyal to him and to his cause. I have to trust somebody, and I put you on your honor not to mention what I am telling you. I have just learned that Freddi is in Dachau——"

She stopped in her tracks and gasped: "In *Dachau!*"

"He has been there for several months."

"How do you know it?"

"I am not free to say. But I am fairly certain."

She started to walk again, but he thought she was unsteady on her feet. "It means so much to me," she said, "because Ludi and Freddi were arrested together."

"I didn't know that Ludi had been arrested. What has happened to him?"

"I have heard nothing from him or concerning him since the Nazis came and dragged them both away from our home."

"What was Freddi doing there?"

"He came because he had been taken ill, and had to have some place to lie down. I knew it was dangerous for him, but I couldn't send him away."

"The Nazis were looking for Ludi?"

"We had gone into hiding and were doing illegal work. I happened to be away from home at the time and a neighbor warned me. The Nazis tore everything in the place to pieces, as if they were maniacs. Why do you suppose they took Freddi to Dachau?"

"It's a long story. Freddi is a special case, on account of being a Jew, and a rich man's son."

It seemed to Lanny that the young woman was weak, perhaps from this shock, perhaps from worry and fear, and not getting enough to eat. He couldn't suggest that they sit on some step, because it would make them conspicuous. He said: "Let me carry that bundle."

"No, no," she replied. "It's all right."

But he knew that it wasn't, and in the land of his forefathers men did not let women carry the loads. He said: "I insist," and thought that he was being polite when he took it out of her arms.

Then right away he saw why she hadn't wanted him to have it. It was wrapped like a bundle of clothing, and was soft like such a bundle, but its weight was beyond that of any clothing ever made. He tried to guess: did the bundle contain arms of some sort, or was it what the comrades called "literature"? The latter was more in accord with Trudi's nature, but Irma had pointed out that one couldn't count upon that. A small quantity of weapons might weigh the same as a larger quantity of printed matter. Both would be equally dangerous in these times; and here was Lanny with an armful of either or both!

VIII

They must keep on walking and keep on talking. He asked: "How far do you have to go?"

"Many blocks."

"I have a car, and I could get it and drive you."

"A car must not stop there, nor can I let you go to the place."

"But we ought to have a talk. Will you let Irma and me meet you somewhere and take you for a drive? That way we can talk safely."

She walked for a space without speaking. Then she said: "Your wife is not sympathetic to our ideas, Genosse Budd."

"She does not agree with us altogether," he admitted; "but she is loyal to me and to the Robins."

"Nobody will be loyal in a time like this except those who believe in the class struggle." They walked again in silence; then the young artist continued: "It is hard for me to say, but it is not only my life that is at stake, but that of others to whom I am pledged. I would be bound to tell them the situation, and I know they would not consent for me to meet your wife, or to let her know about our affairs."

He was a bit shocked to discover what the comrades had been thinking about his marriage; but he couldn't deny Trudi's right to decide this matter. "All right," he said. "I won't mention you, and don't you mention me. There might be a spy among your group, I suppose."

"It's not very likely, because our enemies don't wait long when they get information. They are efficient, and take no chances. It is dangerous for you to be walking with me.'"

"I doubt if it could make serious trouble for an American; but it might cost me my chance to save Freddi if it became known that I was in touch with Socialists."

"It is certainly unwise for us to meet."

"It depends upon what may happen. How can we find each other in case of need?"

"It would not do for you to come where I am. If I need to see you, I'll send you an unsigned note. I read in the papers that you were staying at the Adlon."

"Yes, but I'm leaving tomorrow or the next day for Munich, where I'll be at the Vier Jahreszeiten. Letters will be forwarded, however."

"Tell me, Genosse Lanny," she exclaimed, in a tense voice; "do you suppose there could be any chance for you to find if Ludi is in Dachau?"

"I can't think of any way now; but something might turn up. I must have some way to get word to you."

"Notice this corner ahead of us; remember it, and if you have any news for me, walk by here on Sunday, exactly at noon. I'll be watching for you, and I'll follow you to your car. But don't come unless you have something urgent."

"You mean that you will come to this corner every Sunday?"

"So long as there's any chance of your coming. When you leave Germany, I can write you to Juan-les-Pins."

"All right," he said; and then, as a sudden thought came to him: "Do you need money?"

"I'm getting along all right."

But he knew that propagandists can always use money. He didn't take out his billfold, that being a conspicuous action; he reached under his coat, and worked several bills into a roll, and slipped them into the pocket of that well-worn brown coat. He was becoming expert in the art of distributing illicit funds. What he gave her would be a fortune for Social-Democrats, underground or above. He would leave it for her to explain how she had got it.

When he returned to the hotel, Irma said: "Well! You must have found some paintings that interested you!"

He answered: "A couple of Menzels that I think are worth Zoltan's looking at. But the works by the Maris brothers were rather a disappointment."

IX

The period of the Detaze show in Berlin corresponded with an election campaign throughout the German Reich; assuredly the strangest election campaign since that contrivance had been born of the human brain. Hitler had wiped out all other political parties, and all the legislative bodies of the twenty-two German states; by his methods of murder and imprisonment he had destroyed democracy and representative government, religious toleration and all civil rights; but being still the victim of a "legality complex," he insisted upon having the German people endorse what he had done. A vote to say that votes had no meaning! A Reichstag to declare that a Reichstag was without power! A completely democratic repudiation of democracy! Lanny thought: "Has there ever been such a madman since the world began? Has it ever before happened that a whole nation has gone mad?"

Living in the midst of this enormous institute of lunacy, Lanny Budd tried to keep his balance and not be permanently stood upon his head. If there was anything he couldn't comprehend, his Nazi friends were eager to explain it, but there wasn't a single German from whom he could hear a sane word. Even Hugo Behr and his friends who were planning the "Second Revolution" were all loyal Hitlerites, co-operating in what they considered a sublime demonstration of patriotic fervor. Even the members of smart society dared give no greater sign of rationality than a slight smile, or the flicker of an eyelash so faint that you couldn't be sure if you had seen it. The danger was real, even to important persons. Only a few days later they would see Herzog Philip Albert of Württemberg imprisoned for failing to cast his vote in this sublime national referendum.

Hitler had raised the issue in the middle of October when the British at Geneva had dared to propose a four years' "trial period" before permitting Germany to rearm. The Führer's reply was to withdraw the German delegates from both the League of Nations and the Conference for Arms Limitation. In so doing he issued to the German people one of those eloquent manifestoes which he delighted to compose; he told them how much he loved peace and how eager he was to disarm when the other nations would do the same. He talked to them about "honor"—he, the author of *Mein Kampf*—and they believed him, thus proving that they were exactly what he had said they were. He proclaimed that what the German people wanted was "equal rights"; and, having just deprived them of all rights, he put to them in the name of the government this solemn question:

"Does the German people accept the policy of its National Cabinet as enunciated here and is it willing to declare this to be the expression of its own view and its own will and to give it holy support?"

Such was the "referendum" to be voted on a month later. In addition, there was to be a new Reichstag election, with only one slate of candidates, 686 of them, all selected by the Führer, and headed by the leading Nazis: Hitler, Göring, Goebbels, Hess, Röhm, and so on. One party, one list—and one circle in which you could mark your cross to indicate "yes." There was no place for you to vote "no," and blank ballots were declared invalid.

For that sort of "election" the Fatherland was kept in a turmoil for four weeks, and more money was spent than had ever been spent by all the forty-five parties in any previous Reichstag election. The shows and spectacles, the marching and singing, the carrying of the "blood banners," the ceremonies in honor of the Nazi martyrs; the posters and proclamations, the torchlight processions, the standing at attention and saluting, the radio orations with the people assembled in the public squares to listen to loud-speakers—and a few sent to concentration camps for failing to listen. Hitherto the business of standing silent had been reserved as an honor for the war dead; but now all over Germany the traffic came to a halt and people stood in silence with bared heads; all the factories ceased work and thirty million workers stood to listen to the voice of Adolf Hitler, speaking in the dynamo hall of the enormous Siemens-Schuckert Electrical Works in Berlin. Afterward they stayed and worked an hour overtime, so that they and not their employers might have the honor and glory of making a sacrifice for the Fatherland!

X

On a bright and pleasant Sunday in mid-November, great masses of the German *Volk* lined up in front of polling-places all over the land, and even in foreign lands, and in ships upon the high seas. They voted in prisons and even in concentration camps. Late in the day the Stormtroopers rounded up the lazy and careless ones; and so more than forty-three million ballots were cast, and more than ninety-five per cent voted for the Hitler Reichstag and for the solemn referendum in favor of their own peace and freedom. Irma read about it, the next day and the days thereafter, and was tremendously impressed. She said: "You see, Lanny, the Germans really believe in Hitler. He is what they want." When she read that the internees of Dachau had voted twenty to one for the man who had shut them up there, she said: "That seems to show that things can't be so very bad."

The husband replied: "It seems to me to show that they are a lot worse."

But he knew there was no use trying to explain that. It would only mean an argument. He was learning to keep his unhappiness locked up in his soul. His wife was having a very good time in Berlin, meeting brilliant and distinguished personalities; and Lanny was going about tormenting himself over the activities and the probable fates of a little group of secret conspirators in a Berlin slum!

He could guess pretty well what they were doing; he imagined a small hand-press in the back of the tailor shop, and they were printing leaflets, perhaps about the *Brown Book* and its revelations concerning the Reichstag fire, perhaps quoting opinions of the outside world, so as to keep up the courage of the comrades in a time of dreadful anguish. Probably Trudi was carrying some of this "literature" to others who would see to its distribution. All of them were working in hourly peril of their lives; and Lanny thought: "I ought to be helping them; I am the one who could really accomplish something, because I could get money, and bring them information from outside, and carry messages to their comrades in France and England."

But then he would think: "If I did that, I'd ruin the happiness of my mother and my wife and most of my friends. In the end I'd probably wreck my marriage."

24

Die Juden Sind Schuld

I

A PLEASANT thing to leave the flat windy plain of Prussia at the beginning of winter and motor into the forests and snug valleys of South Germany. Pleasant to arrive in a beautiful and comparatively modern city and to find a warm welcome awaiting you in an establishment called the "Four Seasons of the Year" so as to let you know that it was always ready. Munich was a "Four Seasons of the Year" city; its life was a series of festivals, and the drinking of beer out of *Masskrügen* was a civic duty.

The devoted Zoltan had come in advance and made all arrangements for the show. The Herr Privatdozent Doktor der Philosophie Aloysius Winckler zu Sturmschatten had applied his arts, and the intellectuals of Munich were informed as to the merits of the new school of representational painting; also the social brilliance of the young couple who were conferring this bounty upon them.

In the morning came the reporters by appointment. They had been provided with extracts from what the Berlin press had said about Detaze, and with information as to the Barnes fortune and the importance of Budd Gunmakers; also the fact that Lanny had been on a shooting trip with General Göring and had once had tea with the Führer. The young couple exhibited that affability which is expected from the land of cowboys and movies. Lanny said yes, he knew Munich very well; he had purchased several old masters here— he named them, and told in what new world collections they had found havens. He had happened to be in the city on a certain historic day ten years ago and had witnessed scenes which would make the name of Munich forever famous. Flashlight bulbs went off while he talked, reminding him of those scenes on the Marienplatz when the Nazi martyrs had been shot down.

The interviews appeared in due course, and when the exhibition opened on the following afternoon the crowds came. An old story now, but the people were new, and those who love greatness and glory never tire of meeting Herzog und Herzogin Überall und Prinz und Prinzessin Undsoweiter. A great thing for art when ladies of the highest social position take their stand in a public gallery to pay tribute to genius, even though dead. While Parsifal Dingle went off to ask the spirit of the dead painter if he was pleased with the show, and while Lanny went to inspect older masters and dicker over prices, Beauty Budd and her incomparable daughter-in-law were introduced to important personages, accepted invitations to

lunches and dinners, and collected anecdotes which they would re-
tail to their spouses and later to their relatives and friends.

There was only one thing wrong between this pair; the fact that
Marcel Detaze had died when Irma was a child and had never had
an opportunity to paint a picture of her. Thus Beauty got more
than her proper share of glory, and there was no way to redistribute
it. The mother-in-law would be humble, and try not to talk about
herself and her portraits while Irma was standing by; but others
would insist upon doing so, and it was a dangerous situation. Beauty
said to her son: "Who is the best portrait painter living?"

"Why?" he asked, surprised.

"Because, you ought to have him do Irma right away. It would
be a sensation, and help to keep her interested in art."

"Too bad that Sargent is gone!" chuckled Lanny.

"Don't make a joke of it," insisted the mother. "It's quite inex-
cusable that the crowds should come and look at pictures of a faded
old woman who doesn't matter, instead of one in the prime of her
beauty."

"Art is long and complexions are fleeting," said the incorrigible
one.

II

A far greater event than the Detaze exhibition came to Munich,
causing the city to break out with flags. The Reichskanzler, the
Führer of the N.S.D.A.P., had been motoring and flying all over his
land making campaign speeches. After his overwhelming triumph
he had sought his mountain retreat, to brood and ponder new poli-
cies; and now, refreshed and reinspired, he came to his favorite city,
the one in which his movement had been built and his crown of mar-
tyrdom won. Here he had been a poor *Schlawiner*, as they called a
man whose means of subsistence they did not know, a *Wand- und
Landstreicher*, who made wild, half-crazy speeches, and people went
to hear him because it was a *Gaudi*, or what you would call in English a "lark." Munich had seen him wandering about town looking
very depressed, uncouth in his rusty worn raincoat, carrying an

oversize dogwhip because of his fear of enemies, who, however, paid no attention to him.

But now he had triumphed over them all. Now he was the master of Germany, and Munich celebrated his arrival with banners. Here in the Braune Haus he had the main headquarters of the party; a splendid building which Adolf himself had remodeled and decorated according to his own taste. He, the frustrated architect, had made something so fine that his followers were exalted when they entered the place, and took fresh vows of loyalty to their leader and his all-conquering dream.

Mabel Blackless, alias Beauty Budd, alias Madame Detaze, had done some conquering in her time, and was still capable of dreams. "Oh, Lanny!" she exclaimed. "Do you suppose you could get him to come to the exhibition? It would be worth a million dollars to us!"

"It's certainly worth thinking about," conceded the son.

"Don't delay! Telephone Heinrich Jung and ask him to come. Pay him whatever he wants, and we'll all stand our share."

"He won't want much. He's not a greedy person."

The young Nazi official was staggered by the proposal. He feared it was something far, far beyond his powers. But Lanny urged him to rise to a great occasion. He had worked hard through the electoral campaign and surely was entitled to a few days' vacation. What better way to spend it than to pay his compliments to his Führer, and take him to see some paintings of the special sort which he approved?

"You can bring them to him if he prefers," said Lanny. "We'll close the show for a day and pick out the best and take them wherever he wishes." He spoke with eagerness, having another scheme up his sleeve; he wasn't thinking merely about enhancing the prices of his family property. "If you can get off right away, take a plane. There's no time to be lost."

"*Herrgott!*" exclaimed the ex-forester. He was in heaven.

Then Lanny put in a long distance call to Kurt Meissner in Stubendorf. Kurt had refused an invitation to Berlin because he couldn't afford the luxury and wasn't willing to be put under obligations. But now Lanny could say: "This is a business matter. You will be doing us a service, and also one for the Führer. You can play your new compositions for him, and that will surely be important for your career. Heinrich is coming, and we'll paint the town brown." He supposed that was the proper National Socialist formula!

Irma took the phone and added: "Come on, Kurt. It will be so good for Lanny. I want him to understand your movement and learn to behave himself." Impossible for an apostle and propagandist to resist such a call. Irma added: "Take a plane from Breslau if that's quicker. We'll have a room reserved for you."

III

Somewhat of an adventure for Beauty Budd. Six years had passed since Kurt had departed from Bienvenu and had failed to return. He had found himself a wife, and she a husband, and now they would meet as old friends, glad to see each other, but with carefully measured cordiality; their memories would be like Marcel's paintings hanging on the walls—but not for public showing.

Parsifal Dingle was here, and he had heard much talk about the wonderful German composer who had lived for so long with the Budds. He hadn't been told that Kurt had been Beauty's lover for eight years, but he couldn't very well have failed to guess. He never asked questions, that being contrary to his philosophy. A wise and discreet gentleman with graying hair, he had found himself an exceptionally comfortable nest and fitted himself into it carefully, taking up no more than his proper share of room. He cultivated his own soul, enjoyed the process, and asked nothing more of life. If a German musician who had read Hegel, Fichte, and others of his country's philosophers wished to ask questions about the inner life, Parsifal would be glad to answer; otherwise he would listen to Kurt play the piano in their suite and give his own meanings to the music.

Friendship to Lanny Budd had always been one of life's precious gifts. Now he was happy to be with Kurt and Heinrich again; yet he was torn in half, because he wasn't really with them, he was lying to them. How strange to be using affection as a camouflage; feeling sympathy and oneness, yet not really feeling it, working against it all the time! Lanny's friendship was for Freddi, and Freddi and these two were enemies. With a strange sort of split personality, Lanny loved all three; his friendship for Kurt and Heinrich was still a living thing, and in his feelings he went back to the old days in Stubendorf, twelve years ago, when he had first met the Oberförster's son. To be sure, Heinrich had been a Nazi even then, but Lanny hadn't realized what a Nazi was, nor for that matter had Heinrich realized it. It had been a vision of German progress, a spiritual thing, constructive and not destructive, a gain for the German *Volk* without any loss for Jews or Socialists or democrats or pacifists—all those whom the Nazis now had in their places of torture.

The three talked about old times and were at one. They talked about Kurt's music, and were still at one. But then Heinrich fell to talking about his work, and recent developments in party and national affairs, and at once Lanny had to start lying. It wasn't enough just to keep still, as he had done earlier; no, when the young party official went into ecstasies over that marvelous electoral victory, Lanny had to echo: "*Herrlich!*" When Kurt declared that the Führer's stand for peace and equality among the nations was a great act of statesmanship, Lanny had to say: "*Es hat was heroisches.*" And all the time in his soul he wondered: "Which of us is crazy?"

No easy matter to stick to the conviction that your point of view is right and that all the people about you are wrong. That is the way not merely with pioneers of thought, with heroes, saints, and martyrs, but also with lunatics and "nuts," of whom there are millions in the world. When one of these "nuts" succeeds in persuading the greater part of a great nation that he is right, the five per cent have to stop and ask themselves: "How come?" Particularly is this true of one like Lanny Budd, who was no pioneer, hero, or saint, and surely didn't want to be a martyr. All he wanted was that his friends shouldn't quarrel and make it necessary for him to choose between them. Kurt and Rick had been quarreling since July 1914, and Lanny had been trying to make peace. Never had he seemed less successful than now, while trying to act as a secret agent for Rick, Freddi, and General Göring all at the same time!

They talked over the problem of approaching the Chancellor of Germany, and agreed that Kurt was the one to do it, he being the elder, and the only one with a claim to greatness. Kurt called the Führer's secretary at the Braune Haus, and said that he wished not merely to play the piano for his beloved leader, but to bring the Führer's old friend, Heinrich Jung, and the young American, Lanny Budd, who had visited the Führer in Berlin several years ago. Lanny would bring a sample of the paintings of Marcel Detaze, who was then having a one-man exhibition and had been highly praised in the press. The secretary promised to put the matter before the Chancellor in person, and the Komponist stated where he could be reached. Needless to say, it added to his importance that he was staying at the most fashionable of Munich's hotels, with its fancy name, "The Four Seasons."

IV

Irma invited Kurt into her boudoir for a private chat. She was in a conspiracy with him against her husband—for her husband's own good, of course; and Kurt, who had had professional training in intrigue, was amused by this situation. A sensible young wife, and it might be the saving of Lanny if he could be persuaded to follow her advice. Irma explained that Lanny had been behaving rationally on this trip, and was doing very well with his picture business, which seemed to interest him more than anything else; but he still had Freddi on his conscience, and was convinced that Freddi was innocent of any offense. "I can't get him to talk about it," said Irma, "but I think somebody has told him that Freddi is a prisoner in a concentration camp. It has become a sort of obsession with him."

"He is loyal to his friends," said the Komponist, "and that's a fine quality. He has, of course, no real understanding of what the Jews have done to Germany, the corrupting influence they have been in our national life."

"What I'm afraid of," explained Irma, "is that he might be tempted to bring up the subject to the Führer. Do you think that would be bad?"

"It might be very unfortunate for me. If the Führer thought that I had brought Lanny for that purpose, it might make it impossible for me ever to see him again."

"That's what I feared; and perhaps it would be wise if you talked to Lanny about it and warned him not to do it. Of course don't tell him that I spoke to you on the subject."

"Naturally not. You may always rely on my discretion. It will be easy for me to bring up the subject, because Lanny spoke to me about Freddi in Stubendorf."

So it came about that Lanny had a talk with Kurt without being under the necessity of starting it and having Kurt think that that was why he had been invited to Munich. Lanny assured his old friend that he had no idea of approaching the Führer about the matter; he realized that it would be a grave breach of propriety. But Lanny couldn't help being worried about his Jewish friend, and Kurt ought to be worried too, having played so many duets with him and knowing what a fine and sensitive musician he was. Lanny said: "I have met one of Freddi's old associates, and I know that he is under arrest. I could never respect myself if I didn't try to do something to aid him."

Thus the two resumed their old intimacy; Kurt, one year or so the elder, still acting as mentor, and Lanny, the humble and diffident, taking the role of pupil. Kurt explained the depraved and antisocial nature of *Juda*, and Lanny let himself be convinced. Kurt explained the basic fallacies of Social-Democracy, one of the Jewish perversions of thought, and how it had let itself be used as a front for Bolshevism—even when, as in the case of Freddi, its devotees were ignorant of what base purposes they were serving. Lanny listened attentively, and became more and more acquiescent, and Kurt became correspondingly affectionate in his mood. At the end of the conversation Kurt promised that if they had the good fortune to be received by the Führer, he would study the great man's moods, and if it could be done without giving offense, he would bring up the subject of Lanny's near-relative and ask the Führer to do the favor of ordering his release, upon Lanny's promise to take him out of Germany and see to it that he didn't write or speak against the Fatherland.

"But don't you bring up the subject," warned Kurt. Lanny promised solemnly that he wouldn't dream of committing such a breach of propriety.

V

They waited in the hotel until the message came. The Führer would be pleased to see them at the Braune Haus next morning; and be sure they would be on hand!

It proved to be one of those early winter days when the sun is bright and the air intoxicating, and they would have liked to walk to the appointment; but they were taking the picture, *Sister of Mercy*, so Lanny would drive them. Heinrich, who had learned as a youth to labor with his hands, offered to carry the burden into the Braune Haus, but Beauty insisted that things had to be done with propriety, by a uniformed attendant from the hotel. She herself called up the management to arrange matters, and they fell over themselves to oblige. No charge, Frau Budd, and a separate car if you wish—what hotel in all Germany would not be honored to transport a picture to the Führer? The word spread like wildfire through the establishment, and the three young men were the cynosure of all eyes. The Führer, they learned, had been a familiar figure in this fashionable hotel; for many years he had been entertained here by two of his wealthy supporters, one of them a piano manufacturer and the other a Prussian *Graf* whose wife was conspicuous because of her extreme friendliness with the bellhops. Irma knew all about this, for the reason that she was practicing her German on one of the women employees of the establishment. One would never lack for gossip in a *grand hôtel* of Europe!

The Braune Haus is on the Briennerstrasse, celebrated as one of the most beautiful streets in Germany; a neighborhood reserved for millionaires, princes, and great dignitaries of state and church. In fact, the palace of the Papal Nuncio was directly across the street, and so the representatives of the two rival faiths of Munich could keep watch upon each other from their windows. The princely delegate of the lowly Jewish carpenter looked across to a square-fronted three-story building set far back from the street and protected by high fences; on top of it a large swastika flag waved in the breeze which blew from the snow-clad Alps; in front of its handsome doorway stood day and night two armed Stormtroopers. If the Catholic prelate happened to be on watch that morning he saw a luxurious Mercédès car stop in front of the Nazi building and from it descend a blond and blue-eyed young Nazi official in uniform, a tall Prussian ex-artillery captain with a long and somewhat severe face, and a fashionably attired young American with brown hair and closely trimmed mustache; also a hotel attendant in a gray uniform with brass buttons, carrying a large framed picture wrapped in a cloth.

These four strode up the walk, and all but the burden-bearer gave the Nazi salute. Heinrich's uniform carried authority, and they came into an entrance hall with swastikas, large and small, on the ceiling, the windows, the doorknobs, the lamp-brackets, the grillework. They were a little ahead of time, so Heinrich led them up the imposing stairway and showed them the Senatorensaal, with memorial tablets for the Nazi martyrs outside the doors. Inside were forty standards having bronze eagles, and handsome red leather armchairs for the "senators," whoever they were—they couldn't have met very often, for the Führer gave all the orders. "*Prachtvoll!*" was the comment of Heinrich and Kurt. Lanny had the traitor thought: "This came out of the deal with Thyssen and the other steel kings!"

The offices of Hitler and his staff were on the same floor, and promptly at the appointed hour they were ushered into the simply decorated study of the head Nazi. They gave the salute, and he rose and greeted them cordially. He remembered Lanny and shook hands with him. "*Willkommen, Herr Budd.* How long has it been since we met—more than three years? How time does fly! I don't have a chance to notice it, to say nothing of enjoying it."

Once more Lanny felt that soft moist hand, once more he looked into those gray-blue eyes set in a pale, pasty face, rather pudgy now. for Adi was gaining weight, in spite of or possibly because of his gall-bladder trouble. Looking at him, Lanny thought once more that here was the world's greatest mystery. You might have searched all Europe and not found a more commonplace-appearing man; this Führer of the Fatherland had everything it took to make mediocrity. He was smaller than any of his three guests, and as he was now in a plain business suit with a white collar and black tie, he might have been a grocery assistant or traveling salesman for a hair tonic. He took no exercise, and his figure was soft, his shoulders narrow and hips wide like a woman's. The exponent of Aryan purity was a mongrel if ever there was one; he had straight thick dark hair and wore one lock of it long, as Lanny had done when a boy. Apparently the only thing he tended carefully was that absurd little Charlie Chaplin mustache.

Watching him in his Berlin apartment, Lanny had thought: "It is a dream, and the German people will wake up from it." But now they were more deeply bemused than ever, and Lanny, trying to solve the riddle, decided that here was the *Kleinbürgertum* incarnate, the average German, the little man, the "man in the street." Thwarted and suppressed, millions of such men found their image in Adi Schicklgruber, understood him and believed his promises. The ways in which he differed from them—as in not eating meat and not getting drunk when he could—these made him romantic and inspiring, a great soul.

VI

The hotel attendant was standing in the doorway, with the picture resting on the floor; he steadied it with his left hand while keeping his right arm and hand extended outward and upward in a permanent salute. The Führer noticed him and asked: "What is this you have brought me?"

Lanny told him, and they stood the picture on a chair, with the attendant behind it, out of sight, holding it firmly. Hitler placed himself at a proper distance, and Lanny ceremoniously removed the cover. Then everybody stood motionless and silent while the great man did his looking.

"A beautiful thing!" he exclaimed. "That is my idea of a work of art. A Frenchman, you say? You may be sure that he had German forefathers. Who is the woman?"

"She is my mother," replied Lanny. He had made that statement hundreds of times in his life—Munich being the fifth great city in which he had assisted at an exhibition.

"A beautiful woman. You should be proud of her."

"I am," said Lanny, and added: "It is called *Sister of Mercy*. The painter was badly wounded in the war, and later killed. You can see that he felt what he was painting."

"Ah, yes!" exclaimed Adi. "I too, have been wounded, and know how a soldier feels about the women who nurse him. It would appear that great art comes only by suffering."

"So your Goethe has told us, Herr Reichskanzler."

A silence, while Hitler studied the painting some more. "A pure Aryan type," he commented; "the spiritual type which lends itself to idealization." He looked a while longer, and said: "Pity is one of the Aryan virtues. I doubt if the lesser races are capable of feeling it very deeply."

This went on for quite a while. The Führer looked, and then made a remark, and no one else ventured to speak unless it was a question. "This sort of art tells us that life is full of suffering. It should be the great task of mankind to diminish it as far as possible. You agree with that, Herr Budd?"

"Indeed I do; and I know that it was the leading idea of Marcel's life."

"It is the task of the master race. They alone can fulfill it, because they have both the intelligence and the good will." Lanny was afraid he was going to repeat the question: "You agree with that?" and was trying to figure how to reply without starting an argument. But instead the Führer went on to inform him: "That should be our guiding thought in life. Here in this room we have three of the world's great nationalities represented: the German, the French, the American. What a gain if these nations would unite to guard their Aryan purity and guarantee the reign of law throughout the world! Do you see any hope for that in our time?"

"It is a goal to aim at, Herr Reichskanzler. Each must do what he can."

"You may be sure that I will, Herr Budd. Tell it to everyone you know."

The master of Germany returned to the seat at his desk. "I am obliged to you for bringing me this portrait. I understand that you are having an exhibition?"

"Yes, Herr Reichskanzler; we should be honored if you would attend; or if you prefer, I will bring other samples of the work."

"I wish I could arrange it. Also"—turning to Kurt—"I was hoping to have you come to my apartment, where I have a piano. But I'm afraid I have to leave for Berlin. I was a happier man when I had only a political party to direct; now, alas, I have a government as well, and therefore a lover of music and art is compelled to give all his time and attention to the jealousies and rivalries of small men."

The picture-viewing was over, and the attendant carried it out, backing away and bowing at every step. The Führer turned to Kurt and asked about his music, and lifted a Komponist to the skies by saying that Kurt had rendered a real service to the cause. "We have to show the world that we National Socialists can produce talent and even genius, equal to the best of the past. Science must be brought to reinforce inspiration so that the *Herrenvolk* may ascend to new heights, and, if possible, raise the lesser tribes after them."

He turned to Heinrich. He wanted to hear all that a young official could tell him concerning the Hitler Jugend and its progress. The efficient head of a great organization was getting data about personalities and procedures over which he had control. He asked probing questions, watching the respondent through half-closed eyes. He could be sure that this official was telling him the truth, but it would be colored by the young man's enthusiastic nature. Heinrich was hardly the one to report upon backstairs intrigue and treachery. "I wish I had more young men like you," remarked the Reichskanzler, wistfully.

"You have thousands of them, mein Führer," replied the enraptured ex-forester; "men whom you have never had an opportunity to meet."

"My staff try to shut me up as though I were an oriental despot," said Adi. "They talk to me about physical danger—but I know that it is my destiny to live and complete my work."

VII

It was quite an interview, and Lanny was on pins and needles for fear the great man might rise and say: "I am sorry, but my time is limited." Nobody could imagine anyone in a better humor; and Lanny looked at Kurt, and would have winked at him, only Kurt was keeping his eyes fixed upon his master and guide. Lanny tried telepathy, thinking as hard as he could: "Now! *Now!*"

"Mein Führer," said Kurt, "before we leave there is something which my friend Budd thinks I ought to tell you."

"What is it?"

"A great misfortune, but not his fault. It happens that his half-sister is married into a Jewish family."

"*Donnerwetter!*" exclaimed Adolf. "A shocking piece of news!"

"I should add that the husband is a fine concert violinist."

"We have plenty of Aryan artists, and no need to seek anything from that polluted race. What is the man's name?"

"Hansi Robin."

"Robin? Robin?" repeated Hitler. "Isn't he the son of that notorious *Schieber*, Johannes?"

"Yes, mein Führer."

"She should divorce him." The great man turned upon Lanny. "My young friend, you should not permit such a thing to continue. You should use your authority, you and your father and the other men of the family."

"It happens that the couple are devoted to each other, Herr Reichs-kanzler; also, she is his accompanist, and is now playing with him in a tour of the United States."

"But, Herr Budd, it is sordid and shameful to admit considerations of worldly convenience in such a matter. Your sister is a Nordic blond like yourself?"

"Even more so."

"Yet she gets upon public platforms and advertises her ignominy! And think of what she is doing to the future, the crime she commits against her children!"

"They have no children, Herr Reichskanzler. They are devoting their lives to art."

"It is none the less an act of racial pollution. Whether she has children or not, she is defiling her own body. Are you not aware that the male seminal fluid is absorbed by the female, and thus her bloodstream is poisoned by the vile Jewish emanations? It is a dreadful thing to contemplate, and if it were a sister of mine, I would rather see her dead before my eyes; in fact, I would strike her dead if I knew she intended to commit such an act of treason to her race."

"I am sorry, Herr Reichskanzler; but in America we leave young women to choose their own mates."

"And what is the result? You have a mongrel race, where every vile and debasing influence operates freely, and every form of degradation, physical, intellectual, and moral, flourishes unhindered. Travel that highway into hell, if you please, but be sure that we Germans are going to preserve our purity of blood, and we are not going to let ourselves be seduced by tricky words about freedom and toleration and humanitarianism and brotherly love and the rest. No Jew-monster is a brother of mine, and if I find one of them attempting to cohabit with an Aryan woman I will crush his skull, even as our Stormtrooper song demands: 'Crush the skulls of the Jewish pack!' Pardon me if I speak plainly, but that has been my life's habit, it is the duty which I have been sent to perform in this world. Have you read *Mein Kampf?*"

"Yes, Herr Reichskanzler."

"You know what I have taught in it: 'The Jew is the great instigator of the destruction of Germany.' They are, as I have called them, 'true devils, with the brain of a monster and not that of a man.' They are the veritable *Untermenschen*. There is a textbook of Hermann Gauch, called *Neue Grundlage der Rassenforschung*, which is now standard in our schools and universities, and which tells with scientific authority the truths about this odious race. Our eminent scientist classifies the mammals into two groups, first the Aryans, and second, non-Aryans, including the rest of the animal kingdom. You have seen that book, by chance?"

"I have heard it discussed, Herr Reichskanzler."

"You do not accept its authority?"

"I am not a scientist, and my acceptance or rejection would carry no weight. I have heard the point raised that Jews must be human beings because they can mate with Aryans and Nordics, but not with non-human animals."

"Dr. Gauch says it has by no means been proved that Jews cannot mate with apes and other simian creatures. I suggest this as an important contribution which German science can make—to mate both male and female Jews with apes, and so demonstrate to the world the facts which we National Socialists have been proclaiming for so many years."

VIII

The master of all Germany had got started on one of his two favorite topics, the other being Bolshevism. Again Lanny observed the phenomenon that an audience of three was as good as three million. The sleepy look went out of the speaker's eyes and they became fixed upon the unfortunate transgressor in a hypnotic stare. The quiet voice rose to a shrill falsetto. Something new appeared in the man, demonic and truly terrifying; the thrust-out finger struck as it were hammer blows upon Lanny's mind. A young American playboy must be made to realize the monstrous nature of the treason he was committing in condoning his sister's defilement of the sacred Aryan blood. Somehow, at once, the evil must be averted; the man who had been commissioned by destiny to save the world must prove his power here and now, by bringing this strayed sheep back into the Nordic fold. "*Gift!*" cried the Führer of the Nazis. "Poison! *Poison!*"

Back in New England, Lanny's Great-Great-Uncle Eli Budd had told him the story of the witch-hunt in early Massachusetts. "Fanaticism is a destroyer of mind," he had said. Here it was in another form—the terrors, the fantasies born of soul torment, the vision of

supernatural evil powers plotting the downfall of all that was good
and fair in human life. Adi really loved the Germans: their *Gemütlichkeit*, their *Treue und Ehre*, their beautiful songs and noble sym-
phonies, their science and art, their culture in its thousand forms.
But here was this satanic power, plotting, scheming day and night
to destroy it all. *Die Juden sind schuld!*

Yes, literally, the Jews were to blame for everything; Hitler
called the roll of their crimes for the ten thousandth time. They
had taught revolt to Germany, they had undermined her patriotism
and discipline, and in her hour of greatest peril they had stabbed
her in the back. The Jews had helped to shackle her by the cruel
Diktat of Versailles, and then had proceeded to rivet the chains of
poverty upon her limbs. They had made the inflation, they had
contrived the Dawes Plan, the Young Plan, the systems of interest
and reparations slavery; the Jewish bankers in alliance with the
Jewish Bolsheviks! They had seduced all German culture—theater,
literature, music, journalism. They had sneaked into the professions,
the sciences, the schools, and universities—and, as always, they had
defiled and degraded whatever they touched. *Die Juden sind unser
Unglück!*

This went on for at least half an hour; and never once did anybody else get in a word. The man's tirade poured out so fast that
his sentences stumbled over one another; he forgot to finish them,
he forgot his grammar, he forgot common decency and used the
words of the gutters of Vienna, where he had picked up his ideas.
The perspiration stood out on his forehead and his clean white collar began to wilt. In short, he gave the same performance which
Lanny had witnessed in the Bürgerbräukeller of Munich more
than a decade ago. But that had been a huge beerhall with two or
three thousand people, while here it was like being shut up in a
small chamber with a hundred-piece orchestra including eight trom-
bones and four bass tubas playing the overture to *The Flying
Dutchman*.

Suddenly the orator stopped. He didn't say: "Have I convinced
you?" That would have been expressing a doubt, which no heaven-
sent evangelist ever admits. He said: "Now, Herr Budd, go and

do your duty. Make one simple rule that I have maintained ever since I founded this movement—never to speak to a Jew, even over the telephone." Then, abruptly: "I have other engagements and have to be excused."

The three quickly said their adieus; and when they were outside, Lanny, in his role of secret agent, remarked: "No one can wonder that he stirs his audiences."

When he was back in the hotel with his wife and mother, he exclaimed: "Well, I know now why Göring is keeping Freddi."

"Why?" they asked, with much excitement.

Lanny answered, in a cold fury: "He is going to breed him with a female ape!"

IX

Lanny had to play out the game according to the rules. He must not let either of these friends discover that he had brought them here solely in the hope of persuading Hitler to release a Jewish prisoner. It was for friendship, for sociability, for music and art. Lanny and Kurt must play piano duets as in the old days. Zoltan must take them through the two Pinakotheks and give them the benefit of his art knowledge. Beauty and Irma must put on their best togs and accompany them to the Hof-und-National Theater for *Die Meistersinger*, and to the Prinz-Regenten Theater for Goethe's *Egmont*. There must be a dinner at which distinguished personalities in the musical world were invited to meet a leading Komponist. After a symphony concert in the Tonhalle, Lanny listened to Kurt's highly technical comments on the conductor and the sounds produced. The tone was hard, cold, and brilliant; it lacked "body," by which Kurt explained that he meant a just proportion of low and middle to high registers. He accused the too-ardent Kapellmeister of exaggerating his nuances, of expanding and contracting his volume unduly, fussing over his orchestra like an old hen with a too-large brood of chicks—certainly an undignified procedure, and by no means suitable to the rendition of Beethoven's *Eroica*.

But to Lanny it seemed more important to try to understand what the composer of that noble symphony was trying to tell him than to worry about details of somebody's rendition. The last time Lanny had heard this work had been with the Robin family in Berlin, and he recalled Freddi's gentle raptures. Freddi wasn't one of those musicians who have heard so much music that they have got tired of it, and can think about nothing but technicalities and personalities and other extraneous matters. Freddi loved Beethoven as if he had been the composer's son; but now father and son had been torn apart. Freddi wasn't fit to play Beethoven, by Heinrich's decree, because he was a Jew; and certainly he wasn't having any chance to hear Beethoven in Dachau. Lanny could think of little else, and the symphony became an appeal to the great master for a verdict against those who were usurping his influence and his name.

In Beethoven's works there is generally a forceful theme that tramples and thunders, and a gentle theme that lilts and pleads. You may take it as pleading for mercy and love against the cruelties and oppressions of the world. You may take it that the grim, dominating theme represents these cruelties, or perhaps it represents that which rises in your own soul to oppose them. Anyhow, to Lanny the opening melody of the *Eroica* became the "Freddi theme," and Beethoven was defending it against the hateful Nazis. The great democrat of old Vienna came into the Tonhalle of Munich and laid his hand on Lanny's burning forehead, and told him that he was right, and that he and his Jewish friend were free to march with Beethoven on the battlefields of the soul and to dance with him on the happy meadows.

Was it conceivable that Beethoven would have failed to despise the Nazis, and to defy them? He had dedicated his symphony to Napoleon because he believed that Napoleon represented the liberating forces of the French revolution, and he had torn up the title page of his score when he learned that Napoleon had got himself crowned Emperor of France. He had adopted Schiller's *Hymn to Joy*, sending a kiss to the whole world and proclaiming that all men became brothers where the gentle wing of joy came to rest. Very certainly he had not meant to exclude the Jews from the human race, and would have spurned those who built their movement out of hate.

That was what this urgent music was about; that was what gave it drive and intensity. The soul of Beethoven was defending itself, it was defending all things German from those who would defile them. The "Freddi theme" pleaded, it stormed and raged, heaving itself in mighty efforts as the kettledrums thundered. The young idealist had told his friends that he wasn't sure if he had within him the moral strength to withstand his foes; but here in this symphony he was finding it; here he would prevail, and rejoice— but then would come the rushing hordes and bowl him over and trample him. When the first movement came to its tremendous climax Lanny's hands were tightly clenched and perspiration stood on his forehead.

The poignant, majestic march was Beethoven walking through the Nazi concentration camps—as Lanny had walked so many times in imagination. It was the grief and suffering of fifty or a hundred thousand of the finest and best-trained minds of Germany. It was Beethoven mourning with them, telling them that the blackest tragedy can be turned to beauty by the infinite powers of the soul. The *finale* of the symphony was a victory—but that was a long way off, and Lanny couldn't imagine how it would come; he could only cling to the hand of the great master like a little child to its father.

After hearing this concert Lanny had to face the fact that his love for Kurt and Heinrich had come to an end. He found it hard to be polite to his old friends; and he decided that being a spy, or secret agent, or whatever you chose to call it, was first and foremost a damnable bore. The greatest of all privileges in this life is saying what you think; and your friends have to be people who can at least give decent consideration to your ideas. Lanny was glad when he got Kurt and Heinrich on their separate trains for home. He thanked them for what they had done, assured them that it had been worth while, and thought: "I am going to get Freddi out of this hell, and then get myself out and stay out."

X

For a week Lanny had been living in close proximity to that mass of human misery known as Dachau; he had pretended to be indifferent to it, and had spoken of it only when he and Irma were alone in their car. Dachau is a small market-town nine miles north-west of the city, and a well-paved highway leads to it. Inevitably their thoughts had turned there, and the car had taken them at the first opportunity. They didn't, like most tourists, inspect the castle on the height; they looked for the concentration camp, which wasn't hard to find, as it occupied a square mile of ground. It had been a World War barracks and training camp, disused since the peace. A concrete wall seven feet high ran around it, having on top a tangle of barbed wire, no doubt electrically charged. Lanny thought about somebody trying to climb that wall; it seemed less possible when he came at night, and saw a blaze of white search-lights mounted in towers, moving continually along the walls.

The report, published in the newspapers, that the Führer had seen the *Sister of Mercy*, filled thousands of Bavarians with a desire to see it, and accordingly it was decided to continue the exhibition another week. But Lanny was tired of telling people about it, and tired of what they said; in fact, he was tired of what everybody said in Nazi Germany. If they said it because they wanted to, he hated them; if they said it because they had to, he was sorry for them; but in neither case could he be interested.

Deciding to take the bull by the horns, he picked out a sunshiny morning when the inmates of Dachau might be outdoors—those who were allowed out. He put in his pocket a newspaper clipping about the Führer having viewed and approved the Detaze painting; also a few of the interviews with himself and Irma, containing his portrait, and mention of his having been a guest of Göring. These ought to be equivalent to a ticket of admission to any place in Nazi-land. Leaving Irma to do some shopping, he drove out the Dachau road, and instead of parking his car like a humble nobody, drove to the main gates and announced his desire to see the Kommandant.

They looked at his car, they looked at his clothes and his Aryan face, and at the engraved card which he gave them. "Mr. Lanning Prescott Budd" might be somebody so important that he didn't bother to put his titles and honors on his card, as was the German custom. They let him through the steel gates, and two Stormtroopers stood guard while a third took his card to the office. In front of him was a drill ground, and at one side a clatter of hammers; they were putting up new buildings, doubtless with the labor of prisoners. Stormtroopers were everywhere, all with their rubber truncheons and automatics; there were now half a million of these fighting men for whom jobs had to be provided.

XI

The Kommandant consented to see Herr Budd, and he was escorted to the private office of a tough young Süddeutscher with a scarred face and a round head with black hair close cropped. Having met Göring, Lanny thought he had no more to learn about toughness. He sat down and came straight to the point:

"Herr Kommandant, I am an American sympathizer who happens to be in Munich because I am interested in an art exhibition. You may have read about it, and possibly about me. I had the honor of spending a morning with the Führer at the Braune Haus a few days ago. I am a friend of Minister-Präsident General Göring, and had the pleasure of accompanying him on a shooting trip last month. I live in France and visit frequently in England and America, where I hear a great deal of propaganda against your *Regierung*—you no doubt know of the charges of cruelty and torturing which are being widely published. I thought it might be a good thing if I could say: 'I have visited one of the large concentration camps and seen conditions with my own eyes.' I appreciate that this is a request you would hardly grant to a stranger; but it happens that I have some clippings from Munich newspapers which will show you who I am—and incidentally they contain pictures of myself, so that you can see I'm not anybody else."

The smiling visitor handed over the clippings; the tough Nazi studied them, and his toughness evaporated like early morning frost in sunshine. This elegant rich foreigner had actually enjoyed the highest privilege which any good Stormtrooper could imagine—of walking into the Führer's private study and discussing art with him! "Certainly, Herr Budd; we are always pleased to show our camp to properly accredited persons. We have taken several foreign journalists through in the past month or two." The Kommandant arose, prepared to do the honors himself—perhaps he could find the secret of how to make friends with the Führer!

So Lanny strolled about and saw what was inside those concrete walls with heavily electrified barbed wire. The officer explained the routine of the camp, and led his visitor over to the corner where the barracks were situated, fenced off from the rest of the grounds with barbed-wire entanglements. They were dismal, unpainted, and half-rotted buildings which had been erected of flimsy materials in wartime and had been neglected ever since. There were numerous cracks in the board walls and some of the windows had missing glass. There were thirteen one-story buildings, each with five connecting rooms, and in each room were fifty or more berths, arranged in three tiers like shelves. The floors were of concrete, and the mattresses were straw sacks. There was one washstand in each room.

Many of the inmates were outside the camp, working on the roads under heavy guard. Others were in the workshops, or building the new barracks, or in the offices. The old and the sick were getting the advantage of the sunshine, the only gift of nature which was still free to them. They sat leaning against the sides of the buildings, or strolling slowly. Apparently they were forbidden to converse; at any rate they weren't doing it. They looked dully at Lanny, and he was ashamed to meet their eyes. Fortunately he had no acquaintances among the Reds and Pinks of Bavaria, so he gave no soul-wounds.

A drab and distressing spectacle the prisoners presented. They had close-cropped heads. They wore the clothes in which they had been arrested; but that had been months ago, in many cases nearly a year, and doubtless they were sleeping in their clothes on these near-winter nights. The intellectuals of Bavaria had evidently not been fond of outdoor sports; some were lean and stoop-shouldered, others were paunched and flabby. Many had white hair, and might have been the grandfathers of their guards, but that earned them no consideration. Ill health and depression were written all over them. They did not know what they were here for, or how long they would have to stay—they who had been free men, free thinkers, the best of the land's intellectuals. They had dreamed of a happier and more ordered world, and this was the punishment which fitted their crime. "We are not running a health resort," remarked the Kommandant.

Lanny kept walking, as long as there was anything to be seen: sixty-five bunk-rooms, several mess-halls, a dozen workshops, and various outdoor constructions. Everywhere he scanned the faces, looking for that of his brother-in-law's brother or that of Trudi Schultz's husband. He saw neither; and after he had covered all the ground he could find out about, he ventured the question: "Don't you have any Jews?"

"Oh, yes," replied the host, "about forty; but we keep them apart, out of consideration for the others."

"They work, I suppose?"

"They work good and hard, you may be sure."

"Could I see them?"

"That, I am sorry to say, is contrary to the regulations."

The man volunteered no more; and Lanny, having asked as many questions as he dared, let himself be led back to his car. "I thank you, Herr Kommandant," he said. "I will be able to tell newspaper reporters that I didn't see any bruised or bloody inmates, or any wire whips or rubber hose for beatings."

"You might have looked still farther and not seen any," replied the tough Nazi. The remark was open to more than one interpretation, and Lanny thought: "Maybe he is like me, and prefers not to lie if he can help it!"

XII

The amateur investigator drove back to the city, wondering how Freddi was standing it. Freddi himself had wondered, did he have the needed courage, could he find in himself the spiritual resources?

Lanny, being of an imaginative temperament, asked the same questions of himself; he lived in those dingy and squalid sheds and felt on his back the lash of those whips which he had not seen.

Then his busy mind began inventing a little story. He went to see the tough Nazi Kommandant, and invited him to see the show, and after that to take a ride. When they were well out in the country Lanny addressed him as follows:

"Herr Kommandant, one of the Jews whom you are providing with plenty of hard work happens to be a sort of relative of mine. He is a harmless young fellow, and if I should take him to my home in France he would be content to play the clarinet for the rest of his life and never do any harm to your glorious movement. It happens that I have just sold some paintings and have cash in a Munich bank. Suppose I were to pay you, say twenty-five thousand marks, in any form and by any method you direct, and you in turn would find some way to let me pick up that prisoner in my car and whisk him up into the mountains and across the Austrian border—would that appeal to you as a good night's work?"

Lanny's fancy created several dénouements for that story. He knew that the Nazi machine was pretty well riddled with graft; Johannes Robin had told many tales of pure Aryan business men who were getting what they wanted by such methods, old as the first despotism. On the other hand, this particular toughie might be a sincere fanatic—it was impossible to tell them apart. Lanny was sure that if Hugo Behr had been in charge of the camp, he would have taken the money; on the other hand, Heinrich Jung would probably have reported him to the grim Gestapo.

And what would happen then? They couldn't very well do worse than escort him to the frontier, as Generalissimo Balbo's men had done in Rome nearly ten years ago. But here was the thing to give Lanny pause: if the Kommandant was a really virtuous Nazi, he might go back to his camp and make it impossible for Lanny to corrupt any weakling among his men, by the simple method of taking Freddi Robin and beating him to death and cremating the body.

"I must think of something better," said the grown-up playboy.

BOOK SIX

Blood Hath Been Shed

25

Grasping at Air

I

CHRISTMAS was coming; and Irma had been away from her darling for more than three months. It was unthinkable to stay longer. What was Lanny accomplishing? What was he hoping to accomplish? Göring was just playing with him. He was trying to get something out of them, and for nothing. He was keeping them quiet, sealing their lips. Not that Irma minded so very much having her husband's lips sealed. If only he wouldn't worry, and fill his mind with horrors so that he started in his sleep!

The Detaze show was over, and a happy development had come. One of the great museums in Dresden had asked to have the paintings for a while; they would treat them in a distinguished way, putting them in a separate room. The art lovers of that *Luxusstadt* would come and admire them, inquiries would be made, and it would be a good thing both from the point of view of art and of money. Zoltan would be coming and going, and inquiring purchasers could be referred to him. Much better than having the pictures stuck away in a storeroom on a private estate!

Beauty and Parsifal were going to London, on account of the strangest development you could imagine. Lady Caillard had sent a dear friend of hers all the way to Munich to persuade the American couple to come again as her guests, on account of a presentiment which had seized her; she was going very soon to rejoin her beloved "Vinnie" in the spirit world, and she wanted Beauty's dear man of love to be in her home at that time to close her eyes and take charge of her funeral which was to be like none other in modern times, a thing of joy and not of mourning. The guests were to wear white, and there would be happy music and feasting, all under the sign of "V.B.X"—Vinnie, Birdie, and a Kiss. "Perhaps she will send us some word about Freddi," said Beauty; and then—a horrid thought: "Perhaps she will leave us some of her money."

The museum in Dresden was attending to the pictures, so Jerry Pendleton was free. Irma and Lanny took him with them through a pass in those snow-covered mountains which make for Munich a setting like a drop curtain. They crossed the narrow belt which the Versailles *Diktat* had left to Austria, and through the Brenner pass which had been included in Italy's share of the loot. There Mussolini's Blackshirts were busily engaged in making Aryans into Mediterraneans by the agency of rubber truncheons and dogwhips. It made bad blood between *Fascismo* and its newborn offspring in the north. Dr. Goebbels's well-subsidized agitators were working everywhere in Austria, and not a few of them were in Italian dungeons. Optimistic young Pinks looked forward to seeing the Fascists and the Nazis devour each other like the two Kilkenny cats.

Home sweet home seemed ever so humble when you had been dwelling and visiting in palaces; but roses were in bloom beside its gates, and down the drive came racing a treasure without price, a tiny creature in a little blue dress, with dark brown hair streaming and dark brown eyes shining—she had been told two days ago that mother and father were on the way, and had been prattling about them and asking questions ever since. She was more than halfway through her fourth year, and it is astounding how fast they grow; you come back after three or four months and a new being confronts you; you cannot restrain your cries of delight, and a watchful expert has to check your ardors, lest you promote the evil quality of self-consciousness. Irma Barnes, who had been brought up in a play-world herself, had a hard time realizing that a child is more than a plaything for two delighted parents. Irma Barnes, who had always had her own way, had to learn to submit to discipline in the name of that very dogmatic new science of "child study."

Yes, indeed; for even a twenty-three-million-dollar baby has to learn to use her hands, and how shall she learn if someone does everything for her and never lets her make any effort? How will

she learn discipline if she always has her own way, and if she gets
the idea that she is the center of attention, more important than any
of those with whom she has to deal? The severe Miss Severne persisted in the notion that her professional authority must be respected;
and likewise the conscientious Miss Addington, no longer needed
as Marceline's governess, but staying on as half-pensioner, half-friend
of the family until she would take charge of Frances. Those two
Church-of-England ladies had been conspiring together, and enlisted
Lanny's help against a doting mother, two rival grandmothers, and
a Provençal cook and major domo—to say nothing of Santa Claus.

I I

A merry Christmas, yet not too much so, for over the household
hangs the shadow of sorrow; nobody can forget those two bereaved
Jewish women and the grief that is in their hearts. Rahel and Mama
try their best to restrain themselves, and not to inflict their suffering upon their friends; but everybody knows what they are thinking about. Really, it would be less sad if Freddi were dead and
buried, for then at least they would be sure he wasn't suffering. But
this way the worst is possible, and it haunts them; they stay by
themselves in the Lodge, their lost one always in the back of their
minds and most of the time in the front. They are touchingly grateful for everything that has been done for them, but there is one
thing more they have to ask; their looks ask it even when their lips
are silent. Oh, Lanny, oh, Irma, *can't* you think of *something* to do
for poor Freddi?

Hansi and Bess are in the Middle West, giving concerts several
times every week. They have cabled money after the first concert,
so Mama and Rahel no longer have to use Irma's money to buy
their food. They have offered to rent a little place for themselves,
but Beauty has said No, why should they—it would be very unkind.
Irma says the same; but in her heart she cannot stifle the thought
that she would like it better if they did. She feels a thunder-cloud
hanging over the place, and wants so much to get Lanny from under
it. She is worried about what is going on in his mind, and doesn't

see why she should give up all social life because of a tragedy they are powerless to avert. Irma wants to give parties, real parties, of the sort which make a social impression; she will put up the money and Beauty and Feathers will do the work—both of them happy to do so, because they believe in parties, because parties are what set you apart from the common herd which cannot give them, at least not with elegance and *chic*.

Then, too, there is the question of two little tots. They are together nearly all the time, and this cannot be prevented; they clamor for it, take it for granted, and the science of child study is on their side. Impossible to bring up any child properly alone, because the child is a gregarious creature; so the textbooks agree. If little Johannes were not available it would be necessary to go out and get some fisherboy, Provençal, or Ligurian or what not. There isn't the slightest fault that Irma can find with the tiny Robin; he is a dream of brunette loveliness, he is gentle and sweet like his father, but he is a Jew, and Irma cannot be reconciled to the idea that her darling Frances should be more interested in him than in any other human being, not excepting herself. Of course, they are such tiny things, it seems absurd to worry; but the books and the experts agree that this is the age when indelible impressions are made, and is it wise to let an Aryan girl-child get fixed in her mind that the Semitic type is the most romantic, the most fascinating in the world? Irma imagines some blind and tragic compulsion developing out of that, later on in life.

Also, it means that the spirit of Freddi Robin possesses the whole of Bienvenu. The frail little fellow looks like his father, acts like him, and keeps him in everybody's thoughts; even the visitors, the guests. Everybody has heard rumors that Johannes Robin has been deprived of his fortune by the Nazis, and that his grandchild is here, a refugee and pensioner; everybody is interested in him, asks questions, and starts talking about the father—where is he, and what do you think, and what are you doing about it? The fate of Freddi Robin overshadows even the Barnes fortune, even the twenty-three-million-dollar baby! Bienvenu becomes as it were a haunted house, a somber and serious place where people fall to talking about politics, and where the frivolous ones do not feel at home. Irma Barnes certainly never meant to choose that kind of atmosphere!

I I I

There wasn't anything definite the matter with Lady Caillard, so far as any doctor could find out; but she had got her mind thoroughly made up that she was going to join her "Vinnie" in the spirit world, and sure enough, in the month of January she "passed on." The funeral was held, and then her will was read. She had left to her friend Mrs. Parsifal Dingle her large clock with the gold and ivory bird that sang; a pleasant memento of "Birdie," and one about which there would be no controversy. The medium to whom the Vickers stock had been promised got nothing but a headache out of it, for the directors of the huge concern were determined to protect Sir Vincent's son and daughter, and they worked some sort of hocus-pocus with the stock; they "called" it, and since the estate didn't have the cash to put up, the company took possession of the stock and ultimately the legitimate heirs got it. There was a lot of fuss about it in the papers, and Lanny was glad his mother and his stepfather were not mixed up in it.

With the proceeds of their dramatic success Nina and Rick had got a small car. Rick couldn't drive, on account of his knee, but his wife drove, and now they brought the Dingles to the Riviera, and stayed for a while as guests in the villa. Rick used Kurt's old studio to work on an anti-Nazi play, based on the *Brown Book*, the stories Lanny had told him, and the literature Kurt and Heinrich had been sending him through the years. It would be called a melodrama, Rick said—because the average Englishman refused to believe that there could be such people as the Nazis, or that such things could be happening in Europe in the beginning of the year 1934. Rick said furthermore that when the play was produced, Lanny would no longer be able to pose as a fellow-traveler of the Hitlerites, for they would certainly find out where the play had been written.

Lanny was glad to have this old friend near, the one person to whom he could talk out his heart. Brooding over the problem of Freddi Robin day and night, Lanny had about made up his mind to go to Berlin, ask for another interview with General Göring, and put his cards on the table, saying: "Exzellenz, I have learned that my brother-in-law's brother is a prisoner in Dachau, and I would like very much to take him out of Germany. I have about two hundred thousand marks in a Berlin bank which I got from sales of my stepfather's paintings, and I have an equal amount in a New York bank which I earned as commissions on old masters purchased in your country. I would be glad to turn these sums over to you to use in your propaganda, in return for the freedom of my friend."

Rick said: "But you can't do such a thing, Lanny! It would be monstrous."

"You mean he wouldn't take the money?"

"I haven't any doubt that he'd take it. But you'd be aiding the Nazi cause."

"I don't think he'd use the money for that. I'm just saying so to make it sound respectable. He'd salt the New York funds away, and spend the German part on his latest girl friend."

"You say that to make it sound respectable to yourself," countered Rick. "You don't know what he'd spend the money for, and you can't get away from the fact that you'd be strengthening the Nazi propaganda. It's just as preposterous as your idea of giving Göring information about British and French public men."

"I wouldn't give him any real information, Rick. I would only tell him things that are known to our sort."

"Göring is no fool and you can't make him one. Either you'd give him something he wants, or you wouldn't get what you want. He has made that perfectly plain to you, and that's why Freddi is still in Dachau—if he is."

"You think I have to leave him there?"

"You do, unless you can work out some kind of jailbreak."

"I'd have to pay somebody, Rick—even if it was only a jailer."

"There'd be no great harm in paying a jailer, because the amount would be small, and you'd be undermining the Nazi discipline. Every prisoner who escapes helps to do that."

"You think I did wrong to help Johannes out?"

"I don't think that made much difference, because Johannes would have given up anyhow; he's that sort of man. He thinks about himself and not about a cause."

"You wouldn't have done it in his place?"

"It's hard to say, because I've never been tortured and I can't be sure how I'd stand it. But what I should have done is plain enough—hang myself in my cell, or open my veins, rather than let Göring get hold of any foreign exchange to use in keeping his spies and thugs at work."

IV

Rick talked along the same line to Mama and Rahel; he was the only one who had the courage to do it. He spoke gently, and with pity for their tears, but he told them that the only way he knew of helping Freddi was by writing an anti-Nazi play. He bade them ask themselves what Freddi would want them to do. There could be no doubt about the answer, for Freddi was a devoted Socialist, and would rather die than give help to the enemies of his cause. Rahel could see that, and said so. Mama could see it, also—but couldn't bring herself to say it.

"Consider this," persisted Rick. "Suppose that what Göring wanted of Freddi was to betray some of his comrades. It's quite possible that that may be happening; and would he pay that price for his freedom?"

"Of course he wouldn't," admitted the young wife.

"Well, money's the same thing. The Nazis want foreign exchange so they can buy weapons and the means to make weapons. They want it so they can pay their agents and carry on their propaganda in foreign lands. And in the end it adds up to more power for Nazism, and more suffering for Jews and Socialists. These Hitlerites aren't through; they never can be through so long as they live, because theirs is a predatory system; it thrives on violence, and would perish otherwise. It has to have more and more victims, and if it gets money from you it uses the money to get more money from the next lot. So whatever resources we have or can get, have to go to fighting them, to making other people understand what Nazism is, what a menace it represents to everything that you and I and Freddi stand for."

Rick spoke with eloquence, more than he usually permitted himself. The reason was that it was a scene from his play. He was writing about people confronted with just such a cruel decision. He didn't say: "Let's all put our money and our labors into getting an anti-Nazi play produced, and use the proceeds to start a paper to oppose the Nazis." But that was what he had in mind, and Rahel knew that if her husband could speak to her, he would say: "Rick is right."

But poor Mama! She was no Socialist, and couldn't make real to herself the task of saving all the Jews in Germany. She kept silence, for she saw that Rick had convinced Rahel and Lanny; but what gave her hope was a letter from Johannes, about to sail for Rio de Janeiro to try to work up business for Budd Gunmakers. "I'm going to get some money again, and then I'll find a way to get Freddi out." That was the sort of talk for a sensible Jewish mother!

V

The Riviera was full of refugees from Germany; all France was the same. Many of these unfortunates tried to get hold of Lanny Budd, but he was afraid even to answer their letters. He was still clinging to the idea that Göring might release Freddi; if not, Lanny was going back to make some sort of effort. Therefore he had to be circumspect. Trying to play the spy makes one spy-conscious. How could he be sure that any refugee who appealed to him for aid might not have come from Göring, to find out how he was behaving, and whether he was a person to be dealt with?

All this suited Irma completely. She didn't care what was the reason, so long as her husband kept away from Reds and troublemakers. She and Beauty and Emily and Sophie consulted and conspired to keep him busy and contented; to provide him with music and dancing and sports, with interesting people to talk to, with

Jerry Pendleton and the faithful Bub Smith to go fishing. Best of all for the purpose was little Frances; Irma got a book on child psychology and actually read every word of it, so as to be able to make intelligent remarks, and keep Lanny interested in what his home had to offer. She made love to him assiduously; and of course he knew what she was doing, and was touched by it. But he took Dachau with him everywhere; at one of Emily's *soirées musicales* a strain of sad music brought tears to his eyes, and then a pro-Nazi remark by one of the ladies of the *haut monde* made the blood rush to his head and ruined his appetite for the delicate viands.

Early in February Robbie Budd arrived in Paris on a business trip. Irma thought that change of scene would help, and she knew that the father would back her point of view; so they put their bags into the car and arrived at the Crillon the evening before Robbie was due. Always a pleasant thing to see that man of affairs, sound and solid, if a little too rotund and rosy. He was taking his loss of the presidency of the company as just one of those things; what can't be cured must be endured, and Robbie was getting along with the new head. A self-made man, well informed on financial conditions, he had won everyone's respect; he didn't try to tell Robbie how to sell goods in Europe, and had taken Robbie's word as to the capabilities of Johannes Robin. Things were going on much as in the old days.

Robbie wanted to hear every detail of what had happened in Germany. It was important for him to understand the Nazis, for they were trying to get credit from Budd's and from the banking group which now had Budd's under its wing. Morals had nothing to do with it—except as they bore on the question whether the Third Reich would meet its notes on time.

Robbie and the two young people discussed the problem of Freddi from every point of view, and Robbie gave his approval of what had been done. He said no more in his son's presence, but when he was alone with Irma he confirmed her idea that the Reds and Pinks of Germany had brought their troubles upon themselves. Nor was he worried about Hitler; he said that all Britain and France had to do was to stand together firmly, and let the Nazis devote

their energies to putting down the Red menace throughout eastern
and central Europe.

Of course it was unfortunate that one of the victims of this conflict had to be a young Jewish idealist. They must try to help the
poor fellow, if only for the family's peace of mind. Robbie, who
usually thought of money first, made the guess that if Freddi really
was in Dachau it was because of Irma's stocks and bonds. Rumor
invariably multiplied a rich person's holdings by three or four, and
sometimes by ten or twenty; the fat General doubtless was expecting to get many millions in ransom. Robbie said that he himself
would offer to go in and see what could be done; but he didn't
propose to see Irma plundered, so the best thing was to wait and
let Göring show his hand if he would. Irma appreciated this attitude, and wondered why Lanny couldn't be as sensible.

One thing Robbie said he was unable to understand: the fact that
they had never received a single line of writing from Freddi in
more than eight months. Surely any prisoner would be permitted to
communicate with his relatives at some time! Lanny told what he
had learned from the Kommandant of Dachau, that the inmates
were permitted to write a few lines once a week to their nearest
relatives; but this privilege was withheld in certain cases. Robbie
said: "Even so, there are ways of smuggling out letters; and certainly there must be prisoners released now and then. You'd think
some one of them would have your address, and drop a note to
report the situation. It suggests to me that Freddi may be dead; but
I don't say it to the Robins."

VI

Hard times were producing in France the same effects they had
produced in Germany; and now the political pot boiled over, making a nasty mess. It was the "Stavisky case," centering about a
swindler of Russian-Jewish descent. "Too bad he had to be a Jew!"
said Irma, and Lanny wasn't sure whether she was being sympathetic or sarcastic. "Handsome Alex," as he was called, had been
engaged in one piece of financial jugglery after another, culminating

in a *tour de force* which sounded like comic opera—he had promoted an extensive issue of bonds for the pawnshops of the town of Bayonne! Altogether he had robbed the French public of something like a billion francs; and it was discovered that he had been indicted for a swindle eight or nine years previously, and had succeeded in having his trial postponed no less than nineteen times. Obviously this meant collusion with police and politicians; either he was paying them money or was in position to blackmail them. When Robbie read the details he said it sounded exactly like Chicago or Philadelphia.

Stavisky had gone into hiding with his mistress, and when the police came for him he shot himself; at least, so the police said, but evidence began to indicate that the police had hushed him up. The Paris newspapers, the most corrupt in the world, printed everything they could find out and twenty times as much. Two groups were interested in exploiting the scandals: the parties of the extreme right, the Royalists and Fascists, who wanted to overthrow the Republic and set up their kind of dictatorship; and the Communists, who wanted a different kind. The two extremes met, and while vowing the deadliest hatred, they made war on the same parliamentary system.

Lanny couldn't afford to visit his Red uncle, but he invited Denis de Bruyne to dinner, and the three Budds listened to the story from the point of view of a French Nationalist. The situation in the de Bruyne family bore an odd resemblance to that between Robbie and his son. Denis belonged to a respectable law-and-order party, and was distressed because his younger son had joined the Croix de Feu, most active of the French Fascist groups. Now Charlot was off somewhere with his fellows, conspiring to overpower the police and seize control of the country's affairs. At any moment he and his organization might come out on the streets, and there would be shooting; the unhappy father couldn't enjoy his dinner, and wanted Lanny to find the crazy boy and try to bring him to his senses. Such were the duties you got in for when you chose a lovely French lady for your *amie!*

Lanny said no; he had tried to influence both boys, and had failed, and now he was out of politics; he had made a promise to his wife. He listened to the innermost secrets of *la république française,* derived from first-hand observation. He learned about Daladier, the baker's son, who had just become Premier, the fourth within a year; what interests had subsidized his career, and what noble lady had become his mistress. He learned about Chiappe, chief of the Paris police, a Corsican known as "the little Napoleon"—he was five feet three inches, and had just been "fired" for being too intimate with Stavisky. He had known all the wholesale crooks, the blackmailers and Jewish *métèques* of France, and had whispered their secrets to his son-in-law, publisher of one of the great gutter-journals of Paris.

Lanny observed that the individuals who awakened the anger and disgust of Denis de Bruyne were the climbers, those struggling for wealth and power to which they had no valid claim. He rarely had any serious fault to find with the *mur d'argent,* the members of the "two hundred families" who had had wealth and power for a long time. They had to pay large sums of money in these evil days, and the basis of Denis's complaint was not the corruption but the increasing cost. The politicians demanded larger campaign funds, and at the same time kept increasing taxes; their idea of economy was to cut the salaries of civil servants—which Denis had discovered was bad for the taxicab business. To make matters worse, the taxicab drivers were on strike! Robbie listened sympathetically, and when his friend got through scolding Daladier, Robbie took a turn at Roosevelt.

VII

Next day Lanny escorted his wife to the Summer Fashion Show. This wasn't a public affair, but one for the trade; an exhibition of the new styles which the manufacturers intended soon to release. Irma was invited as a special honor by the fashion artist to whom she entrusted her social destiny. Lanny went along because, if she endeavored to take an interest in his things, it was only fair that he should do the same for hers. They sat in a hall with many potted palms, gazing at a long ramp with dark blue curtains behind it;

along the ramp paraded beautiful and *chic* young women wearing summer costumes with a strong Japanese flavor, or note, or atmosphere—the journalists groped about for a metaphor. There were bamboo buttons and coolie hats; the ladies' gowns had fan-tails like Japanese goldfish, the afternoon costumes had cut sleeves like kimonos, and the evening wraps had designs resembling Japanese flower prints.

Among the favored guests at this show was an old friend of Lanny's; Olivie Hellstein, now Madame de Broussailles, very lovely daughter of Jerusalem whom Emily had picked out as a proper match for Lanny. That had been some eight years ago, and now Olivie had three or four children, and had become what you called "maternal," a kinder word than "plump." Words which have an unpleasant connotation change frequently in the best society, where people try so hard not to wound one another's feelings.

Olivie was a woman of Irma's type, a brunette with deep coloring, in temperament rather placid, in manner sedate. They had entertained each other, exchanged visits, and satisfied their curiosity. Now they talked about having to wear summer clothing with a strong Japanese flavor, or note, or atmosphere; they would have to wear it, of course—it would never occur to them to rebel against what the fashion creators decided was the fashion.

Lanny, wishing to be polite, remarked: "We were talking about your family last night. My father is having a meeting with your father."

"A business matter?" inquired Olivie.

"Mine is trying to persuade yours that he can deliver certain railroad equipment at Brest at a lower price than it can be manufactured in France."

"It will be pleasant if they become associated," replied the young matron. "My father has a great admiration for American production methods, and wishes they might be imported into France."

Pierre Hellstein was a director in the Chemin de Fer du Nord, and controlled one of the biggest banks in Paris. Robbie had asked Denis about him, and they had discussed this wealthy Jewish family spread widely over Europe; also the position of the railroad, reputed to be run down and overloaded with bonds. The Hellsteins didn't have to worry, because the government covered its deficits; there had been criticism in the Chamber—the French Republic was going broke in order to protect the railroad bondholders. Denis de Bruyne, who owned some of the bonds, resented these criticisms as irresponsible and demagogic. As for Olivie, beautiful, serene, magnificent in a long sable coat, she was perfect evidence of the wisdom of guaranteeing large incomes to a few chosen individuals, in order that they may be free to attend fashion shows and constitute themselves models of elegance and refinement.

VIII

"Oh, by the way," said the daughter of Jerusalem, all at once; "I understand that you were in Germany not long ago."

"Just before Christmas," replied Lanny.

"I do wish you would tell me about it. It must be dreadful."

"In some ways, and for some people. Others hardly notice it."

"Oh, Monsieur Budd," said Olivie, lowering her voice, "may I tell you something without its going any farther? I'm really not supposed to talk, but we are all so worried."

"You may be sure that my wife and I will respect your confidence, Madame."

"We have just learned that the Nazis have arrested my Uncle Solomon. You know him, possibly?"

"I had the pleasure of meeting him at the home of Johannes Robin. Also, I am one of his depositors in Berlin."

"They have trumped up some charge against him, of sending money out of Germany. You know, of course, that a banker cannot help doing that; especially a family like ours, doing business in Austria and Czechoslovakia and Rumania, and so many other countries."

"Of course, Madame."

"We Jews hear the most dreadful stories—really, it makes you quite sick."

"I am sorry to say that many of them are true. They tell you that such things happen in violent social overturns. But I doubt if the Nazis would do physical harm to a man like your uncle. They would be more likely to assess him a very large fine."

"It is all so bewildering, Monsieur Budd. Really, my father cannot be sure whether it would be safe for him to go into Germany to see about it."

"I will make a suggestion, Madame, if you don't mind."

"That is just what I was hoping you might do."

"I ask you to consider it confidential, just as you have asked me. Tell your mother and father, but nobody else."

"Certainly, Monsieur Budd."

"I suggest their sending somebody to interview General Göring. He has a great deal of influence and seems to understand these matters."

"Oh, thank you!" exclaimed Olivie Hellstein. "I am so glad I thought to ask you about it."

Irma put in: "Send somebody who is dignified and impressive-looking, and tell him to be dressed exactly right, and not forget any of the Minister-Präsident General's titles."

IX

Out of duty to the memory of Marie de Bruyne, Lanny made an effort to see her younger son, but found it impossible. Charlot was meeting somewhere with the leaders of his society, and the inquiries of strangers were not welcomed. This Tuesday, the sixth of February, was to be the great night in which all the organizations of the Right in France would "demonstrate" against the government. Marching orders had been published in all the opposition papers, under the slogan: *"A bas les voleurs!* Down with the thieves!" At twilight Charlot would emerge from his hiding place, wearing his tricolor armband with the letters F.C.F., which meant that he was a Son of the Cross of Fire. He would be singing the *Marseillaise;* an odd phenomenon, the battle-song of one revolution becoming the anti-song of the next! In between singing, Charlot and his troop of patriotic youths would be yelling the word

"*Démission!*"—which meant the turning out of the Daladier government. Less politely they would cry: "*Daladier au poteau!*" meaning that they wished to burn him alive.

Lanny drove his wife to the Chamber, going by a circuitous route because the Pont de la Concorde was blocked by gendarmes. For an hour the couple sat in the public gallery and listened to an uproar which reminded Lanny of what he had heard on the floor of the New York Stock Exchange at the height of the panic. Daladier couldn't make his speech; his political enemies hurled at him every abusive name in the extensive French vocabulary, while at the same time the Communists sang the *Internationale*.

When this became monotonous, the Americans went out to have a look at the streets. They couldn't see much from a car, for fear of being caught in fighting, and decided that the best place from which to witness a Paris *démonstration* was from the windows of their hotel suite. Robbie, sensible fellow, was in his rooms, talking business with the head of a French building concern which sometimes bought *ascenseurs*. The two younger people stood on the balcony of their drawing-room, which looked over the great Place de la Concorde, brilliantly lighted, and with an obelisk in the center having floodlights on it. Directly across the Place was the bridge over the Seine to the Palais-Bourbon, where the deputies met; a building in Roman style with many tall pillars brightly shining.

There must have been a hundred thousand people in the Place, and more pouring in by every street. They were trying to get across the bridge, but the police and troops had blocked it with patrol-wagons. The mob started throwing things, and soon there was a pitched battle, with charges and counter-charges going on most of the night. The Fascists hurled whatever they could lay hands on. They pried up stones from the pavement, and tore off the scaffolding from the American Embassy, which was under repair. The railings of the Tuileries gardens provided them with an iron missile, shaped like a boomerang and impossible to see in the dark. When the mounted *gardes républicaines* tried to drive them off the bridge, charging and striking with the flat of their sabers, the mob countered with walking-sticks having razor-blades fastened to the ends, to slash the bellies of the horses. In one attack after another they crippled so many of the police and *gardes* that they came very near getting across the bridge and into the Chamber.

So at last shooting began. The street-lights were smashed, and the floodlights on the obelisk were turned off, so you couldn't see much. An omnibus had been overturned and set afire near the bridge, but that gave more smoke than light, and it soon burned out. The last sight that Lanny saw was a troop of the Spahis, African cavalrymen in white desert robes looking like the Ku Kluxers, galloping up the Champs Élysées and trampling the mob. There came screams directly under where Irma and Lanny were standing; a chambermaid of the hotel had been shot and killed on the balcony. So the guests scrambled in quickly, deciding that they had seen enough of the class war in France.

"Do you think they will raid the hotel?" asked Irma; but Lanny assured her that this was a respectable kind of mob, and was after the politicians only. So they went to bed.

X

"Bloody Tuesday," it was called, and the Fascist newspapers set out to make it into the French "Beerhall Putsch." From that time on they would have only one name for Daladier: "*Assassin!*" They clamored for his resignation, and before the end of the next day they got it; there were whispers that he could no longer depend upon the police and the *gardes*. More than two hundred of these were in the hospitals, and it looked like a revolution on the way. There was wreckage all over Paris, and the Ministry of Marine partly burned. Charlot had got a slash across the forehead, and for the rest of his life would wear a scar with pride. "*La Concorde,*" he would say, referring to the bridge; it would become a slogan, perhaps some day a password to power.

On Wednesday night matters were worse, for the police were demoralized, and the hoodlums, the *apaches*, went on the warpath. They smashed the windows of the shops in the Rue de Rivoli and other fashionable streets and looted everything in sight. It wasn't a pleasant time for visitors in Paris; Robbie was going to Amsterdam on business, so Irma and Lanny stepped into their car and sped home.

But you couldn't get away from the class war in France. The various reactionary groups had been organized all over the Midi, and they, too, had received their marching orders. They had the sympathy of many in the various foreign colonies; anything to put down the Reds. Rick, after hearing Lanny's story, said that *la patrie* was awaiting only one thing, a leader who would have the shrewdness to win the "little man." So far, all the Fascist groups were avowedly reactionary, and it would take a leftish program to win. Lanny expressed the opinion that the French man in the street was much shrewder than the German; it wouldn't be so easy to hoodwink him.

Life was resumed at Bienvenu. Rick worked on his play and Lanny read the manuscript, encouraged him, and supplied local color. In the privacy of their chamber Irma said: "Really, you are a collaborator, and ought to be named." She wondered why Lanny never wrote a play of his own. She decided that what he lacked was the impulse of self-assertion, the strong ego which takes up the conviction that it has something necessary to the welfare of mankind. Uncle Jesse had it, Kurt had it, Rick had it. Beauty had tried in vain to awaken it in her son, and now Irma tried with no more success. "Rick can do it a lot better"—that was all she could get.

Irma was becoming a little cross with this lame Englishman. She had got Lanny pretty well cured of his Pinkness, but now Rick kept poking up the fires. There came a series of terrible events in Austria—apparently Fascism was going to spread from country to country until it had covered all Europe. Austria had got a Catholic Chancellor named Dollfuss, and a Catholic army, the Heimwehr, composed mainly of peasant lads and led by a dissipated young prince. This government was jailing or deporting Hitlerites, but with the help of Mussolini was getting its own brand of Fascism, and now it set out to destroy the Socialist movement in the city of Vienna. Those beautiful workers' homes, huge apartment blocks which Lanny had inspected with such joy—the Heimwehr brought up its motorized artillery and blasted them to ruins, killing about a thousand men, women, and children. Worse yet, they killed the workers' movement, which had been two generations building.

A terrible time to be alive in. Lanny and Rick could hardly eat or sleep; they could only grieve and brood over the tragedy of the time into which they had been born. Truly it seemed futile to work for anything good; to dream of peace and order, justice or even mercy. This wholesale slaughter of working people was committed in the name of the gentle and lowly Jesus, the carpenter's son, the social rebel who had been executed because he stirred up the people! A devout Catholic Premier ordering the crime, and devout Catholic officers attending mass before and after committing it! And not for the first time or the last in unhappy Europe. Rick reminded his friend of that cardinal in France who had ordered the St. Bartholomew massacre, saying: "Kill them all; God will be able to pick out His Christians."

XI

Hot weather came to the Riviera, and the people whom Irma considered important went away. Those who were poor, like the Dingles and the Robins, would stick it out and learn to take a siesta. But Nina and Rick went back to England, and Emily Chattersworth moved her servants to Les Forêts and invited Irma and Lanny to visit her and see the spring Salon and the new plays. It was Irma's idea, to keep her husband's mind off the troubles of the world. They went, and after they had played around for a couple of weeks, Irma had a letter from her mother, begging them to come to Shore Acres and bring Baby Frances for the summer. Really it was a crime to have that magnificent place and never use it; also it was grossly unfair that one grandmother should have her heart's desire all the time and the other not at all. "I don't believe that Beauty cares for the child anything like as much as I do," wrote the Queen Mother; a sentence which Irma skipped when she read the letter aloud.

The couple talked over the problem. Irma was reluctant to take her precious darling on board a steamer; she hadn't got over her memories of the Lindbergh kidnaping, and thought that an ocean liner was an ideal place for a band of criminals to study a twenty-three-million-dollar baby, her habits and entourage. No, it would be better to spend the summer in England's green and pleasant land, where kidnapers were unknown. Let Mother be the one to brave the ocean waves! Irma hadn't spent any money to speak of during the past year, and now interest on bonds was being paid and dividends were hoped for. She said: "Let's drive about England, the way we did on our honeymoon, and see if we can find some suitable place to rent."

Nothing is more fun than doing over again what you did on your honeymoon; that is, if you have managed to keep any of the honeymoon feeling alive after five years. "There are so many nice people there," argued the young wife. Lanny agreed, even though he might not have named the same persons.

He knew that Rick's play was nearly done, and he wanted to make suggestions for the last act. Then there would be the job of submitting it to managers, and Lanny would want to hear the news. Perhaps it might be necessary to raise the money, and that wouldn't be so easy, for it was a grim and violent play, bitter as gall, and would shock the fashionable ladies. But Lanny meant to put up the money which he had earned in Germany—all of it, if necessary, and he didn't want Irma to be upset about it. They were following their plan of keeping the peace by making concessions, each to the other and in equal proportions.

They crossed the Channel and put up at the Dorchester. When their arrival was announced in the papers, as it always would be, one of the first persons who telephoned was Wickthorpe, saying: "Won't you come out and spend the week end?"

Lanny replied: "Sure thing. We're looking for a little place to rent this summer. Maybe you can give us some advice." He said "little" because he knew that was good form; but of course it wouldn't really be little.

"I have a place near by," responded his lordship. "I'll show it to you, if you don't mind."

"Righto!" said Lanny, who knew how to talk English to Englishmen.

When he told Irma about it, she talked American. "Oh, heck! Do you suppose it'll have tin bathtubs?"

XII

But it didn't. It was a modern villa with three baths, plenty of light and air, and one of those English lawns, smooth as a billiard table, used for playing games. There was a high hedge around the place, and everything lovely. It was occupied by Wickthorpe's aunt, who was leaving for a summer cruise with some friends. There was a staff of well-trained servants who would stay on if requested. "Oh, I think it will be ducky!" exclaimed the heiress. She paid the price to his lordship's agent that very day, and the aunt agreed to move out and have everything in order by the next week end. Irma cabled her mother, and wrote Bub Smith and Feathers to get everything ready and bring Baby and Miss Severne and the maid on a specified date. Jerry Pendleton would see to the tickets, and Bub would be in charge of the traveling, Feathers being such a featherbrain.

So there was a new ménage, with everything comfortable, and no trouble but the writing of a few checks and the giving of a few orders. A delightful climate and many delightful people; a tennis court and somebody always to play; a good piano and people who loved music; only a few minutes' drive to the old castle, where Lanny and his wife were treated as members of the family, called up and urged to meet this one and that. Again Lanny heard statesmen discussing the problems of the world; again they listened to what he had to tell about the strange and terrifying new movement in Germany, and its efforts to spread itself in all the neighboring countries. Englishmen of rank and authority talked freely of their empire's affairs, telling what they would do in this or that contingency; now and then Lanny would find himself thinking: "What wouldn't Göring pay for *this!*"

Zoltan had been in Paris, and now came to London. It was the "season," and there were exhibitions, and chances to make sales. An art expert, like the member of any other profession, has to hear the gossip of his *monde;* new men are coming in and old ones going out, and prices fluctuating exactly as on the stock market. Lanny and his partner still had money in Naziland, and lists of pictures available in that country, by means of which they expected to get their money out. Also, there was the London stage, and Rick to go with them to plays and tell the news of that world. There was the fashion rout, with no end of dances and parties. Dressmakers and others clamored to provide Irma with costumes suited to her station; they would bring them out into the country to show her at any hour of the day or night.

Good old Margy Petries, Dowager Lady Eversham-Watson, had opened her town house, and begged the young couple to make it their headquarters whenever they came to town; she telegraphed Beauty and Sophie to bring their husbands and come and have a good old-fashioned spree. When Mrs. Barnes arrived, she, too, was "put up"; that was the custom in Kentucky, and Margy still called herself a blue-grass-country girl, even at the age of fifty-five.

So it was just like Bienvenu at the height of midwinter; so many things going on that really you had a hard time choosing, and would rush from one event to the next with scarcely time to catch your breath. It was extremely difficult for Lanny to find time to brood over the fate of the world; and that was what his wife had planned. She saw that she was winning out, and was happy, and proud of her acumen. Until one Saturday noon, arriving at their villa for a week end, Lanny found a telegram from Bienvenu, signed "Rahel" and reading:

"Letter from Clarinet in place you visited most distressing circumstances he implores help am airmailing letter."

26

Out of This Nettle, Danger

I

THE argument started as soon as Irma read the telegram and got its meaning clear. She knew exactly what would be in her husband's mind; she had been thinking about it for more than a year, watching him, anticipating this moment, living through this scene. And she knew that he had been doing the same. They had talked about it a great deal, but she hadn't uttered all of her thoughts, nor he of his; they had dreaded the ordeal, shrinking from the things that would be said. She knew that was true about herself, and guessed it was true about him; she guessed that he guessed it about her—and so on through a complication such as develops when two human souls, tied together by passionate love, discover a basic and fundamental clash of temperaments, and try to conceal it from each other and even from themselves.

Irma said: "Lanny, you can't do it! You can't, you can't!" And he replied: "Darling, I have to! If I didn't I couldn't bear to live!"

So much had been said already that there was nothing to gain by going over it. But that is the way with lovers' quarrels; each thinks that if he says it one time more, the idea will penetrate, it will make the impression which it so obviously ought to make, which it has somehow incomprehensibly failed to make on previous occasions.

Irma protested: "Your wife and child mean nothing to you?"

Lanny answered: "You know they do, dear. I have tried honestly to be a good husband and father. I have given up many things that I thought were right for me, when I found they were wrong for you. But I can't give up Freddi to the Nazis."

"A man is free to take up a notion like that—and then all his family duties become nothing?"

"A man takes up a notion like that when there's a cause involved; something that is more precious to him than his own life."

"You're going to sacrifice Frances and me for Freddi!"

"That's rather exaggerated, darling. You and Frances can stay quite comfortably here while I go in and do what I can."

"You're not asking me to go with you?"

"It's a job for someone who believes in it, and certainly not for anyone who feels as you do. I have no right to ask it of you, and that's why I don't."

"What do you suppose will be my state of mind while you are in there risking your life with those dreadful men?"

"It will be a mistake to exaggerate the danger. I don't think they'll do serious harm to an American."

"You know they have done shocking things to Americans. You have talked about it often."

"What happened in those cases was accidental; they were mix-ups in street crowds and public places. You and I have connections in Germany, and I don't think the authorities will do me any harm on purpose."

"Even if they catch you breaking their laws?"

"I think they'll give me a good scare and put me out."

"You know you don't believe that, Lanny! You're only trying to quiet me down. You will be in perfectly frightful danger, and I will be in torment."

She broke down and began to weep. It was the first time he had seen her do that, and he was a soft-hearted man. But he had been thinking it over for a year, and had made up his mind that this would be the test of his soul. "If I funk this, I'm no good; I'm the waster and parasite I've always been called."

There was no way to end the argument. He couldn't make her realize the importance of the matter to him; the duty he owed to what he called "the cause." He had made Freddi Robin into a Socialist; had taught him the ideal of human brotherhood and equality, what he called "social justice." But Irma hated all these high-sounding words; she had heard them spoken by so many disagreeable persons, mostly trying to get money, that the words had become poison to her. She didn't believe in this "cause"; she believed that brotherhood was rather repulsive, that equality was another name for envy, and social justice an excuse for outrageous income and inheritance taxes. So her tears dried quickly, and she grew angry with herself for having shed them, and with him for making her shed them.

She said: "Lanny, I warn you; you are ruining our love. You are doing something I shall never be able to forgive you for."

All he could answer was: "I am sorry, darling; but if you made me give up what I believe is my duty, I should never be able to forgive either you or myself."

II

The airmail letter from Juan arrived. Freddi's message had been written in pencil on a small piece of flimsy paper, crumpled up as if someone had hidden it in his mouth or other bodily orifice. It was faded, but Rahel had smoothed it out and pasted the corners to a sheet of white paper so that it could be read. It was addressed to Lanny and written in English. "I am in a bad way. I have written to you but had no reply. They are trying to make me tell about other people and I will not. But I cannot stand any more. Do one thing for me, try to get some poison to me. Do not believe anything they say about me. Tell our friends I have been true."

There was no signature; Freddi knew that Lanny would know his handwriting, shaky and uncertain as it was. The envelope was plain, and had been mailed in Munich; the handwriting of the address was not known to Lanny, and Rahel in her letter said that she didn't know it either.

So there it was. Irma broke down again; it was worse than she had imagined, and she knew now that she couldn't keep Lanny from going. She stopped arguing with him about political questions, and tried only to convince him of the futility of whatever efforts he might make. The Nazis owned Germany, and it was madness to imagine that he could thwart their will inside their own country. She offered to put up money, any amount of money, even if she had to withdraw from social life. "Go and see Göring," she pleaded. "Offer him cash, straight out."

But Rick—oh, how she hated him all of a sudden!—Rick had persuaded Lanny that this was not to be done. Lanny wouldn't go near Göring, or any of the other Nazis, not even Kurt, not even Heinrich. They wouldn't help, and might report him and have him watched. Göring or Goebbels would be sure to take such measures. Lanny said flatly: "I'm going to help Freddi to escape from Dachau."

"Fly over the walls, I suppose?" inquired Irma, with bitterness.

"There are many different ways of getting out of prison. There are people in France right now who have managed to do it. Sometimes they dig under the walls; sometimes they hide in delivery wagons, or are carried out in coffins. I'll find somebody to help me for a price."

"Just walk up to somebody on the street and say: 'How much will you charge to help me get a friend out of Dachau?'"

"It's no good quarreling, dear. I have to put my mind on what I mean to do. I don't want to delay, because if I do, Freddi may be dead, and then I'd blame myself until I was dead, too."

So Irma had to give up. She had told him what was in her heart, and even though she would break down and weep, she wouldn't change; on the contrary, she would hold it against him that he had made her behave in that undignified fashion. In her heart she knew that she hated the Robin family, all of them; they were alien to her, strangers to her soul. If she could have had her way she would never have been intimate with them; she would have had her own yacht and her own palace and the right sort of friends in it. But this Socialism business had made Lanny promiscuous, willing to meet anybody, an easy victim for any sort of pretender, any slick, canting "idealist"—how she loathed that word! She had been forced to make pretenses and be polite; but now this false "cause" was going to deprive her of her husband and her happiness, and she knew that she heartily despised it.

It wasn't just love of herself. It was love of Lanny, too. She wanted to help him, she wanted to take care of him; but this "class struggle" stepped in between and made it impossible; tore him away from her, and sent him to face danger, mutilation, death. Things that Irma and her class were supposed to be immune from! That was what your money meant; it kept you safe, it gave you privilege and security. But Lanny wanted to throw it all away. He had got the crazy notion that you had no right to money; that having got it, you must look down upon it, spurn it, and thwart the very purposes for which it existed, the reasons why your forefathers had worked so hard! If that was not madness, who could find anything that deserved the name?

III

All social engagements were called off while this duel was fought out. Irma said that she had a bad headache; but as this affliction had not been known to trouble her hitherto, the rumor spread that the Irma Barneses were having a quarrel; everybody tried to guess what it could be about, but nobody succeeded. Only three persons were taken into the secret; Rick, and the mothers of the two quarrelers. Rick said: "I wish I could help you, old chap; but you know I'm a marked man in Germany; I have written articles." Lanny said: "Of course."

As for Fanny Barnes, she considered it her duty to give Lanny a lecture on the wrongness of deserting his family on account of any Jew or all of them. Lanny, in turn, considered it his duty to hear politely all that his mother-in-law had to say. He knew it wasn't any good talking to her about "causes"; he just said: "I'm sorry, Mother, but I feel that I have incurred obligations, and I have to repay them. Do what you can to keep Irma cheerful until I get back." It was a rather solemn occasion; he might not come back, and he had a feeling that his mother-in-law would find that a not altogether intolerable solution of the problem.

As for Beauty, she wasn't much good in this crisis; the sheer horridness of it seemed to paralyze her will. She knew her boy's feeling for the Robin boys, and that it couldn't be overcome. She knew also that he suspected her concern about Irma's happiness as being not altogether disinterested. The mother dared not say what was in the deeps of her heart, her fear that Lanny might lose his ultra-precious wife if he neglected her and opposed her so recklessly. And of all places to leave her—on the doorstep of Lord Wickthorpe! Beauty developed a *crise des nerfs*, with a real head-ache, and this didn't diminish the gossip and speculation.

Meanwhile, Lanny went ahead with his preparations. He wrote Rahel to have a photograph of Freddi reduced to that small size which is used on passports, and to airmail it to him at once; he had a reason for that, which she was at liberty to guess. He wrote Jerry Pendleton to hold himself in readiness for a call to bring a *camion* to Germany and return the Detaze paintings to their home. That would be no hardship, because the tourist season was over and Cerise could run the office.

Lanny gave his friend Zoltan a check covering a good part of the money he had in the Hellstein banks in Berlin and Munich; Zoltan would transfer the money to his own account, and thus the Nazis wouldn't be able to confiscate it. In case Lanny needed the money, he could telegraph and Zoltan could airmail him a check. The ever discreet friend asked no questions, and thus would be able to say that he knew nothing about the matter. Lanny talked about a picture deal which he thought he could put through in Munich, and Zoltan gave him advice on this. Having been pondering all these matters for more than a year, Lanny was thoroughly pre-pared.

When it came to the parting, Lanny's young wife and Lanny's would-be-young mother both broke down. Both offered to go with him; but he said No. Neither approved his mission, and neither's heart would be in the disagreeable task. He didn't tell the plain truth, which was that he was sick of arguments and excitements; it is one of the painful facts about marital disputes that they cause each of the disputants to grow weary of the sound of the other's voice, and to count quiet and the freedom to have one's own way as the greatest of life's blessings. Lanny believed that he could do this job himself, and could think better if he didn't have opposition. He said: "No, dear," and "No, darling; I'm going to be very careful, and it won't take long."

IV

So, bright and early one morning, Margy Petries's servants deposited his bags in his car, and not without some moisture in his eyes and some sinkings in his inside, he set out for the ferry to Calais, whose name Queen Mary had said was written on her heart, and which surely existed as some sort of scar on Lanny's. He went by way of Metz and Strasbourg, for the fewer countries one entered in unhappy Europe, the less bother with visas and customs declarations. How glorious the country seemed in the last days of June; and how pitiful by contrast that *Missgeburt* of nature which had developed the frontal lobes of its brain so enormously, in order to create new and more dreadful ways of destroying millions of other members of its own species! "Nature's insurgent son" had cast off chain-mail and dropped lances and battle-axes, only to take up bombing-planes and Nazi propaganda.

The blood of millions of Frenchmen and Germans had fertilized this soil and made it so green and pleasant to Lanny's eyes. He knew that in all these copses and valleys were hidden the direful secrets of the Maginot Line, that series of complicated and enormously expensive fortifications by which France was counting upon preventing another German invasion. Safe behind this barricade, Frenchmen could use their leisure to maim and mangle other Frenchmen with iron railings torn from a beautiful park. Where Lanny crossed the Rhine was where the child Marie Antoinette had come with her train of two or three hundred vehicles, on her long journey from Vienna to marry the Dauphin of France. All sorts of history around here, but the traveler had no time to think about it; his mind was occupied with the history he was going to make.

Skirting the edge of the Alps, with snow-clad peaks always in view, he came to the city of Munich on its little river Isar. He put up at a second-class hotel, for he didn't want newspaper reporters after him, and wanted to be able to put on the suit of old clothes which he had brought, and be able to walk about the city, and perhaps the town of Dachau, without attracting any special attention. At the Polizeiwache he reported himself as coming for the purpose of purchasing works of art; his first act after that was to call upon a certain Baron von Zinszollern whom he had met at the Detaze show and who had many paintings in his home. This gentleman was an avowed Nazi sympathizer, and Lanny planned to use him as his "brown herring," so to speak. In case of exposure this might sow doubts and confusion in Nazi minds, which would be so much to the good.

Lanny went to this art patron's fine home and looked at his collection, and brought up in his tactful way whether any of the works could be bought; he intimated that the prices asked were rather high, but promised to cable abroad and see what he could do. He did cable to Zoltan, and to a couple of customers in America, and these messages would be a part of his defense in case of trouble. All through his stay in Munich he would be stimulating the hopes of a somewhat impoverished German aristocrat, and diminishing the prices of his good paintings.

V

Upon entering Germany the conspirator had telephoned to Hugo Behr in Berlin, inviting that young Nazi to take the night train to Munich. Lanny was here on account of pictures, he said, and would show his friend some fine specimens. Hugo had understood, and it hadn't been necessary to add, "expenses paid." The young sports director had doubtless found some use for the money which Lanny had paid him, and would be pleased to render further services.

He arrived next morning, going to a different hotel, as Lanny had directed. He telephoned, and Lanny drove and picked him up on the street. A handsome young Pomeranian, alert and with springy step, apple-cheeked and with wavy golden hair, Hugo was a walk-

ing advertisement of the pure Nordic ideal. In his trim Brownshirt
uniform, with insignia indicating his important function, he received a salute from all other Nazis, and from many civilians wishing to keep on the safe side. It was extremely reassuring to be with
such a man in Germany—although the "Heil Hitlers" became a bit
monotonous after a while.

Lanny drove his guest out into the country, where they could
be quiet and talk freely. He encouraged the guest to assume that
the invitation was purely out of friendship; rich men can indulge
their whims like that, and they do so. Lanny was deeply interested
to know how Hugo's movement for the reforming of the Nazi
party was coming along, and as the reformer wanted to talk about
nothing else, they drove for a long time through the valleys of the
Alpine foothills. The trees were in full splendor, as yet untouched
by any signs of wear. A beautiful land, and Lanny's head was full
of poetry about it. *Die Fenster auf, die Herzen auf! Geschwinde,
geschwinde!*

But Hugo's thoughts had no trace of poetic cheerfulness. His
figure of a young Hermes was slumped in the car seat, and his
tone was bitter as he said: "Our Nazi revolution is *kaput*. We
haven't accomplished a thing. The Führer has put himself completely into the hands of the reactionaries. They tell him what to
do—it's no longer certain that he could carry out his own program,
even if he wanted to. He doesn't see his old friends any more, he
doesn't trust them. The Reichswehr crowd are plotting to get rid
of the Stormtroopers altogether."

"You don't really mean all that, Hugo!" Lanny was much distressed.

"Haven't you heard about our vacation?"

"I only entered Germany yesterday."

"All the S.A. have been ordered to take a vacation during the
month of July. They say we've been overworked and have earned
a rest. That sounds fine; but we're not permitted to wear our uniforms, or to carry our arms. And what are they going to do while
we're disarmed? What are we going to find when we come back?"

"That looks serious, I admit."

"It seems to me the meaning is plain. We, the rank and file, have done our job and they're through with us. We have all been hoping to be taken into the Reichswehr; but no, we're not good enough for that. Those officers are Junkers, they're real gentlemen, while we're common trash; we're too many, two million of us, and they can't afford to feed us or to train us, so we have to be turned off—and go to begging on the streets, perhaps."

"You know, Hugo, Germany is supposed to have only a hundred thousand in its regular army. Mayn't it be that the Führer doesn't feel strong enough to challenge France and Britain on that issue?"

"What was our revolution for, but to set us free from their control? And how can we ever become strong, if we reject the services of the very men who have made National Socialism? *We* put these leaders in power—and now they're getting themselves expensive villas and big motor-cars, and they're afraid to let us of the rank and file even wear our uniforms! They talk of disbanding us, because the Reich can't afford our magnificent salaries of forty-two pfennigs a day."

"Is that what you get?"

"That is what the rank and file get. What is that in your money?"

"About ten cents."

"Does that sound so very extravagant?"

"The men in our American army get about ten times that. Of course both groups get food and lodgings free."

"Pretty poor food for the S.A.; and besides, there are all the levies, which take half what anybody earns. Our lads were made to expect so much, but now all the talk is that the Reich is so poor. The propaganda line has changed; Herr Doktor Goebbels travels over the land denouncing the *Kritikaster* and the *Miessmacher* and the *Nörgler* and the *Besserwisser*—" Hugo gave a long list of the depraved groups who dared to suggest that the Nazi *Regierung* was anything short of perfect. "In the old days we were told there would be plenty, because we were going to take the machinery away from the *Schieber* and set it to work for the benefit of the common folk. But now the peasants have been made into serfs, and the workingman who asks for higher pay or tries to change his job is treated as a criminal. Prices are going up and wages falling, and what are the people to do?"

"Somebody ought to point these things out to the Führer," suggested Lanny.

"Nobody can get near the Führer. Göring has taken charge of his mind—Göring, the aristocrat, the friend of the princes and the Junker landlords and the gentlemen of the steel *Kartell*. They are piling up bigger fortunes than ever; I'm told that Göring is doing the same—and sending the money abroad where it will be safe."

"I've heard talk about that in Paris and London," admitted Lanny; "and on pretty good authority. The money people know what's going on."

V I

They were high up in the foothills, close to the Austrian border. *Auf die Berge will ich steigen, wo die dunkeln Tannen ragen!* The air was crystal clear and delightfully cool, but it wasn't for the air that Lanny had come, nor yet on account of Heine's *Harzreise*. They sat on an outdoor platform of a little inn looking up a valley to a mountain that was Austria; Lanny saw that the slopes about him were not too precipitous, nor the stream in the valley too deep. He remarked to his companion: "There's probably a lot of illegal traffic over these mountain paths."

"Not so much as you might think," was the reply. "You don't see the sentries, but they're watching, and they shoot first and ask questions afterward."

"But they can't do much shooting on a stormy night."

"They know where the paths are, and they guard them pretty closely. But I've no doubt some of the mountaineers take bribes and share with them. The Jews are running money out of Germany by every device they can think of. They want to bleed the country to death."

That didn't sound so promising; but Lanny had to take a chance somewhere. When they were back in the car, safe from prying ears, he said: "You know, Hugo, you're so irritated with the Jews,

and yet, when I hear you talk about the ideals of National Socialism, it sounds exactly like the talk of my friend Freddi Robin whom
I've told you about."

"I don't deny that there are good Jews; many of them, no doubt;
and certainly they have plenty of brains."

"Freddi is one of the finest characters I have ever known. He is
sensitive, delicate, considerate, and I'm sure he never had a vice.
He was giving all his time and thought to the cause of social justice,
exactly as you believe in it and have explained it today."

"Is he still in Dachau?"

"I want to talk to you about him, Hugo. It's so important to
me; I can't have any peace of mind while the situation stands as
it is, and neither can anybody who knows Freddi. I'd like to take
you into my confidence, and have your word that you won't
mention it to anybody else, except by agreement with me."

"I don't think it'll be possible to get me to take an interest in the
affairs of any Jew, Lanny. I don't even care to know about him,
unless I can have your word that you won't tell anybody that you
have told me."

"You certainly can have that, Hugo. I have never mentioned
your name to anyone except my wife, and this time I didn't even
tell her that I was planning to meet you. I've told everybody I was
coming for the purpose of buying some pictures from Baron von
Zinszollern."

On that basis the young Aryan athlete consented to risk having
his mind sullied, and Lanny told him he had positive information
that Freddi was being tortured in Dachau. Lanny intimated that
this news had come to him from high Nazi sources; Hugo accepted
this, knowing well that the rich American had such contacts.
Lanny drew a horrifying picture, using the details which Göring
had furnished him; Hugo, a fundamentally decent fellow, said it
was a shame, and what did they expect to accomplish by such proceedings? Lanny answered that some of the big Nazis had learned
that Lanny's wife had a great deal of money, and were hoping to
get a chunk of it—money they could hide in New York, and have
in case they ever had to take a plane and get out of Germany. Irma

had been on the verge of paying; but Lanny's English friend, Rick, had said No, those men were betraying the Socialist movement of the world, and nobody should furnish them with funds. It had occurred to Lanny that he would rather pay money to some of the honest men in the movement, those who took seriously the second half of the party's name, and would really try to promote the interests of the common man.

In short, if Hugo Behr would spend his vacation helping to get Freddi out of Dachau, Lanny would pay him five thousand marks at the outset, and if he succeeded would pay him another five thousand, in any form and any manner he might desire. Hugo might use the money for the movement he was building, and thus his conscience would be clear. Lanny would be glad to put up whatever additional sums Hugo might find it necessary to expend in order to interest some of the proletarian S.A. men in Dachau in bringing about the escape of a comrade who had the misfortune to have been born a Jew. They, too, might use the money to save National Socialism.

"Oh, Lanny!" exclaimed the young sports director. "That's an awfully serious thing to be trying!"

"I know that well. I've been hesitating and figuring it for a year. But this news about the torturing decided me—I just can't stand it, and I'm willing to run whatever risk I have to. It's something that ought to be stopped, Hugo, and every decent Nazi ought to help me, for the good name of the party. Is that guard you told me about still there?"

"I'd have to make sure."

"I don't ask you to tell me anything you're doing, or thinking of doing. I have complete confidence in your judgment. It'll be up to you to make some friends in the camp and decide who are the right ones to trust. Don't mention me to them, and I won't mention you to anybody, now or later. We'll carry this secret to our graves."

"There'll be the question of getting your man over the border."

"You don't have to bother about that part of it. All I ask is for you to deliver Freddi to me on some dark night at a place agreed upon, and without anybody to stop me or follow me. I don't want to rush you into it—take your time, think it over, and ask me all the questions you want to. Let's have a complete understanding, so that you'll know exactly what you're getting in for, and each of us will know exactly what we're promising."

VII

Hugo did his thinking right there in the car. He said it was a deal; but when Lanny asked him how he wanted his first payment, he was afraid to take the money. He said he wouldn't dare to carry such a sum on his person, and he had no place to hide it; he was a poor man, and had no right to have money, but Lanny, a rich man, did, so keep it for him until the job was done and the danger was over. Lanny said: "I am touched by your confidence."

They worked out their arrangements in detail. Neither would ever visit the other's hotel. When Hugo wanted Lanny he would telephone, and always use the code name of "Boecklin." They agreed upon a certain spot on a well-frequented street, and whenever they were to meet, Lanny would stop at that spot and Hugo would step into the car. They would do all their talking in the car, so there could never be any eavesdropping. All this having been agreed upon, Lanny drove his fellow conspirator to Dachau and left him near the concentration camp, so that he might start getting in touch with his friend.

The art expert telephoned the American consul in Munich. He had taken the precaution to meet that gentleman on his previous visit and to invite him to the Detaze show. Now he took him to dinner, and over a bottle of good wine they chatted about the affairs of Germany and the outside world. Lanny contributed an account of the riots in Paris, and the consul said that this kind of thing proved the need of a strong government, such as Hitler was now furnishing to the German people. The official was sure that the excesses of the *Regierung* had no great significance; National Socialism would soon settle down and get itself on a living basis with the rest of Europe. Lanny found this a sensible point of view, and his conversation showed no faintest trace of Pinkness.

Incidentally he mentioned that he was in Munich to arrange for a picture deal with Baron von Zinszollern. He wondered if the consul knew anything about this gentleman, and his reputation in the community. The reply was that the baron bore an excellent reputation, but of course the consul couldn't say as to his financial situation. Lanny smiled and said: "He is selling, not buying." He knew that the consul would take this inquiry as the purpose for which he had been invited to dine; it was a proper purpose, it being the duty of consuls to assist their fellow countrymen with information. They parted friends, and the official was satisfied that Lanny Budd was in Munich for legitimate reasons, and if later on Lanny should get into any sort of trouble, the representative of his country would have every reason to assist him and vouch for him.

Lanny stayed in his room the rest of the evening and read the *Münchner Neueste Nachrichten* from page one to the end. He learned a little of what was happening in Germany, and still more of what the Nazis wanted the Germans to believe was happening. The Reichsführer was in the Rheinland, attending the wedding of one of his Gauleiter. He was stopping at the Rhein Hotel in Essen, and had visited the Krupp works and conferred with several of the steel magnates. That was in accord with what Hugo had said; and so was the fact that Minister-Präsident General Göring was accompanying him. Flying in the rear cabin in a plane was the best of occasions for one man to whisper into another man's ear; and what was Göring telling Adi about plots against him, and the urgent need to disband the S.A. and avert the "Second Revolution"? Lanny put his imagination to work; for it was a part of his job to point out these things to Hugo and have Hugo pass them on to discontented members of the S.A. in Dachau. From the leading editorial in the newspaper Lanny followed the campaign now going on against those evil persons who were described by the German equivalents of grouches, knockers, and smart Alecks, soreheads, muckrakers, and wet blankets.

VIII

Late at night Lanny was summoned to the telephone. There being none in his room, he went downstairs, and there was the voice of "Boecklin," saying: "Can I see you?" Lanny replied, "*Ja, gewiss*," which in American would have been "Sure thing!"

He went to his car and picked up his friend at the place agreed upon. "Well," said Hugo, "I believe it can be arranged."

"Oh, good!" exclaimed the other.

"I promised not to name any names, and there's no need of your knowing the details, I suppose."

"None in the world. I just want to know that I can come to a certain place and pick up my friend."

"There's only one trouble: I'm afraid it will cost a lot of money. You see, it can't be done by a common guard. Somebody higher up has to consent."

"What do you think it will cost?"

"About twenty thousand marks. I can't be sure what will be demanded; it might be twenty-five or thirty thousand before we get through."

"That's all right, Hugo; I can afford it. I'll get the cash and give it to you whenever you say."

"The job ought to be put through as soon as it's agreed upon. The longer we wait, the more chance of somebody's talking."

"Absolutely. I have certain arrangements to make, and it's hard for me to know exactly how long it will take, but I'm pretty sure I can be ready by Friday night. Would that be all right?"

"So far as I can guess."

"If something went wrong with my plans I might have to put it off till Saturday. Whenever you are ready for the money, you have to let me know before the bank closes."

All this was assented to; and after dropping his friend on a quiet street Lanny went to one of the large hotels where he would find a telephone booth, and there put in a call for Jerry Pendleton, Pension Flavin, Cannes. It takes time to achieve such a feat in

Europe, but he waited patiently, and at last heard his old pal's sleepy voice.

Lanny said: "The Detazes are ready, and I'm waiting in Munich for you. I am buying some others, and want to close the deal and move them on Friday. Do you think you can get here then?"

"By heck!" said Jerry. It was Wednesday midnight, and his voice came suddenly awake. "I can't get visas until morning."

"You can hunt up the consul tonight and pay him extra."

"I'll have to go and make sure about Cyprien first." That was a nephew of Leese, who did truck-driving for Bienvenu.

"All right, get him or somebody else. Make note of my address, and phone me at noon tomorrow and again late in the evening, letting me know where you are. Come by way of Verona and the Brenner, and don't let anything keep you from being here. If you should have a breakdown, let Cyprien come with the truck, and you take a train, or a plane if you have to. I have somebody here I want you to meet on Friday."

"O.K." said the ex-tutor and ex-soldier; he sort of sang it, with the accent on the first syllable, and it was like a signature over the telephone.

IX

Baron von Zinszollern possessed an Anton Mauve, a large and generous work portraying a shepherd leading home his flock in a pearly gray and green twilight. It seemed to Lanny a fine example of that painter's poetical and serious feeling, and he had got the price down to thirty thousand marks. He had telegraphed Zoltan that he was disposed to buy it as a gamble, and did his friend care to go halves? His friend replied Yes, so he went that morning and bought the work, paying two thousand marks down and agreeing to pay the balance within a week. This involved signing papers, which Lanny would have on his person; also, an influential Nazi sympathizer would have an interest in testifying that he was really an art expert. Incidentally it gave Lanny a pretext for going to the Munich branch of the Hellstein Bank, and having them pay him thirty thousand marks in Nazi paper.

At noon the dependable Jerry telephoned. He and Cyprien and the *camion* were past Genoa. They would eat and sleep on board, and keep moving. Lanny told him to telephone about ten in the evening wherever they were. Jerry sang: "O.K."

A little later came a call from "Boecklin," and Lanny took him for a drive. He said: "It's all fixed. You're to pay twenty-three thousand marks, and your man will be delivered to you anywhere in Dachau at twenty-two o'clock tomorrow evening. Will you be ready?"

"I'm pretty sure to. Here's your money." Lanny took out his wallet, and handed it to his friend beside him. "Help yourself."

It was improbable that Hugo Behr, son of a shipping clerk, had ever had so much money in his hands before. The hands trembled slightly as he took out the bundle of crisp new banknotes, each for one thousand marks; he counted out twenty-three of them, while Lanny went on driving and didn't seem to be especially interested. Hugo counted them a second time, both times out loud.

"You'd better take your own, also," suggested the lordly one. "You know I might get into some trouble."

"If you do, I'd rather be able to say you hadn't paid me anything. I'm doing it purely for friendship's sake, and because you're a friend of Heinrich and Kurt."

"Lay all the emphasis you can on them!" chuckled Lanny. "Mention that Heinrich told you how he had taken Kurt and me to visit the Führer last winter; and also that I told you about taking a hunting trip with Göring. So you were sure I must be all right."

Hugo had got some news about Freddi which the other heard gladly. Apparently Lanny had been right in what he had said about the Jewish prisoner; he had won the respect even of those who were trying to crush him. Unfortunately he was in the hands of the Gestapo, which kept him apart from the regular run of inmates. A prison inside the prison, it appeared! The rumor was that they had been trying to force Freddi to reveal the names of certain

Social-Democrats who were operating an illegal press in Berlin; but he insisted that he knew nothing about it.

"He wouldn't be apt to know," said Lanny. To himself he added: "Trudi Schultz!"

It had been his intention to make a casual remark to his friend: "Oh, by the way, I wonder if you could find out if there's a man in Dachau by the name of Ludwig Schultz." But now he realized that it was not so simple as he had thought. To tell Hugo that he was trying to help another of the dreaded "Marxists" might sour him on the whole deal. And for Hugo to tell his friends in the concentration camp might have the same effect upon them. Lanny could do nothing for poor Trudi—at least not this trip.

X

He drove the car to Dachau, and they rolled about its streets, to decide upon a spot which would be dark and quiet. They learned the exact description of this place, so that Hugo could tell it to the men who were going to bring Freddi. Hugo said he had an appointment to pay the money to a man in Munich at twenty o'clock, or 8:00 p.m. according to the American way of stating it. Hugo was nervous about wandering around with such an unthinkable sum in his pocket, so Lanny drove him up into the hills, where they looked at beautiful scenery. The American quoted: "Where every prospect pleases and only man is vile." He didn't translate it for his German friend.

Hugo had been talking to some of his party comrades in Munich, the birthplace of their movement, and had picked up news which didn't get into the *gleichgeschaltete Presse*. There was a terrible state of tension in the party; everybody appeared to be quarreling with everybody else. Göring and Goebbels were at daggers drawn over the question of controlling policy—which, Lanny understood, meant controlling Hitler's mind. Goebbels had announced a program of compelling industry to share profits with the workers, and this, of course, was criminal to Göring and his friends the industrialists. Just recently von Papen, still a Reichsminister, had made a speech demanding freedom of the press to discuss all public questions, and Göring had intervened and forbidden the publication of this speech. A day or two ago the man who was said to have written the speech for the "gentleman jockey" had been arrested in Munich, and the town was buzzing with gossip about the quarrel. It was rumored that a hundred and fifty of Goebbels's personal guards had mutinied and been sent to a concentration camp. All sorts of wild tales like this, and who knew what to believe?

They had come to the Tegernsee, a lovely mountain lake, and there was a road-sign, reading: "Bad Wiessee, 7 km." Hugo said: "The papers report that Röhm is having his vacation there. I hear he's had several conferences with the Führer in the past week or two, and they've had terrible rows."

"What's the trouble between them?" inquired the gossip-hungry visitor.

"The same old story. Röhm and his friends want the original party program carried out. Now, of course, he's wild over the idea of having his Stormtroopers disbanded."

Lanny could credit the latter motive, if not the former. He had heard the red-headed Chief of Staff speak at one of the Nazi *Versammlungen*, and had got the impression of an exceedingly tough military adventurer, untroubled by social ideals. Perhaps that was due in part to his battle-scars, the upper part of his nose having been shot away! Röhm wanted the powers of his Brownshirts increased, and naturally would fight desperately against having them wiped out.

Seven kilometers was nothing, so Lanny turned his car in the direction indicated by the sign. A lovely little village with tree-shaded streets, and cottages on the lakefront. In front of one of the largest, and also of the Gasthaus Heinzlbauer, were parked a great many fancy cars. Hugo said: "They must be having a conference. Only our leaders can afford cars like those." The note of bitterness indicated that he didn't trust his new Führer much more than his old.

"Do you know him?" asked Lanny.

"I know one of the staff members in Berlin, and he has told the Chief that I am working on his behalf."

"Would you like to go in and meet him?"

"Do *you* know him?" countered Hugo, startled.

"No; but I thought he might be interested to meet an American art expert."

"*Aber,* Lanny!" exclaimed the young sports director, whose sense of humor was not his strongest suit. "I really don't think he has much time to think about art right now!"

"He might take a fancy to a magnificent young athlete like yourself, Hugo."

"*Gott behüte!*" was the reply.

It seemed almost blasphemy to talk about this subject while under the shadow of Röhm and his entourage; but when the American put the question point blank, Hugo admitted that he had heard about the habits of the Sturmabteilung Chief of Staff. Everybody in Germany knew about them, for Hauptmann Röhm, while acting as a military instructor in Bolivia, had written a series of letters home admitting his abnormal tastes, and these letters had been published in the German press. Now, said Hugo, his enemies gave that as the reason for not taking him and his staff into the regular army. "As if the Reichswehr officers were lily-white saints!" exclaimed the S.A. man.

XI

Back in the city, Lanny took a long walk in the Englischer Garten, going over his plans and trying to make all possible mistakes in advance. Then he went back and read the co-ordinated newspapers, and picked up hints of the struggle going on—you could find them if you were an insider. It looked very much as if the N.S.D.A.P. was going to split itself to pieces. Lanny was tempted by the idea that if he waited a few days, Freddi Robin might come out from Dachau with a brass band leading the way!

At the appointed hour Jerry Pendleton called; he was rolling on, and all was well. It was slow on the mountain roads, but he thought he could make it by noon the next day. "What is the deadline?" he asked, and Lanny replied: "Two o'clock." Jerry sang: "O.K." and Lanny lay down and tried to sleep, but found it difficult, because he kept imagining himself in the hands of the Gestapo, who had prisons inside of prisons. What would he say? And more important yet, what would they do?

Next morning the conspirator received a telephone call from "Herr Boecklin," and drove to meet his friend and receive some bad news; one of the men concerned was demanding more money, because the thing was so very dangerous. Lanny asked how much, and the answer was, another five thousand marks. Lanny said all right, he would get it at once; but Hugo wanted to change the arrangement. He hadn't paid out the money, and wanted to refuse to pay more than half until the prisoner was actually delivered. His idea now was to drive to Dachau with Lanny at the appointed time, and to keep watch near by. If Freddi was produced and everything seemed all right, he would emerge and pay the rest of the money.

Lanny said: "That's a lot more dangerous for you, Hugo."

"Not so very," was the reply. "I'm sure it's not a trap; but if it were, they could get me anyhow. What I want to do is to keep you from paying the money and then not getting your man."

XII

Lanny went back to his hotel and waited until early afternoon, on pins and needles. At last came a telephone call; Jerry Pendleton was at the hotel in Munich to which Lanny had told him to come. "Everything hunkydory, not a scratch."

Lanny said: "Be out on the street; I'll pick you up."

"Give me ten minutes to shave and change my shirt," countered the ex-lieutenant from Kansas.

Delightful indeed to set eyes on somebody from home; somebody who could be trusted, and who didn't say "Heil Hitler!" The ex-lieutenant was over forty, his red hair was losing its sheen and he had put on some weight; but to Lanny he was still America, prompt, efficient, and full of what it called "pep," "zip," and "ginger." A lady's man all his life, Lanny was still impressed by the masculine type, with hair on its chest. Though he would have died before admitting it, he was both lonely and scared in Naziland.

Driving in the traffic of the Ludwigstrasse, he couldn't look at his ex-tutor, but he said: "Gee whiz, Jerry, you're a sight for sore eyes!"

"The same to you, kid!"

"You won't be so glad of my company when you hear what I'm in this town for."

"Why, what's the matter? I thought you were buying pictures."

"I am buying Freddi Robin out of the Dachau concentration camp."

"Jesus Christ!" exclaimed Jerry.

"He's to be delivered to me at ten o'clock tonight, and you've got to help me smuggle him out of this goddam Nazi country!"

27

A Deed of Dreadful Note

I

JERRY had known that Freddi Robin was a prisoner in Germany, but hadn't known where or why or how. Now, in the car, safe from eavesdroppers, Lanny told the story and expounded his plan. He was proposing to take his own photograph from his passport and substitute that of Freddi Robin which he had brought with him. Then he would pick up Freddi in Dachau, drive to some other part of the town and get Jerry, and let Jerry drive Freddi out of Germany under the name of Lanning Prescott Budd. Such was the genial scheme.

"At first," Lanny explained, "I had the idea of fixing up your passport for Freddi to use, and I would drive him out. But I realized, there's very little danger in the driving part—the passports will be all right, and once you get clear of Dachau everything will be O.K. But the fellow who's left behind without a passport may have a bit of trouble; so that's why I'm offering you the driving part."

"But, my God!" cried the bewildered Kansan. "Just what do you expect to do about getting out?"

"I'll go to the American consul and tell him my passport has been stolen. I have made friends with him and he'll probably give me some sort of duplicate. If he won't, it'll be up to me to find a way to sneak out by some of the mountain passes."

"But, Lanny, you're out of your mind! In the first place, the moment Freddi's escape is discovered they'll know he's heading for the Austrian border, and they'll block the passes."

"It'll take you only an hour or two to get to the border from Dachau, and you'll be over and gone. You're to drive my car, understand, not the *camion*."

"But there will be the record of the Lanny Budd passport and of mine at the border."

"What then? They'll draw the conclusion that you are the man who stole my passport. But it's not an extraditable offense."

"They'll know it was a put-up job! You're the brother-in-law of Freddi's brother and you've been trying to get him released. It'll be obvious that you gave me your papers."

"They won't have a particle of evidence to prove it."

"They'll sweat it out of you, Lanny. I tell you, it's a bum steer! I could never look your mother or your father or your wife in the face if I let you put your foot into such a trap." As ex-tutor, Jerry spoke for the family.

"But I have to get Freddi out of Germany!" insisted the ex-pupil. "I've been a year making up my mind to that."

"All right, kid; but go back to your original idea. *You* steal *my* passport and drive Freddi out."

"And leave you in the hole?"

"That's not nearly so bad, because I'm not related to the prisoner and I'm not known. I'm a fellow you hired to get your paintings, and you played a dirty trick on me and left me stuck. I can put up a howl about it and stick to my story."

"They'd sweat you instead of me, Jerry."

So the two argued back and forth; an "Alphonse and Gaston" scene, but deadly serious. Meanwhile the precious time was passing in which exit permits and visas had to be got. There appeared to be a deadlock—until suddenly an inspiration came to the ex-tutor. "Let's both go out with Freddi, and leave Cyprien to face the music. I'll steal *his* passport in earnest."

"That would be a rotten deal, Jerry."

"Not so bad as it seems. Cyprien's a French peasant, who obviously wouldn't have the brains to think up anything. He'll be in a rage with us, and put on a fine act. I'll get him loaded up with good Munich beer and he'll be smelling of it when the police come for him. When we get to France you can telegraph some money to the French consul here and tell him to look after his own. When Cyprien gets home with his truck you can give him a few thousand francs and he'll think it was the great adventure of his life."

Lanny didn't like that plan, but his friend settled it with an argument which Lanny hadn't thought of. "Believe me, Freddi Robin looks a lot more like the name Cyprien Santoze than like the name Lanning Prescott Budd!" Then, seeing Lanny weakening: "Come on! Let's get going!"

II

Jerry took the truckman to get their exit permits and to have their passports "visaed" for Switzerland—he thought it better not to trust themselves in Mussolini's land. Lanny went separately and did the same, while Jerry treated Cyprien to a square meal, including plenty of good Munich beer. The Frenchman, who hadn't grown up as saintly as his mother had named him, drank everything that was put before him, and then wanted to go out and inspect the girls of thirteen years and up who were offering themselves in such numbers on the streets of Munich. His escort said: "Those girls sometimes pick your pockets, so you'd better give me your papers to keep." The other accepted this as a reasonable precaution.

Lanny drove his friend out to Dachau to study the lay of the land. He pointed out the spot where the prisoner was to be delivered, and made certain that Jerry knew the street names and landmarks. It was the Kansan's intention to "scout around," so he said; he would find a place from which he could watch the spot and see that everything went off according to schedule. Hugo would be doing the same thing, and Lanny wasn't at liberty to tell Jerry about Hugo or Hugo about Jerry. It sufficed to warn his friend that there would be a Nazi officer watching, and Jerry said: "I'll watch *him*, too!"

One serious difficulty, so far as concerned the ex-tutor, and that was, he knew only a few words of German. He said: "Tell me, how do you say: 'Hands up!'?"

Lanny answered: "What are you thinking about, idiot? Have you got a gun?"

"Who? Me? Who ever heard of me carrying a gun?" This from one who had been all through the Meuse-Argonne in the autumn of 1918!

"You mustn't try any rough stuff, Jerry. Remember, murder is an extraditable offense."

"Sure, I know," responded the other. "They extradited a couple of million of us. You remember, the A.E.F., the American Extraditable Force!" It was the old doughboy spirit.

Lanny knew that Jerry owned a Budd automatic, and it was likely he had brought it along with him in the truck. But he wouldn't say any more about it; he just wanted to learn to say: "*Hände hoch!*"

They studied the map. They would drive north out of Dachau,

then make a circle and head south, skirt the city of Munich and streak for the border. When they had got the maps fixed in mind, they went over the streets of Dachau, noting the landmarks, so as to make no mistake in the dark. All this done, they drove back to Munich and had a late supper in a quiet tavern, and then Jerry went to his hotel. There were a few things he didn't want to leave behind, and one or two letters he wanted to destroy. "I didn't know I was embarking upon a criminal career," he said, with a grin.

At the proper hour he met his pal on the street and was motored out to Dachau and dropped there. It was dark by then, a lovely summer evening, and the people of this workingclass district were sitting in front of their homes. Lanny said: "You'll have to keep moving so as not to attract attention. See you later, old scout!" He spoke with assurance, but didn't feel it inside!

III

Back in Munich, the playboy drove past the spot where he was accustomed to meet Hugo, in front of a tobacco shop on a well-frequented street. Darkness had fallen, but the street was lighted. Lanny didn't see his friend, and knowing that he was ahead of time, drove slowly around the block. When he turned the corner again, he saw his friend not far ahead of him, walking toward the appointed spot.

There was a taxicab proceeding in the same direction, some thirty or forty feet behind Hugo, going slowly and without lights. Lanny waited for it to pass on; but the driver appeared to be looking for a street number. So Lanny went ahead of it and drew up by the curb, where Hugo saw him and started to join him. Lanny leaned over to open the door on the right side of the car; and at the same moment the taxicab stopped alongside Lanny's car. Three men sprang out, wearing the black shirts and trousers and steel helmets of the Schutzstaffel. One of them stood staring at Lanny, while the other two darted behind Lanny's car and confronted the young sports director in the act of putting his hand on the car door.

"Are you Hugo Behr?" demanded one of the men.

"I am," was the reply.

Lanny turned to look at the questioner; but the man's next action was faster than any eye could follow. He must have had a gun in his hand behind his back; he swung it up and fired straight into the face in front of him, and not more than a foot away. Pieces of the blue eye of Hugo Behr and a fine spray of his Aryan blood flew out, and some hit Lanny in the face. The rest of Hugo Behr crumpled and dropped to the sidewalk; whereupon the man turned his gun into the horrified face of the driver.

"*Hände hoch!*" he commanded; and that was certainly turning the tables upon Lanny. He put them high.

"*Wer sind Sie?*" demanded the S.S. man.

It was a time for the quickest possible answers, and Lanny was fortunate in having thought up the best possible. "I am an American art expert, and a friend of the Führer."

"Oh! So you're a friend of the Führer!"

"I have visited him several times. I spent a morning with him in the Braune Haus a few months ago."

"How do you come to know Hugo Behr?"

"I was introduced to him in the home of Heinrich Jung, a high official of the Hitler Jugend in Berlin. Heinrich is one of the Führer's oldest friends and visited him many times when he was in the Landsberg fortress. It was Heinrich who introduced me to the Führer." Lanny rattled this off as if it were a school exercise; and indeed it was something like that, for he had imagined interrogations and had learned his *Rolle* in the very best German. Since the S.S. man didn't tell him to stop, he went on, as fast as ever: "Also on the visit to the Reichsführer in the Braune Haus went Kurt Meissner of Schloss Stubendorf, who is a Komponist and author of several part-songs which you sing at your assemblies. He has known me since we were boys at Hellerau, and will tell you that I am a friend of the National Socialist movement."

That was the end of the speech, so far as Lanny had planned it. But even as he said the last words a horrible doubt smote him: Perhaps this was some sort of anti-Nazi revolution, and he was sealing his own doom! He saw that the point of the gun had come down, and the muzzle was looking into his navel instead of into his face; but that wasn't enough to satisfy him. He stared at the S.S. man, who had black eyebrows that met over his nose. It seemed to Lanny the hardest face he had ever examined.

"What were you doing with this man?"—nodding downward toward what lay on the pavement.

"I am in Munich buying a painting from Baron von Zinszollern. I saw Hugo Behr walking on the street and I stopped to say *Grüss Gott* to him." Lanny was speaking impromptu now.

"Get out of the car," commanded the S.S. man.

Lanny's heart was hitting hard blows underneath his throat; his knees were trembling so violently he wasn't sure they would hold him up. It appeared that he was being ordered out so that his blood and brains might not spoil a good car. "I tell you, you will regret it if you shoot me. I am an intimate friend of Minister-Präsident General Göring. I was on a hunting trip with him last fall. You can ask Oberleutnant Furtwaengler of Seine Exzellenz's staff. You can ask Reichsminister Goebbels about me—or his wife, Frau Magda Goebbels—I have visited their home. You can read articles about me in the Munich newspapers of last November when I conducted an exhibition of paintings here and took one of them to the Führer. My picture was in all the papers——"

"I am not going to shoot you," announced the S.S. man. His tone indicated abysmal contempt of anybody who objected to being shot.

"What are you going to do?"

"Take you to Stadelheim until your story is investigated. Get out of the car."

Stadelheim was a name of terror; one of those dreadful prisons about which the refugees talked. But it was better than being shot on the sidewalk, so Lanny managed to control his nerves, and obeyed. The other man passed his hands over him to see if he was armed. Then the leader commanded him to search the body of Hugo, and he collected a capful of belongings including a wad of bills which Lanny knew amounted to some fifteen thousand marks.

Apparently they meant to leave the corpse right there, and Lanny wondered, did they have a corpse-collecting authority, or did they leave it to the neighborhood?

However, he didn't have much time for speculation. "Get into the back seat," commanded the leader and climbed in beside him, still holding the gun on him. The man who had got out on Lanny's side of the car now slipped into the driver's seat, and the car sprang to life and sped down the street.

I V

Lanny had seen Stadelheim from the outside; a great mass of buildings on a tree-lined avenue, the Tegernsee road upon which he had driven Hugo Behr. Now the walls of the place loomed enormous and forbidding in the darkness. Lanny was ordered out of the car, and two of his captors escorted him through the doorway, straight past the reception room, and down a stone corridor into a small room. He had expected to be "booked" and fingerprinted; but apparently this was to be dispensed with. They ordered him to take off his coat, trousers, and shoes, and proceeded to search him. "There is considerable money in that wallet," he said, and the leader replied, grimly: "We will take care of it." They took his watch, keys, fountain-pen, necktie, everything but his handkerchief. They searched the linings of his clothing, and looked carefully to see if there were any signs that the heels of his shoes might be removable.

Finally they told him to put his clothes on again. Lanny said: "Would you mind telling me what I am suspected of?" The reply of the leader was: "*Maul halten!*" Apparently they didn't believe his wonder-tales about being the intimate friend of the three leading Nazis. Not wishing to get a knock over the head with a revolver butt, Lanny held his mouth, as ordered, and was escorted out of the room and down the corridor to a guarded steel door.

The head S.S. man appeared to have the run of the place; all he had to do was to salute and say: "*Heil Hitler!*" and all doors were swung open for him. He led the prisoner down a narrow flight of stone stairs, into a passage dimly lighted and lined with steel doors.

Old prisons have such places of darkness and silence, where deeds without a name have been done. A warder who accompanied the trio opened one of these doors, and Lanny was shoved in without a word. The door clanged behind him; and that, as he had learned to say in the land of his fathers, was that.

V

In the darkness he could only explore the place by groping. The cell was narrow and had an iron cot built into the stone wall. On the cot were two sacks of straw and a blanket. In the far corner was a stinking pail without a cover; and that was all. There was a vile, age-old odor, and no window; ventilation was provided by two openings in the solid door, one high and one low; they could be closed by sliding covers on the outside, but perhaps this would be done only if Lanny misbehaved. He didn't.

He was permitted to sit on the straw sacks and think, and he did his best to quiet the tumult of his heart and use his reasoning powers. What had happened? It seemed obvious that his plot had been discovered. Had the would-be conspirators been caught, or had they taken the money and then reported the plot to their superiors? And if so, would they shoot Freddi? No use worrying about that now. Lanny couldn't be of any use to Freddi unless he himself got out, so he had to put his mind on his own plight, and prepare for the examination which was bound sooner or later to come.

Hugo's part in the jailbreak had evidently been betrayed; but Hugo had never named Lanny, so he had said. Of course this might or might not have been true. They had found a bunch of thousand-mark notes on Hugo, and they had found some on Lanny; suddenly the prisoner realized, with a near collapse of his insides, what a stupid thing he had done. The clue which a criminal always leaves! He had gone to the bank and got thirty new thousand-mark bills, doubtless having consecutive serial numbers, and had given some of these to Hugo and kept some in his own wallet!

So they would be sure that he had tried to buy a prisoner out of Dachau. What would the penalty be for that crime? What it would

have been under the old regime was one thing, and under the Nazis
something else again. As if to answer his question there came terrifying sounds, muffled yet unmistakable; first, a roll of drums, and
then shooting somewhere in those dungeon depths or else outside
the walls. Not a single shot, not a series of shots, but a volley, a
closely-packed bunch of shots. They were executing somebody, or
perhaps several bodies. Lanny, who had started to his feet, had to
sit down again because his legs were giving way.

Who would that be? The S.A. man in Dachau with whom Hugo
had been dealing? The man higher up who had demanded more
money? The plot must have been betrayed early, for it couldn't be
much after ten o'clock, and there had hardly been time for the
jailbreak to have been attempted and the guilty parties brought from
Dachau to this prison. Of course it might be that this was some
execution that had nothing to do with Dachau. Shootings were
frequent in Nazi prisons, all refugees agreed. Perhaps they shot
people every night at twenty-two o'clock, German time!

After the most careful thought, Lanny decided that the Nazis
had him nailed down; no chance of wriggling out. He had come
to Germany to get Freddi Robin, and the picture-dealing had been
only a blind. He had had a truck brought from France—they would
be sure he had meant to take Freddi out in that truck! And there
was Jerry—with two one-thousand-mark bills which Lanny had
handed him! Also with the passport of Cyprien Santoze, having the
picture of Freddi Robin substituted! Would they catch the meaning
of that?

Or would Jerry perhaps get away? He would be walking about,
passing the appointed spot, waiting for the prisoner and for Lanny
to appear. Would the Nazis be watching and arrest anybody who
passed? It was an important question, for if Jerry escaped he'd
surely go to the American consul and report Lanny as missing.
Would he tell the consul the whole truth? He might or he might
not; but anyhow the consul would be making inquiries as to the
son of Budd Gunmakers.

VI

More drum-rolls and more shooting! Good God, were they killing people all night in German prisons? Apparently so; for that was
the way Lanny spent the night, listening to volleys, long or short,
loud or dim. He couldn't tell whether they were inside or out. Did
they have a special execution chamber, or did they just shoot you
anywhere you happened to be? And what did they do with all the
blood? Lanny imagined that he smelled it, and the fumes of gun-
powder; but maybe he was mistaken, for the stink of a rusty old
slop-pail can be extremely pungent in a small cell. An art expert
had seen many pictures of executions, ancient and modern, so he
knew what to imagine. Sometimes they blindfolded the victims,
sometimes they made them turn their backs, sometimes they just
put an automatic to the base of their skulls, the medulla; that was
said to be merciful, and certainly it was quick. The Nazis cared
nothing about mercy, but they surely did about speed.

Every now and then a door clanged, and Lanny thought: "They
are taking somebody to his doom." Now and then he heard footsteps, and thought: "Are they coming or going?" He wondered
about the bodies. Did they have stretchers? Or did they just drag
them? He imagined that he heard dragging. Several times there were
screams; and once a man going by his door, arguing, shouting pro-
tests. What was the matter with them? He was as good a Nazi as
anyone in Germany. They were making a mistake. It was *eine gott-
verdammte Schande*—and so on. That gave Lanny something new
to think about, and he sat for a long time motionless on his straw
pallet, with his brain in a whirl.

Maybe all this hadn't anything to do with Freddi and a jailbreak!
Maybe nothing had been discovered at all! It was that "Second
Revolution" that Hugo had been so freely predicting! Hugo
had been shot, not because he had tried to bribe a Dachau guard,
but because he was on the list of those who were actively working
on behalf of Ernst Röhm and the other malcontents of the Sturmabteilung! In that case the shootings might be part of the putting
down of that movement. It was significant that Lanny's captors had

been men of the Schutzstaffel, the "élite guard," Hitler's own chosen ones. They were putting their rivals out of business; "liquidating" those who had been demanding more power for the S.A. Chief of Staff!

But then, a still more startling possibility—the executions might mean the success of the rebels. The fact that Hugo Behr had been killed didn't mean that the S.S. had had their way everywhere. Perhaps the S.A. were defending themselves successfully! Perhaps Stadelheim had been taken, as the Bastille had been taken in the French revolution, and the persons now being shot were those who had put Lanny in here! At any moment the doors of his cell might be thrown open and he might be welcomed with comradely rejoicing!

Delirious imaginings; but then the whole thing was a delirium. To lie there in the darkness with no way to count the hours and nothing to do but speculate about a world full of maniacal murderers. Somebody was killing somebody, that alone was certain, and it went on at intervals without any sign of ending. Lanny remembered the French revolution, and the unhappy aristocrats who had lain in their cells awaiting their turn to be loaded into the tumbrils and carted to the guillotine. This kind of thing was said to turn people's hair gray over night; Lanny wondered if it was happening to him. Every time he heard footsteps he hoped it was somebody coming to let him out; but then he was afraid to have the footsteps halt, because it might be a summons to the execution chamber!

He tried to comfort himself. He had had no part in any conspiracy of the S.A. and surely they wouldn't shoot him just because he had met a friend on the street. But then he thought: "Those banknotes!" They would attach a still more sinister meaning to them now. They would say: "What were you paying Hugo Behr to do?" And what should he answer? He had said that he hadn't known what Hugo wanted of him. They would know that was a lie. They would say: "You were helping to promote a revolution against the N.S.D.A.P." And that was surely a shooting offense— even though you had come from the sweet land of liberty to do it!

Lanny thought up the best way to meet this very bad situation.

When he was questioned, he would talk about his friendship with the great and powerful, and wait to pick up any hint that the questioner had made note of the bills, or had found out about Freddi Robin. If these discoveries had been made, Lanny would laugh—at least he would try to laugh—and say: "Yes, of course I lied to those S.S. men on the street. I thought they were crazy and were going to shoot me. The truth is that Hugo Behr came to me and asked for money and offered to use his influence with the S.A. in Dachau to get my friend released. There was no question of any bribe, he said he would put the money into the party funds and it would go for the winter relief." One thing Lanny could be sure of in this matter—nothing that he said about Hugo could do the slightest harm to the young sports director.

VII

Footsteps in the corridor; a slot at the bottom of Lanny's door was widened, and something was set inside. He said, quickly: "Will you please tell me how long I am to be kept here?" When there was no reply, he said: "I am an American citizen and I demand the right to communicate with my consul." The slot was made smaller again and the footsteps went on.

Lanny felt with his hands and found a metal pitcher of water, a cup of warm liquid, presumably coffee, and a chunk of rather stale bread. He wasn't hungry, but drank some of the water. Presumably that was breakfast, and it was morning. He lay and listened to more shooting off and on; and after what seemed a very long time the slot was opened and more food put in. Out of curiosity he investigated, and found that he had a plate of what appeared to be cold potatoes mashed up with some sort of grease. The grease must have been rancid, for the smell was revolting, and Lanny came near to vomiting at the thought of eating it. He had been near to vomiting several times at the thought of people being shot in this dungeon of horrors.

A bowl of cabbage soup and more bread were brought in what he assumed was the evening; and this time the warder spoke. He said:

"Pass out your slop-pail." Lanny did so, and it was emptied and passed back to him without washing. This sign of humanity caused him to make a little speech about his troubles. He said that he had done nothing, that he had no idea what he was accused of, that it was very inhuman to keep a man in a dark hole, that he had always been a lover of Germany and a sympathizer with its struggle against the Versailles *Diktat*. Finally, he was an American citizen, and had a right to notify his consul of his arrest.

This time he managed to get one sentence of reply: "*Sprechen verboten, mein Herr.*" It sounded like a kind voice, and Lanny recalled what he had heard, that many of the permanent staff of these prisons were men of the former regime, well disciplined and humane. He took a chance and ventured in a low voice: "I am a rich man, and if you will telephone the American consul for me, I will pay you well when I get out."

"*Sprechen verboten, mein Herr,*" replied the voice; and then, much lower: "*Sprechen Sie leise.*" Speaking is forbidden, sir; speak softly! So the prisoner whispered: "My name is Lanny Budd." He repeated it several times: "Lanny Budd, Lanny Budd." It became a little song. Would that it might have wings, and fly to the American consulate!

VIII

For three days and four nights Lanny Budd stayed in that narrow cell. He could estimate the number of cubic feet of air inside, but he didn't know what percentage of that air was oxygen, or how much he needed per hour in order to maintain his life. His scientific education had been neglected, but it seemed a wise precaution to put his straw sacks on the floor and lie on them with his mouth near the breathing hole.

Saturday, Sunday, Monday—he could tell them by the meal hours —and during a total of some eighty-two hours there were not a dozen without sounds of shooting. He never got over his dismay. God Almighty, did they do this all the time? Had this been going on ever since the National Socialist revolution, one year and five months ago? Did they bring all the political suspects of Bavaria to

this one place? Or was this some special occasion, a Nazi St. Bartholomew's Eve? "Kill them all; God will be able to pick out His
Christians!"

Lanny, having nothing to do but think, had many and varied
ideas. One was: "Well, they are all Nazis, and if they exterminate
one another, that will save the world a lot of trouble." But then:
"Suppose they should open the wrong cell door?" An embarrassing
thought indeed! What would he say? How would he convince
them? As time passed he decided: "They have forgotten me. Those
fellows didn't book me, and maybe they just went off without a
word." And then, a still more confusing possibility: "Suppose they
get shot somewhere and nobody remembers me!" He had a vague
memory of having read about a forgotten prisoner in the Bastille;
when the place was opened up, nobody knew why he had been put
there. He had had a long gray beard. Lanny felt the beginnings of
his beard and wondered if it was gray.

He gave serious study to his jailers and their probable psychology.
It seemed difficult to believe that men who had followed such an
occupation for many years could have any human kindness left in
their systems; but it could do no harm to make sure. So at every
meal hour he was lying on the floor close to the hole, delivering a
carefully planned speech in a quiet, friendly tone, explaining who
he was, and how much he loved the German people, and why he
had come to Munich, and by what evil accident he had fallen under
suspicion. All he wanted was a chance to explain himself to somebody. He figured that if he didn't touch the heart of any of the
keepers, he might at least get them to gossiping, and the gossip
might spread.

IX

He didn't know how long a person could live without food. It
wasn't until the second day that he began to suffer from hunger,
and he gnawed some of the soggy dark bread, wondering what was
in it. He couldn't bring himself to eat the foul-smelling mash or the
lukewarm boiled cabbage with grease on top. As for the bitter-
tasting drink that passed for coffee, he had been told that they put

sal soda into it in order to reduce the sexual cravings of the prisoners. He didn't feel any craving except to get out of this black hole. He whispered to his keepers: "I had about six thousand marks on me when I was brought in here, and I would be glad to pay for some decent food." The second time he said this he heard the kind voice, which he imagined coming from an elderly man with a wrinkled face and gray mustaches. "*Alles geht d'runter und d'rüber, mein Herr.*" . . . "Everything topsy-turvy, sir; and you will be safer if you stay quiet."

It was a tip; and Lanny thought it over and decided that he had better take it. There was a civil war going on. Was the "Second Revolution" succeeding, or was it being put down? In either case, an American art lover, trapped between the firing lines, was lucky to have found a shell-hole in which to hide! Had the warder been a Cockney, he would have said: "If you knows of a better 'ole, go to it!"

So Lanny lay still and occupied himself with the subject of psychology, which so far in his life he had rather neglected. The world had been too much with him; getting and spending he had laid waste his powers. But now the world had been reduced to a few hundred cubic feet, and all he had was the clothes on his back and what ideas he had stored in his head. He began to recall Parsifal Dingle, and to appreciate his point of view. Parsifal wouldn't have minded being here; he would have taken it as a rare opportunity to meditate. Lanny thought: "What would Parsifal meditate about?" Surely not the shooting, or the fate of a hypothetical revolution! No, he would say that God was in this cell; that God was the same indoors as out, the same yesterday, today, and forever.

Then Lanny thought about Freddi Robin. Freddi had been in places like this, and had had the same sort of food put before him, not for three days but for more than a year. What had he said to himself all that time? What had he found inside himself? What had he done and thought, to pass the time, to enable him to endure what came and the anticipation of what might come? It seemed time for Lanny to investigate his store of moral forces.

X

On Tuesday morning two jailers came to his cell and opened the door. " *'Raus, 'raus!*" they said, and he obeyed to the best of his ability; he was weak from lack of food and exercise—not having dared to use up the air in that cell. Also his heart was pounding, because all the psychology exercises had failed to remove his disinclination to be shot, or the idea that this might be his death march. Outside the cell he went dizzy, and had to lean against the wall; one of the jailers helped him up the flight of stone stairs.

They were taking him toward an outside door. They were going to turn him loose!—so he thought, for one moment. But then he saw, below the steps, a prison van—what in America is called "Black Maria," and in Germany "Grüne Minna." The sunlight smote Lanny's eyes like a blow, and he had to shut them tight. The jailers evidently were familiar with this phenomenon; they led him as if he were a blind man and helped him as if he were a cripple. They put him into the van, and he stumbled over the feet of several other men.

The doors were closed, and then it was mercifully dim. Lanny opened his eyes; since they had been brought to the condition of an owl's, he could see a stoutish, melancholy-looking gentleman who might be a businessman, sitting directly across the aisle. At Lanny's side was an eager little Jew with eyeglasses, who might be a journalist out of luck. Lanny, never failing in courtesy, remarked: "*Guten Morgen*"; but the man across the way put his finger to his lips and nodded toward the guard who had entered the van and taken his seat by the door. Evidently "*Sprechen verboten*" was still the rule.

But some men have keen wits, and do not hand them over when they enter a jail. The little Jew laid his hand on Lanny's where it rested on the seat between them. He gave a sharp tap with his finger, and at the same time, turning his head toward Lanny and from the guard, he opened his mouth and whispered softly: "*Ah!*" just as if he were beginning a singing lesson, or having his throat examined for follicular tonsillitis. Then he gave two quick taps, and whispered: *"Bay!"* which is the second letter of the German alphabet. Then three taps: *"Tsay!"*—the third letter; and so on, until the other nodded his head. Lanny had heard tapping in his dungeon, but hadn't been sure whether it was the water-pipes or some code which he didn't know.

This was the simplest of codes, and the Jew proceeded to tap eighteen times, and then waited until Lanny had calculated that this was the letter R. Thus slowly and carefully, he spelled out the name "R-O-E-H-M." Lanny assumed that the little man was giving his own name, and was prepared to tap "B-U-D-D," and be glad that it was short. But no, his new friend was going on; Lanny counted through letter after letter: "E-R-S-C-H-O-S—." By that time the little Jew must have felt Lanny's hand come alive beneath his gentle taps, and realized that Lanny had got his meaning. But he finished the word to make sure. It took twice as long as it would have taken in English: *"Röhm shot!"*

XI

That simple statement bore a tremendous weight of meaning for Lanny. It enabled him to begin choosing among the variety of tales which he had constructed for himself in the past three days and four nights. If Ernst Röhm, Chief of Staff of the Sturmabteilung, had been shot, it must mean that the much-talked-of "Second Revolution" had failed. And especially when the tapping continued, and Lanny counted out, letter by letter, the words "in Stadelheim." That was a flash of lightning on a black night; it told Lanny what all the shooting had been about. The S.A. Chief of Staff and his many lieutenants who had been gathered for a conference! They must have been seized, carried from Wiessee, and shot somewhere in the grim old prison! The quick finger tapped on, and spelled the name of Heines, followed again by the dread word *"erschossen."* Lanny knew that this was the police chief of Breslau, who had led the gang which had burned the Reichstag; he was one of the most notorious of the Nazi killers, and Hugo had named him as one of Röhm's fellow-perverts, and a guest at the Wiessee villa.

And then the name of Strasser! Lanny put his hand on top of the little Jew's and spelled the name "Otto"; but the other wiggled away and spelled "Gr——" so Lanny understood that it was Gregor Strasser, whom he had heard getting a tongue-lashing from the Führer, and whom he and Irma had heard speaking at a *Versammlung* in Stuttgart. Otto Strasser was the founder of the hated "Black Front," and was an exile with a price on his head; but his elder brother Gregor had retired from politics and become director of a chemical works. Lanny had been surprised when Hugo had mentioned him as having had conferences with Röhm.

The little Jewish intellectual was having a delightful time breaking the rules and gossiping with a fellow-prisoner, telling him the meaning of the terrific events of the past three days. Even into a prison, news penetrates and is spread; and never in modern times had there been news such as this! The eager finger tapped the name of Schleicher; the one-time Chancellor, the self-styled "social general" who had tried so hard to keep Hitler out of power; who had thwarted von Papen, and then been thwarted in turn. Of late he had been dickering with the malcontents, hankering to taste the sweets of power again. "*Schleicher erschossen!*" A high officer of the Reichswehr, a leading Junker, one of the sacred ruling caste! Lanny looked at the face of the stoutish gentleman across the aisle, and understood why his eyes were wide and frightened. Could he see the little Jew's finger resting on Lanny's hand, and was he perhaps counting the taps? Or was he just horrified to be alive in such a world?

Lanny had heard enough names, and began tapping vigorously in his turn. "*Wohin gehen wir?*" The answer was: "Munich Police Prison." When he asked: "What for?" the little Jew didn't have to do any tapping. He just shrugged his shoulders and spread his two hands, the Jewish way of saying in all languages: "Who knows?"

28

Bloody Instructions

I

IN THE city jail of Munich Lanny was treated like anybody else; which was a great relief to him. He was duly "booked": his name, age, nationality, residence, and occupation—he gave the latter as *Kunstsachverständiger*, which puzzled the man at the desk, as if he didn't get many of that kind; with a four days' growth of brown beard Lanny looked more like a bandit, or felt that he did. He was, it appeared, under "protective arrest"; there was grave danger that somebody might hurt him, so the kindly Gestapo was guarding him from danger. By this device a Führer with a "legality complex" was holding a hundred thousand men and women in confinement without trial or charge. The American demanded to be allowed to notify his consul, and was told he might make that request of the "inspector"; but he wasn't told when or how he was to see that personage. Instead he was taken to be fingerprinted, and then to be photographed.

All things are relative; after a "black cell" in Stadelheim, this city jail in the Ettstrasse seemed homelike and friendly, *echt süddeutsch-gemütlich*. In the first place, he was put in a cell with two other men, and never had human companionship been so welcome to Lanny Budd. In the next place, the cell had a window, and while it was caked with dust, it was permitted to be open at times, and for several hours the sun came through the bars. Furthermore, Lanny's money had been credited to his account, and he could order food; for sixty pfennigs, about fifteen cents, he could have a plate of cold meat and cheese; for forty pfennigs he could have a shave by the prison barber. For half an hour in the morning while his cell was being cleaned he was permitted to walk up and down in the corridor, and for an hour at midday he was taken out into the exercise court and allowed to tramp round and round in a large circle, while from the windows of the four-story building other inmates looked down upon him. Truly a *gemütlich* place of confinement!

One of his cell-mates was the large business man who had been his fellow-passenger in the *Grüne Minna*. It turned out that he was the director of a manufacturing concern, accused of having violated some regulation regarding the payment of his employees; the real reason, he declared, was that he had discharged an incompetent and dishonest Nazi, and now they were going to force him out and put that Nazi in charge. He would stay in prison until he had made up his mind to sign certain papers which had been put before him. The other victim was a Hungarian count, who was a sort of Nazi, but not the right sort, and he, too, had made a personal enemy, in this case his mistress. Lanny was astonished to find how large a percentage of prisoners in this place were or thought they were loyal followers of the Führer. Apparently all you had to do in order to get yourself into jail was to have a quarrel with someone who had more influence than yourself, then you would be accused of any sort of offense, and you stayed because in Naziland to be accused or even suspected was worse than being convicted.

Lanny discovered that having been in a "black cell" of Stadelheim for three days and four nights had made him something of a distinguished person, a sort of Edmond Dantès, Count of Monte Cristo. His cell-mates fell upon him and plied him with questions about what he had seen and heard in those dreadful underground dungeons. Apparently they knew all about the killings; they could even tell him about the courtyard with a wall against which the shooting was done, and the hydrant for washing away the blood. Lanny could add nothing except the story of how he had lain and listened; how many drum-rolls and volleys he had heard, and about the man who had argued and protested, and Lanny's own frightful sensations. It was a relief to describe them, he found; his Anglo-Saxon reticence broke down in these close quarters, where human companionship was all that anybody had, and he must furnish his share of entertainment if he expected others to furnish it to him.

II

Newspapers had been forbidden in the prison during this crisis; but you could get all sorts of things if you had the price, and the Hungarian had managed to secure the *Münchner Zeitung* of Monday. He permitted Lanny to have a look at it, standing against the wall alongside the door, so as to be out of sight of any warder who might happen to peer through the square opening in the door; if he started to unlock the door Lanny would hear him and slip the paper under the mattress or stuff it into his trousers. Under these romantic circumstances he read the flaming headlines of a radio talk in which his friend Joseph Goebbels had told the German people the story of that dreadful Saturday of blood and terror. Juppchen had been traveling about the Rheinland with the Führer, dutifully inspecting labor-camps, and he now went into details, in that spirit of melodrama combined with religious adoration which it was his job to instill into the German people. Said crooked little Juppchen:

"I still see the picture of our Führer standing at midnight on Friday evening on the terrace of the Rhein Hotel in Godesberg and in the open square a band of the Western German Labor Service playing. The Führer looks seriously and meditatively into the dark sky that has followed a refreshing thunderstorm. With raised hand he returns the enthusiastic greetings of the people of the Rheinland . . . In this hour he is more than ever admired by us. Not a quiver in his face reveals the slightest sign of what is going on within him. Yet we few people who stand by him in all difficult hours know how deeply he is grieved and also how determined to deal mercilessly in stamping out the reactionary rebels who are trying to plunge the country into chaos, and breaking their oath of loyalty to him under the slogan of carrying out a 'Second Revolution.' "

Dispatches come from Berlin and Munich which convince the Führer that it is necessary to act instantly; he telephones orders for the putting down of the rebels, and so: "Half an hour later a heavy tri-motored Junkers plane leaves the aviation field near Bonn and disappears into the foggy night. The clock has just struck two. The Führer sits silently in the front seat of the cabin and gazes fixedly into the great expanse of darkness."

Arriving in Munich at four in the morning they find that the traitorous leaders have already been apprehended. "In two brisk sentences of indignation and contempt Herr Hitler throws their whole shame into their fearful and perplexed faces. He then steps to one of them and rips the insignia of rank from his uniform. A very hard but deserved fate awaits them in the afternoon."

The center of the conspiracy is known to be in the mountains, and so a troop of loyal S.S. men have been assembled, and, narrates Dr. Juppchen, "at a terrific rate the trip to Wiessee is begun." He gives a thrilling account of the wild night ride, by which, at six in the morning "without any resistance we are able to enter the house and surprise the conspirators, who are still sleeping, and we arouse them immediately. The Führer himself makes the arrest with a courage that has no equal . . . I may be spared a description of the disgusting scene that lay before us. A simple S.S. man, with an air of indignation, expresses our thoughts, saying: 'I only wish that the walls would fall down now, so that the whole German people could be a witness to this act.' "

The radio orator went on to tell what had been happening in Berlin. "Our party comrade, General Göring, has not hesitated. With a firm hand he has cleared up a nest of reactionaries and their incorrigible supporters. He has taken steps that were hard but necessary in order to save the country from immeasurable disaster."

There followed two newspaper columns of denunciation in which the Reichsminister of Popular Enlightenment and Propaganda used many adjectives to praise the nobility and heroism of his Führer, "who has again shown in this critical situation that he is a Real Man." A quite different set of adjectives was required for the "small clique of professional saboteurs," the "boils, seats of corruption, the symptoms of disease and moral deterioration that show themselves in public life," and that now have been "burned out to the flesh."

"The Reich is there," concluded Juppchen, "and above all our Führer."

III

Such was the story told to the German people. Lanny noticed the curious fact that not once did the little dwarf name one of the victims of the purge; he didn't even say directly that anybody had been killed! As a specimen of popular fiction there was something to be said for his effusion, but as history it wouldn't rank high. Lanny could nail one falsehood, for he knew that Hugo Behr had been shot at a few minutes after nine on Friday evening, which was at least three hours before the Führer had given his orders, according to the Goebbels account. The jail buzzed with stories of other persons who had been killed or arrested before midnight; in fact some had been brought to this very place. Evidently somebody had given the fatal order while the Führer was still inspecting labor camps.

It was well known that Göring had flown to the Rheinland with his master, and had then flown back to Berlin. Hermann was the killer, the man of action, who took the "steps that were hard but necessary," while Adi was still hesitating and arguing, screaming at his followers, threatening to commit suicide if they didn't obey him, falling down on the floor and biting the carpet in a hysteria of bewilderment or rage. Lanny became clear in his mind that this was the true story of the "Blood Purge." Göring had sat at Hitler's ear in the plane and terrified him with stories of what the Gestapo had uncovered; then, from Berlin, he had given the orders, and when it was too late to reverse them he had phoned the Führer, and the latter had flown to Munich to display "a courage that has no equal," to show himself to the credulous German people as "a Real Man."

The official statement was that not more than fifty persons had been killed in the three days and nights of terror; but the gossip in the Ettstrasse was that there had been several hundred victims in Munich alone, and it turned out that the total in Germany was close to twelve hundred. This and other official falsehoods were freely discussed, and the jail buzzed like a beehive. Human curiosity broke down the barriers between jailers and jailed; they whispered news to one another, and an item once put into circulation was borne by busy tongues to every corner of the institution. In the corridors you were supposed to walk alone and not to talk; but every time you passed other prisoners you whispered something, and if it was a tidbit you might share it with one of the keepers. Down in the exercise court the inmates were supposed to walk in silence, but the man behind you mouthed the news and you passed it on to the man in front of you.

And when you were in your cell, there were sounds of tapping; tapping on wood, on stone, and on metal; tapping by day and most of the night; quick tapping for the experts and slow tapping for the new arrivals. In the cell directly under Lanny was a certain Herr Doktor Obermeier, a former Ministerialdirektor of the Bavarian state, well known to Herr Klaussen. He shared the same water-pipes as those above him, and was a tireless tapper. Lanny learned the code, and heard the story of Herr Doktor Willi Schmitt, music critic of the *Neueste Nachrichten* and chairman of the Beethoven-Vereinigung; the most amiable of persons, so Herr Klaussen declared, with body, mind, and soul made wholly of music. Lanny had read his review of the *Eroica* performance, and other articles from his pen. The S.S. men came for him, and when he learned that they thought he was Gruppenführer Willi Schmitt, a quite different man, he was amused, and told his wife and children not to worry. He went with the Nazis, but did not return; and when his frantic wife persisted in her clamors she received from Police Headquarters a death certificate signed by the Bürgermeister of the town of Dachau; there had been "a very regrettable mistake," and they would see that it did not happen again.

Story after story, the most sensational, the most horrible! Truly, it was something fabulous, Byzantine! Ex-Chancellor Franz von Papen, still a member of the Cabinet, had been attacked in his office and had some of his teeth knocked out; now he was under "house arrest," his life threatened, and the aged von Hindenburg, sick and near to death, trying to save his "dear comrade." Edgar Jung, Papen's friend who had written his offending speech demanding freedom of the press, had been shot here in Munich. Gregor Strasser had been kidnaped from his home and beaten to death by S.S. men in Grunewald. General von Schleicher and his wife had been riddled with bullets on the steps of their villa. Karl Ernst, leader of the Berlin S.A., had been slugged unconscious and taken to the city. His staff leader had decided that Göring had gone crazy, and had flown to Munich to appeal to Hitler about it. He had been taken back to Berlin and shot with seven of his adjutants. At Lichterfelde, in the courtyard of the old military cadet school, tribunals under the direction of Göring were still holding "trials" averaging seven minutes each; the victims were stood against a wall and shot while crying: *"Heil Hitler!"*

IV

About half the warders in this jail were men of the old regime and the other half S.A. men, and there was much jealousy between them. The latter group had no way of knowing when the lightning might strike them, so for the first time they had a fellow-feeling for their prisoners. If one of the latter had a visitor and got some fresh information, everybody wanted to share it, and a warder would find a pretext to come to the cell and hear what he had to report. Really, the old Munich police prison became a delightfully sociable and exciting place! Lanny decided that he wouldn't have missed it for anything. His own fears had diminished; he decided that when the storm blew over, somebody in authority would have time to hear his statement and realize that a blunder had been made. Possibly his three captors had put Hugo's money into their own pockets, and if so, there was no evidence against Lanny himself. He had only to crouch in his "better 'ole"—and meantime learn about human and especially Nazi nature.

The population of the jail was in part common criminals—thieves, burglars, and sex offenders—while the other part comprised political suspects, or those who had got in the way of some powerful official. A curious situation, in which one prisoner might be a blackmailer and another the victim of a blackmailer—both in the same jail and supposedly under the same law! One man guilty of killing, another guilty of refusing to kill, or of protesting against killing! Lanny could have compiled a whole *dossier* of such antinomies. But he didn't dare to make notes, and was careful not to say anything that would give offense to anybody. The place was bound to be full of spies, and while the men in his own cell appeared to be genuine, either or both might have been selected because they appeared to be that.

The Hungarian count was a gay companion, and told diverting stories of his *liaisons;* he had a passion for playing the game of Halma, and Lanny learned it in order to oblige him. The business man, Herr Klaussen, told stories illustrating the impossibility of conducting any honest business under present conditions; then he would say: "Do you have things thus in America?" Lanny would reply: "My father complains a great deal about politicians." He would tell some of Robbie's stories, feeling certain that these wouldn't do him any harm in Germany.

Incidentally Herr Klaussen expressed the conviction that the talk about a plot against Hitler was all *Quatsch;* there had been nothing but protest and discussion. Also, the talk about the Führer's being shocked by what he had discovered in the villa at Wiessee was *Dummheit,* because everybody in Germany had known about Röhm and his boys, and the Führer had laughed about it. This worthy *Bürger* of Munich cherished a hearty dislike of those whom he called *die Preiss'n*—the Prussians—regarding them as invaders and source of all corruptions. These, of course, were frightfully dangerous utterances, and this was either a bold man or a foolish one. Lanny said: "I have no basis to form an opinion, and in view of my position I'd rather not try." He went back to playing Halma with the Hungarian, and collecting anecdotes and local color which Eric Vivian Pomeroy-Nielson might some day use in a play.

V

Lanny had spent three days as a guest of the state of Bavaria, and now he spent ten as a guest of the city of Munich. Then, just at the end of one day, a friendly warder came and said: "*Bitte, kommen Sie, Herr Budd.*"

It would do no good to ask questions, for the warders didn't know. When you left a cell, you said *Adé*, having no way to tell if you would come back. Some went to freedom, others to be beaten insensible, others to Dachau or some other camp. Lanny was led downstairs to an office where he found two young S.S. men, dapper and correct, awaiting him. He was pleased to observe that they were not the same who had arrested him. They came up, and almost before he realized what was happening, one had taken his wrist and snapped a handcuff onto it. The other cuff was on the young Nazi's wrist, and Lanny knew it was useless to offer objections. They led him out to a courtyard, where he saw his own car, with another uniformed S.S. man in the driver's seat. The rear door was opened. "*Bitte einsteigen.*"

"May I ask where I'm being taken?" he ventured.

"It is not permitted to talk," was the reply. He got in, and the car rolled out into the tree-lined avenue, and into the city of Munich. They drove straight through, and down the valley of the Isar, north-eastward.

On a dark night the landscape becomes a mystery; the car lights illumine a far-stretching road, but it is possible to imagine any sort of thing to the right and left. Unless you are doing the driving, you will even become uncertain whether the car is going uphill or down. But there were the stars in their appointed places, and so Lanny could know they were headed north. Having driven over this route, he knew the signposts; and when it was Regensburg and they were still speeding rapidly, he made a guess that he was being taken to Berlin.

"There's where I get my examination," he thought. He would have one more night to do his thinking, and then he would confront that colossal power known as the Geheime Staats-Polizei, more dark than any night, more to be dreaded than anything that night contained.

The prisoner had had plenty of sleep in the jail, so he used this time to choose his *Ausrede*, his "alibi." But the more he tried, the worse his confusion became. They were bound to have found out that he had drawn thirty thousand marks from the Hellstein bank in Munich; they were bound to know that he had paid most of it to Hugo; they were bound to know that some sort of effort had been made to take Freddi out of Dachau. All these spelled guilt on Lanny's part; and the only course that seemed to hold hope was to be frank and naïve; to laugh and say: "Well, General Göring charged Johannes Robin his whole fortune to get out, and used me as his agent, so naturally I thought that was the way it was done. When Hugo offered to do it for only twenty-eight thousand marks, I thought I had a bargain."

In the early dawn, when nobody was about except the milkman and the machine-gun detachments of the Berlin police, Lanny's car swept into the city, and in a workingclass quarter which he took to be Moabit, drew up in front of a large brick building. He hadn't been able to see the street signs, and nobody took the trouble to inform him. Was it the dreaded Nazi barracks in Hedemannstrasse, about which the refugees talked with shudders? Was it the notorious Columbus-Haus? Or perhaps the headquarters of the Feldpolizei, the most feared group of all?

"*Bitte aussteigen,*" said the leader. They had been perfectly polite, but hadn't spoken one unnecessary word, either to him or to one another. They were machines; and if somewhere inside them was a soul, they would have been deeply ashamed of it. They were trying to get into the Reichswehr, and this was the way.

They went into the building. Once more they did not stop to "book" the prisoner, but marched him with military steps along a corridor, and then down a flight of stone stairs into a cellar. This time Lanny couldn't be mistaken; there was a smell of blood, and there were cries somewhere in the distance. Once more he ventured a demand as to what he was being held for, what was to be done to him? This time the young leader condescended to reply: "*Sie sind ein Schutzhäftling.*"

They were telling him that he was one of those hundred thousand persons, Germans and foreigners, who were being held for their own good, to keep harm from being done to them. "*Aber,*" insisted

Lanny, with his best society manner, "I haven't asked to be a *Schutzhäftling*—I'm perfectly willing to take my chances outside."

If any of them had a sense of humor, this was not the place to show it. There was a row of steel doors, and one was opened. For the first time since these men had confronted Lanny in the Munich jail the handcuff was taken from his wrist, and he was pushed into a "black cell" and heard the door clang behind him.

VI

The same story as at Stadelheim; only it was more serious now, because that had been an accident, whereas this was deliberate, this was after two weeks of investigation. Impossible to doubt that his plight was as serious as could be. Fear took complete possession of him, and turned his bones to some sort of pulp. Putting his ear to the opening in the door, he could have no doubt that he heard screaming and crying; putting his nose to the opening, he made sure that he smelled that odor which he had heretofore associated with slaughter-houses. He was in one of those dreadful places about which he had been reading and hearing, where the Nazis systematically broke the bodies and souls of men—yes, and of women, too. In the *Brown Book* he had seen a photograph of the naked rear of an elderly stout woman, a city councilor of the Social-Democratic party, from her shoulders to her knees one mass of stripes from a scientific beating.

They weren't going to trouble to question him, or give him any chance to tell his story. They were taking it for granted that he would lie, and so they would punish him first, and then he would be more apt to tell the truth. Or were they just meaning to frighten him? To put him where he could hear the sounds and smell the smells, and see if that would "soften him up"? It had that effect; he decided that it would be futile to try to conceal anything, to tell a single lie. He saw his whole past lying like an open book before some *Kriminalkommissar*, and it was a very bad past indeed from the Nazi point of view; every bit as bad as that which had brought Freddi Robin some fourteen months of torture.

Whatever it was, it was coming now. Steps in the corridor, and they stopped in front of his door; the door was opened, and there were two S.S. men. New ones—they had an unlimited supply, and all with the same set faces, all with the same code of *Blut und Eisen.* Black shirts, black trousers, shiny black boots, and in their belts an automatic and a hard rubber truncheon—an unlimited supply of these, also, it appeared.

They took him by the arms and led him down the corridor. Their whole manner, the whole atmosphere, told him that his time had come. No use to resist; at least not physically; they would drag him, and would make his punishment worse. He was conscious of a sudden surge of anger; he loathed these subhuman creatures, and still more he loathed the hellish system which had made them. He would walk straight, in spite of his trembling knees; he would hold himself erect, and not give them the satisfaction of seeing him weaken. He dug his nails into the palms of his hands, he gritted his teeth, and walked to whatever was beyond that door at the end of the corridor.

VII

The sounds had died away as Lanny came nearer, and when the door was opened he heard only low moans. Two men were in the act of leading a beaten man through a doorway at the far side of the room. In the semi-darkness he saw only the dim forms, and saw one thrown into the room beyond. Apparently there were many people there, victims of the torturing; moans and cries came as from a section of Dante's inferno; the sounds made a sort of *basso continuo* to all the infernal events which Lanny witnessed in that chamber of horrors.

A room about fifteen feet square, with a concrete floor and walls of stone; no windows, and no light except half a dozen candles; only one article of furniture, a heavy wooden bench about eight feet long and two feet broad, in the middle of the room. From end to end the bench was smeared and dripping with blood, and there was blood all over the floor, and a stench of dried blood, most sickening. Also there was the pungent odor of human sweat, strong, ammoniacal; there were four Nazis standing near the bench, stripped to the waist, and evidently they had been working hard and fast, for their smooth bodies shone with sweat and grease, even in the feeble light. Several other Nazis stood by, and one man in civilian clothes, wearing spectacles.

Lanny had read all about this; every anti-Nazi had learned it by heart during the past year and a half. He took it in at a glance, even to the flexible thin steel rods with handles, made for the purpose of inflicting as much pain as possible and doing as little permanent damage. If you did too much damage you lost the pleasure of inflicting more pain—and also you might lose important evidence. Lanny had read about it, heard about it, brooded over it, wondered how he would take it—and now here it was, here he was going to find out.

What happened was that a wave of fury swept over him; rage at these scientifically-trained devils, drowning out all other emotion whatsoever. He hated them so that he lost all thought about himself, he forgot all fear and the possibility of pain. They wanted to break him; all right, he would show them that he was as strong as they; he would deny them the pleasure of seeing him weaken, of hearing him cry out. He had read that the American Indians had made it a matter of pride never to groan under torture. All right, what an American Indian could do, any American could do; it was something in the climate, in the soil. Lanny's father had hammered that pride into him in boyhood, and Bub Smith and Jerry had helped. Lanny resolved that the Nazis could kill him, but they wouldn't get one word out of him, not one sound. Neither now nor later. Go to hell, and stay there!

It was hot in this underground hole, and perhaps that was why the sweat gathered on Lanny's forehead and ran down into his eyes. But he didn't wipe it away; that might be taken for a gesture of fright or agitation; he preferred to stand rigid, like a soldier, as he had seen the Nazis do. He realized now what they meant. All right, he would learn their technique; he would become a fanatic, as they. Not a muscle must move; his face must be hard, turned to stone with defiance. It could be done. He had told himself all his life that he was soft; he had been dissatisfied with himself in a hundred ways. Here was where he would reform himself.

He was expecting to be told to strip, and he was ready to do it. His muscles were aching to begin. But no, apparently they knew that; their science had discovered this very reaction, and knew a subtler form of torture. They would keep him waiting a while, until his mood of rage had worn off; until his imagination had had a chance to work on his nerves; until energy of the soul, or whatever it was, had spent itself. The two men who led him by the arms took him to one side of the room, against the wall, and there they stood, one on each side of him, two statues, and he a third.

VIII

The door was opened again, and another trio entered; two S.S. men, leading an elderly civilian, rather stout, plump, with gray mustaches, a gray imperial neatly trimmed; a Jew by his features, a business man by his clothes—and suddenly Lanny gave a start, in spite of all his resolutions. He had talked to that man, and had joked about him, the rather comical resemblance of his hirsute adornments to those of an eminent and much-portrayed citizen of France, the Emperor Napoleon the Third. Before Lanny's eyes loomed the resplendent drawing-room of Johannes Robin's Berlin palace, with Beauty and Irma doing the honors so graciously, and this genial old gentleman chatting, correct in his white tie and tails, diamond shirt-studs no longer in fashion in America, and a tiny square of red ribbon in his buttonhole—some order that Lanny didn't recognize. But he was sure about the man—Solomon Hellstein, the banker.

Such a different man now: tears in his eyes and terror in his face; weeping, pleading, cowering, having to be half dragged. "I didn't do it, I tell you! I know nothing about it! My God, my God, I would tell you if I could! Pity! Have pity!"

They dragged him to the bench. They pulled his clothes off, since he was incapable of doing it himself. Still pleading, still protesting, screaming, begging for mercy, he was told to lie down on the bench. His failure to obey annoyed them and they threw him down on his belly, with his bare back and buttocks and thighs looming rather grotesque, his flabby white arms hanging down to the floor. The four shirtless Nazis took their places, two on each side, and the officer in command raised his hand in signal.

The thin steel rods whistled as they came down through the air; they made four clean cuts across the naked body, followed by four quick spurts of blood. The old man started up with a frightful scream of pain. They grabbed him and threw him down, and the officer cried: "Lie still, *Juden-Schwein!* For that you get ten more blows!"

The poor victim lay shuddering and moaning, and Lanny, tense and sick with horror, waited for the next strokes. He imagined the mental anguish of the victim because they did not fall at once. The officer waited, and finally demanded: "You like that?"

"*Nein, nein! Um Himmel's Willen!*"

"Then tell us who took that gold out!"

"I have said a thousand times—if I knew, I would tell you. What more can I say? Have mercy on me! I am a helpless old man!"

The leader raised his hand again, and the four rods whistled and fell as one. The man shuddered; each time the anguish shook him, he shrieked like a madman. He knew nothing about it, he would tell anything he knew, it had been done by somebody who had told him nothing. His tones grew more piercing; then gradually they began to die, they became a confused babble, the raving of a man in delirium. His words tripped over one another, his sobs choked his cries.

Of the four beaters, the one who was working on the victim's shoulders apparently held the post of honor, and it was his duty to keep count. Each time he struck he called aloud, and when he said "*Zehn*" they all stopped. Forty strokes had been ordered, and the leader signed to the civilian in spectacles, who proved to be a doctor; the high scientific function of this disciple of Hippocrates was to make sure how much the victim could stand. He put a stethoscope to the raw flesh of the old Jew's back, and listened. Then he nodded and said: "*Noch eins.*"

The leader was in the act of moving his finger to give the signal when there came an interruption to the proceedings; a voice speaking loud and clear: "You dirty dogs!" It rushed on: "*Ihr dreckigen Schweinehunde, Ihr seid eine Schandfleck der Menschheit!*"

For a moment everybody in the room seemed to be paralyzed. It was utterly unprecedented, unprovided for in any military regulations. But not for long. The officer shouted: "*'Rrraus mit ihm!*" and the two statues besides Lanny came suddenly to life and led him away. But not until he had repeated loudly and clearly: "I say that you dishonor the form of men!"

IX

Back in his cell, Lanny thought: "Now I've cooked my goose!" He thought: "They'll invent something special for me." He discovered that his frenzy, his inspiration, whatever it was, had passed quickly; in darkness and silence he realized that he had done something very foolish, something that could do no good to the poor old banker and could do great harm to himself. But there was no undoing it, and no good lamenting, no good letting his bones turn to pulp again. He had to get back that mood of rage and determination, and learn to hold it, no matter what might come. It was a psychological exercise, a highly difficult one. Sometimes he thought he was succeeding, but then he would hear with his mind's ears the whistle of those terrible steel rods, and he would find that a disgraceful trembling seized him.

Waiting was the worst of all; he actually thought he would feel relief when his cell door was opened. But when he heard the steps coming, he found that he was frightened again, and had to start work all over. He must not let them think that they could cow an American. He clenched his hands tightly, set his teeth, and looked out into the corridor. There in the dim light was the S.S. man to whom he had been handcuffed for a whole night—and behind that man, looking over his shoulder, the deeply concerned face of Oberleutnant Furtwaengler!

"Well, well, Herr Budd!" said the young staff officer. "What have they been doing to you?"

Lanny had to change his mood with lightning speed. He was busily hating all the Nazis; but he didn't hate this naïve and worshipful young social climber. "Herr Oberleutnant!" he exclaimed, with relief that was like a prayer.

"Come out," said the other, and looked his friend over as if to see if he showed any signs of damage. "What have they done to you?"

"They have made me rather uncomfortable," replied the prisoner, resuming the Anglo-Saxon manner.

"It is most unfortunate!" exclaimed the officer. "Seine Exzellenz will be distressed."

"So was I," admitted the prisoner.

"Why did you not let us know?"

"I did my best to let somebody know; but I was not successful."

"This is a disgraceful incident!" exclaimed the other, turning to the S.S. man. "Some one will be severely disciplined."

"*Zu Befehl, Herr Oberleutnant!*" replied the man. It conveyed the impression: "Tell me to shoot myself and I am ready."

"Really, Herr Budd, I don't know how to apologize."

"Your presence is apology enough, Herr Oberleutnant. You are, as we say in America, a sight for sore eyes."

"I am sorry indeed if your eyes are sore," declared the staff officer, gravely.

It was like waking up suddenly from a nightmare, and discovering that all those dreadful things had never happened. Lanny followed his friend up the narrow stone stairway, and discovered that there were no more formalities required for his release than had been required for his arrest. Doubtless the officer's uniform bore insignia which gave him authority. He said: "I assume responsibility for this gentleman," and the S.S. man repeated: "At command, Herr Oberleutnant."

They went out to the official car which was waiting. Rain was falling, but never had a day seemed more lovely. Lanny had to shut his eyes from the light, but he managed to get inside unassisted. Sinking back in the soft seat he had to struggle to make up his mind which was real—these cushions or that dungeon! Surely both couldn't exist in the same city, in the same world!

29

Too Deep for Tears

I

LANNY was living in a kaleidoscope; one of those tubes you look into and observe a pattern, and then you give it a slight jar, and the pattern is gone, and there is an utterly different one. He was prepared for anything, literally anything. But when he heard his friend give the order: "Seine Exzellenz's residence," he came to with a start, and became what he had been all his life, a member of the *beau monde*, to whom the proprieties were instinctive and inescapable. "Surely," he protested, "you're not taking me to Seine Exzellenz in this condition! Look at my clothes! And my beard!" Lanny ran his hand over it, wondering again if it was gray.

"Where are your clothes, Herr Budd?"

"When last heard from they were in a hotel in Munich."

"A most preposterous affair! I will telephone for them this morning."

"And my money?" added the other. "That was taken from me in Stadelheim. But if you will drive me to the Adlon, I am sure they will cash my check."

The orders were changed, and the young staff officer entered with amusement into the enterprise of making his friend presentable by the magic of modern hotel service. While the guest bathed himself, a valet whisked his clothes away to sponge and press them, and a bellboy sped to the nearest haberdashers for a shirt, tie, and handkerchief. A barber came and shaved him—and collected no gray hairs. In half an hour by the Oberleutnant's watch—Lanny had none—he was again the picture of a young man of fashion, ready to meet all the world and his wife.

It was truly comical, when they were motored to the official residence of the Minister-Präsident of Prussia and escorted up to his private apartments. This mighty personage had all the sartorial appurtenances of his office: blue trousers with a broad white stripe; a coat of lighter blue with a white belt and broad white sash from one shoulder crossing his chest; numerous gold cords and stars, epaulets and insignia of his rank—but it was a blazing hot day in mid-July, and all this honorificabilitudinitatibus had become intolerable to a fat man. He had it hung on a chair near-by, and was sitting at his desk in his shorts and that large amount of soft white skin with which nature had endowed him. Beads of perspiration stood out on the skin, and before Lanny's mind flashed the vision of a Jewish banker. Impossible to keep from imagining this still larger mass of flesh and fat laid out on a blood-soaked and slimy bench, bottom up!

II

It was the General's intention to take Lanny Budd's misadventure as a comic opera *divertissement* in the midst of very grave business; and it was up to Lanny to be a good sport and do the same. "*Ja aber, mein lieber Herr Budd!*" cried Seine Exzellenz, and caught Lanny's hand in a grip that showed he was by no means all fat. "*Was ist Ihnen denn passiert?*"—he insisted upon hearing all about a playboy's misadventures. "Were you afraid?" he wanted to know; and Lanny said: "Wait until your turn comes, Exzellenz, and see if you're not afraid."

That wasn't so funny. The great man replied: "You had the misfortune to get caught in the traffic at a very busy hour. We have some wild fellows in our party, and it was necessary to teach them a lesson. I think they have learned it thoroughly."

Lanny had done a bit of thinking while he was in the bathtub at the hotel. He would never trust any Nazi again. It seemed unlikely that the head of the Prussian state had no information as to what had been happening to one who claimed to be his friend; almost incredible that his efficient secret police had failed to send him any report during the past two weeks. A thousand times more likely that there had been some purpose in what had befallen an American visitor; also in this sudden change of front, this explosion of friendliness and familiarity. Last-minute rescues belong in melodramas, where they are no accidents, but have been carefully contrived. Lanny had begun to suspect this particularly hair-raising dénouement.

The Minister-Präsident of Prussia didn't keep him long in suspense. There was a large stack of papers on his desk and he was obviously a busy fat man. "*Jawohl, Herr Budd!*" he said. "You had the opportunity of studying our penal institutions at first hand; also our methods of dealing with Jew *Schieber!* You can testify that they are effective."

"I had no opportunity to observe the outcome, Exzellenz."

"I will see that you are informed about it, if you so desire. Do you have any idea who that Jew was?"

"It so happens that I had met him in Berlin society."

"Indeed? Who was he?"

"His name is Solomon Hellstein."

"*Ach!* Our *weltberühmter* Shylock! You will indeed have an interesting story to tell the outside world."

Lanny thought he saw a hint. "You will remember, Exzellenz, that you asked me to say nothing to the outside world about the case of Johannes Robin. Fourteen months have passed, and still I have not done so."

"I have made a note of the fact, Herr Budd, and appreciate your good judgment. But now there is a quite different set of circumstances. We have a saying in German: *Es hängt ganz davon ab.*"

Lanny supplied the English: "It all depends."

"*Also, Herr Budd!* Would you be greatly embarrassed if I should suggest that you narrate the story of what you saw this morning?"

"I should be somewhat puzzled, Exzellenz."

"It is a bright idea which occurs to me. Are you still interested in that *Jude Itzig* of yours?" This is a German name of jeering derived from the Hebrew word for Isaac, which is Yitzchock.

"If you mean the son of Johannes Robin, I am still deeply interested, Exzellenz."

"I have recently learned that he is in the *Lager* at Dachau. Would you like to have him turned loose?"

"*Aber natürlich, Exzellenz.*"

"*Na, also!* I offer him to you in exchange for a small service which you may render me. Go to Paris and tell the members of the Hellstein family what you have seen happening to their Berlin representative. You know them, possibly?"

"It happens that I know them rather well."

"I will explain to you: This *Dreck-Jude* has succeeded in shipping a fortune out of Germany, and we were not so fortunate as in the case of Robin, we do not know where the money is. The family is scattered all over Europe, as you know. We have no claim to their money, but we intend to have Solomon's, every mark of it— if we have to flay him alive."

"You wish me to tell them that?"

"They know it already. All you have to tell is what you saw with your own eyes. Make it as realistic as you know how."

"Am I to mention that you have asked me to tell them?"

"If you do that, they may suspect your good faith. It will be better not to refer to me. Simply tell what happened to you and what you saw."

"And then, Exzellenz?"

"Then I will release your pet Jew."

"How am I to let you know that I have done my part?"

"I have my agents, and they will report to me. The story will be all over Paris in a few hours. It will be a good thing, because our rich *Schieber* have got the idea that we dare not touch them, and they think they can bleed Germany to death."

"I get your point, Exzellenz. How will I know where I am to get Freddi Robin?"

"Leave your Paris address with Furtwaengler, and within a day or two after you have talked with the Hellsteins he will telephone you and arrange to ship your precious *Itzig* to the French border. Is that according to your wishes?"

"Quite so, Exzellenz. I can see no reason why I shouldn't comply with your request."

"*Abgemacht!* It is a deal. It has been a pleasure to meet you, Herr Budd; and if, after you think it over, you wish to do more business with me, come and see me at any time."

"*Danke schön, Exzellenz.* I will bear your suggestion in mind and perhaps avail myself of the opportunity."

"*Dem Mutigen ist das Glück hold!*" The fat commander had risen from his chair to speed his parting guest, and now favored him with a staggering slap upon the back, and a burst of merriment which left the visitor uncertain whether he was being laughed with or at.

III

So Lanny went out from the presence of this half-naked free-booter, and was courteously driven back to his hotel by the young staff officer. Evidently Lanny's papers had been brought along on the trip from Munich, for Furtwaengler put his passport and his six thousand marks into his hands; also an exit permit. He promised to have Lanny's clothes and other belongings forwarded to Juan. The American didn't lay any claim to the money which had been found on the body of Hugo Behr!

His car had been delivered to the hotel, and the Oberleutnant assured him that it had been properly serviced and supplied with a tank full of petrol. They parted warm friends; and Lanny stayed in Berlin only long enough to pay his hotel bill and send telegrams to Rahel in Juan, to his father in Newcastle, to his mother and his wife in England: "Leaving for Crillon Paris hopeful of success notify friends all well." He dared say no more, except to ask Irma to meet him in Paris. He knew that they must have been in an agony of dread about him, but he wouldn't make any explanations until he was out of Germany and had got Freddi out. There would be a

chance that an old-style Teutonic freebooter might get some additional information and change his mind. The Hellstein family in
Paris might "come across," or the Gestapo in Munich might unearth
the story of the attempted jailbreak.

Or had they already done so, and had the Minister-Präsident of
Prussia tactfully refrained from mentioning the subject? No chance
to fathom the mind of that master of intrigue, that wholesale killer
of men! At some time in the course of the past two weeks of madness and murder he had found time to take note that he had an
American playboy in his clutches, and to figure out a way to make
use of him. Lanny shook with horror every time he recalled those
minutes in the torture-chamber; nor was the experience a particle
less dreadful because he now perceived that it had been a piece of
stageplay, designed to get his help in extorting some millions of
marks, possibly some scores of millions of marks, from a family of
Jewish bankers.

IV

Lanny didn't feel very much like driving, but he didn't want to
leave his car to the Nazis, so he stuck it out, and drove steadily,
with a mind full of horrors, not much relieved by hope. The Nazi
General, who had cheated him several times, might do it again; and
anyhow, Lanny had come to a state of mind where he wasn't satisfied to get one Jewish friend out of the clutches of the terror. He
wanted to save all the Jews; he wanted to wake up Europe to the
meaning of this moral insanity which had broken out in its midst.
The *gemütliche* German *Volk* had fallen into the hands of gangsters, the most terrible in all history because they were armed with
modern science. Lanny echoed the feelings of the "simple S.A. man"
of whom Goebbels had told, who had wanted the walls of Röhm's
bedroom to fall down, so that the German people might see. Lanny
wanted the walls of that torture chamber to fall down, so that all
the world might see.

He crossed the border into Belgium in the small hours of the
morning and went to a hotel and had a sleep, full of tormenting
dreams. But when he awakened and had some breakfast, he felt bet-

ter, and went to the telephone. There was one person he simply couldn't wait to hear from, and that was Jerry Pendleton in Cannes —if he *was* in Cannes. Lanny's guess proved correct, and his friend's voice was the most welcome of sounds.

"I am in Belgium," said the younger man. "I'm all right, and I just want a few questions answered—with no names."

"O.K.," sang Jerry.

"Did you see our friend that evening?"

"I saw him brought out; but nobody came for him."

"What happened then?"

"I suppose he was taken back; I had no way to make sure. There was nothing I could do about it. I was tempted to try, but I didn't see how I could get away without a car."

"I was afraid you might have tried. It's all right. I have a promise and have some hopes."

"I was worried to death about you. I went to the American authority and reported your absence. I went again and again, and I think he did everything he could, but he was put off with evasions."

"It was serious, but it's all right now. What did you do then?"

"I couldn't think of anything to do for you, so I came out to report to the family. They told me to come home and wait for orders, and I did that. Gee, kid, but I'm glad to hear your voice! Are you sure you're all right?"

"Not a scratch on me. I'm leaving for Paris."

"I just had a wire from your wife; she's on the way to meet you at the Crillon. She's been scared half out of her wits. There's been a lot in the papers, you know."

"Thanks, old sport, for what you did."

"I didn't do a damn thing. I never felt so helpless."

"It's quite possible you saved me. Anyhow, you've got an interesting story coming to you. So long!"

V

The traveler reached Paris about sunset, and surprised Irma in the suite she had taken. She looked at him as if he were a ghost; she seemed afraid to touch him, and stood staring, as if expecting to find him scarred or maimed. He said: "I'm all here, darling," and took her in his arms.

She burst into tears. "Oh, Lanny, I've been living in hell for two weeks!" When he started to kiss her, she held off, gazing at him with the most intense look he had ever seen on her usually calm face. "Lanny, promise me—you *must* promise me—you will never put me through a thing like this again!"

That was the way it was between them; their argument was resumed even before their love. It was going to be that way from now on. He didn't want to make any promises; he didn't want to talk about that aspect of the matter—and she didn't want to talk about anything else. For two weeks she had been imagining him dead, or even worse, being mutilated by those gangsters. She had had every right to imagine it, of course; he couldn't tell her that she had been foolish or unreasonable; in fact he couldn't answer her at all. She wanted to hear his story, yet she didn't want to hear it, or anything else, until her mind had been put at rest by a pledge from him that never, never would he go into Germany, never, never would he have anything to do with that hateful, wicked thing called the class struggle, which drove men and women to madness and crime and turned civilized life into a nightmare.

He tried his best to soothe her, and to make her happy, but it couldn't be done. She had been thinking, and had made up her mind. And he had to make up his mind quickly. For one thing, he wouldn't tell her the whole story of what happened to him in Hitlerland. That would be for men only. He would have to tell the Hellstein ladies about the torturing; but only Robbie and Rick would ever know about his deal with Göring. Rumors of that sort get twisted as they spread, and Lanny might get himself a name that would make him helpless to serve the movement he loved.

Now he said: "Control yourself, darling; I'm here, and I'm none the worse for an adventure. There's something urgent that I have to do, so excuse me if I telephone."

Her feelings were hurt, and at the same time her curiosity was aroused. She heard him call Olivie Hellstein, Madame de Broussailles, and tell her that he had just come out of Germany, and had seen her Uncle Solomon, and had some grave news for her; he thought her mother and father also ought to hear it. Olivie agreed to cancel a dinner engagement, and he was to come to her home in the evening.

He didn't want to take Irma, and had a hard time not offending her. What was the use of subjecting her to an ordeal, the witnessing of a tragic family scene? He had to tell them that the Nazis were cruelly beating the brother of Pierre Hellstein to get his money; and of course they would weep, and perhaps become hysterical. Jews, like most other people, love their money; also they love their relatives, and between the two the Hellstein family would suffer as if they themselves were being beaten.

Then, of course, Irma wanted to know, how had he been in position to see such things? He had a hard time evading her; he didn't want to say: "Göring had me taken there on purpose, so that I might go and tell the Hellsteins; that is the price of his letting Freddi go." In fact, there wasn't any use mentioning Freddi at all, it was clear that Irma didn't care about him, hadn't asked a single question. What she wanted to know was that she was going to have a husband without having to be driven mad with fear; she looked at Lanny now as if he were a stranger—as indeed he was, at least a part of him, a new part, hard and determined, insistent upon having its own way and not talking much about it.

"I owe Olivie Hellstein the courtesy to tell her what I know; and I think it's common humanity to try to save that poor old gentleman in Berlin if I can."

There it was! He was going on saving people! One after another —and people about whom Irma didn't especially care. He was more interested in saving Solomon Hellstein than in saving his wife's peace of mind, and their love, which also had been put in a torture chamber!

VI

The scene which took place in the very elegant and sumptuous home of Madame de Broussailles was fully as painful as Lanny had foreseen. There was that large and stately mother of Jerusalem who had once inspected him through a diamond-studded lorgnette to consider whether he was worthy to become a progenitor of the Hellstein line. There was Pierre Hellstein, father of the family, stoutish like the brother in Berlin, but younger, smarter, and with his mustaches dyed. There was Olivie, an oriental beauty now in full ripeness; she had found Lanny a romantic figure as a girl, and in her secret heart this idea still lurked. She was married to a French aristocrat, a gentile who had not thought it his duty to be present. Instead there were two brothers, busy young men of affairs, deeply concerned.

Lanny told the story of the dreadful scene he had witnessed, sparing them nothing; and they for their part spared him none of their weeping, moaning, and wringing of hands. They were the children of people who had set up a Wailing Wall in their capital city, for the public demonstration of grief; so presumably they found relief through loud expression. Lanny found that it didn't repel him; on the contrary, it seemed to be the way he himself felt; the tears started down his cheeks and he had difficulty in talking. After all, he was the brother-in-law of a Jew, and a sort of relative to a whole family, well known to the Hellsteins. He had gone into Germany to try to save a member of their race, and had risked his life in the effort, so he couldn't have had better credentials. He told them that he had expected to be the next victim laid on the whipping-bench, and had been saved only by the good luck that an officer friend had got word about his plight and had arrived in time to snatch him away. They did not find this story incredible.

Lanny didn't wait to hear their decision as to the payment of ransom to the Nazis. He guessed it might require some telephoning to other capitals, and it was none of his affair. They asked if the story he had told them was confidential, and he said not at all; he thought the public ought to know what was happening in Naziland, but he doubted if publicity would have any effect upon the extortioners. Olivie, in between outbursts of weeping, thanked him several times for coming to them; she thought he was the bravest and kindest man she had ever known—being deeply moved, she told him so. Lanny was tempted to wish she had said it in the presence of his wife, but on second thought he decided that it wouldn't really have helped. Nothing would help except for him to conduct himself like a proper man of fashion, and that seemed to be becoming more and more difficult.

VII

Lanny's duty was done, and he had time to woo his wife and try to restore her peace of mind. When she found that he was trying not to tell her his story, her curiosity became intensified; he made up a mild version, based upon his effort to buy Freddi out of Dachau, which Irma knew had been his plan. He said that he and Hugo had been arrested, and he had been confined in the very *gemütlich* city jail of Munich. He could go into details about that place and make a completely convincing story; his only trouble had been that they wouldn't let him communicate with the outside world. It was on account of the confusion of the Blood Purge; Irma said the papers in England had been full of that, and she had become convinced that she was a widow.

"You'd have made a charming one," he said; but he couldn't get a smile out of her.

"What are you waiting for now?" she wanted to know. He told her he had had a conference with Furtwaengler, and had a real hope of getting Freddi out in the next few days. He couldn't think of any way to make that sound plausible, and Irma was quite impatient, wanting to be taken to England. But no, he must stay in this hotel all day—the old business of waiting for a telephone call that didn't come! She wanted to get away from every reminder of those days and nights of misery; and this included Freddi and Rahel and all the Robin family. It made her seem rather hard; but Lanny realized that it was her class and racial feeling; she wanted to give her time and attention to those persons whom she considered important. Her mother was in England, and so was Frances; she had new stories to tell about the latter, and it was something they could talk about and keep the peace. It was almost the only subject.

There being more than one telephone at the Crillon, Lanny was able to indulge himself in the luxury of long-distance calls without a chance of delaying the all-important one from Berlin. He called his mother, who shed a lot of tears which unfortunately could not be transmitted by wire. He called Rick, and told him in guarded language what were his hopes. He called Emily Chattersworth and invited her to come in and have lunch, knowing that this would please Irma. Emily came, full of curiosity; she accepted his synthetic story, the same that he had told his wife. The episode of Solomon Hellstein was all over Paris, just as Göring had predicted; Emily had heard it, and wanted to verify it. Lanny explained how he had been under detention in Berlin, and there had got the facts about what was being done to the eldest of the half dozen banking brothers.

Also Lanny wrote a long letter to his father, telling him the real story; a shorter letter to Hansi and Bess, who had gone to South America, along with Hansi's father—the one to sell beautiful sounds and the other to sell hardware, including guns. The young Reds hadn't wanted to go, but the two fathers had combined their authority. The mere presence in Europe of two notorious Reds would be an incitement to the Nazis, and might serve to tip the scales and defeat Lanny's efforts to help Freddi. The young pair didn't like the argument, but had no answer to it.

VIII

Early in the morning, a phone call from Berlin! The cheerful voice of Oberleutnant Furtwaengler announcing: "*Gute Nachrichten, Herr Budd!* I am authorized to tell you that we are prepared to release your friend."

The man at the Paris end of the wire had a hard time preserving his steadiness of voice. "Whereabouts, Herr Oberleutnant?"

"That is for you to say."

"Where is he now?"

"In Munich."

"You would prefer some place near there?"

"My instructions are that you shall name the place."

Lanny remembered the bridge by which he had crossed the river

Rhein on his way to Munich; the place at which the child Marie Antoinette had entered France. "Would the bridge between Kehl and Strasbourg be acceptable to you?"

"Entirely so."

"I will be on that bridge whenever you wish.".

"We can get there more quickly than you. So you set the time."

"Say ten o'clock tomorrow morning."

"It is a date. I won't be there personally, so this is to thank you for your many courtesies and wish you all happiness."

"My wife is in the room, and desires to send her regards to you and your wife."

"Give her my greetings and thanks. I am certain that my wife will join in these sentiments. *Adieu*." Such were the formulas; and oh, why couldn't people really live like that?

IX

"Now, dear," said Lanny to his wife, "I think we can soon go home and have a rest."

Her amazement was great, and she wanted to know, how on earth he had done it? He told her: "They were trying to find the whereabouts of some of Freddi's friends and comrades. My guess is, they've got them by now, so he's of no use to them. Also, it might be that Göring thinks he can make some use of me in future."

"Are you going to do anything for him?"

"Not if I can help it. But all that's between you and me. You must not breathe a word of it to anybody else, not even to your mother, nor to mine." It pleased her to feel that she stood first in his confidence, and she promised.

He went to the telephone and put in a call for his faithful friend in Cannes. "Jerry," he said, "I think I'm to get Freddi out, and here's another job. Call Rahel at Bienvenu and tell her to get ready; then get her, and motor her to Strasbourg. Don't delay, because I have no idea what condition Freddi will be in, and she's the one who has to handle him and make the decisions. You know the sort of people we're dealing with; and I can't give any guarantees, but I believe

Freddi will be there at ten tomorrow, and it's worthwhile for Rahel to take the chance. Get Beauty's car from Bienvenu, if you like. I advise you to come by way of the Rhone valley, Besançon and Mulhouse. Drive all night if you can stand it and let Rahel sleep in the back seat. I will be at the Hotel de la Ville-de-Paris in Strasbourg."

Lanny had another problem, a delicate one. He didn't want to take Irma on this trip, and at the same time he didn't want to hurt her feelings. "Come if you want to," he said, "but I'm telling you it may be a painful experience, and there won't be much you can do."

"Why did you ask me to Paris, Lanny, if you didn't want my help?"

"I asked you because I love you, and wanted to see you, and I thought you would want to see me. I want your help in everything that interests you, but I don't want to drag you into something that you have no heart for. I haven't seen Freddi, and I'm just guessing: he may look like an old man; he may be ill, even dying; he may be mutilated in some shocking way; he may be entirely out of his mind. It's his wife's job to take care of him and nurse him back to life; it's not your job, and I'm giving you the chance to keep out of another wearing experience."

"We'll all be in it, if they're going to live at Bienvenu."

"In the first place, Rahel may have to take him to a hospital. And anyhow, we aren't going back until fall. Hansi and Bess are making money, and so is Johannes, I have no doubt, and they'll want to have a place of their own. All that's in the future, and a lot of it depends on Freddi's condition. I suggest leaving you at Emily's until I come back. I'm having Jerry bring Rahel in a car, so he can take her wherever she wants to go, and then you and I will be free. There's a *maison de santé* here in Paris, and a surgeon who took care of Marcel when he was crippled and burned; they're still in business, and I phoned that I might be sending them a patient."

"Oh, Lanny!" she exclaimed. "How I would enjoy it if we could give just a little time to our own affairs!"

"Yes, darling," he said. "It's a grand idea, and England will seem delightful after I get this job off my hands. I'm eager to see what

Rick has done with his last act, and maybe I can give him some hints."

It wasn't until he saw Irma's *moue* that he realized what a slip he had made. Poor Lanny, he would have a hard time learning to think about himself!

X

Irma was duly deposited at the Château les Forêts, an agreeable place of sojourn in mid-July. In fifteen years the noble beech forests had done their own work of repair, and the summer breezes carried no report of the thousands of buried French and German soldiers. Since Emily had been a sort of fostermother to Irma's husband, and had had a lot to do with making the match, they had an inexhaustible subject of conversation, and the older woman tried tactfully to persuade a darling of fortune that every man has what the French call *les défauts de ses qualités*, and that there might be worse faults in a husband than excess of solicitude and generosity. She managed to make Irma a bit ashamed of her lack of appreciation of a sweet and gentle Jewish clarinetist.

Meanwhile Lanny was speeding over a fine highway, due eastward toward the river Rhein. It was in part the route over which the fleeing king and queen had driven in their heavy "berlin"; not far to the south lay Varennes, where they had been captured and driven back to Paris to have their heads cut off. Human beings suffer agonies, and their sad fates become legends; poets write verses about them and playwrights compose dramas, and the remembrance of past grief becomes a source of present pleasure—such is the strange alchemy of the spirit.

The traveler had supper on the way, and reached his destination after midnight. There was no use looking at an empty bridge, and he wasn't in the mood for cathedrals, even one of the oldest. He went to bed and slept; in the morning he had a breakfast with fruit, and a telegram from Jerry saying that they were at Besançon and coming straight on. No use going to the place of appointment ahead of time, so Lanny read the morning papers in this town which had changed hands many times, but for the present was French. He read that Adolf Hitler had called an assembly of his tame Reichstag in the Kroll Opera House, and had made them a speech of an hour and a half, telling how he had suffered in soul over having to kill so many of his old friends and supporters. When he was through, he sat with head bowed, completely overcome, while Göring told the world how Hitler was the ordained Führer who was incapable of making a mistake; to all of which they voted their unanimous assent.

With thoughts induced by this reading Lanny drove three or four miles to the Pont de Kehl, parked his car, and walked halfway across. He was ahead of time, and standing by the railings he gazed up and down that grand old river. No use getting himself into a state of excitement over his own mission; if it was going to succeed it would succeed, and if it didn't, he would go to the nearest telephone and get hold of the Oberleutnant and ask why. No use tormenting himself with fears about what he was going to see; whatever Freddi was would still be Freddi, and they would patch it up and make the best of it.

Meantime, look down into the depths of that fast-sliding water and remember, here was where the Rheinmaidens had swum and teased the dwarf Alberich. Perhaps they were still swimming; the *motif* of the Rheingold rang clear as a trumpet call in Lanny's ears. Somewhere on the heights along this stream the Lorelei had sat and combed her golden hair with a golden comb, and sung a song that had a wonderfully powerful melody, so that the boatman in the little boat had been seized with a wild woe, and didn't see the rocky reef, but kept gazing up to the heights, and so in the end the waves had swallowed boatman and boat; and that with her singing the Lorelei had done. Another of those tragic events which the alchemy of the spirit had turned into pleasure!

Every minute or two Lanny would look at his watch. They might be early; but no, that would be as bad as being late. "*Pünktlich!*" was the German word, and it was their pride. Just as the minute hand of Lanny's watch was in the act of passing the topmost mark of the dial, a large official car would approach the center line of the bridge, where a bar was stretched across, the east side of the bar being German and the west side French. If it didn't happen exactly so, it would be the watch that was wrong, and not *deutsche Zucht und Ordnung*. As a boy Lanny had heard a story from old Mr. Hackabury, the soapman, about a farmer who had ordered a new watch by mail-order catalogue, and had gone out in his field with watch and almanac, announcing: "If that sun don't get up over that hill in three minutes, she's late!"

XI

Sure enough, here came the car! A Mercédès-Benz, with a little swastika flag over the radiator-cap, and a chauffeur in S.S. uniform, including steel helmet. They came right up to the barrier and stopped, while Lanny stood on the last foot of France, with his heart in his mouth. Two S.S. men in the back seat got out and began helping a passenger, and Lanny got one glimpse after another; the glimpses added up to a gray-haired, elderly man, feeble and bowed, with hands that were deformed into claws, and that trembled and shook as if each of them separately had gone mad. Apparently he couldn't walk, for they were half-carrying him, and it wasn't certain that he could hold his head up—at any rate, it was hanging.

"*Heil Hitler!*" said one of the men, saluting. "Herr Budd?"

"*Ja,*" said Lanny, in a voice that wasn't quite steady.

"*Wohin mit ihm?*" It was a problem, for you couldn't take such a package and just walk off with it. Lanny had to ask the indulgence of the French police and customs men, who let the unfortunate victim be carried into their office and laid on a seat. He couldn't sit up, and winced when he was touched. "They have kicked my kidneys loose," he murmured, without opening his eyes. Lanny ran and got his car, and the Frenchmen held up the traffic while he turned it around on the bridge. They helped to carry the sufferer and lay him on the back seat. Then, slowly, Lanny drove to the Hotel de la Ville-de-Paris, where they brought a stretcher and carried Freddi Robin to a room and laid him on a bed.

Apparently he hadn't wanted to be freed; or perhaps he didn't realize that he was free; perhaps he didn't recognize his old friend.

He didn't seem to want to talk, or even to look about him. Lanny waited until they were alone, and then started the kind of mental cure which he had seen his mother practice on the broken and burned Marcel Detaze. "You're in France, Freddi, and now everything is going to be all right."

The poor fellow's voice behaved as if it was difficult for him to frame sounds into words. "You should have sent me poison!" That was all he could think of.

"We're going to take you to a good hospital and have you fixed up in no time." A cheerful "spiel," practiced for several days.

Freddi held up his trembling claws; they waved in the air, seemingly of their own independent will. "They broke them with an iron bar," he whispered; "one by one."

"Rahel is coming, Freddi. She will be here in a few hours."

"No, no, no!" They were the loudest sounds he could make. "She must not see me." He kept that up for some time, as long as his strength lasted. He was not fit to see anybody. He wanted to go to sleep and not wake up. "Some powders!" he kept whispering.

Lanny saw that the sick man was weakening himself by trying to argue, so he said, all right. He had already called for a doctor, and when the man came he whispered the story. Here on the border they knew a great deal about the Nazis, and the doctor needed no details. He gave a sleeping powder which quieted the patient for a while. The doctor wanted to examine him, but Lanny said no, he would wait until the patient's wife had arrived to take charge. Lanny didn't reveal that he had in mind to get an ambulance and take the victim to Paris; he could see that here was a case that called for a lot of work and he wanted it done by people whom he knew and trusted. He was sure that Rahel would agree with this.

XII

A moment not soon to be forgotten when the two travelers arrived, and Freddi's wife came running into the hotel suite, an agony of suspense in her whole aspect; her face, gestures, voice. "He's here? He's alive? He's ill? Oh, God, where is he?"

"In the next room," replied Lanny. "He's asleep, and we'd better not disturb him."

"How is he?"

"He needs to be gone over by a good surgeon and patched up; but we can have it done. Keep yourself together, and don't let him see that you're afraid or shocked."

She had to set her eyes upon him right away; she had to steal into the room, and make it real to herself that after so many long months he was actually here, in France, not Germany. Lanny warned her: "Be quiet, don't lose your nerve." He went with her, and Jerry on the other side, for fear she might faint. And she nearly did so; she stood for a long while, breathing hard, staring at that gray-haired, elderly man, who, a little more than a year ago, had been young, beautiful and happy. They felt her shuddering, and when she started to sob, they led her out and softly closed the door.

To Lanny it was like living over something a second time, as happens in a dream. "Listen, Rahel," he said: "You have to do just what my mother did with Marcel. You have to make him want to live again. You have to give him hope and courage. You must never let him see the least trace of fear or suffering on your face. You must be calm and assured, and just keep telling him that you love him, and that he is going to get well."

"Does he know what you say to him?"

"I think he only half realizes where he is; and perhaps it's better so. Don't force anything on him. Just whisper love, and tell him he is needed, and must live for your sake and the child's."

The young wife sat there with her whole soul in her eyes. She had always been a serious, intellectual woman, but having her share of vigor and blooming. Now she was pale and thin; she had forgotten to eat most of the time; she had dined on grief and supped on fear. It was clear that she wanted only one thing in the world, to take this adored man and devote her life to nursing him and restoring him to health. She wouldn't rebel against her fate, as Beauty Budd, the worldling, had done; she wouldn't have to beat and drive herself to the role of Sister of Mercy. Nor would she have herself painted in that role, and exhibit herself to smart crowds; no, she would just go wherever Freddi went, try to find out what Freddi needed and give it to him, with that consecrated love which the saints feel for the Godhead.

Lanny told her what he had in mind. They would take him in an ambulance to Paris, quickly but carefully, so as not to jar him. Rahel could ride with him, and talk to him, feed him doses of courage and hope, even more necessary than physical food. Jerry and Lanny would follow, each in his own car; Jerry would stay in Paris for a while, to help her in whatever way he could. Lanny would instruct the surgeon to do everything needed, and would pay the bill. He told Jerry to go and get some sleep—his aspect showed that he needed it, for he had driven five or six hundred miles with only a few minutes' respite at intervals.

XIII

Lanny had food and wine and milk brought to the room, and persuaded Rahel to take some; she would need her strength. She should give Freddi whatever he would take—he probably had had no decent food for more than a year. Preparing her for her long ordeal, he told more of the story of Marcel, the miracle which had been wrought by love and unfailing devotion. Lanny talked as if he were Parsifal Dingle; incidentally he said: "Parsifal will come to Paris and help you, if you wish." Rahel sat weeping softly. With half her mind she took in Lanny's words, while the other half was with the broken body and soul in the next room.

Presently they heard him moaning. She dried her eyes hastily, and said. "I can never thank you. I will do my best to save Freddi so that he can thank you."

She stole into the other room, and Lanny sat alone for a long while. Tears began to steal down his cheeks, and he leaned his arms upon the table in front of him. It was a reaction from the strain he had been under for more than a year. Tears because he hadn't been able to accomplish more; because what he had done might be too late. Tears not only for his wrecked and tormented friend, not only for that unhappy family, but for all the Jews of Europe, and for their tormentors, just as much to be pitied. Tears for the unhappy people of Germany, who were being lured into such a deadly trap, and would pay for it with frightful sufferings. Tears for this unhappy continent on which he had been born and had lived most of his life. He had traveled here and there over its surface, and everywhere had seen men diligently plowing the soil and sowing dragon's teeth—from which, as in the old legend, armed men would some day spring. He had raised his feeble voice, warning and pleading; he had sacrificed time and money and happiness, but all in vain. He wept, despairing, as another man of gentleness and mercy had wept, in another time of oppression and misery, crying: .

"O Jerusalem, Jerusalem, thou that killest the prophets, and stonest them which are sent unto thee, how often would I have gathered thy children together, even as a hen gathereth her chickens under her wings, and ye would not! Behold, your house is left unto you desolate."

BOOKS BY UPTON SINCLAIR

PRESIDENTIAL AGENT
WIDE IS THE GATE
DRAGON'S TEETH
BETWEEN TWO WORLDS
WORLD'S END
EXPECT NO PEACE
YOUR MILLION DOLLARS
LITTLE STEEL
OUR LADY
THE FLIVVER KING
NO PASARAN!
THE GNOMOBILE
CO-OP: A NOVEL OF LIVING TOGETHER
WHAT GOD MEANS TO ME: AN ATTEMPT
   AT A WORKING RELIGION
I, CANDIDATE FOR GOVERNOR AND HOW I
   GOT LICKED
THE EPIC PLAN FOR CALIFORNIA
I, GOVERNOR OF CALIFORNIA
THE WAY OUT: WHAT LIES AHEAD FOR
   AMERICA
UPTON SINCLAIR PRESENTS WILLIAM FOX
AMERICAN OUTPOST: AUTOBIOGRAPHY
THE WET PARADE
ROMAN HOLIDAY
MENTAL RADIO
MOUNTAIN CITY
BOSTON
MONEY WRITES!
OIL!

THE SPOKESMAN'S SECRETARY
LETTERS TO JUDD
MAMMONART
THE GOSLINGS—A STUDY OF THE AMERICAN
   SCHOOLS
THE GOOSE-STEP—A STUDY OF AMERICAN
   EDUCATION
THE BOOK OF LIFE
THEY CALL ME CARPENTER
100%—THE STORY OF A PATRIOT
THE BRASS CHECK
JIMMIE HIGGINS
KING COAL, A NOVEL OF THE COLORADO
   COAL STRIKE
THE PROFITS OF RELIGION
THE CRY FOR JUSTICE
DAMAGED GOODS
SYLVIA'S MARRIAGE
SYLVIA
LOVE'S PILGRIMAGE
THE FASTING CURE
SAMUEL, THE SEEKER
THE MONEYCHANGERS
THE METROPOLIS
THE MILLENNIUM
THE OVERMAN
THE JUNGLE
MANASSAS, A NOVEL OF THE CIVIL WAR
THE JOURNAL OF ARTHUR STIRLING

Plays

PRINCE HAGEN
THE NATUREWOMAN
THE SECOND STORY MAN
THE MACHINE
THE POT-BOILER
HELL

SINGING JAILBIRDS
BILL PORTER
OIL! (DRAMATIZATION)
DEPRESSION ISLAND
MARIE ANTOINETTE

Printed in the United States
203547BV00001B/379/A